and the
business pages...

DIARY OF A WORKING GIRL

Diary of a Working Girl

DANIELLA BRODSKY

BERKLEY BOOKS, NEW YORK

B

A Berkley Book
Published by The Berkley Publishing Group
A division of Penguin Group (USA) Inc.
375 Hudson Street
New York, New York 10014

Copyright © 2004 by Daniella Brodsky
Book design by Kristin del Rosario
Cover design by George Long
Cover art by Kim Johnson

First Edition: April 2004

Library of Congress Cataloging-in-Publication Data

Brodsky, Daniella.
  Diary of a working girl / Daniella Brodsky.—1st ed.
    p. cm.
  ISBN 0-429-19422-1
    1. Freelance journalism—Fiction. 2. New York (N.Y.)—Fiction. 3. Mate
selection—Fiction. 4. Single women—Fiction. I. Title.

PS3602.R635D53 2004
813'.6—dc22   2003070389

Printed in the United States of America

10   9   8   7   6   5   4   3   2   1

For Aunt Tiny—
on behalf of everyone she inspired.

One

Once Upon a Time

I am turning over a new leaf in life. Starting right now—at this very second in time—3 P.M., March 15, I will get out of my work rut, stop allowing fantasies of finding Mr. Right (and bouts of depression about not finding him) to invade almost every second of my life. I will start down the road to award-winning, top-notch freelance writer, rather than third-rate, barely-paying-the-rent freelance writer—as I have formerly been.

I know very well that I have said this before. And the reason I know this very well is because, when I called my friend Joanne a moment ago, she reminded me of just that. She called off specific dates and everything. "Well there was September fifteenth, and then October fifteenth, and then of course you swore this exact thing to me on November fifteenth . . ." and by the time she got all the way through to last month, she said, "Darling, isn't that the day you get your rent bill every month?" Okay, so there is a pattern. But what she doesn't realize is that *this time* is different.

I. Am. Going. To. Change. My. Life.

I am ready.

Perhaps it took me a while to get here.

But, *now*, I am ready.

I can just feel creativity and energy oozing from every single cell in my body.

I am equipped with the essentials for embarking upon the path to success. My tools, as I sit down with them at my couch, are one brand-new red suede-covered journal, a purple gel pen, and my sharp-as-a-whip journalistic mind. You need a new notebook if you are going to begin your career anew. You can't very well start fresh on a crinkled page in a notebook that has served as the palette for hundreds of rejected article ideas. For someone who does this for a living, a notebook like this is an investment. You need to surround yourself with beautiful, creative things if you ever hope to write beautiful, creative things. The government agrees with this, because you can even write those beautiful, creative things off on your taxes.

Gently, I turn back the spine to the first crisp, gold-leafed page to begin brainstorming article ideas. I breathe in. I breathe out. I pick up my pen and sit poised, like that famous statue, *The Thinker*, but with a pen—I am *The Freelance Thinker*. No, *The Creative Thinker*. Perhaps I am not *The Thinker* so much as *The Writer*. Yes, that's it, exactly. I am *The Writer*. I love the way that sounds.

I have to say that everyone loves the way that sounds. When I meet people, they are uniformly impressed with my profession. And then, of course, they ask me exactly what I write, and this is where the men usually drop right out of the conversation. This is because they are completely uninterested in the new spring fashions, the fact that big belts have made a comeback, or that pink is *the* color for lips this season. But the next question is even worse, because that is inevitably, "So which magazines do you write for?" It's not that I write for *Penthouse* or something you need to be ashamed of in a moral way. It's just that nobody has ever heard of the magazines I write for, like *Love Your Hair*, or *For Her*.

I'm sure you understand, then, that sometimes—not very often—I find myself embellishing the truth a bit. That is to say, rather than name the magazines that I actually write for, I name the magazines that I have most recently pitched for. But I always follow it up with, "Freelance writers are constantly pitching. You never know what's just around the corner." This makes me look like a fly-by-the-seat-of-your-pants girl, rather than a how-sad-she-can't-give-up-the-ghost girl. And then I can just go into all of the cool people that I've met along the way, and men, especially, get drawn into the exciting lifestyle I (supposedly) lead.

But after today's work, I will never have to "embellish" again. Never. I begin by putting today's date at the top. Surely, when I look back at this page, from my new desk, in my new SoHo loft, which I will buy the moment *Vogue* hires me on as a permanent columnist, I will sit back, a vision in preseason Prada samples and custom-designed Manolo Blahniks, and remember this day with joy.

I peruse some old magazines I've got in hopes of stirring the creative juices and lose myself in admiration of a stunning charcoal bias-cut gown. The girl in the picture is draped over a velvet sofa, a mass of pearls twisted around her neck, one black beaded pump dangling from one very elegant foot. I can't help it. I picture myself in the dress, only with crystal-beaded sandals to match (I think that would go much better), my highlights glistening in an explosion of paparazzi flashbulbs. I'm waving and smiling in that polite way I've noticed royalty do all these years. Yes, it's all coming clear:

My purse will be one of those Lulu Guinness flowerpots, with the adorable sayings embroidered inside like a little secret only you know about.

My breath quickens, grows shallower, like I can't get enough air. My eyes go fuzzy. All at once I feel it, that overwhelming urge in my gut to know just how I can have this dress. Because if I get it, I'll feel different than I ever have before. I'll be glamorous in that everything-in-its-place way that has always managed to elude me in the past. When I open my silky flowerpot, I'll know exactly where my lip gloss is for the first time in my life; and it won't be that play-it-safe pink I always wear. It will be red, because once you've become that woman in that dress you'll be that woman who can pull off crimson lips, too. If I want to pass a business card to someone, it will be precisely where it should be. I'll be taller, more slender than ever before when I wear it; my eyes will somehow look greener than they ever have before. My eye makeup (always tastefully done) will be applied with a bit more drama, maybe with some smudging around the lash line and a shimmery bronze in the crease. It's as if my whole life has been one big training session leading up to this one purchase. Now I feel this dress and everything it will mean so close in my reach; I am suddenly positive it will actually be mine—that it was destined to be mine—just because I want it that much.

I turn ravenously to the back of the book for the buying information. I estimate with sharp, rapid breaths of the sort only the "have-nots" with serious "have" tastes are familiar with just how much the dress will cost with a description like "price available upon request." I figure in the mile and a half of silk, and embroidered roses on each and every inch. Finally, I conclude I could definitely afford it if I exist solely on a diet of ketchup packets and free drinks and sell every item in my possession on eBay. I begin tossing said possessions into a "sell" pile. It is only after I estimate the value of most of my belongings that I realize the magazine is two years old.

Devastation overtakes me and I am ready to call it quits on the changing my life thing when it hits me. This sort of experience could make for a fantastic personal essay for a magazine like, say, *Bazaar*. "In Search of the Charcoal Gown," I could call it. I begin writing, "When one woman falls for Badgley Mischka vintage, absolutely nothing less will do." Those are the sorts of tiny descriptions you need to write with your pitch to explain what the article would be like and in what style you would write it. I leave out the part about the slight heart attack I suffered at learning the price was "available upon request" as *Bazaar* readers somehow always have budgets for such things ("I bought one in every color!"), and instead take on the air of a wealthy society woman as I always do with such sophisticated publications.

These things come to me almost instantaneously. All I have to do is look at a pair of shoes, watch a television show, overhear a conversation and—*poof!*—there's my idea. This is why I am positive that I will make it. But then I send out the ideas and nothing ever comes of them and then I am even more positive that I will *never* make it. Depending on the day, my outlook can vary drastically. Mysteriously, the outlook pattern has an inverse relationship to the chocolate intake pattern: outlook up, chocolate intake down and vice versa.

I make some mental notes about the cute adjectives used in lipstick descriptions: slick, pouty, glossy, shimmery—words that lend themselves to magazine writing, but most definitely not for everyday banter. Imagine being greeted pre-caffeination by some coworker with, "My you are looking so slick-lipped today!" It's no mystery what you'd think of that person. Magazines should come with a disclaimer, "Kids, do not try these words at home!" Still, they are my words and I absolutely love mastering them despite the fact that I am more than aware of how dorky that is.

Twenty minutes later I am truly engrossed by a story of romance on page eighty-seven in the June issue of *Vogue*. It turns out this stunning princess (who can really pull off that tiara look like a star) and her debonair shiny husband have been married for fifty years and wanted to share their story with the world. Theirs—like all true loves—was born of the most star-crossed of circumstances. She was meant to have tied the knot with some highly decorated, scarcely interesting older man from a neighboring nation. He was merely a dressmaker. For years and years, the princess had come to his atelier where he would admire the curve of her spine, the angle of her shoulder, and with every pin inserted, every tape measure pulled taut, she would shudder. Never a word was spoken between princess and dressmaker—yet he knew exactly which dresses to bring her each and every time she came to him. She always loved what he put her in—simple, long silhouettes that paid homage to shoulders, neck, long slender arms, and that is because he lovingly designed each with her in mind.

"Cutting patterns, slicing through the most rare crepe de chine with the precision of a surgeon to perfectly envelope a hip, a breast, I felt I was with her; we were making love in the most magical, mystical way. We were always together, even when apart. There was never another."

He had no need for measurements or even to see her (these were merely excuses to be near her)—he knew the dresses would encase her ins and outs, rounds and straights with the delicate intricacy of a glove, as each was crafted from love and knowledge of her each and every inch. After fifteen years of silence, they fled to Madagascar and there have lived ever since.

Under one photo in which the couple sits before a sparkling blue sea, the caption reads: " 'We love the mussels there!' they both declare in unison. The ex-designer turns to the princess and with one brow raised in mock-suspicion admits, 'But we cannot share them because she eats them up so quickly I never have a chance!' The princess's smile betrays her."

This story holds me in a trance. I read it once. Twice. Three times. It strikes me as the most beautiful story I've ever come upon. I search to find something about bronzing powder that could inspire so much passion in readers. Although the right shade could drastically revitalize a winter-worn complexion, or for that matter, give a girl the beauty boost that just might help her survive a lethal bout of PMS, it still doesn't provide the same high the princess love story offers. I should just skip right past this story and back into safer territory—how to wear hats, new fragrances for yoga—but I can't draw myself from the idea of romance. It pulls me in, beckons me to follow.

I'd always dedicated a large portion of my personal time to thoughts of romance, and at an increasing rate, since my youthful ideals seem to be weathering and decaying and daring me to abandon them. Especially lately as I have spent the better part of the month mourning the one-day, one-week, two-week, and one-month anniversaries of the day I broke up with James. My mourning ritual has consisted mainly of drinking cheap red wine, and, well, whining—to anyone who'd listen—about my hopeless, lonely, boyfriend-less existence.

Unfortunately for her, my friend Joanne just happens to be "anyone who'll listen." Most of my other friends have rather quickly tired of my treatment of Bridget Jones as an actual human being, and henceforth, a bona fide point of comparison to my own predicament: "I can't believe she (wine slurp) wound up with a rich lawyer with a great personality (wine slurp) *and* an English accent and he truly was her Magic Man (failed attempt at wine slurp as no more wine to slurp)."

"Her what?" Joanne had asked.

"You know, her Magic Man. There was something there and, of course, it was there all along, but it took them a while to figure it out and so she almost lost him, but then they realized it and he was perfectly magical."

Well, over time (and wine slurps) Magic Man became MM and eventually, the similarities between the perfect man and the perfect candy of the same initials (you only need a couple every day to get your fill; melts in your mouth, not in your hand) were discovered and MM became M&M and now I see that the name is perfect as it represents comfort and home and happiness and simplicity and sweetness. And if you eat enough of them—the candies, that is— and chant "I want my M&M, I want my M&M," while crunching, it eventually starts to sound like "mmmmm" which is exactly the cry of the satisfied and of the (ahem) "satisfied," which is why that tiny ancient woman next door has probably been looking at me strangely.

James is one of a long line of men who turned out not to be my M&M. And hence, turned out to be another ideal-weathering beckon towards reality. Needless to say, I have been eating more than my fair share of M&M's—the candy—to make up for my lack of The M&M—the man.

So, now, in addition to receiving blubbering I'll-never-find-my-M&M telephone calls that can only be classified as pathetic attempts to get her to spend some time with me (ironically they were more than likely the actual reason she "couldn't" come over), Joanne now receives blubbering you're-my-only-friend-in-the-world phone calls from me, too.

I need to get back to the more practical matters of Mediterranean-inspired lipsticks and the benefits/hindrances of high waistlines on variously flawed figures (and, of course, that most tragic of all categories, "thin"), and so I turn to a British magazine, *Beautiful*, which is famous for never addressing anything of a serious nature (and would in fact encourage Badgley-Mischka-induced heart attack chronicles). Here I am inspired to pitch "Beauty on the Go: What to Take, How to Pack; Hairstyling and Makeup How-to from the Jet Set." After exhausting the host of related themes: "Beauty in a Flash," "The Spring Face," and "Facial Index," I once again find myself searching out that princess love story.

Was there something in the eye of the princess that could teach me to find true love? Her face had a superhuman strength (in a strictly Katharine Hepburn not Hulk Hogan way) in just about all of the accompanying photos. If you looked at her with your head cocked to the right, turned her portrait ninety degrees to a horizontal position, and squinted your left eye, she *definitely* appeared in possession of a secret. Why had the secret evaded me?

Outside my window it appears everyone but me is qualified to write a story about love. I count thirty-five happy couples who happen to be qualified on account of menacing actions such as hand-holding, talking, and laughing even—all of which are quite obviously efforts exerted for my benefit.

"People can see you!" I scream because, well, I can't exactly say why.

And that's when I hear the cry, "What?"

Taken off guard, I quickly withdraw my head from the window and begin to feel an intense blush at the sort of mortification one can only suffer when one has just been called on asocial, unstable behavior. But when my doorbell rings and my upstairs neighbor Chris screams through the door, "Are you sitting by the window counting couples again?" I rip myself from my embarrassment coma with the comforting knowledge that Chris is already well versed in my weakness in the rational arena.

"No, absolutely not! I am working!" Was there not a notebook lying open on my table? Had I not come up with lots of great ideas?

"Well, then let me come in and see what you've done." I scan the room. The bed is unmade. There are junk food and candy wrappers where there used to be the top of a coffee table. Blankets I had piled around me all morning are still strewn about the couch. I panic, lest Chris think I have somehow sacrificed another day to *The Young and the Restless*. I have to act like I've been working hard all day. Otherwise, I'll never hear the end of how "resilient" I am. Chris can be rather sarcastic, especially when it comes to my breakups and the idea of M&M's. ("They will will just make you fat.") So, to keep up appearances and prevent him from drawing any connection between the princess love story and my current mind-set, I close the notebook, shove the magazines under a sofa cushion, scramble some papers on my desk, jiggle the mouse to get my laptop off sleep mode, open a document I'd written ages ago, and jam a pen behind my ear. Now, that looks like a busy workingwoman who *never* draws parallels between her own life and those of *The Young and the Restless* characters, I think, glancing in the mirror. That is, except for the greasy hair propped up in a wild bun and the snowman-printed pajama pants, and, of course, the bit of ketchup on my cheek.

When I finally let him in, after he'd spent a moment clearing his throat in the hallway, he says, "So you really are working on some real, saleable story ideas, huh? You haven't just opened some old document, shimmied some papers around your desk, and stuck a pen behind your ear, right?" Although Chris is a photographer, he would really be better suited to manning a psychic hotline. If he'd seen the magazines, he'd be able to flip right to the princess story and repeat back, word for word, what I'd been thinking. I walk over to the cushion currently concealing them to sit on top just in case.

He looks stunning, as always. His dark hair is perfectly combed back so it's just beginning to fall by his ears—in the sort of way that, on a straight man, would make you want to run your hands through it to push it back. But, as often as I've wished he were, Chris is not a straight man. Once I learned (the hard way) that he would not show any romantic interest in me, even if I rang his bell wearing only the cutest Agent Provocateur teddy beneath my coat, and holding a bottle of champagne and two flutes, I began to take him for what he is—a fantastic friend with fabulous insight into the male psyche, and someone who lets me run my hands through his hair when I am feeling especially deficient in the area of male tresses for such a purpose. He also functions as mother, father, brother, sister, therapist, superintendent, personal chef, and date. He glances at my coffee-cum-buffet table and shakes his head despairingly.

"My darling, what are we going to do with you?"

"I don't know what you mean. This?" I ask, waving my hand *The Price Is Right*-style, at what would be a very unfabulous prize. He doesn't answer, only lowers his lids to half-mast as a way of saying he isn't buying what I am sloppily attempting to unload in lieu of the truth.

I continue anyway, "This is—er, the research for an article I'm working on. Yes. It's *research*."

"So what exactly are you researching? The fastest way to put on twenty pounds? Or is it a home-brewed recipe for a creamy pity soup with artichoke and . . . Oh, Lanie, barbecue chicken wings? Yuckk. C'mon. Pull yourself together and get your head out of this . . . this bag of salt and vinegar potato chips. What is this, kettle style? Any good? (Crunch.) Not bad, actually. Still, when was the last time you actually had an article published? Not to be the bearer of bad news, but you know the rent is due soon."

I can't prove he actually has telepathic powers or that his taste test wasn't some sort of sleight of hand just to set this whole thing up, but it seems like an awfully big coincidence that the bag of potato chips just happens to come crashing down into a carbohydrate avalanche at exactly the same moment he finishes this sentence.

For some reason, I hate when Chris knows how awful I feel. He's just so practical. Like, I'll go on and on about spending Christmas or New Year's or even Valentine's Day alone and he'll be so sweet—making me dinner or wrapping thoughtful gifts in gorgeous wallpaper remnants with regal ribbon-work and strands of antique glass beads—and all the while never say anything about his being alone, too. He'll make me feel pathetic, like I should be thankful for the life I have. But it doesn't matter what I say, he always knows the truth anyhow, so either way I walk away feeling bad about having felt bad, which makes me feel even worse because I hate that I can't be as strong as Chris.

"For your information, I am actually working on an article right now—about the favorite clothes of this famous writer-woman—in addition to this food research thingy I'm doing," I say, defending my existence.

"Well, I was about to see if you wanted to go out and get a breath of fresh air, but I see you're busy, so I'll just leave you to it."

"Thank you. Yes, I am *extremely* busy today." And with that, I nudge him through the door. "But don't forget to call me later," I scream down the hall.

Two

A Sign of the Times

When I wake Monday morning, still on my couch, it takes a second to figure out where I am. In my dream, I had been shacked up in the most beautiful St. Lucian cliffside villa with a faceless, but definitely Latin, Enrique Iglesias–type.

Unimaginatively typecast or not (I can't be blamed for my unconscious mind) he turned out to be a fantastic lover—the sort that knows exactly what to say, and how to tug at your hair and linger at the insides of your thighs until you are positive that you are the sexiest woman in America (needless to say my thighs were of spectacular Victoria's Secret caliber in this dream) and therefore you toss aside all inhibitions in pursuit of a single goal: having a raging orgasm.

When finally my eyes flicker open to full capacity, I look around myself in disgust. The remains of my million-calorie weekend feast, now smelling pretty bad, are strewn around the television unit, an altar to my depression. My blanket and I have long since parted, the blanket preferring a more southerly climate—the floor. Yet I am somehow rivaling a hormonally charged adolescent boy in the sweat department. I am not sure how the glittery poster reading "Anti-fairy-tale-ism" got on my bed.

Slowly, I attempt to rise and make my way to the bathroom. The mirror lets me know, quite harshly, that I have looked better. My hair, normally ironed out to perfection has attained such volume it would give Fran Drescher a run for her *Nanny* residuals. My face is so pasty I fear people will start singing bad Ray Parker Junior movie scores when they see me. The arches of my brows have unmistakably disappeared and been replaced by two fluffy caterpillar-type formations above my bloodshot eyes, which are accompanied by two cases of dark luggage that sag and puff beneath them.

If I told some random person on the street that I am the one instructing them on skincare and hairstyling in magazines (okay, most people you run into haven't read *Celebrity Hairstyles*, but still, I'm trying to make a point here) they would swear off glossies for good. Hah! That is actually kind of funny, I muse, trying to drag a comb through my hair and failing miserably (and painfully).

You know what would be really funny? If I started writing about relationships. Now that would be absolutely hysterical, I think as I brush my teeth, quickly smooth some soap around my face and neck, and prepare to shower off the effects of a lonely, unproductive stint that has run entirely too long a course. Peach Blossom seems to be a perfect shower gel choice, although I can't exactly explain why.

I have to begin an article I am writing for a woman's magazine that nobody has ever heard of. It is my only assignment for the week. The job is to interview one famous woman about her favorite articles of clothing. This sort of article normally makes me depressed because the women I interview have the most amazing wardrobes, and, to make matters worse, I have to actually go and walk through their closets, which are the size of my apartment, while they whine about needing more space to squeeze in all of their Alaïa originals, Jimmy Choos, and Manolo Blahniks. But then, I rationalize, I have my health! I am so lucky! I live in the best city in the world! Somehow, that never works.

I try to concentrate on my health and the benefits of my geographical location and remember that I promised myself today would be the day I rejoin the living as an active member of society. But as I reach and unlock my door, ready to venture out to interview Lisa McLellon, I instead begin to amuse myself with what *Inside Edition* might say when Lane Silverman, relationship columnist, is sighted home alone on a Saturday night: "Before you consider taking any advice from a relationship expert, you may want to peer through the windows of five hundred and fifty-five West Thirteenth Street, where Lane Silverman, scribe responsible for 'Want Love? Go Get It!' was seen this Saturday boiling ramen noodles and trying—in futility—to master a Britney Spears dance routine, singing into a round brush in front of her mirror—*alone*. Story at eight."

"Ouch!" I scream, partially in hopes that someone (maybe the cute guy down the hall) might come scoop me up from the heap I am now lying in, after tripping right over my Sunday *Times*. Couldn't I once look forward to tripping over a paper with my story on the cover? Couldn't some kind neighbor have removed the paper so the world wouldn't know I hadn't even opened my door yesterday? I feel the physical presence of the head-shaking and deep sighs this evidence of my gross self-pity no doubt produced from passersby all morning. The hall smells of people with places to go and people to see and I want them all to know that I am now, as they say, leaving the building.

"Ouch!" I scream once more, a bit louder, to make sure they all hear.

When nobody comes and my leg is starting to get tingly, I leave the paper, totally ignoring the fact that along with a reminder of my piteous weekend the broadsheet also serves as a symbol of failure. Just last week I wondered for twenty minutes whether or not to hit the "send" button to a thus-far response-impaired editor from the *Times*; yet again I was pitching some trend that will go in and out of style and be mentioned in every other publication without the likelihood of even a form rejection letter seeing the interior of my mailbox. My peach-scented trail now comes in handy to cover any residuals of mortification the episode may produce.

The woman I am scheduled to interview is one of the most successful freelance magazine writers in New York. She contributes to all the big glossies, *Vogue, Bazaar, Elle, Glamour*. I met her at a press event for a new line of cosmetics, Lovely!, and she is very nice. We bonded while laughing over, and attempting to score, a second microscopic (editor-friendly!) portion of rosemary chicken served at the lunch.

When I arrive at her Upper West Side apartment, I am awestruck. It is mammoth. I get the urge to skip around like a little kid in a museum. That's how big it is. I could definitely fit my apartment in here four, no, five times. Maybe six. As a matter-of-fact, they could probably reassemble the entire Natural History Museum dinosaur collection right in her living room. There are all sorts of antique furnishings from the fifties and sixties, like a chrome desk and a real Eames chair. I could write such beautiful words in here! The words would just flow from me, as I sat in my fur-trimmed negligee, sipping cognac from a crystal glass and admiring the wainscoting.

"So do you want to see it?" she asks.

"See what?" I am so astounded I don't even remember why I'm here. Oh. The interview. Right. Her closet. "Sure. Let's get right to it!"

"So, what's this magazine again? *Her Life?* I don't think I've ever heard of it before." As she turns toward the staircase, the amethyst golf ball on her finger temporarily blinds me.

"Actually it's called *For Her,*" I say, blinking away the big violet blob that won't seem to disappear from view. Defending the magazine, and, well, my pride, which is shrinking faster than an overstock of Marc Jacobs army jackets at a Barneys warehouse sale, I go on with the spiel I have all but memorized by now. "It's actually a really fantastic magazine. It's very new, which is why you are probably not familiar with it, but it has the most fabulous photography, and every time I read it, it just gets better and better. It's really going to be very successful."

"Well, that is great. It must be nice to work for such a cute little magazine like that." She didn't mean that as badly as it came out. I know she didn't, because as I said, she is very nice. She is just looking for something nice to say about it, but there isn't really that much that's nice to say about it. She's trying.

We're walking through her bedroom, which is right out of the pages of *Elle Décor.* Really, it is—January 2001 issue—and I am admiring the caramel-colored suede pillows and the modular end tables, when I turn to see it. It is breathtaking. And I don't mean that in a figurative way. I mean, when I reach the entryway of her closet, I literally cannot breathe.

And, apparently, I am turning blue, because Lisa says, "Honey, are you turning blue?"

I try to get the word "No" out, but, instead, a throaty, dry sound comes from deep down somewhere, and I am incapable of coming out with anything else.

"Sevilla, can you fetch me a glass of water for Ms. Lane, please?" she screams down the stairs to the kitchen, where her housekeeper has been polishing silver statues since I arrived. I never think to polish my silver statues, but, of course, mine are from Target. And they aren't actually silver. And the one time I did accidentally spray a bit of Windex on the one "silver" bookend I have, I actually rubbed off some of the "silver."

Sevilla, that's pronounced Sa-vee-ya, appears so fast—holding an elegant cylindrical glass, probably from ABC Carpet and Home, filled to the rim with water—that I think she may have gone through a time warp to get here. I take a big sip, as Lisa looks at me with her head cocked and a sweet smile on her face, which seems to say, "I've been there." And, I swear to God, even the water tastes better here than mine does, and it's ever so faintly infused with peach, like my bath gel, I note, quickly find the coincidence interesting and then as quickly realize it may not actually be that interesting. And, before I know it, I am back to breathing like a normal person. But, thinking about what has just happened, I feel less like a normal person than I ever have in my life.

"Are you alright now?" Lisa asks.

"I'm fine," I say, standing up and brushing myself off. "Thank you."

"I remember the first time I had to write an article about some rich woman's wardrobe. I was so nervous that I tore the sleeve off of Polly Mellen's bouclé Chanel suit. Right at the shoulder." She shakes her head, and with the wisdom and security of success says, "Don't worry about it at all."

And, with that, I feel more at ease. Lisa McLellon was once like me. And now, she has all this. My jealousy gives way to faith. I can do this, too, I find myself thinking. I just know I can.

The interview goes very well. I ask all the right questions. That means my questions got her engaged and speaking in an animated tone about all sorts of topics you could never have planned to ask. Lisa is very impressed with my fashion knowledge. At a football field's distance, I can spot an Alaïa sheath, a Gucci blazer. I know the year each was made. She takes me lovingly through the contents of her closet, which is fitted with a moving rack system, pointing out a Chloe blouse she is eternally devoted to, because she got her first *Vogue* assignment when she was wearing it, a Prada blossom-printed A-line dress she wore the first time she went to Paris for the fashion shows, and tons of other pieces that, together, really weave together the history of her fascinating life. At this moment, I love my job. I could just stand here all day and hear stories about Kate Moss and André Leon Talley and parties at Le Cirque. And the best thing about Lisa is that she doesn't ever forget for a second where she came from. Lisa worked her way all the way up from an assistant to the assistant of the assistant editor at *Vanity Fair*, fetching coffees and undergarments for her superiors. And look where she is now.

Three hours later, I really don't want to leave. So when we are through with her closet and all of the "sportif," "dress," "vixen," and "everyday" shoes are back in their pristine Lucite boxes—a mosaic of Swarovski crystals, buckskin, crocodile, and satin—and all of the garments are resting for their next outing on satin hangers, I am delighted when she asks, "Do you have a few minutes to drink a cappuccino with me? The weather is so nice, and I would love to sit on the veranda for a bit."

"I would love to," I say. When we have both lit cigarettes and Sevilla appears, again in seconds flat, with our steaming cappuccinos, I realize that I really need to ask some practical advice of Lisa. You don't get opportunities like this every day. So, I venture, "Lisa, would you mind if I asked you a professional question?"

"Sure, shoot."

She is really so sweet, and that gives me hope that there are many good people in this world, and then I feel bad again for having envied her wardrobe. I try to push that away, but when I realize this is not going to happen, I accept that I can be both jealous and thankful at the same time. So, I continue, "Well, I always read your articles, they are all so great, by the way, and, I have to ask, where do you get your ideas?"

A yellow bird alights on the iron scrollwork separating us from Fifth Avenue. Lisa takes no notice, and I think feathered friends stopping over for a visit must be an everyday sort of thing in this world as she takes a long, silent sip, her pinky pointing out gracefully, and says, "A lot of people ask me that question. And I always say that all you really have to do is keep your eyes and ears open. The ideas are all around you. And then, what you have to do is ask questions about those things. For instance, I just broke the heel of my favorite pair of Manolos, and I was literally jetting off to Spain that evening. And so I had to get them fixed, because they go with that—"

"Alaïa dress," I finish her sentence. I just can't help myself.

"Yes, that's the one." She flashes her extremely white teeth here. "And I'm sure you can tell why I needed to pack that dress. So, I researched the best place to go for same-day repairs, and then asked about what types of things they can fix and which ones they can't, and so on. And then I pitched a story about that. They used it in *Vogue*."

"I see. Okay. So, I just have to really think about every single thing that is going on around me. Real-life stuff." I am thinking this is horrible, common-sense sort of advice that will not help me in the least, nor anyone else who hasn't the connections that Lisa does, and I don't feel so bad about the wardrobe-envy anymore. Don't I do this already? Hadn't I just pitched a story about hair color after I got my color done? And hadn't it been rejected? "That is great advice. Thanks so much," I offer anyway, since she is such a great connection and she has been so nice. I can't very well say, "Thanks for nothing."

To maintain my sanity, I again reiterate to myself that her success with this strategy, and my failure with it, has to do with connections—both wealth and lack of, respectively. She has them, and I don't. That's my problem. It can really be the only answer. This last discourse leaves me feeling hopeless and almost entirely wipes out the ray of hope that had been with me during my stay here.

"Just keep your eyes open for the signs," Lisa reminds me as Sevilla begins her pedicure with a hot soak right there on the veranda. She picks up the *Times*, by way of ending the meeting—and again, this isn't rude, this is just Lisa—and after a second, lifts her head to the sun and says as I turn to go, "That is what takes time, my dear, knowing what to look for."

Back at my apartment, I unlock the door, and scoop up the *Times* with my two spare fingers and it seems amazing that both Lisa McLellon and myself have possession of something as commonplace as the same newspaper. My balancing act with the paper works fine until it is not working fine, which is to say until the *Times* falls to the floor, sections spilling out all over. "Shit," I say, resuming my solo hallway act of curses and exclamations. Again, this does nothing to rouse cute neighbors or even not-so-cute neighbors.

Once inside my apartment, I turn all of my current negativity toward the printed pages. But, still whirling from Lisa's wardrobe, I am operating in a heightened state of discovery and taking note of each and every detail with the sort of wonder an infant would encounter with, say, a torn scrap of gift wrap. Taking a quick look at the Sunday Styles section, I glance through the topics, already clucking my tongue at my stupidity for not having thought of the various stories and the paper's stupidity for having chosen topics so close in nature to those I sent in, only about entirely different products under entirely different pretenses. After about ten minutes of this, I pile the rest of the useless sections on top. The last is the Business section. I have never opened this section in my life. I don't think I would like anyone who reads this section. What is even inside of it?

Taking a glance at the cover, a picture of Oscar de la Renta jumps out at me. In the business section? I can't believe it. Style in the business pages? I am drawn into a long story about how Oscar's company is faring these days, and when I get to the end of the first page, I turn to page sixteen, as instructed. At the end of the story I glance at the next page, which is filled with boxed job listings. I suddenly feel bad for people who have to look for jobs. The little ads seem so boring. *Assist head of accounts department in collecting debt. Word and Excel a plus. Managing Director, Mergers and Acquisitions, seeks diligent assistant to organize, type correspondence, and maintain schedule.* How mundane. How tiresome. How could anyone wake up, day after day to type correspondence and maintain schedules? *Fifty thousand dollars starting?* Oh. My. God. Maybe it's not that bad.

You could get a whole new wardrobe of cute pants suits and ruffly blouses with cuffs that stick out from the sleeves. Brooches. Heels. Sophisticated strands of beads, twisted twice about your neck. A camel-colored overcoat tied at a nipped waist, an unused-but-integral-to-the-look-buckle dangling from a perfect knot. I have always wanted one of those. I picture myself in a smart getup, beneath my camel-colored overcoat, an oversize Gucci tote, swinging light as air at my shoulder, walking into a glittering skyscraper with one of those clip-on badges that everyone wears these days, amongst throngs of suited men. *Wait*. Suited men. What I'm saying here is, *men*. In suits. Hundreds of them.

Why has this never occurred to me before? Of course! I never meet those sorts of motivated businessmen, because I have never worked with them. In my industry the only sort of men I socialize with have an acute awareness of the percentage of cashmere used in a cashmere-cotton blend sweater. What I mean to say is, they are all gay. And while that may do wonders for my wardrobe, and would give me a fantastic sounding board if I actually had a love life, it does nothing to help me to get a love life.

Between the realization that I am so far out of Lisa McLellon's league that the fact we share the same planet even resonates oddly and the sort of obvious all-along discovery that I never meet men because I don't work on Wall Street, I am almost in tears. "Where are the *signs* Sevilla?" I ask aloud in Lisa-speak just because, well, just because. I wonder where I can go from here as I scrutinize the contents of my desk for potential inspiration.

Sevilla may actually have been channeled in a sort of crosstown momentary opening in the universe because just then the new e-mail jingle sounds.

It's Page Six. Yay! I love Page Six. Some famous person who looks too perfect, apparently is too perfect, which is to say, partially plastic, and her boyfriend, upon finding out, is suing her for misrepresentation, as he fell in love with her on the sole principle that her boobs were, in fact, real. I wonder if, like me, the dumped star indulged in a feast of fried foods and chocolate. While she may be skinnier, I momentarily get a shallow rise out of the knowledge that my boobs are real. When that rise begins to dip, I click on the fashion link so I can kick myself over more story ideas that were staring me in the face.

Big belts are back. I knew that! Basket bags are in for spring. I just visited the accessories show at the Javitz Center! I saw all of those. I'd even inquired about purchasing one. Oh, well. As Joanne would say, you can't cry over spilled milk. I go for my horoscope—the *Post* has the best horoscopes:

> With Saturn in your house, you are on the verge of a new opportunity. You have to think very carefully about the opportunity, as things will be happening rather quickly, and a mistake can be detrimental at this time. But, if you don't take the offer right away, you will not get a second chance. Finally, remember that the silence will be broken.

Wow. How will I know which opportunities are the right ones if I have to figure it out immediately? Why are horoscopes always so nonspecific? They should really give you a little more of a hint, like those starting with the letter *B* are safe; but whatever you do, stay away from anything beginning with the letter *T*.

Shifting back to idea mode I feel I must be on to something with such a celestial reading, and I get that tingle of happiness at being the lucky one whose horoscope outlines something fantastic that is sure to come. For that moment everything feels pregnant with possibility. But then that second is over and all I see is a somewhat unhygienic desk, with countless coffee cups, crumbs forming quite a collection underneath computer keys and God knows where else, and enough unsorted paper to make me feel some personal responsibility for destroying our planet's forests.

Messy desks, how to keep them in order? Cigarette smoking, why is it so addictive? Computers, why is it so difficult to keep up with the payments? "Dumb. Dumb. Dumber," I say to the pencil balancing between my upper lip and nose. And then I pick up the job market section of the paper, now sitting on my desk. Jobs. Hmmm. Jobs. What's new and cool with jobs? Er, no. With both hands, I tear the section open to the job listings and clear my throat with the abruptness of an important business sort. Changing careers? No hook. Making ends meet in a bad economy? Obviously I don't know the first thing about that. I put the paper down. It drapes the entire width of my desk, covering my computer, papers, the sacrificed trees, as if they never even existed—a living metaphor of the fact that I have gotten nowhere.

"Hello?" I say into the phone when it rings, happy for the distraction. Even if it were a telephone salesman, I would have found the time to be friendly today.

"What's up?"

It's Joanne. Yay! My best friend! I am back to loving her.

"Hi!" I squeak into the receiver.

"What the hell are you so excited about?" she asks.

I must sound like I haven't had human contact for months. This feels like an accurate description, even though I have just gotten home and had that somewhat magical contact with Sevilla since.

"Oh, I just missed you!" It's amazing how much you take your friends for granted when you are one half of a couple. Weeks, even months can go by, and you barely see them at all. And, both of you say things like, "It's so great that we are such close friends that we don't even need to see each other." But, then as soon as you are boyfriendless you begin grilling them for not spending time with you and you hate them for being happy when you're not. It is quite convenient, though, because you can take out all of your frustration on your best friend, as if the sole reason you are sitting home on a Saturday night is because she is wrapped up in her life.

So, after she tells me all about her romantic Saturday dinner, I berate her out of jealousy, explaining that I am not interested in the way Pete "did this thing with his tongue where he curled it up and . . ." She apologizes when I start crying. This is a horrible stunt, but it's the only way with her and I need to find an outlet for this unique talent to cry on demand. I begin to feel a bit better again. With that out of the way, the conversation turns more helpful. I begin complaining about a lack of cash flow. And a lack of boyfriends. And a lack of human interaction. I am on "complain control." A car has "cruise control," and I have "complain control." The switch is flipped and the stuff just comes out; I am merely a conductor for the negativity. I glance at the job listings again. I bounce the idea of getting a corporate job off of Joanne.

"I think it's a great idea. You can get out of the house and stop calling me every eight seconds. Maybe you can meet some *other*-people, too. Maybe even some men, so you could stop complaining about the fact that there are no men in your industry!"

I think about what she says. Perhaps it's a bit self-motivated, but she definitely shares the same view I do, if I am honest with myself for about half a second and realize that I am not making ends meet as a writer. She says something else about "writing an article about that," but I am too distracted by the visions of corporate life to listen. You see, I'd thought about supplementing my income with jobs before, but it always seemed like a bad investment if you think about the time you're not going to be able to spend trying to get writing jobs that will pay a lot more than Duane Reade could. That and the little humungous feeling that having a plastic strip punched with my name stuck onto a Duane Reade tag would have the distinct smell of failure. But this corporate thing. This is a different thing altogether.

You have to understand that in this industry, talent does not nec-

essarily equal success. What equals success is talent plus connections. You can pitch stories until the cows come home, but the person on the receiving end has five girlfriends who are freelance
writers calling and asking for assignments. And they are the ones
getting the assignments. Without a face, you are just a number. I
don't need to explain this to Joanne, because I have, probably about
five million times before on complain control. I have wanted to be
a writer ever since I could shimmy a pencil around on paper. My
mother still tells people (and by people I mean the supermarket
checkout girl and the mailman) the story about when I was in the
third grade and my teacher asked what I wanted to be when I grow
up and I said, "Judy Blume."

And then all of a sudden, I am not listening to Joanne at all anymore. Her silence is broken for the first time in, well, ever, with
presumably all manner of friendly advice and tender caring (not
sure where the words "Soundfactory" and "Webster Hall" fit in
there but I'm new to this Joanne talking, me ignoring thing) and
I'm not listening. The world is on its head. I've zoned out in a
flurry of instant genius. Lisa's words come back to me: "The ideas
are all around you." And it hits me, like a ray of sunlight through
the clouds. I suddenly know exactly how Benjamin Franklin felt
when he discovered electricity. I see a printout of my name, taped
to a front-row seat at fashion week. My driver, who will be named
Smithers (what else?) My breakup, the *Times* falling open to reveal
the job listings, Joanne "breaking the silence," and even the pile of
bills on my desk—they are suddenly revealing themselves as signs.

I now have the groundbreaking journalistic idea that will make
my career.

The story is (drumroll, please) . . . switching careers to find
love.

I will do the research by getting a job in a big corporation, where I will meet a wonderful, suited hottie, make some money, get insurance (maybe even dental!), and everything will be just sublime. It's perfect. I love it! It's so *Never Been Kissed* meets *Working Girl*. I can do anything! Thank you Lisa. Thank you *New York Times*. Thank you God!

"Hello? Are you there?" she asks, after I've been quiet for a while.

I fill Joanne in on my revelation, and when I'm through I take a deep breath, waiting for her to tell me how Einstein-like I have become in the past twenty-four hours.

"Uh, Lane, why does that sound so familiar?"

I'm not sure what she's talking about, but really I can't shake the feeling I have about this article idea. I feel positive, driven, in a way I haven't in a long, long time.

Joanne breaks the silence again. "But you do realize there's a chance you won't meet anyone?"

Why shouldn't I meet someone with all of those men around? It doesn't even make sense. Joanne is not in this industry, so she doesn't really understand, so I don't put too much stock in this response.

She must realize this, because she goes on to say, "Honey, all I'm saying is don't put all of your eggs in one basket."

Don't count your chickens before they hatch. A bird in the hand is worth two in the bush. Joanne is a vast source of wisdom, if you could ever decipher what it is she's trying to say.

"Listen, people in glass houses shouldn't throw stones," I say.

"Well, people in glass houses want to know if you are free for a drink tonight. I'd say you're in need of one. Morgan Bar, around seven?"

We always go to the Morgan Bar, located in the Morgan Hotel, on the notion (well, my notion, really) that we will meet some rich European businessmen staying there. I spend hours dressing just so, worrying over the brown eye shadow or the nude shade. It never really matters what I wear or how I look, since we just wind up talking to each other, and nobody speaks to us, except for the waiter—but, of course, he has to. Since Joanne already has a boyfriend, it doesn't make it very easy, as she is never concerned with meeting anyone and so says very nonsexy things very loud that could turn away even the most aggressive pickup artist. ("So, did I tell you about that awful yeast infection I had last week?")

We agree to meet at seven, and I get started calling around with my story idea. Normally you write in, but since I am so impatient, and ready to start on this project immediately, I just start calling editors directly. They already have me on file from all of the stories they have rejected in the past. I start with *Marie Claire*. Sorry, we're actually concentrating more on women who will do anything anyone asks them to, like ride a horse naked down Fifth Avenue or marry and divorce three men in a month—and even for that we're booked with stories until . . . until (paper rifling) February 2010. Why don't you try back then? *Vogue*. Love is so last season, daahling. It's all about bittersweet right now. But, of course, your name would have to be *instantly* recognizable to our readers in order to be considered. You're not the one from that movie with Corey Feldman are you? *Woman's Day*. We'll get back to you in a few months and if you could somehow work that into a cookie recipe *and* get a really good celebrity to come and cook it with you . . . No, you know what? We already did that one. *Us Weekly*. I have just one question for you. Do pictures of J. Lo or Ben fit into this story anywhere?

It's all feeling pretty hopeless until I get the *Cosmo* features editor on the phone. In a very uncomfortable split-second decision, I decide to use Lisa's name to get in the door and hopefully prevent another railroading rejection. I feel horrible, but I just know she

wouldn't mind. She's such a smart businesswoman, she'd probably
be shocked I haven't used it before.

"Oh, a friend of Lisa's, eh?" After providing me with a gener-
ous "fifteen seconds to describe your idea, start-inggggg—now!" I
barrel my way through the pitch, feeling with every word that
maybe the idea wasn't as great as I thought and that I am the stupidest person on this earth and why, oh why, does anybody in the
world let me speak, ever, and when I'm through I am absolutely
shocked because Karen says, "Maybe. Yes, maybe. We'll have to
think about it."

Although no *maybe* responses have, as yet, ever morphed into assignments for me, I have also never as of yet been known as a friend
of Lisa McLellon's and the laws of creatively applied positive
thinking clearly state that I can apply "feelings" and "hunches" to
motivate myself at any time I deem appropriate. It is just this sort
of positive thinking that keeps me from stapling my fingers to
the desk after quite definite and, well, abrasive "no's" minus
any "thank-you's," excuses, or similar pleasantries—and, in one
case, the addition of a "how did you get this number?"—from
Bazaar, Shape, Glamour, Mademoiselle. I'm thinking this all over, and
decide, maybe I will take a break and begin calling about some of
those jobs in the paper.

The first place asks that I fax over a resume. This means I have
to get my resume in order. Shit. I forgot about this. Writing a resume is possibly the most irritating task one can perform. Since
you just alter everything to make it say what you want anyway, I
don't see the point. It's basically a page of lies. Everyone knows
that. They should just do away with the resume altogether. I begin
thinking about things I'd rather be doing. Going shopping. Going
on a date. With a good-looking exec in a pinstripe suit. Kissing me
in the taxi on the way to Daniel. Placing his hand on my back as he

leads me to our table. Revealing a tiny turquoise box over a warm chocolate torte with crème fraîche.

Suddenly, I feel inspired to get a jump-start on the article. These romantic imaginings should not be wasted. I minimize the window with my resume on it. So far, I've changed the font, played with several type sizes for my name and address, decided to write out the word "apartment" rather than use the abbreviation, and changed the completion date of my last job from "to present" to "January '99" to "January 1999."

I am so sure I will be able to use this dreamy stuff in my Working-Girl-Finds-Love article that I type in the bits I have thought up rather than concentrate on my resume. I read it over, remarking that I like the use of "thoughtful kisser," and "elegant inappropriateness." I am more "excited" about this project than ever, so much so that I am actually a bit embarrassed when my bell rings.

It's a messenger with a press release and, I note with joy, a tiny shopping bag of beauty product samples. This is my favorite part of my job. I get lots of presents. Reading over the release and smelling the beautifully packaged bath and body products (This is so great, since I'm just running out of lotion), I press myself to think of an article idea from this faintly fig-scented collection.

But, there are so many bath and body lines already. What is different about this one? Fig is yesterday's news. Where is the story? I look at the ingredients to see if there is anything new inside that may be of interest. But the list is printed in French. And, although I took French for eleven years, I have never learned any chemistry words, and so this is no help to me. After cursing my $120,000 education, which I am still (not) paying for, I smooth the lotion on to see if perhaps it feels any different from other lotions. Nothing. It is rather soft and creamy though. But they are all soft and creamy.

Maybe I can write about the fact that it is from France. But isn't everything these days?

I toss the press release on the now three-foot-high pile of releases that I have never used for story ideas, but refuse to throw away on the principle that I will one day think of something to do with them.

It occurs to me that I need to finish my resume. It's really done. Well not *done* done. All I really have to do is spruce it up. It's not that big a deal, honestly. But, then my stomach makes a sound, and I realize that I haven't eaten yet today. You can't work on an empty stomach! Everyone knows that. You'll miss details. Forget the little things. What was I thinking? Not eating—really!

After indulging in a meal representing carbohydrates in each and every form that can in the best possible light only be described as escapist, I get back to my home office.

My desk is piled high with papers, folders, computer junk, notebooks, magazines, and an extraordinary number of pens bearing the brand name of everything from "Ralph Lauren" to "Galderma Labs"—most of which do not work. There are neat little officey things like Post-it notes that say, "Dr. Gesta is always available for interviews; remember him for lipo, microdermabrasion, and breast augmentation!"; stamps in a cute tin box with the words, "Remember to write to Maybelline when you're writing a beauty story!"; a calculator which insists that "Covergirl is the leading cosmetics brand in the world. Numbers don't lie!"; and paper clips in a box that says, "We'll help you *bring it all together* with makeup artists and hairstylists from across the globe—Global Public Relations."

All this stuff is positioned very close to my bed. Okay. It's touching and spilling onto my bed, which sometimes results in office product findings in some very unwelcome areas.

I ignore the mess and tell myself I will get right back to the resume, as soon as I check my phone messages. Ooh. But first I notice I have a little envelope on my computer screen, announcing a new e-mail message. I love that. There's always a chance that it will be some big magazine saying, "We absolutely love the story idea you have sent in. You are a complete genius. We hope it will not be too inappropriate for us to offer you four dollars a word to write sixteen hundred words on the topic." But, of course it never is.

It's just another press release. "We would like to tell you all about Kim Holbrook, the Hair Color guru from France who is coming to America to open her very first stateside salon. We hope you will join us for cocktails and a free blow-dry to celebrate." Sure, I would love a free blow-dry. And maybe, instead of thinking of a bigger story idea, I will just pitch it as a small bit, announcing that the Hair Color guru from France is coming to the Big Apple. Let's see. "French Hair Color Guru Dyes the Big Apple Red, Blonde, and Even Gives a Head of Shimmering Highlights." That sounds very cute. I'll send it to the usual Nobody's-Ever-Heard-of-Them publications I write for, and then maybe a couple of bigger ones.

I get started. Boy, I am a work machine today. I ignore the possibility that perhaps I am just motivated by the fact that I have no desire to finish this resume and take computer tests at a job placement agency.

It's 4 P.M. by the time I have put together three packets pitching the idea to some of the big-name glossies, along with copies of other articles I've written for the no-namers, and my list of assignments, which is quite long, despite the fact that all of the publications are so unimportant. Gosh, how many magazines are there in this world? Unbelievable that I can't make ends meet. Maybe I am at fault. Perhaps I am not meant to be a writer. Staggering to consider that out of the millions of people who want to do this for a living I think I will make it.

I am feeling blah. Hopelessness overtakes me. The only thing that will make me feel better is chocolate. I quickly consider eating that fake frozen yogurt that has no calories and no fat and no carbs (what the hell is in there anyway?), but then remember reading that when you have cravings, you should just indulge in the real thing, otherwise you will be on your way to a binge of Grand Canyon proportions. Of course, I have been binging since I broke up with James, but, still, every opportunity to do the right thing is an opportunity for a fresh start. And, I'm going to the gym tomorrow. And, after this I will eat like a saint, or a celebrity rather, (in paintings those saints always seem to be surrounded by food) for the rest of my life.

I am just unlocking my door, chewing on the most delicious chocolate croissant I have ever eaten (still warm!), when I hear my phone ringing. I try to say "Hello," but with the croissant still in mid-chew, it's more like, "Re-ro."

"Is this Lane Silverman?" the voice asks. Oh, no. Which bill have I not paid now? I look at the unopened pile on my desk and realize that this call could pretty much be about any of them.

"Who's calling?" I say in that bitchy voice I reserve for bill collectors. I can't believe they have the audacity to call me in the middle of my workday. Don't they know how busy I am? I mean, really. How am I supposed to get anything done?

"This is Karen, from *Cosmopolitan*. Is this a bad time?"

Oops. Note to self: Refrain from using bitchy bill-collector voice until you are sure you are speaking with a bill collector deserving of bitchy bill-collector voice. *Cosmopolitan*. Okay, don't panic. *Cosmopolitan* has just called *me*.

Trying to be as nice as possible to make up for the not-so-nice opening, I defer to mortifyingly spineless ass-kisser mode, "No, not at all. How can I help you? I just want to tell you that I have been reading *Cosmo* ever since we got off the phone and I absolutely love it so—"

"Listen, I am really busy and I don't have time to chat but I've just gotten back from one hell of an editorial meeting—we had to pull a huge story on women who enjoy having sex with relatives called 'Kissing Cousins' because our biggest advertiser thinks the story is too racy and has threatened to pull their ad pages—no ad pages, no money, no magazine—so do you think you could have the story ready by May fifteenth for the August issue?" Really she says that all in one long sentence; no stops or pauses or anything and so it takes me a moment to comprehend the whole thing and realize that she wants me to write the story.

This is the story that I knew was somehow different, would somehow do something to alter my life forever, that my horoscope said would come and that I would have to decide upon immediately and, of course, that that decision had to be the correct one. And now that I have thought this whole thing through in the apparently contagious frenzied manner that Karen has just presented it to me—no stops, no pauses—I realize the worst part of the whole thing. The day she wants the story is May fifteenth, which wouldn't be too bad if today were December fifteenth or January fifteenth or even February fifteenth, for that matter. But it is not. It is now March fifteenth and that is just two months away from May fifteenth. That is just sixty-one days. In the past, this hasn't proven nearly enough time to find my misplaced lacy black tank top, much less the man I will love for the rest of my life and have two kids with and fly kites on the beach with and pose in front of a mantel with for photo holiday cards. May 15. I haven't even gotten my resume ready yet. I'd have to get a job, find a man-target, and land him in just two months.

Oh. My. God.

But, it's *Cosmo*. And they really want me. (And I have just, for the first time in my life, used the words "land him.") *And*, if I'm honest with myself for just about two seconds, I will realize that if I don't have the energy to pitch this story to anyone else right now, I am never going to have the energy to pitch this story again ever, and then it will just end up with the pile of other ideas I've had and tossed over the last couple of years.

"Hello? Are you still there?" Since it has only been a second since I last spoke, I figure she must be talking to someone in her office. I wait for her to finish, but she doesn't say anything else.

"Hello? Lane?" Lane, that's me—the one who has the tiny pressure upon her to make the right decision immediately or suffer the consequences. The one whose shaking hand has landed croissant crumbs in a formation that, if looked at in the right way and slid around just a teensy bit, could look *exactly* like a heart (if with one hump up top, rather than two) and who, without time to be choosy, decides this "heart" will serve just perfectly as The Sign.

"Yes. Yes. I'm here. I'll do it. How many words?"

"Three thousand. We want it to be a cover story. We can pay you two dollars and fifty cents a word."

Two dollars and fifty cents a word times three thousand words is . . . a lot! "I'll do it. Corporate world, here I come."

"Great. We're so excited about it. I'm here for support if you need me. We're actually all here for you. You've picked a topic that definitely hits home for everyone here. This industry is impossible for meeting men. All those parties, all those drinks. The gift bags are great, but you can't very well cuddle up with one of those, can ya?" And then, as if she realizes she is showing too much emotion, she clears her throat and continues, "We're rooting for you, Lane. But, remember, you *have* to meet somebody. No pressure. But that's the story."

The first thing I do is consult my calculator. I do it again. This cannot be right. For *one* story—$7,500! I can pay off all of those bills, plus have some money to buy some new shoes and smart outfits. It will be great. And, I'm going to get paid an actual salary from the job I get, too. Cha-ching! I can't believe this!

I can't believe this. I have to get a job. I have to meet a man. Not just any man. I have to meet The One. The One who, after twenty-six years, has still not shown his face. But now I only have two months in which to find his face. What have I gotten myself into? It's 5 P.M. Too late to send my resume in today. I'll finish it up tomorrow first thing, bright and early. Momentarily a vision of myself, rising at the cock's crow, facing the day bright-eyed and bushy-tailed races through my mind's eye. Then the girl in the mental image barks, "Who are you kidding with this?" So, I settle on first thing, whether or not it's bright and early.

My schedule for the following day all straightened out, I shift my energies to the present, where I have to take a shower and get ready to meet Joanne, so I can tell her how freaked out I am, have her advise me on why I should be happy, ignore her, and continue on with the same line of thinking.

When I wobble into my apartment that evening, filled to the brim with the power of three cosmos, I call my voice mail. Well, actually, first I call some guy named Swen, whose number is quite similar to the voice mail number.

"Late night again?" Swen asks. He recognizes me by the same

question I always ask, "Why isn't this working?" because I never really listen, I just press the numbers, and then wait for the messages, until Swen says, "You've got the wrong number again honey." I always picture Swen in a smoking jacket, all patience and fluidity, running his fingers through his shoulder-length blond hair, sitting by a crackling fire after a long day on the slopes, even though I know there are no slopes in Manhattan.

"Yeah, sorry," I say. And that's when I usually hang up. Except for when either Swen or I are feeling chatty. And, tonight both Swen and I are feeling chatty.

"How are things, lovely?" he asks.

"Swen, if you really want to know, I've made quite a mess of things today." I explain the whole story to him—the article, the fact that if history repeats itself there is a possibility that there is nobody who can claim the title of The One. I tell him about the resume I have to put together and the fact that it is teeming with what *some* may construe to be lies. Swen proves a good listener, which is to say, he doesn't simply fit the "ahas" and "rights" into the proper pauses, but actually takes it all in and produces an opinion.

"If you really believe in your heart that you can do it, then you can. You can do anything. It sounds to me like you have a warm, trusting heart, and that you just might be one of the last of a dying breed that believes in true love. And that is a fantastic place to be. And now, you'll just have more of a reason to trust that heart of yours. Just research this project the way you would research anything. And you'll be prepared." Like a horoscope, sounding all wise, but without the specifics. Until he says, "And if you really need to find love, I'm right here for you, darling."

Sure, me and every other girl who dials his number rather than voice mail late at night.

Being that I imagine him such a ladies' man, who most probably just read that entire speech from a well-handled booklet of "perfect pickups," I think he might have some insight into what men find attractive and therefore he might prove helpful in the sartorial advice department. When I mention the camel-colored overcoat I'm thinking of investing in, he says it's a good idea, and adds, "I always like a woman in a black dress and heels. It's sexy, timeless." This advice is so good I find myself wondering if Swen is gay, rather than a womanizing playboy. I shake the image from my mind. It's nice to have him on hand for a fantasy or two, when one is needed.

As if sensing my hesitation, he leaves me with, "Don't forget I'll always be your M&M."

Just how many times *have* I called him?

After I hang up with Swen, I try the voice mail again. This time I listen to hear the instructions, "Please enter your password," before keying in the numbers. "You have six new messages," the automaton female says on the other end. Six. That is amazing. Perhaps wind of my success has gotten out and now everyone wants me to write for them. I'll probably be sent directly to Paris and Milan to cover the fashion shows. I'll have to get a vanity case and Evian Mist to travel with on the plane. I'll probably be Anna Wintour's best friend by summer. She'll be sending me e-mails informing me, before anyone else is aware, that gray is the new black. If I'm that busy, maybe I won't have to do the *Cosmo* piece after all.

One: "Lane, pick up, it's Mom." Or, maybe I will have to do the *Cosmo* piece after all. Two: "La-yne, c'mon. Just pick up the phone." She never quite comprehends the fact that voice mail, unlike an answering machine, does not allow you to hear the person as they leave a message. Three: "Lay-ne, I'm getting very worried about you. It's bad enough that I have to worry about my daughter being all alone in the world. You who never thinks any man is good enough for her. I wish I could sleep soundly knowing that you are with James. I hope you're happy because my heart is palpitating. I might wind up in the hospital. Pick up." (I smile here. No matter how irritating, and awful, it is still nice to know that somebody is worrying about you.) Four: "Lane, I've called all of the police precincts in your area to find out if you are okay. Call your mother!" Five: "Lane, the hospitals haven't heard anything from you either. Call me!"

I don't even bother considering a phone call. This is just what my mother does. She'll have forgotten all about it in the morning. She hasn't really called the police or hospitals. She just says that for effect. This is her way of convincing me to get back together with James, accept the fact that he is a good, decent man—the perfect type for marrying. She wants me to settle down already, instead of filling my head with "unrealistic fantasies named after crisp chocolate candies." I'm just ready to skip past message six, which, if history serves as any sort of indication, will probably have to do with the fire department, when Joanne's voice comes on.

"Lane, I'm on my way home, and I just want to make sure that you know—before you stay up all night worrying about this whole thing—that you can do this. You will do this. Just have confidence in yourself. I'm not saying the whole predicament isn't a bit ridiculous—because it is—but I think it will do you good to get out among the living again and see that you are a fabulous, worthy woman. Now go to sleep."

How very un-Joanne. But, how very needed and appreciated. If I ever felt the urge to use that awful expression, now's the time—Grrrl power!

Despite Joanne's fabulous advice, I am not yet ready to go to sleep. I haven't seen Chris in way too long, and the last few times I have, I've been a horribly selfish girl, only thinking about myself and my problems. A visit is in order. So, I grab my keys and head up to his apartment. He doesn't sleep, which serves as a thoroughly awful condition for him, but serves as a wonderful condition for me, should I wake up in the middle of the night, unable to get back to dreamland.

"Come in," he screams when I knock at the door. He knows it's me, because I am the only one who comes to his door in the middle of the night.

"Hey," I say and we swap double air-kisses—not so much because we are fabulous, but because we are both part of the fabulous world and love/hate it together. I drop into my "spot," his extremely cozy chair-and-a-half and slip my shoes off. "What's shakin' bacon?" he asks.

"Oh this and that," I say.

"And which this are we upset about now?" He looks up from the photos he's looking through on his table.

"Actually, none at all."

And this time he turns from the table and walks right up to me. "Lane, am I sensing that you are happy?"

You know what? I am. And although it is somewhat to do with the possibility of meeting a man, it's much more to do with a sense of purpose. I have a big responsibility and I feel something I haven't felt in a while—great. "I am, my darling."

"Well, I'm uncorking the bubbly. It is definitely time to celebrate," he says. Chris keeps these fabulous champagne glasses in his apartment, which he only uses on the most special occasions, and he pulls them down from the rack above his sink now.

"The special flutes?" I ask.

"My darling, I am so glad to have you back."

It's amazing how much you take your friends for granted sometimes, when you can't think of anything but being alone. But, when you get out of that horrible stage and into life again, for

some reason, they are still there and willing to forget how insuffer-
able you have been.

So, I tell Chris the whole story and if it's possible, he is more excited about it than I am. And, unlike Joanne, Chris has been to the
Traveler's Building and has seen the throngs of men walking
around. "You, my dear, are going to have a blast," he assures me.
The rest of the evening is spent in a thoroughly enjoyable fashion—playing poker using a currency of Polaroid shots of bare-
chested male models Chris will be shooting next week.

"I'll raise you one Tyson."

"I'll see your Tyson and raise you a Marcus and a Scott."

You might not understand the value of one over the other, but
believe me, we surely do. It only takes eyes, and we have been playing this game for so long that we don't ever dispute the worth.
During fashion week, when others are taking pictures of the
clothes to remember the looks they'd liked when order or article-
writing time rolls around, Chris and I snap faces, asses and, if visible, bare chests that we'd like to order.

Three

You're Gonna Make It After All

Two cups of coffee and fifteen cigarettes into the following morning, I am faxing my resume to the Financial Professional Recruiting Agency, to the attention of a Ms. Banker. When I telephone an hour later to make sure that she has received it and to schedule a meeting, the first thing I ask is, "Isn't it such a coincidence that your name is Ms. Banker? Do people ask you that all of the time?"

"I'm not sure I know exactly what you mean, Ms. Silverman, but I think we have more important things to discuss."

"Do you have something for me, then?" I knew it. See, when you just put your mind to it, you can do absolutely anything. So quick and painless. Success, love, riches, here I come.

"Not so quickly, Ms. Silverman. Do you think people trust the Financial Professional Recruiting Agency because we throw just anyone into positions at the finest financial institutions in the city?"

Is this a trick question? "Er, no?"

"That's right. First we'll need you to come in and perform some computer skills tests. You do know Word, Excel, and PowerPoint, correct?" When I was typing Excel and PowerPoint into the computer skills section of my resume, I was a bit worried, only because I have never used either one in my lifetime, but since all of the job listings in the *Times* had called for them, I'd figured I ought to just add them, and then learn them if the need ever arose. How hard could it be really? They make Windows applications so simple that a monkey could use them. I mean, look at that America Online commercial with the monkey. He had no problems whatsoever sending a message to his friend to announce he'd passed his driving test.

"Of course," I say with such authority that *I* actually believe that I could sit right down and figure out quadratic equations with my eyes shut.

"Great. Can you come in this afternoon? Say two o'clock?"

In the advertisements for these agencies, they should really warn you how depressing the offices are. It's all puke green cinderblock walls, like in a prison, boring office carpeting that doesn't even match, and a receptionist so rude that I can't imagine a recruiting agency hasn't found a better replacement. The worst part, though, is this one painting on black felt of a single clown, frowning as he looks up at his balloon that's drifted up out of reach. Someone should do an article about this. "Job Hunting Nightmares," or better yet, "Recruiting Agency Blues."

After I dash through my application and pass it on to the receptionist (that is, once she's through telling the person on the other end of the telephone about this blouse that she bought at Joyce Leslie that rang up for only $6, even though the tag said $25, what color it was, the type of cut, what she'll pair it with, and when she's thinking of wearing it), I say I am ready to take my tests now. "What do you think all of these other people are waiting for? To get to the pearly gates?"

Okay. A simple "you'll have to wait" would have been just fine, but I smile and take my seat in the sweetest way possible. Don't bite the hand that feeds you, Joanne's voice says in my head.

Perhaps I should just ask some people here about their feelings regarding job hunting through a recruiter, to get a bit of research for a possible article. I might as well pitch the story to one of the daily papers. What's the worst they could say? Lord knows I've heard that N word before. I look around the room at the job hunters to find one that would be a good candidate for the story. To me, a good candidate is the kind of person who will see things the way I do. Perhaps this is not the best way to go about writing a story, but if they don't say what I think they will, then the piece won't work.

The first thing I do is look at shoes. I see a pair of scuffed up stack-heeled Mary Janes—cute, but unfortunately, very obviously plastic. I mean, you can't very well hope to get a job if you come to an interview wearing plastic shoes. It's all about impressions, which is why I am wearing the black leather pants I purchased for my last job interview at *Jane*, paired with a smart black and white tweed blazer, which I also bought for that interview. So, I didn't get the job. But I looked the part. I really did. I shift my gaze to another corner of the room and spot a very stylish pair of natural-colored, point-tip stiletto boots, peeking from beneath a smart brown pantsuit. There's my girl.

"Hi. How are you?" I ask, a bit too cheery-voiced for this particular waiting room. I'm like a clown in the ICU unit of a hospital.

"O-kaay," she says hesitantly, probably wondering exactly why I am talking to her.

"I am researching an article and I'm wondering if I can perhaps ask you a couple of questions about using job recruiters."

"For which publication?" she asks.

Shoot, a smart one. I hate this part, because now I have to explain that I don't exactly have the assignment, but that I would like to pitch it to the daily papers in the city, and her input would really be helpful.

Normally, when I'm trying to get together information for a beauty or fashion story without actually having an assignment, big companies cut me off here, and explain that they don't have time to speak with someone who may or may not be writing an article for some publication or another. But in this bleak environment, where the only other form of entertainment is a thoroughly dog-eared, two-year-old issue of *Biography* or an even more abused coverless issue of *People*, it's an easier sell.

When I'm done with my spiel she says, "Sure. I'm Samantha, by the way. What would you like to know?"

The words just come to me. I am a natural. "This office seems so sober to me. Everyone is wearing a frown. Does this have any effect on you?" I ask, sounding rather professional. "I'm Lane, by the way," I add as an afterthought.

I begin jotting down notes as she says, "I'm so glad that you said that. This is the third place I've been to in the past two weeks, and they're all like this. And then, after waiting for about two hours, you take these awful tests which are, like, the most difficult things in the world, and then after you fail miserably, some woman behind a desk says with the most high and mighty tone you've ever heard, 'Sorry. We don't have anything for you.' And then you feel like the biggest loser in the entire world, and even though you graduated from college with honors, you don't think you'll ever find work anywhere."

I've made Samantha cry. Her head is convulsing in all of these tiny jerks and her mascara is quickly making its way from high-lighting her lashes to highlighting the bags under her eyes. I run to the receptionist (still on the phone) and grab the tissue box from her desk. "It's okay, Samantha. We all feel like that," I say, starting to get worried for myself. She doesn't sound all that different from me. I hope I can pass the tests.

I rub her back, looking around the room, and notice that most everyone there is shaking their heads in agreement—even the girl in the plastic stack-heel Mary Janes. And some people begin vocalizing their views. This seems to calm Samantha down, and she goes on to tell me the rest of her story. It seems that the people who work in the recruiting agencies don't always consider your skill set properly, and so make you feel like a moron because you can't balance accounts in Excel—even if you were the valedictorian of your class. After I've finished interviewing her, and we've exchanged telephone numbers to grab a drink together some time (misery does love company), other people begin approaching *me* to participate in the story. Whether it's the five minutes of fame, or the us-against-them force that has everyone excited, it doesn't matter one bit to me. People are fired up about this story. And so am I. By the time I am called in for my test, I have practically penned the entire article. Lane Silverman, star reporter. It does have a certain ring to it.

I can't quite get my head around how everything happened to work out so well at the recruiting agency (despite the fact that Ms. Banker is, in person, as nasty as she was on the telephone), but I am beaming by the time I get home.

And, I am radiant in my new camel-colored overcoat. I probably shouldn't have used my Saks card, but I just had to start my new executive life with a new executive look. And the sling-back chocolate croc pumps were just the perfect corporate shoes. I wore them both on the way home, just to break them in (okay, really because I couldn't help myself). I stuffed all of the tags and boxes inside my new attaché case. It was on sale, okay?

The job Ms. Banker is considering me for is in the Mergers and Acquisitions department of Salomon Smith Barney. It is the one I'd seen advertised in the paper. My duty would be to support one of the Managing Directors. I can do that! No problem. And after we'd spoken about how glowingly perfect I am (according to my resume and alleged computer skills), I've almost forgotten that I have to take the tests at all.

"Before you run into the testing center," Ms. Banker explains in a wide-eyed manner, "I'd like you to meet the man you'd be reporting to. He actually just came in to meet with me about his particular requirements, and I asked him to stay for a moment to meet you. Please do not embarrass the Financial Professional Recruiting Agency or yourself."

I am glad at this opportunity, because I'm always great with interviews—I do this for a living! As I glance at her thumbtack-hung posters—waves crashing off pointed rocks under a crystal blue sky, above the word, "Success;" another depicting a skier doing the downhill underneath the word, "Compete,"—I wonder why, if she thought she was helping people so much, she felt the need to act like a mean know-it-all. Fingering Ms. Banker's Precious Moments figurine of a girl wearing glasses at a desk, which seemed almost sinister, given the situation (you know, resting on the desk of a mean cow), I picture the balding, stout man, stuffed into a cheap-looking suit, sporting a record-breaking comb-over, who would most likely walk through that door. He'd probably take one look at a young, pretty thing like myself and hire me on the spot.

"Thomas Reiner, meet Lane Silverman," says Ms. Banker as she came back into her inspiration-filled office with him. I stand up to shake his hand, noting that he is not, in fact, old at all. My guess—about thirty-two. His full head of soft brown hair is neatly shaved at the back and sides and just the right length up top. He looks like someone you would glance at, but never look twice at in a bar; the sort of man you would describe as "nice." His female friends probably tried to fix him up all the time, selling him with phrases like, "He is the nicest man I know and so smart!" I feel a wave of pity for him.

We both take the vinyl seats on the interrogation end of her desk, and Ms. Banker props herself up, back perfectly straight (straighter than when she'd met with me, I note) in her own high-backed Staples special, hands folded in prayer position.

"So, Lane, Ms. Banker tells me your computer skills are excellent, and I see you've graduated from NYU and spent lots of time as a freelance writer. All very impressive. Writing skills are highly regarded for positions like this. But, I must ask why you are choosing to switch careers at this particular time?"

"Well, I just want to meet men, really," I say, smiling to show it was a joke. A joke. Of course, it's a joke. Of course. Ms. Banker's brows scrunch up so tightly, they virtually disappear. But when Reiner's face breaks into a gleaming smile (he has very white teeth) and he begins laughing, she lets them ease back into two separate entities again and even manages an under-her-breath laugh/sigh to show she is obviously in agreement with popular opinion—her important, paying client's popular opinion.

"Obviously, you have very good interpersonal schmoozing skills," he says. "Is that what you studied in college?"

"Well, that was my minor, but English was my major." I try to communicate levity with my eyes rather than my hands in the spirit of smooth calm. Nevertheless, of their own will, they make half gestures in my lap that could have gotten me confused with a sign language translator.

"You'd never tell from where I wound up, but I actually studied literature in my undergrad days as well. Big American lit fan, too?"

"Sure, I love Faulkner and Hemingway," I say. This is my standard reply. That was the only course I actually took that went into any lengthy detail on authors. They were all right, but probably not really my favorites. Those would be Sophie Kinsella, Helen Fielding, Jane Austen, the Brontës, anyone who writes about love and provides a happy ending and fodder for my M&M search. Hemingway's male love interests always get thwarted, have sexual dysfunctions or get freaked out when their wives transform into men—not really my cup of tea.

"Big bullfighting aficionado?" he replies—in complete mastery of the eye levity thing, hands statue-still over one knee—and continues, "Anyhow, let me tell you a bit about the position. You're obviously more than qualified." And then, as if only to please Ms. Banker, he adds, "You do know what mergers and acquisitions is, right?"

"Well, sure, it's when two companies want to m-erggge (I bent my head a bit here as the word slid slowly out. His eyes followed until it looked as if our heads would crash. And in a flash it came to me.) to put their . . . assets together to . . . to . . . increase profits."

Tada! It sounds like common sense to me. I look over to Ms. Banker to pooh-pooh her lack of confidence in me, but she isn't smiling. In fact just the opposite. I get that awful body-floating-off-to-sea feeling that so often accompanies shoe-in-mouth syndrome.

"Ha, ha," I snicker, in case what I said is more appropriate as a cute little joke and readjust my hair behind my ear.

"Yes, on a small scale, that's it exactly. Basically, mergers and acquisitions are just one product area in investment banking that we offer clients as strategic advice. If we see that a certain industry is consolidating for any number of reasons, we will present our best ideas to specific clients regarding what we feel makes sense as a long-term growth plan for shareholders. For a company to hire *us* rather than a competitor takes years of building relationships and credibility." That's what he says.

What I hear is, "Yes, blah, blah, blah, blah, blah."

Was that even in English?

I don't worry about the heretofore-unmentioned "foreign language" requirement. I remember from my college temp days, it didn't really matter if you understand what's going on when you're an assistant. As long as you can type and ask questions when you aren't sure if something makes sense the way you've typed it, you're fine. When you're not really a key player at a company and realize that from the menial tasks you are asked to perform every day ("Lane, can you find out if this notebook comes with the spiral *on top*, rather than on the side?" or "While you're at it, can you pull all of the files out and stamp each with 'FILED' and then put them back exactly the same, except retype the tabs in Courier New ten point?"), it's easy to get depressed about your worth.

One day you step back and wonder exactly how you've gone so far off track that you are torturing yourself over mistakenly having chosen "standard" manila over "nouveau" manila folders and that's when you start implementing Third Reich nicknames for your superiors, maintaining a steady habit of bringing up things like the cost of your education and the honors you were granted at graduation, and adopting a bad case of finger-waving-hand-on-hip syndrome during "happy" hour over five-too-many margaritas.

Although those wonderful olden days were flooding back in Ms. Banker's fuzzy corporate presence, this time at least I know I am returning with my own stable of goals. And so I hope going from master-of-my-own-domain to underpaid, underappreciated, I'll-show-you (by hoarding, at home, every last number two pencil, rubber stamp, and novelty Post-it flag set I can get my hands on) status wouldn't set me back too far on the emotionally-prepared-for-a-high-school-reunion scale.

But I have the feeling that Tom isn't the sort of guy who would scream at the top of his lungs: "You are the stupidest girl I have ever met!" He seems to get the fact that I could do the job in my sleep. I am nodding comprehension, as he continues to go into the splendors of investment banking—a spiel I've heard and attempted to stay conscious through before at midtown bars during weekdays between the hours of five and ten P.M. I am sure the information will take the same route it has before—in through one ear and, at warp speed, out the other.

"That is fascinating," I say. (Again, much practice in this sort of reply from midtown happy hours.)

(Possible article: "Everything I Needed to Know About Financial Job Interviews I Learned at Sutton Place.")

One side of his mouth traveled north a bit, in a mock smile, and I get the feeling that although he acted like he was buying my shtick by the wagonload, he can really see right through me to the neon marquee flashing "Zzzzzz." You have to respect a guy like that. He sees I can do the job, and doesn't get bogged down in all of the snooze-inducing details that anyone with passing marks in playtime can surely pick up along the way. I never could understand those bosses who allotted two hours in the conference room to explain office supply order form procedure. I'm guessing Mr. Reiner couldn't either.

He seemed so cool and yet looked so uncool. I mentally shook my head. Too bad he was wearing a tie with pairs of golf clubs crossed all over it. That's actually one of the top five things on my list of no-way-in-hell guys:

#4. Never date a guy who wears ties with golf clubs on them.

I am getting all caught up in thinking about how guys are always just one or the other—nice, or cool and sexy—never both, never all the items on the checklist (I have my M&M checklist all neatly typed up and photocopied one hundred times in a pretty, spiral-bound book with a furry pink cover, so that each time I meet someone with M&M potential, I'll have a clean checklist with which to properly write out an assessment of him)—when everything goes silent.

I notice both Ms. Banker (who I swear, does not want me to get a job, no matter how many posters of successful waves or competitive skiers she had tacked on her wall) and Mr. Reiner are looking at me in anticipation. The former has a smirk on which you could literally see the words "I thought so," and the latter is wearing that one-sided smile again.

Mr. Reiner saves me. "So, do you think a bit of organizing, filing, scheduling, and telephone answering is something a smart gal like you could handle?"

Gal? Who the heck uses that word? *Oy*. He could have been using it sort of jokingly, which would be kind of cute. But still, if you are going to talk like that you might as well shave off all your hair, grow a round belly, and move to Boca.

"Sure."

I smile and he stands up at that, sticking out his hand, which was not manicured and a bit on the dry side, for me to shake. "We'll see you Monday. Eight-thirty A.M."

"Can't wait," I say, and this time both sides of his lips turn up in a full smile, and I am almost sure that he could see right through to my brain, where my little assignment sits front and center and I am mentally swapping his tie for a beautiful subtle silk one.

Imagine how simple this whole thing would be if Mr. Reiner had been The One!

I am almost embarrassed for big, old Ms. Banker, when she gets up to escort Mr. Reiner out of the office, her polyester pants shirring with each stride. She looks like she is trying so hard to impress in a way that shows she doesn't know the first thing about how to do it. There is hair-fluffing and blouse straightening and forced giggling at comments that aren't meant to be funny. I can't help thinking about giving her a makeover—taking her to the gym, a whistle strung around my neck as she chugged along on the treadmill; coaching her through Bloomingdale's, pointing out stylish clothing that actually enhanced her looks; snapping a pointer at her fingers when she gravitated towards tapered slacks. ("Remember the crashing waves! Success! Success! Say it with me, Banker!") She does have quite beautiful eyes and a nice, tiny nose.

But when I get up to follow them, and she turns around with a silent "Na-ah, we're not done yet," I am back to visually rapping her hand. This time I added a gaggle of highlighted beauty editors coming at her virgin brows with tweezers, chanting, "This won't hurt a bit! *Hoooh-hoooh, haaaahhhhh-haaaaah-haaaah*."

So she puts me to the test by running the computer skills evaluations. And I am not exaggerating when I say that these are awful, horrible tests that are designed to massacre self-esteem and chuck confidence into the East River. After you fail to know what the vaguest little button on Microsoft Word does (which obviously can't be too important, since that is the only application I have been using every day for years and I haven't had the need for it yet) a window disguised as cute and innocent with a bold font and pretty colors, says things like, "Sorry, that is the wrong answer," and "Are you sure that is what you want your final answer to be?" in such a dehumanizing way that you really have to fight off the urge to pick the monitor up and hurl it out the window.

I fail miserably.

When I meet with her again in her "inspired" office, Ms. Banker looks smugger than she had earlier.

"Do you think it funny to lie on your resume?" she asks.

This time I am sure it was not the sort of question that required an answer.

"Our clients trust us to provide them with excellent staffers, and you have taken that responsibility and stomped all over it." Ms. Banker appears thrilled at the opportunity to reprimand me thus. It's like when you go to McDonald's and ask the underpaid, caste system–conscious cashier to "Biggie Size" your meal, and avenging themselves for every time they've been forced to ask "Would you like fries with that?" they act like they haven't a clue what you're talking about, until you realize you're using Wendy's terminology in McDonald's and correct yourself by saying, "Um, sorry, I mean Supersize." And then, as if in epiphany, they say, "Oh," like they hadn't known what you'd meant all along.

It is clear that Ms. Banker has feelings for me like the ones people normally reserve for penny-pinching landlords and shoplifters—in sum, not the good kind. Who knows the cause? Youth? A difference of 120 pounds, maybe? And I am okay with it, too, just as long as she can find it in whatever she had in place of a heart to let me keep the job with Mr. Reiner.

"But since Mr. Reiner is so set on hiring you, I'm going to let you take the tutorials to learn the programs now."

I am shocked. I can barely speak. Is she actually being *nice* to me? Maybe this is what she thought her role in inspiring people is all about. You knock them down first, and then you show them that you, and you alone hold the tools to pick them up—and then they're eternally grateful. It seems like a strange way to make yourself feel important. But I am not about to argue. And you know what? Those tutorials broke everything down so simply that I figured it all out in no time, retested and passed with flying colors. I have to admit that I did feel a bit inspired. I am not about to grab a surfboard and a ticket to Hawaii, but still.

In the end, Ms. Banker shakes my hand, smiling, I might add, and says that she is very proud of me.

I like the sound of that.

Four

The Trial, the Men,
and the Wardrobe

Since I am to arrive at 8:30 A.M. I set my alarm for 7 A.M. Howard Stern wakes me up talking about the size of someone's boobs. I look down at mine and wonder what he would think. I fare on the bigger side, and that seems to be his thing. I shake this thought from my head and wonder why the hell I am even considering this point in the first place.

I chalk it up to the unnatural necessity of waking up so early in the morning. If you need an artificial device like a clock radio to get out of bed, then can it possibly be good for the natural, normal way your body functions? I should write an article about that, "Snoozers Rejoice" or "Ten Reasons Why You Should Chuck Your Alarm Clock." To regain some normalcy, I throw sweatpants over my nightgown and run down to the deli for coffee.

The guy behind the counter makes some remark about "joining the living today," since I don't think I have ever been here before nine. I laugh it off, but it does seem to ring true. It's been a long while since I worked in an office, and although I normally make a habit of laughing at and feeling superior to the throngs of people squishing into the subway during rush hour (metaphors involving cattle often play in here), today I am proud to be one of them. The new shoes and camel-colored coat don't hurt, either.

I look very smart in a knee-length red pencil skirt and a printed Chloe top that I bought on eBay for one hundred dollars this winter. The floral chiffon top has the tiniest buds with the same brownish hue as my shoes and so the whole ensemble comes together beautifully. Normally, I am a total moron when it comes to practical dressing (I'm ready for any last-minute invitation requiring a pink taffeta ballerina skirt with crinoline underlay, but I wouldn't exactly "blend in" on the North Fork), but everything just seems to be working out effortlessly today. Maybe I don't have little birds and squirrels putting together my outfit, but this is a very Cinderella-esque moment in my life. When I press the elevator button, the doors open immediately. Never has the elevator been waiting for me in the entire three years I have lived here. I buy a newspaper (after going back and forth between impersonating a professional with the *Times* or being true to myself by indulging in a bit of gossip with the *Post*, I go for the latter—I've already got the job, so there's no longer a need to impress), fold it under my arm, all working-woman-like and descend underground.

I am going to Tribeca. I have been there for parties at design shops, to review bars with velvet ropes outside, to perchance catch Ed Burns coming out of his apartment, but I've never gone by train or walked around the area for any length of time. And if you know anything about the "Triangle Below Canal" then you know it is a maze of a district, with street names that taxi drivers rarely know and, as if that's not enough, two Broadways, a regular old one and another with the word West before it, which is enough to leave even the most street savvy running around in circles like a tourist and feeling the need, when forced to ask directions, to explain that you are indigenous to the city, but you *never* make it down this far.

So perhaps it would have been a better idea for me to take a trial run to the office yesterday, rather than spend hours on the phone with Joanne going over the profile of what my M&M will look like, using the Polaroids I'd won in the poker game as guides. But, gosh, how often do you get to spend a Sunday in such a pleasant way as that—so pregnant with possibilities and hopes?

When I emerge from the train at Franklin Street, the sidewalks are overflowing with suits and all manner of corporate casualites shuffling off in this direction and that, all knowing exactly where to go. I am dumbfounded. I don't even know east from west, north from south over here. I normally go with the "we" trick—west to your left, east to your right if I can figure out which way is north, but I can't find any points of reference. I'm straining to see the Empire State Building, but it's out of my view. I think I see water in the distance, but is that the west or east side? Tom had told me to ask someone where The Travelers Building is, but I can't imagine anyone would know a building by name.

"Do you know where Greenwich Street is?" I ask one good-looking man, carrying a briefcase. No time like the present to begin my mission; now that I've an assignment I'm really interested in, I am a true workaholic.

Only I don't notice that his other hand is laced through the hand of a woman, and, taking one look at me, she tugs him away before he can even answer. Aghast (it's not as if I'd inquired whether he could perform oral sex on me right there on the street corner); I turn to look for another suitable (and preferably suited) direction-giving candidate. Only, my foot will not move with me, the occasion for the human pretzel (even if one dressed in a beautiful overcoat and real Chloe top) I am now attempting to Mac-Gyver my way out of.

I am not panicking, but it seems that my shoe may be stuck, and, unlike the charming chain of events set off after this happens to Jennifer Lopez in *The Wedding Planner,* I am all alone in my predicament. Looking down, I see that my heel is lodged between the grooves of one of those subway grates. I have never in my life stepped on one of those—never. I am always so careful about this. In fact, I remember moaning aloud while watching that movie, "Yeah right! Nobody walks right over those in heels!"

I am still trying to keep my cool, while twisting and yanking to free myself of the damn grate, but nothing's happening. Shit! People are starting to stare, and I can feel my cheeks turning crimson. This is unbelievable. I am the one in need, and they should be embarrassed for not coming to my rescue, and I'm the one blushing.

From somewhere behind, I finally hear someone ask if I need help, and like a lunatic, I scream, "I'm fine! I'm fine!" because I am so busy being angry at the lack of humanitarianism in our society that I don't realize this is my way out.

But I'm not fine, and now I have to bend down to remove my shoe and jiggle it free. Only once I loosen my foot from the shoe, I step on something with my bare foot, and my stocking snags, and as I try to pull that free, I feel the distinct tickle of nylon tearing up my calf, as the run makes a warp-speed vertical climb.

"Always carry two pairs of stockings," I've advised in articles. But when you're deciding between one pair of the really nice kind that make you feel like a million bucks and two of the practical pairs that put together don't even make you feel like fifty cents, you somehow convince yourself that the expensive ones never run.

Okay, I'll just run into a store and grab any old pair of stockings. That is, if I don't die here, trying to pull my shoe from the grate. Surely there's a shop around. I'm trying to pull the gorgeous Jimmy Choo croc heel from the grate with the delicacy one would afford the crown jewels when all of a sudden, the shoe comes free, sending me sailing back to the ground on my butt.

I look at my shoe, ready to kiss it, really, for coming out in one piece, when I realize that it is not, in fact, in one piece at all. Well, rather *I* have one piece—and some subway rat is now scurrying off with the other piece—the quintessential piece—the heel, which has descended down into the disgusting depths of subway hell. I briefly hope that I haven't hit a homeless person in the head with it. I have seen specials about the millions of people living down there. Maybe not millions, but lots. And a heel that sharp may be quite a useful weapon in the underworld. Great. Now I've (if fashionably) armed someone.

It is 8:20 A.M. and I have a heel-less shoe and a run in my stocking and may be responsible for the death of an innocent human being via stiletto stabbing. I am not off to the greatest of starts. The only thing I do have is a cell phone and a number for my boss.

"Hello?" he answers.

I was hoping for his voice mail, and now he's on the line, I'm not sure what to say. I opt for the truth. "Mr. Reiner. Hi. It's Lane here."

"Oh. Hi, Lane. You can call me Tom, you know. Everything alright?"

"Well, actually, *Tom*, I've had a bit of a mishap here with a subway grate and my shoe, so I've just got to pop back home and get another pair that actually has two heels, okay? I won't be more than a half hour."

I am pretty sure I hear a muffling sound, like when you put your hand over the receiver, and then a deep laugh in the background, before he says, "No problem, Lane. Do the best you can. We're still getting everything all set for you anyway."

"Thanks," I say, and forget again to ask him how to get there. I'll just have to take a taxi.

After I hang up, I realize I am pretty close to Century 21. Not around the corner close, but since I am all the way downtown, it will take me less time to get down there and buy another pair of brown shoes, than to go all the way back to my apartment and re-consider my whole outfit, which was built entirely around this pair of shoes.

I can't believe how crowded this shop is so early in the morning. People know how nuts it gets here and want to get a chance to scavenge the merchandise before everyone else. But since so many people have this same tactic in mind, it is not very effective any-more. I head straight for the shoe department and feel the electric-ity pulsing through my veins. I spot a pair of Clergerie platforms for only seventy dollars. It should be illegal to have so many beau-tiful things on sale for such little money. I am saddened that I can only buy a pair of work shoes, rather than fun platform sandals that would normally cost around $500. And they have the most adorable crystals embroidered on faux gold leafy-twisty things around the ankle (I know that this bohemian look is going to be HUGE this summer) and so, I just decide to try them on. They are spectacular.

Maybe I can write an article about my experience buying these shoes, and then I can write them off on my taxes, and then they would really only cost—well, how much of it do you actually get back?—less, yes, much less than even the seventy dollars which is, undeniably, an extraordinary deal, anyway. I hold the box in my hands, because in this shop, people are eyeing what you've got, just waiting for you to put it back, under the idea that if someone else wants it, it's got to be great, right? This is the sort of thinking that causes catastrophic trends like those humongous jeans guys started wearing years ago, and oversize sunglasses, and anything by Gaultier.

Halfway down the aisle, a miracle happens. A miracle in chocolate crocodile. The very same pair of Jimmy Choos I had broken is sitting right there. In a box. In. My. Size. It is a veritable miracle (since they are from this season) and makes me think that maybe, just maybe, miracles really do happen, and that the story of Hanukkah is actually true, and the oil really *did* last for eight nights. And they are only eighty dollars. It's a sign from God, and maybe I will found my own holiday to commemorate this day and this miracle. Someone is smiling down on me anyhow.

Perhaps the day will get off on a better foot now (no pun intended), I'm thinking as I pass by some adorable earrings at the checkout. They're ten dollars so I toss them onto the counter with the rest of my purchases, which, after having scanned the clothing department, fill up two hefty shopping bags. I'll be having lots of long days at the office, and who knows what I can expect in the sartorial disaster area, after today's start? I'm just preparing. And I'll be making so much money, I'll be able to pay this credit card bill, no problem, I surmise as the cashier swipes my card through and I'm crossing my fingers that it won't be declined.

The only problem, I realize, as the cab pulls up in front of a very large office tower with an adorable sculpture of a red umbrella outside, is that I now have two shopping bags from Century

21, which, I'm not sure will make the greatest impression, especially now that I am late. How late am I? A quick glance at my cell phone tells me it is now ten o'clock. Not quite the half hour I implied.

I am waiting for my change and receipt when I really take in the scene at this building. There is a huge courtyard in front with trellised overhanging walkways and all form of greenery; to the side lots of benches are set up like a quaint little park. And on every inch of this property, and I do mean every single inch, there is something infinitely more wonderful than anything Mother Nature could ever produce. Something that would cause any living, breathing woman's jaw to drop down to her ankles.

And that majestic, fantastic, utterly unbelievable something is men. Men in button-down shirts in various modes of buttoned— all the way up, one open at the top, two open at the top. There are men in ties, men with no ties, men with ties tossed over their shoulders.

But wait, there's more.

There are tall men, short men, men with glasses, men without glasses. I spy men in sports coats, long overcoats, suits. Men with briefcases, backpacks, messenger bags, holding files, plastic bags. Some men are alone; some are in groups. There are men standing, sitting, walking, running, *bending over to pick things up.*

And the best part?

There are very few women.

"Miss! Miss! Do you want your change or not?"

"Huh?" I wave my hand around to grab for the contents in his outstretched palm, unable to shift my gaze from this fantastic scene, and finally stand up gripping the spoils of my shopping spree, and slam the door shut.

Picture me, if you will, standing in front of this massive structure, men literally oozing out all over the place (so this is where they have been all this time!), the sun shining, a gentle breeze blowing (and whipping hairs right into my gooey lip gloss, of course), just beaming at the fact that my hunch was one thousand percent correct. If anything, this phenomenon is more glorious than anything I could have ever hoped for when I'd pitched the article.

I do *know* this place though. I have been enraptured by its booty before. I have picked through its litter, so to speak. But at the time, I was in deep REM sleep. Only this Nirvana surpasses anything I have ever dreamed up (and I maintain a rather vivid dream life, mind you).

So, I do what any soon-to-be-famous magazine writer, who is now one and a half hours late, overflowing with inexplicable shopping bags, would do. I take note of the absolutely humongous smile that has formed on my face (and will probably necessitate a nimble surgeon's removal), lower my sunglasses from my head to my eyes, run for a seat on the low wall that runs along one of the walkways and whip my phone out to call Joanne.

"Holy Fucking Shit!" I whisper-scream into the receiver.

"What? What?" she asks.

"You are not going to fucking believe how many men there are here. One just looked at me! Oh my God, and another one is checking me out right now! This is insane. Abso-fucking-lutely insane!" Now it is not like me to curse this much. Okay, yes it is, but I try to reserve the profanities for situations that truly require it. But I'm sure I don't need to make excuses to you for my fucking awe-inspired cursing. Can you just imagine? Can you just *fucking* imagine?

For a girl, who prior to this day, only had daily contact with the men on her block—the mailman, the FedEx man, a messenger, the guys at the deli, the superintendent, perhaps the odd delivery boy

I'd scare as he attempted to shove a menu under my door—this is one utterly fantastic moment.

"Can I come meet you for lunch one day?" she asks.

"Ha!" I say, because I am so giddy and can't think of anything else.

"You sound like you've just won the lottery."

"I think I have," I say. "Do you have a second to talk while I smoke a cigarette?"

"Sure, my boss isn't here," she says, not because her boss gets mad when she talks on the phone, but because he sits right across from her and has this annoying habit of asking "What? What did she say? What's so funny?" every time Joanne laughs, replies or says virtually anything at all into the phone.

"Holy shit."

"What? What?" she's asking, sounding, I think, a bit like her boss. "What's going on?"

"What isn't going on?" I reply. "This is incredible. And I haven't even gone inside yet."

"Why not? It's pretty late, isn't it?"

"Well, I had a little incident with my heel and a subway grate this morning." I'm talking kind of loudly now, because I'm sort of hoping some guy will overhear my conversation and think me wildly amusing and, well, sexy. One does, I'm guessing from the way his eyes rest on me as he's walking past, and the way his head turns to look back at me after.

Now, lest you think this only happens to the most gorgeous women in the entire world, let me give you a bit of a clearer picture of me. I am a pretty girl. That is to say, in this world—the normal world, or rather, the one outside of the beauty and fashion businesses. And if you're not familiar, "the industry," as we insiders refer to it, is a microcosm in the universe where everyone has access to the best beauty services in the entire world: the hair color gurus; the biweekly blowout (daily in many instances); the BaByliss flatiron (bye-bye frizz); Paula Dorf makeup; lessons on how to use the Paula Dorf makeup (it's all about contouring); the clothes (free!); the trainers; the wires to shut your jaw up with to drop twenty pounds; the Zone to deliver healthy meals to your home every day; the eyebrow artistes; and then, of course, the breast enhancements; the Ursule Beaugeste pocketbooks; the Chanel shades; the BOTOX; the endermologie; microdermabrasion; airbrushed self-tanner; laser hair removal; and on and on and on. And although I, through connections, have access to many of those things, there are many more women who have many more of those things (and, let's face it, longer legs and smaller noses, tighter abs, skinnier arms). And so this causes me to fare on the bottom end of the spectrum of their "fabulous, daahling" kingdom.

Press lunches at Barneys oftentimes bring on such raging attacks of ugliness and insecurity that I can't even bring myself to go. Those that serve cocktails normally allow me to at least take the edge off enough to speak to the goddesses whom I need to mingle with in order to succeed in my career.

But in this world, the world of finance, where the words "remède" and "Decleor" are laughed off as overly exotic appetizers, and answered with "No, thanks, I'm allergic to fish," and women are *just beginning* to understand the power of a pointy toe, I am truly beautiful. And I can tell from the way these men are looking at me that this is not just in my head. I feel taller, my nose barely visible, my legs are long, willowy branches gracefully swaying from my torso. My hair is long and smooth and doubtless reflecting the rays of the sun in the majestic manner of Gueneveire riding through Camelot on a white horse. My hazel eyes are so green I may have to change their description on my license. People have always said I have great cheekbones (little do they know this is simply another shading trick), and when I remember this, I suck my cheeks in a bit now to make them even better. I glance down at my nails—slightly square shaped, and finished in a barely-there hue and even those are absolutely alluring. I have never felt more desirable in my life.

I mumble something into the receiver about Century 21 and shopping bags, but I'm not really all that interested in this conversation anymore. I just wanted to gloat and share my unbelievable discovery with someone, and that being done with, I need to get going on conquering the kingdom. "Yeah, I'm done gloating now. Nothing left to say here. There are men to meet!" I say, and with a laugh, Joanne hangs up. She must be thrilled I'm not complaining about something for once.

I figured I would just go on up in an elevator and be seated at my desk in no time. This was a serious oversimplification on my part (not unlike the train of thought that had me believing I would find my way to work without a hitch). Everyone is showing ID cards to the security guard.

"Hi," I say when it's my turn.

"Hi," he says back. Even saying that word feels sexy. The idea of all of this security feels sexy. This entire fucking place is one big orgy.

"I don't have an ID card. It's my first day," I say, feeling that perhaps what I've said is X-rated in some way.

"Okay, any picture ID will do, and then just go to that desk (pointing) and they'll call your boss and get you a card."

I'm fumbling through my handbag and trying to balance the shopping bags when suddenly I feel the whole load lighten up.

"Can I help you with these?" Someone speaks out from the Sea of Man behind me and grabs for the second group of shopping bag handles currently digging red marks into my left hand.

"Sure," I say, in a way-too-excited manner, as I am still stunned from this scene, and the fact that this is surely not reality. If I read this in a book I'd be mumbling to myself out loud about how "unrealistic" and "ridiculous" this description is. I'd chide the author for having gone over the edge.

The lobby is even more unbelievable than the exterior. There are so many men that your eye doesn't know where to look. The marble, swirling imperially, here, there, and everywhere, seems exquisite. I am an elegant Audrey Hepburn or Plum Sykes (beautiful, fashionable *Vogue* writer) in someplace like the Plaza Hotel. And my spontaneous rise to fabulousness is enhanced in a bit of a shallow (but human, really) moment, as I realize that the women passing to and fro, scarce as they are, have really put in very minimal effort. They're wearing ponytails, flats! I see bare lips everywhere. Not one contoured-through-blusher-and-highlighter cheek, not a single slim white suit with black shell, no trace of a freshly blown-out head of hair. With all these men? They must be out of their minds! They really must. I can see no other alternative. Do they not read magazines? Have they no televisions?

"First day, really?" the bag-carrier is asking as he follows me through the metal detector and on towards the check-in desk (now *that* is a desk with a fantastic view, I can't help thinking). I can barely concentrate on keeping a conversation going with him (adorable as he is—in one of those blue shirts, which are really heaven-sent and should be subsidized by the government in an effort to make the world a more beautiful place), as I am simply overstimulated. There goes another, and another, and one with blond hair, and one with brown, and black. Oh my God. Unreal.

"I'm Tim," he says, putting his hand out. (A John Cusack look-alike and a shorter Mel Gibson walk by.)

"Lane." I reach for his hand thinking how I now know what people mean when they use the phrase "a kid in a candy store." It is unprecedented. I may volunteer my free time as a job counselor at a college. I will only handle female students and I will tell them all the very same thing: "Get a job in finance! That is it. Whatever else you want to do, you can do it later."

"May I help you, miss?" asks this poor woman in an unfortunate shiny nylon top—*oy!*—and the frizziest hair I have ever seen. I want to reach out to her, work through her sartorial ignorance, really I do, but that feeling goes away and I just feel so glorious and beautiful and desirable in comparison. Who *am* I?

I see behind her an enormous American flag and I think, feeling extremely patriotic, I am an American. And at this moment, feeling so happy with my world, my job, my fellow MEN, I can't think of a better thing to be. I balk at the urge to belt out the national anthem.

"Well, you're busy here I see. I'll catch you around." And Tim gingerly drops the bags in a semicircle around me, joins his friend, whom he'd ignored this entire time, and I hear the distinct clap of a high five, and I am flattered.

This is going to be a piece of cake. I can probably finish the article in a week and then it will be smooth sailing with lunchtime rendezvous and supply-closet nookie the rest of the time. I can just enjoy the view for the final month and three weeks. Maybe I won't even quit at the end of the two months. Maybe I'll stay here forever until I get old and gray and retire. Maybe it's not really that I'm meant to be a writer, but that I just didn't know any other life before, like when you've been eating your steak well-done your whole lifetime because you consider a hunk of bloody meat to be repulsive, and then you finally take your first bite of medium-rare and you can't believe how stupid you have been.

The poorly dressed attendant calls Tom Reiner and instructs me to wait by the side of the counter. I find no problem with this at all. I could stand here and watch this fantastically erotic bustle for the rest of my life and feel that I have indubitably lived. Ooh! One with dimples. I love that! One with floppy layers of hair on top! Blue eyes! Green! I would not be surprised in the least if I am swimming in a pool of my own drool. As it is, my cheeks are already hurting from stretching around my full-teeth smile.

I'm not paying attention to much aside from the apparently bottomless supply of men, and when I feel a tickle on my foot, I look down with surprise to see that someone has knocked over one of my bags. I'm reaching over to pick up my highly fashionable mess, when the heretofore slowly rising panic level associated with the fact that I have no way of hiding (or explaining) the spoils of a conspicuously monstrous shopping spree that has caused me to be an hour and a half (now an hour and forty-five minutes actually) late suddenly accelerates and reaches a heart-stopping crescendo.

I momentarily consider putting each and every garment on my body, in layers, and tucking each of the wedges into a pocket of my coat. I am just picking up my new adorable pink Cosabella lowrider thong (I hope/fear this may cause a horrible man-pileup collision, and smile wickedly), considering whether I should ball them up and hide them in my purse, when someone says my name. It's none other than Mr. Thomas Reiner.

Although I don't meet his eyes first, only spy a tie covered over in miniature spinning globes (the double lines around them indicate the spinning, raised blue stitching represents the watery bits), but as I rise to a standing position, I can recognize him from this telltale sign. And when I shift my gaze up to see his face, we compliment each other at the same time:

"Nice tie," I say.

"Nice color for you," he says, indicating the incriminating underwear. And despite the fact that you are probably holding your hand up to cover your face right now (and if you are on the subway, yes, everyone thinks you are crazy), this is actually a good thing, because Tom happens to be the sort of guy who flushes at the sight of his new assistant's underpants.

And so, despite the fact that there are doubtless a number of questions looming in his mind, he decides to push them aside and instead, excuses himself from the situation by saying, "I'm running out for a meeting. I've left some instructions with John Tansford, in my department, and I think he can keep you all covered up (megablush) while I'm out." And while coming from someone else's mouth, this might sound snippy, from him it is just fine for some reason. "And I hope you're as good at your job as you apparently are at bargain-hunting. Ask the receptionist to buzz John for you. When I get back I will take you on a tour and to the glamorous (waving his hand loftily here) cafeteria for lunch."

I follow his image as it disappears through the doors ahead and I am alone, already wondering if John Tansford will be my M&M, or the guy who carried my bags, or the one who winked at me, or the one with the dimples. . . . How does anyone get any work done here?

As I stand, and wait, I am delirious to see that every turn of the head reveals a new man, a new opportunity to meet my M&M. I am a true genius. I must e-mail Karen as soon as possible to let her know what a great start I am off to. Although, if I do, she may come and get a job here and then she won't be an editor and then they may not run my story, and although I've never met her, I gather she is one of those beautiful editor types, and then I'll have competition. With each male passing through the turnstiles (a checked shirt, a white shirt, a black shirt), I am wondering which one will be the hopefully enchanting, single and scrumptious John Tansford.

"Ms. Silverman?" asks the tallest, skinniest man in the world, which to me, now consists of this building and its surrounding grounds. It is a miracle he can even stand up without tipping over. Looking down, I see this is in no small part thanks to his colossal feet. In actuality, he looks less like a man, and more like a boy, albeit a very tall one, all big-eyed and rosy-cheeked. When I stand (all of five feet four inches—despite how willowy and long my legs now seem), he makes a conscious effort to hunch over—in hopes, apparently, of apologizing for his height and to maintain eye contact with the always predictable, never embarrassing floor. It isn't difficult to see which side of the sexy/nice line John makes his home on.

"Yes. John, is it?" I ask, shaking his hand, which he takes in his with a grip so light, I can barely feel it at all.

"Yes, John Tansford. Nice to meet you. I hear you had some problems getting here this morning," he says, his face scrunching up in a questioning way at Mr. Floor as I gather my bags. "Can I get those for you?" he offers.

No matter what people say about the cutthroat world of business, I have to say, if this were an editorial office, there would be no way I would have gotten through my first day walking in with the spoils of a shopping spree an hour and forty-five minutes late. My firing papers would have been filed before I even arrived. And while they had me filling them out, someone would probably have taken my Clergerie platforms as part of the money I somehow owed them for arriving late and wasting their time. But here I am, being escorted with my own personal porter to the ID station as though I am Julia Roberts in that scene in *Pretty Woman* where she's just had that divine shopping spree and whirlwind makeover. (I briefly toy with the idea of purchasing a wide-brimmed straw hat of my own.)

Everything is so organized and professional here. You get your ID processed immediately. That is, after showing about five forms of ID, and going through all of these security checks, which run just shy of inquiring how many sexual partners you've had, the last time you've gone to the bathroom, and how often you fight with your mother.

Unfortunately it is not a clip-on, and when I ask the ID man if there is a possibility they can order a clip for me, he thinks this is a joke and begins going off into hysterics.

"That's a good one. 'Can you order one for me?' Ha!" He elbows John (who has barely looked me in the face yet) in the ribs, and it looks like my waiflike coworker may actually be punctured from the jab.

But my picture looks great (and I swear I have never looked good in a picture before—when people view my license they normally make a face like they've just seen a hideous rotting corpse) and at least I have a beautiful Gucci wallet to stow it in. (Serious splurge: still not paid off.)

We make our way up twenty-six flights and for some reason, into the stairwell and down one flight, then through the mostly open-format office strewn with cubicles, divided with horribly unfashionable colored cloth modular walls in maroons and grays, which in any other spot would probably seem depressing. But here, just as a slicked-back ponytail and toned-down makeup can actually highlight a boisterous ensemble on the runway, the drab colors just make the men seem to pop out even more. I note, once again, that women are sparse. I do catch the random "Happy Birthday, Tiffany!" sign here, and the telltale candy dish there, but the tokens of female life are few. And those women that I do regard are in suits or androgynous pants and tops of the Express variety. And even that isn't enough to stop me from feeling like part of one, big happy family with each and every one of them. These are my people. I am drunk with being part of something big, (with lots of men involved). I am mentally taking note of each and every detail for my article.

My cubicle is right outside of Tom's office and right next to John's cubicle. Although it does have those maroon walls, I am sure I can work some magic and transform it into an adorable respite. It's got plenty of space for me to hang things on, and lots of great storage bins and work surfaces. I wish I could come to a space like this to do my regular job. With all of these people working, and the distance from my bed, I'm sure I'd get so much more work done. It's buzzing here, with telephones ringing, people going to the water-cooler, typing away, and drawers opening and closing. It's like a real office in here. So inspiring! So lively! So, well, filled with men! Now, I know I sound like a little kid who's never seen the big working world before, but that's kind of how I feel, since I have been holed up in my apartment for so long. I don't think I realized how far removed from society I had been. I don't think I will ever feel the need to sit on my couch and devour a meal made for twenty ever again.

Tom has left a beautiful arrangement of lilies and orchids on my desk with a little card that reads, "We are so glad to have you." I couldn't be more pleased, and feel a bit amused by the fact that Tom has omitted the exclamation point here, where most likely any other human being would place one. Reading it as a straight sentence, without the lilt at the end that an exclamation point would require, does make one take the statement more seriously. You know, I think Tom has got something there. No wonder he is a Managing Director of Mergers and whatever that other thing is. It does sound like a pretty serious job.

"Shall I leave you to settle in for a bit? Tom's left all sorts of notes here for you about filling out your paperwork and meeting with HR about benefits and all. I'll be right over the wall if you need me." He knocks on our dividing line and raises his eyebrows in wait of my response. If the fidgeting and crimson cheeks serve as any indication, it looks like he just might faint if I require his presence for a moment longer.

"Sounds gre—" I go to lift my voice, as if there is an exclamation point, and then, stop myself, clear my throat, and repeat, in a monotone, professional way, "Sounds great." John nods his head and disappears behind the maroon wall. I think I can hear a sigh of relief coming from the other side.

My computer appears to be brand new. I take my coat off and hang it on the side of my mock doorway. It's so beautiful, I think it will make a nice first impression to passersby. Sitting at my new chair, which has a comfy, high back, and, I note, as I lean back into it, a fantastic rocking option—a nice change to the cheap, uncomfortable chair I use at home—I actually feel very much at home here.

One mountain of paperwork and the most boring meeting of my life later, I'm fidgeting with my computer, which won't allow much fidgeting before a dialogue box prompts me to enter a password. Passwords remind me of voicemail and voicemail gets me wondering if there are people leaving me messages at home, left and right, offering me assignments for the first time in my life. I get a sinking feeling, realizing that I am not there to answer the calls. So I dial my voicemail number.

While I'm waiting for the call to go through, I scream to John over the wall, "How do I get a computer password?"

I can barely hear John's response over a voice shouting in my ear, "Lane!"

I takes me a second to realize the voice is coming from the phone. "Oh Swen! Sorry, *again*," I whisper when it all becomes clear.

"No worries, my sweet. I'm just coming in from the steam room." Swen—otherworldly, fantastical, Swen. "So how's the new job going?"

"You wouldn't even believe it if I told you." Lowering my voice, and cupping my hand over the receiver, I whisper, "There are, like, a million, trillion men here." Again, I attempt to avoid silly exclamation points.

He asks, "What are you wearing?" I briefly wonder if I am feeding a fantasy he may be scheduling after high tea, but describe the whole outfit and the croc-shoe debacle anyway (sometimes the mileage you get out of a great story is worth the hassle of actually going through the experience), when that hideous globe tie appears before me once again.

"I see you're settling in nicely," Tom says, when I hang up the phone. And, I note, he glances—with a bit of a rosy cheek—to where I've propped his little note from the flowers atop my computer monitor.

"Thanks for the flowers. That was awfully sweet of you. How'd your meeting go?" And to seem extremely professional, I ask, "Are there any notes you'll need me to transcribe?"

"Well, if you haven't any more shopping to do this afternoon, that would be a great help," he says and hands me a couple of sheets of yellow legal paper. "I've got you a password already. It's really a lot of trouble for nothing, and I figured I'd save you the hassle. It's (and he lowers his voice to a whisper here) Faulkner."

I type in the notes quickly, calling Tom every once and again to ask what "MD" (managing director) and "IBD" (Investment

Banking Division) stand for, and embarrassingly, once to ask what
"TR" is—"Um, that's, um, me," he replies, not wanting to hurt my
feelings. I roll back in my chair to peek at him through the plates
of clear glass that serve as his office wall when he says this, attempting to convey a "duh" expression in the cutest way possible.

He smiles and says, "I gotta go, there's some girl staring at me
through my window."

When I go to grab the sheets off the printer, I take in my new
department. There are about one hundred people right in my surrounding area, and I am already picturing all of us going out for
happy hour, complaining that "numbers are down" or whatever it
is these people complain about. There is, I have already noticed, a
bunch of semiboisterous guys a few desks down, who keep walking
around to give each other papers and files and things—and more
than once, I have noticed them whispering and pointing in my direction. I am intrigued.

When I bring the papers to Tom, he gives them a once-over
and, nodding his head approvingly says, "You do nice work."

"Thank you," I say, feeling that first wave of pride you get from
a job well-done. I'm a kitten who's mastered the litter box.

"You ready for your tour?" he asks.

God am I ever. I get to go around once again—taking it all in,
top to bottom—all of those strong legs, backs, arms. "Let me just
grab my notebook," I say, not wanting to miss anything I can possibly use for my article.

Now Tom has professional reasons for showing me the building,
but I have my own reasons for touring it, so taking it all in is not
the easiest thing in the world. First we go around our floor.

"This entire floor is investments. And most of it is Mergers and
Acquisitions. Most of the guys in the cubicles are the number
crunchers. You know, the guys who play with the figures to see

what companies would look like combined, to find out who's in trouble, who can afford to acquire another company. There are about one hundred and fifty of those guys on this floor. They are called analysts, and they are assigned to different projects that the managing directors and vice presidents are working on."

I'm trying to get this info down, and note (in code, of course) which ones are cute and which ones have checked me out, and which cologne it is that is wafting up into my nose and causing heat to emanate from my neck.

He continues, "Now there are lots of managing directors. That's MDs. No, not the medical type. About ten right now, and they are all working on different projects in various sectors of the market-place. So, over here," he says, waving over a section midway down this corridor of open-front offices, "the trafficking segment of our department makes sure that nobody is contacting the same companies to suggest different deals. Otherwise we would all look like we don't know what the hell is going on."

I have always found it boring when men talk about the world of finance, when I've met them in bars or at parties, but Tom, talking this way, in his element (even with that awful tie) seems so regal, important.

"So what kind of deals do you put together?" I ask, and surprisingly, I find, I am actually interested in hearing the answer.

"Well, it can be anything. Say Barneys is doing really well and looking to grow their remainders and discounting business, and Daffy's is not doing so well. We'll have the analysts put together a prospectus of what a Barneys /Daffy's company would look like and present it to them."

Barneys and Daffy's? That sounds like a deal I could really get excited about. But Barneys would never want to be associated with a bargain-basement store like Daffy's. Come on. Anyone knows that. It's like *Vogue* merging with *Family Circle*. That conference room would be left a tattered battlefield strewn with tufts of perfectly flattened blond hair and torn strings of outsize Chanel faux-pearls on the one side, and Lycra and polyester blends on the other side of the enemy line.

When I mention this, Tom just smiles and says, "Excellent point."

The whole floor is coming to life before my eyes, as I imagine the important negotiations, intimidation tactics, and fiscal something or others currently in progress.

Tom opens a door that leads to a stairwell, and explains the mysterious path John led me through earlier. "Since we are on twenty-five, and the elevators are divided into two towers—one to twenty-five and twenty-six to thirty-nine—the fastest way to get to our floor from the lobby is to take the express straight up to twenty-six, rather than stopping on every floor all the way up to twenty-five. Same when you go down."

I follow him up the one flight, smiling at the two women chatting here (my coworkers); they get very quiet when they notice Tom, and I remark to myself that he must be pretty important.

"Now, the first thing everyone learns in this building is that there are no arrows above the elevators to indicate whether they are going up or down. Instead, the red light means up, white down."

"Why? Wouldn't it be easier just to have arrows?" I ask.

"That's just the way it is. Feel free to draft a letter of concern to the management office, but I'm sure you'll figure it out."

"Tom, nice to see you," says an older man in the elevator.

"Jim," Tom says and nods. "This is my new assistant Lane." He introduces me, and Jim sticks his (hairy) hand in my direction.

I shake it. "Nice to meet you," I say.

"A pleasure," he says, smiling.

And before we get to our destination—the conference floor on thirty—the elevator stops to let in one bespectacled man, a couple of casually dressed guys in jeans and tees, one skinny, and two blond men. Wow. Wow. Wow.

"Tom, which—" I want to clarify once again which is down and which is up, and he stops me and says, "Red, up." I smile.

"Thanks." I am taking notes and Tom screws up his face, probably wondering what the heck I could possibly be writing down, and considering that if it is the elevator instructions then perhaps he hasn't made the best choice in hiring me. Of course, this is exactly what I'm writing down, because my mind is so cluttered with all of the men that I'm sure I won't remember, and so I cup my hand over my paper, like someone who is afraid a classmate is cheating off of their exam paper. I shake my head when he tries to peek over. Tom finds this utterly amusing.

The conference floor is exactly what it sounds like—a floor lined with conference rooms. Outside of each room are tables of food, soda cans, bottled water, and appropriate amounts of garnish, for those meeting inside. Those rooms that have meetings in session have signs outside indicating which potential mergers or acquisitions are being discussed: "Verizon and Time Warner;" "Macy's and Marshalls;" "Starbucks and Tealuxe."

Tom takes on a hushed tone here to indicate that we need to be quiet. "So this is where it all happens. When we have meetings I'll need you to come in and take the minutes down. It's not that bad—at least you'll get a free lunch."

I haven't eaten yet, and I spy a cookie that looks fantastic, but resist the urge to grab for it. This isn't so hard to do, as there are so many men standing around and walking past, that the last thing I want to do is stuff my face like a pig. (Another article idea? "The

Man Diet.") And there goes another, and another, and that one looks really important. Where have I seen him before?

I catch a smidge of a conversation. "With the resources we had three years ago . . ." It trails off as they walk into one of the rooms.

We follow a square route around until we once again reach the glass doors that lead to the elevators, and Tom says, "Okay, here's your test. We're going down to the first floor. Let's see if you can get into the right elevator, Lane."

And I am starting to get embarrassed. I mean, okay, so I asked once, but obviously it's not that hard. What kind of moron does he think I am anyway? So there I am, all pissed off that my boss thinks I can't figure out something as simple as a white light indicating a descending elevator, when the doors of an elevator with a red light open up and a breathtakingly handsome man is revealed, and I can't help myself from walking right through the doors.

"Lane, that's not us," Tom says, saving me just as the door is about to close me inside. The handsome one smiles, and I feel that even if I piddle on the floor men here will adore me and stroke me, like a good little girl who's just said her first word.

"Sorry," I say.

"Rite of passage," he assures me.

Enter proper elevator; join ridiculous amount of men; exchange looks; get the feeling Tom may be silently laughing at my probably now obvious point-of-view; doors open.

"And this is where you came in," he reminds me, as we pass by a lobby shop with tons of magazines (maybe something I've written is in there?), Snapples, candy, greeting cards. "And this is the coffee shop," he indicates with an outstretched hand. It is an adorable little station below a sign that reads JAVA CITY with lines of (what else?) men, waiting, to the sounds of frothing, for cappuccinos and lattes. I have never in my life found a coffee shop so exhil-arating. "And behind there is the cafeteria, which we will see in a second. But first I want to show you where it all happens." We make our way toward the mysterious "it" down an escalator and around a corridor, with, I see, a long table and some vending ma-chines—a great spot for an intimate lunch for two?

Now, before I divulge the scene on the trading floor, I need to tell you what Tom later tells me, when we get to know each other a little better, that these guys sit here all day long staring at com-puter screens and listening to these thingies called "squawk boxes," and their lives are all about gambling and taking risks. So they get all antsy sitting there, with all that pent-up excitement and energy, and when women—who are even more rare here than elsewhere in this fantastical place—walk down the aisles, there is much atten-tion to be garnered.

It is loud in here. There are stock quotes running along black LCD screens. There must be millions of computers—and each one is fitted with its very own man. "This is one of the largest trading floors on Wall Street," teacher Tom says. "There are millions of dollars worth of computers in here. And here's where it gets inter-esting—there are strict rules about the investment side and the trading side sharing information. That is to say, they cannot. They say there are 'firewalls' between both sides. So picture a wall that neither side can cross."

This sounds so mysterious and Gorden Gecko–esque and *Boiler Room* all in one, I can barely contain my excitement. Espionage, intrigue—so fucking sexy. All the guys here are dressed really casu-ally, and next to Tom, they seem so . . . young, I guess is the word.

As we're walking out, and Tom is winding down the tour and heading me to the cafeteria for lunch, he asks, "Well, what do you think?"

And for the first time I make my slip. It comes out before I even process it. And this is probably because I feel like I have just had sex for about two hours. I am flushed, having trouble breathing, and not really on planet earth yet.

"There are so many men!" As soon as it's out, I cup my hand over my mouth, afraid I look like an ass. Perhaps I have blown my cover. But Tom, as I'm learning is his style, takes everything in stride.

"Yeah. That's what they all say," he says. "After a while you won't even notice them anymore."

Sure. Right.

"So," he resumes his mock-professional tone here. "This is the cafeteria."

Men. Men. Men.

"And more men," he says, and my breath catches in my throat, and then eases once again as he raises his eyebrows to suggest a joke. "And you take a box," he instructs, handing me a flattened cardboard box. "And this is the salad bar," he grabs a bowl and passes one in my direction to see if I would like a salad.

I accept.

"And this is the lettuce. And this is the tomato, and these are the carrots, and this is the celery, and this is the green pepper," he introduces each one to me as we make our way down the line.

As I pile on bits from the different bowls, I find it funny that someone as important as Tom does something as trivial as eat lunch.

"And I skip the dressing, because I'm trying to eat right," he says. I consider following his lead, but practicality has never really been my forte, so I opt for extra Italian and shrug my shoulders as he shakes his head and clucks his tongue in dramatic disapproval.

He adds a hot pretzel to his box and we head to the register. "Allow me," he says, as the cashier weighs the salads and tallies up the total.

"You know," I say, "if you're trying to stay in shape, a hot pretzel is probably the worst thing you can eat."

"Why's that?" he asks.

"Carbs, carbs, carbs—they are the enemy," I inform him. "So can I have a little piece?" I ask, never one known to possess the strength to resist a simple carbohydrate.

He shakes his head, no.

"Why not?" I ask.

"Well, I don't want to be responsible for you eating a microscopic pretzel bite, so you can come back in two weeks and blame an extra ounce on me."

"I would never." I am Betty Boop, lashes working overtime.

"Oh, I've heard that one before," he says, still holding the pretzel out of my reach.

"Fine, be like that." I do my best to affect indifference, focusing on my exciting heap of salad bar selections.

"Fine, I will," he says, unwavering. "Mmmmm," he murmurs, closing his eyes after he takes the first bite of the pretzel. "You would not believe how good this tastes."

"I hope you get fat," I retort.

"I'm sure you do," he says.

So, you see, my welcome at the Mergers and A—gosh I keep forgetting that word—department at Salomon Smith Barney was really very sweet. By five o'clock, I'm pretty much settled into my "cubey," which I like to call it, and now like referring to it as even better, because every time I do, Tom says, "It's a cubi-*cle*, Lane." And I can tell he enjoys making those sorts of corrections, even though he realizes I obviously know the difference.

I already have a nickname, something I've wanted for years now, really ever since I shed the last one I garnered in college. It was a horrible moniker: Lame, which was attained for obvious reasons, but which, for similarly obvious reasons, did not suit my fancy when used during introductions at parties and other social functions.

My new nickname, Ab Fab, which Tom christened me with over our lunch, as I told him more about my magazine writing, did not have so much to do with the fact that the characters on the show are, and I quote, "Obnoxious, spoiled women." He insisted that it was more "the whole fashion world thing, and the fact that it is just a combination of words that really suits you."

I could see why Tom would have been an English major. He really does delight in words.

Everyone in the cubicles around me seems to pile out between five and six, which I guess is because they come in so early. And when it starts clearing out, Tom tells me that I can leave for the day if I wish. But since he is staying, and I am feeling really good all around (and partially because I can't bring myself to go back to the real world just yet for fear I will find the whole thing was a mere dream), I opt to stay and write about my day's experiences.

I have decided at the end of each day I will write down everything that's happened, so that at least I'm staying in practice *and* I'll have a chance to dissect every encounter I have, every single professional arm, leg, butt, face, neck, and ear. That way I can see if any M&Ms have crossed my path undetected. Also, maybe I'll stumble upon some other themes over the next couple of months that I can use for other articles.

And I can't help but notice once again that in this traditional workspace, actually doing work comes much easier. Which is much more than I can say for my own office at home, which normally inspires me to run to the deli for coffee, to flirt with the guy who owns it, if only in pursuit of human interaction. Appearing studious to the men around me also makes me feel quite desirable (odd, true).

I am just starting the *fourth* page of my work journal, probably

the longest thing I've written in . . . in . . . ever, which I have enti-
tled on yet another crisp, gold leaf page, is *Diary of a Working Girl*,
which I really like the sound of, when John raps on my cubey wall.

"I'm heading home. You're really making me look bad here," he
says, smiling, and then, perhaps realizing he should be nervous,
catches himself and looks down as if attempting to decipher some
Beautiful Mind–type code buried deep within the carpet.

"Well, Tom's still here, too," I plead, rejoicing in the fact that my
studious act is working.

"Yeah, but that's because he doesn't want to go home to his evil
girlfriend," John says, still decoding the carpet, but definitely
warming up, adding a "*woooh*," in an attempt to indicate spookiness. Two fingers of each hand inch up from the sides of his pants
legs, as if he would make the corresponding international gesture
of spookiness, but they drop before even getting close to their
headside destination. He wasn't quite there yet.

"Really? An evil girlfriend? But he seems like such a nice guy."
The kind of nice guy that is sensitive to carbohydrate conse-
quences; the sort of nice guy who has spinning worlds on his tie.
This is the species of nice guy you don't come across every day.
This is the last person you'd expect to have an evil girlfriend.

"I've gone out with them a couple of times; one day I'll tell you
about the 'spaghetti incident.'"

Just as I'm wondering how long "one day" will be when I don't
even know John's eye color after spending a full day with him, he
surprises me.

"But you didn't hear any of this from me," he says, catching my
eye for a quick second (yay! they're blue, by the way) and turning
to make sure Tom's door is still closed, which it is. He shrugs his
shoulders and bids me, "Sayonara," and I swear, ducks his head to
stop it from hitting the ceiling as he walks down the corridor.

Back to my journal, I record this bit of info, and then realize as I'm writing it, that this news about Tom is very surprising.

And isn't the "*Spaghetti Incident*" the name of a really bad Guns 'n' Roses CD? I wonder if there was a stain... hmmm...or maybe a disapproved slurp. Wait. Maybe Tom ordered the spaghetti and the girlfriend wanted that but refused to order the same thing and so she screamed at him until he changed to the penne.

Realizing this train of thought probably will not be very useful to my article, or future articles (although I am growing quite fond of the title 'spaghetti incident' and wondering if it could make for a really cool fashion shoot; it could be all mod, with weathered seventies furniture and strands of spaghetti hanging off the side of the table, from counters, olive green colanders, orange floral printed bowls . . .), I move on to more important issues.

I am absolutely in love with my department. I am in love with the fact that I have a department. I am in love with the fact that I will soon hopefully be able to say things like, "I am having drinks with my department." Day One and already there is a very sweet man named John, whom I know so well already that I am making it my own personal goal to have him open up to me (you NEVER find out that sort of stuff about the FedEx or UPS guys—NEVER) and there is the very intriguing issue of the 'spaghetti incident.' Only last week I...I...

I can't stop thinking what that incident might be! I will not waste time and creative energy, though, writing about it.

But wait. Maybe the girlfriend sent back her spaghetti because it wasn't good, only it <u>was</u> good and she just didn't want to eat the carbs—only wanted to smell them and see what it felt like to order them, savor the sounds of the syllables—spa-ghett-i—as they rolled from her tongue. That could be why he was so sensitive about the pretzel. Maybe it wasn't the light, innocent joke I first assumed.

Why, Ms. Lane Silverman, are you wasting the pages of your diary with such thoughts about pasta and its involvement with a woman you don't even know?!!!!? You will not, cannot get lazy with this project on your first day. Now where were you?

Just last week, I thought I was moving on by utilizing my overdraft account to shop for practical meals for one (a single chicken breast, a lamb chop that he never liked, Mueslix—it's supposed to be healthy); when the reality of my miserable, lonely existence came up and whacked me in the face. I was waiting on line for some diet cheese when it happened.

He was tasting a cube of fresh mozzarella from a platter; she was reminding him of that special report they'd watched about how unsanitary those tasting platters are—unwashed hands grabbing, no refrigeration. I know it doesn't sound very lovey-dovey, but it was the intimacy that grabbed me. The fact that they'd watched the special report together, that she cared enough to warn him against eating from the tray, that he smiled and shook his head affecting that he knew her ways and loved them, no matter how quirky. It was then that I looked down at my basket full of meals for one and realized there were tears running down the bag that held my single orange, on my small container of milk, on my produce bag containing four mushrooms—all tiny portions because anything bigger would spoil in a refrigerator opened and closed by only one pair of hands. I realized that if any of the items in my basket were harmful to my health, I had no one to advise me against them. I might have been buying the makings of my final meal. I only hoped that someone would notice if I died by the papers piled outside my door.

Today, however, the world is filled with possibility. Papers could never pile outside my door. I have somewhere to be!

Being that this seems (if I do say so myself) quite a great start to an article draft, and I wouldn't want to jinx myself by making predictions, I close the diary for the day.

I have already become familiar with the e-mail system here (okay I've not turned into a computer genius overnight, it's the same one I use at home), and, with the help of a stereotypically dorky Information Technology guy, figured out how to check my home e-mail account. So I pull this account up now, to see if anything new has come in.

There is one message, from an address that ends in nypost.com! I am already sure it is a rejection to the article I pitched last week about the temp agency horrors as I click to open it.

Dear Lane,

I am delighted, after having rejected your submissions a record fifty times, to inform you that you have finally hit the nail on the head. The piece you sent in about temp agencies is absolutely perfect. We would like to offer you seventy-five dollars to print it in this Friday's paper. Please e-mail me a list of your sources for our fact-checker.

Best,

Brian Allen

This absolutely, positively cannot be. I am speechless. That is, until I scream "Yay!" and begin jumping up and down in my maroon cubicle. I am considering wearing my pink panties atop my head, but then remember that this is not my home, when Tom emerges from his office, bobbing his head up and down to the rhythm of my jumping.

"I got the feeling you liked it here, but this joy is unprecedented in Smith Barney history."

It is so nice to have someone to share good news with, rather than dancing around your apartment telling yourself "Congratulations!" (Even if I cannot put my panties on top of my head.)

"Looks like we have a star reporter in our midst," Tom says after my *Post* briefing, patting me on the back, and demanding we share a mini bottle of Pommerey champagne he's been keeping in his office for a special occasion. ("That is an order.") "Don't tell human resources," he says, placing his pointer across his mouth. "It's against the rules to drink on the job."

It's warm, which doesn't do much to help champagne, but it's sweet enough, and by the time we finish it, I am a bit light-headed.

It feels so cool to be sitting in an office, overlooking the water, the Statue of Liberty, and just hanging out after work like this. The champagne loosens my lips a bit, and I tell Tom about how boring his ad in the *Times* looked and how I'd first come across it (stopping short, of course, at the reason I finally followed through with calling). I decide to give him a bit of advice.

"You should make the ads witty and cute, so that people will be enticed to call," I say.

And at first he looks as if he's going to crack up, but then, his face takes on a serious look, and he says, "You know Ab Fab, that's not such a bad idea at all."

When, finally, an hour later, Tom's phone rings, I take a moment to get acquainted with his desk. It's nice and tidy—the way I always wish mine could be—with very few decorative objects to clutter things. In fact, there is just the one—a frame I can only see the back of from where I'm sitting.

When curiosity gets the better of me (can this be the evil girlfriend of the spaghetti incident fame?), I get up to act as if I'd like to take in the view at the window behind his desk.

He rolls his eyes at the person on the other end and makes that duck quack gesture with his fingers as if the caller may never cease talking. When he turns around and starts to jot down some notes, I'm pretty sure I'll have a second to safely check out the photograph in question.

It's all I can do to stop myself from sprinting to the phone to call Joanne and scream, "OH MY GOD." The photo of the evil girlfriend is so far from anything you'd expect to see within ten miles of Tom that I do a double take, hoping when I turn toward it again it will look completely different.

The photo is unmistakably a Glamour Shot, the sort they're always trying to sell at suburban malls. She's got a hazy soap-opera glow about her eyes and a feather boa floating around her neck. The sparkly cowboy hat tragically elevates the whole thing into another realm.

In a gag reflex, I choke on a sip of champagne. Tom turns around and I quickly transfer my gaze from the photo and before it's too late, mouth to him that I'm heading home. As he waves me through, pointing at the phone and sticking his tongue out like he's so sorry to be interrupting fun with work, I think how amazing it is that his job is so demanding, yet he handles himself in such a light, pleasant manner. And I'm considering this as I pack my bag up, shut my computer down, and make the journey up the stairwell to twenty-six to take the express down.

"Red or white?" Despite the fact that this might possibly make me the perfect candidate for the Most Scatterbrained Girl in the World Award, I cannot remember. I am flipping through my little notebook, and while I can't locate the information in question, I can clearly see that I chronicled Tom's introduction to the salad bar.

And this is the lettuce, and here is the tomato.

I hadn't even realized I wrote that down. I wonder what he'd say now that I can't remember how the stupid elevator works again. Ha! I bet he would really be laughing about that.

I smile, instead of grunt when I take a chance—wrongly—and find myself sailing up towards the higher floors, because I have someone to share this with in the morning.

Finally, I make my way down and through the turnstile and past the security guards, and when I'm outside lighting up a cigarette, I can't help but wonder if the whole experience was just a dream. I fear that when I come back tomorrow, I'll happen upon an empty lot, rather than a tower of wonder where dreams come true.

When I return home that evening to my tiny apartment, I feel like I haven't been there in ages. I think the separation did us both good; I find a new appreciation for my sofa as I sink into it, working a pair of chopsticks through a warm tin takeout tray of steamed chicken and mixed vegetables. (I need to look amazing every day now since being attractive is part of my job, so I am eating celebritylike.) I have a newfound understanding of characters on my favorite television shows, as I now get what all of the corporate jokes are about—nine-to-five living and all that. Smoking outside with the boss; that Rachel on *Friends* is something else (knee-slap).

It has only been one day, but I feel so much has happened already. A new phase of my life is beginning. I can feel it all around me, like those childhood moments when you just knew the slowly heating popcorn was about to start popping madly.

Rather than go right to sleep—I am too excited for this tonight—I have a revelation. I decide to input the information from the pile of press releases on my floor into my computer, and then I throw the actual papers in the trash. I had been inputting lots of corporate information into my database at work all day, and I don't see why the same system wouldn't work here. It gets rid of the mess, that's for sure. I don't finish the whole pile, but I take a very big bite from it, and when I drag the huge garbage bag down to the basement to recycle, I decide to press seven rather than five and visit with Chris before turning in for the night.

"How's my little Mary Tyler Moore?" he asks, taking in my outfit. I am still wearing the (second pair of) croc heels and he stops at them, asking, "Choos?"

"Yes," I say, almost ashamed, as I am so used to having no money, and being questioned about indulgent purchases that seem to wind up in my possession anyway. But then I remember I am actually making money—good money—now.

I haven't exactly seen any of the money yet. But unlike the freelance gigs, where you have to call and call and put all of your pride aside and make your entire personal life public (I have to pay my rent, I need to eat, I blew all my money like a complete moron on this wool Mayle dress with the most adorable antique lace because the forgotten feel of actual cash in my hands brought on such insanity I couldn't think straight, etc.) just so they can act as if they are really doing you such a huge favor by promising to mail a check that's already five months late, I now know at the end of two weeks a check for a set amount of money is on the way and will continue to be on the way—for a little while, anyhow.

And, of course, he knows all of this and so, like the mom you wished for your whole life, he smiles, and says, "Well, I guess you've earned them now, haven't you, you little corporate diva?"

It feels funny to be with someone from the other world—meaning the fashion one, rather than the corporate one—which is funny, since it has been my world for so long. There is such a different M.O.: the words, the manner of speech. In the fashion language, "divine," "genius," and "bisoux" are Day One required vocabulary words. And don't get me started on the double kisses. I can never remember a second one is on the way and run a very high risk rate of accidentally kissing people right on the lips when they swing around to plant the surprise bonus no-actual-contact kiss on the opposite cheek.

I had become desensitized to the Planet Double Bisoux after so many years of being smack in the middle, or rather, trying to get smack in the middle of it.

But now the difference is rather striking. Still, Chris, despite walking the walk (hand out, palm down; chin up, lids down), and talking the talk ("That sportif collection by Dolce was brilliant"), is still the sweetest man alive. He can play the role when necessary, but in such a way that it is apparent he is really so above and beyond the brand-name game and the attitude showcase showdowns.

"I know this sounds crazy, but you seem like an entirely different woman. At the risk of sounding like Sheryl Crow, I really think this change has done you good. Twirl for me darling, you must twirl."

And so I do just that, the champagne, as little as I may have drunk, still holds its grip on my head a bit (probably because for the first time in a while, food without fat has made up my entire daily intake), and so, it doesn't take much coaxing for me to swivel my hips as I make my rotation and move on to an unprompted cat-walk-like journey across the room.

Later, as I curl up in my bed, after tackling two hundred sit-ups I might add, I am happier than I have been in months. And think-ing over the last half-hour, I am delighted Chris noticed a change because I was beginning to think I was crazy to feel like such a dif-ferent person in, really, just one day. At first, I thought the happiness factor was on account of the barrage of men who surrounded me all day and the possibility that any of them could be The One (for both professional and personal reasons), but, when I further con-sider everything, it dawns on me what the biggest change has been.

After hundreds of rejections; months and months of dragging myself out of bed to spend hours coming up with never-to-be-used article ideas; running off copies of my published articles from magazines nobody's ever heard of (and unwaveringly hoping I would magically come upon one I'd written for *Vogue* or *Elle*); composing pitch letters (this time funny, this time serious, this time mentioning a cousin's friend's sister's ex-boyfriend the editor had once met at a cocktail party) to make myself look bigger and better than my roundup of experience allows me to, only to be appeased by answers like, "Yes, we've received your packet. We'll call if we need anything. Thank you."—I am actually being praised.

And, it's not just the *Cosmo* article. It's Tom and Chris, and now even the *Post*. And I know it sounds funny, but even the fact that I am good at typing up notes and organizing files (who knew?) and answering the telephone in a pleasing manner makes me feel great when somebody actually recognizes it.

When the word "no" becomes so familiar to you, when it barely even fazes you anymore, it takes a toll on you. All of that energy and pride you have when you first start out, that gets peeled away, like the layers of an onion, and with each bit that's removed, the tears become less and less, because you actually get used to it. And maybe, after years of dealing with such acidic stuff, you kind of enjoy the expectation of the rejection, even if it's just for the I-knew-it value. Conversations with peers in the same boat, during which we complain and complain about so-and-so who got an assignment at a magazine just because she is friends with the editor (even though she is a *terrible* writer: "I mean, did you see that intro? And was this even edited?") become so enjoyable that entire friendships are built around them. You can spend a whole day lying in a pile of the *terrible*-but-connected writer's published articles, discussing via telephone her unacceptable abuse of commas, counting each and every infraction as if it will somehow get you closer to your goal.

But that's a bad place to be—and it hadn't even occurred to me before. And despite the fact that I do have talent (which has been difficult to continue telling myself), I have allowed all of those no's to peel away at me until almost nothing was left. When you're not getting to use your talent on a regular basis, it leaves you fearing, perhaps, that your talent was fleeting. Sometimes, I wake in the middle of the night, positive I will no longer be able to string a sentence together. I'll sit on the side of my tub for hours paralyzed with fear that I won't even be capable of writing the story I've just pitched, should they—by some miracle—decide to assign it to me.

And, as if that's not scary enough, the negativity, not unlike a bad self-image, spills over into basically everything you do. I never think a date will go well or that a trip (not that I'd taken one any-time recently) or a party will pass enjoyably—it's always a shock when something does.

Go figure. I got all that from a mini bottle of warm champagne, a bunch of flowers, and a pat on the back.

Five

The Princess and the Paper Jam

The next day, I get to work on time (well, five minutes late, but that's really on time—everyone knows there's a fifteen minute cushion on promptness); thankfully without snagging any heels or hose. The morning brings with it another chance to stand in wonder at the male population scurrying here and there in black loafers, brown loafers, and (now seeing things with a more discerning eye) sneakers of the traders, and that same excitement ignites inside of me. I decide to smoke a cigarette before heading in, and once again take a seat on the low wall. As this is my second day, I know exactly where I'm going, who to show my ID to, and which elevator is going up (hopefully), and so I get that delightful sensation of belonging to all of this activity. It's nice. It makes me feel chatty, so I glance next to me and see a girl I recognize as the Tiffany of the "Happy Birthday, Tiffany!" sign fame.

"You're Tiffany, right?" I ask when our eyes meet (which they often do when smokers are sitting around smoking together).

"Yeah, you're Tom's new assistant, right?" she asks, putting her hand out.

"That's right. Lane," I say as we shake. She's got her dark hair back in one of those lazy buns you normally reserve for the gym or an evening in.

"This is a great place to work, isn't it?" I ask.

"It's okay," she says in that way only someone with years of familiarity with a place can, and so I'm left wondering if she's blind despite the eye contact. A job at a mall store can be okay. A position waiting tables can be okay. But a job living, breathing, doing just about anything amongst all this testosterone—well, that can't be described as anything less than spectacular.

"What do you do here?" I ask, taking in her outfit—slightly pilled black pants and a loose gray top.

"I assist Larry Waters, one of the VPs," she says, after a long exhale.

I figure this could be a good opportunity to gain a bit of insight into the dating scene around here. "I can't believe how many men there are here," I venture, omitting, almost without effort now, the verbal exclamation point at the end. Which I hope does wonders to conceal the exclamation point now contained in a permanent bubble over my head.

"Yeah, but they're all assholes," she says, again with that tone of experience. She rolls her eyes for emphasis and taps one finger on her cigarette, which sends a little tornado of ashes spiraling up over the two of us.

"They can't *all* be assholes," I shrug. I hate people who overgeneralize. And then I realize I have probably been overgeneralizing ever since I laid eyes on this place.

"Yes. They can," she retorts, stating a fact as one might note four quarters equal one dollar. "But," she continues, "that doesn't stop people from making out in the stairwell or hooking up at happy hour. I'm sure you'll see."

I'm never one to be swayed by other opinions, especially when they run so contrary to the one I want to be correct. And even doubly when the very idea of such a thing might stamp out everything I'm working towards here before I've even begun working towards it.

"Hey, you going up?" I ask.

"Yeah," she drops her cigarette to the ground and stomps it out.

Ten men look to see what the women are doing. I think perhaps someone might push her out of the way and say, "Allow me, please."

"Why don't we eat lunch together later?" she asks, in her first positive note, before we part at her cubicle. And her face lights up even further when she says, "I can let you in on *all* the gossip."

"Sure, that would be great," I say, excited to be initiated into that other sacred office life rite—gossip. Heading over to my cubey I imagine Tiffany's gossip has got to top any I'd participated in at home. "Did you hear they're getting a new brand of sport drink at the deli?" and "Our mailman was fired because he was too slow," isn't exactly the stuff that inspires remembering, much less recounting.

In the end, I had to take a rain check on the lunch date with Tiffany. My smart and well-traveled boss hasn't had an assistant for a couple of months now and the mountain of receipts growing on his desk nearly touches the ceiling.

When he first introduced me to the Leaning Tower of Pisa that is his overdue expense receipts, Tom confessed, "I wanted to wait until day two to tell you about this; otherwise, I thought you might run screaming."

With hands raised and waving in the international sign for running scared, I managed to score some guilt from my thoughtful but apparently sneakier-than-he-might-look boss.

"Fine. You're right. I should have warned you."

I shake my head; the assistant scorned.

"Although technically this was in the job description, I'll make it up to you. Let's see . . . lunch?" I thought the idea of another lunch spent fighting over pretzel bites could be considered enjoyable. But then I thought of that tie. And that evil girlfriend. And that Tom, as sweet and smart and funny as he was, was just not my type. Still, I could enjoy lunch with him.

"Lunch is on me. Order in from wherever you like. The menus are in the bottom drawer on the left side of your cub-*icle*. You can even have them bring you a glass of wine. I gather you'll need it."

Of course. He meant I could *order* lunch. Not us having lunch *together*. Thank God. Really, I would have just gone to be nice anyway.

Still I was strangely happy to find the no-drinking rule not strictly enforced.

However, I realize later, maybe it isn't so much that the rule is not strictly enforced as it is just reserved for times when one really needed to bend it. The problem isn't so much that the pile could serve as a life-sized model of a floor-to-ceiling bookcase, but rather the fact I can barely count to ten, much less learn to convert pounds and yen(s?) into dollars to figure out how much Tom's really spent on his international trips. I decide to start with the neat taping of all the receipts onto letter-sized paper, organized by each week, which in itself is rather simple and cathartic, and after a few hours, mind-numbing and, well, dangerous—if you consider the three Band-Aids that now serve as accessories to my ensemble (today, adorable white Hugo Boss pants suit from the Century 21 extravaganza—only eighty dollars!—and a black shell, black kitten-heeled mules, beaded turquoise necklace, and simple silver drop earrings).

I am just finished with taping the first three weeks of receipts, and although Tom is the picture of appreciativeness, popping his head in with lunch menu suggestions, treats from the vending machines, and little paper signs that say "Thank You" with poor attempts at stars and hearts, I need to take a break from the monotony. And so I head to the copy room for the utterly riot-a-minute task of running this first bit through for Tom's records.

The "Law of Offices" tacked up over the copier on an appropriately post-paper-jam crinkled sheet of copy paper dictates: "Whenever you need to copy something, this stupid machine always breaks."

I am knee deep in the thing, doors and drawers open everywhere, when I realize the Law of Offices may be less of a joke than a matter of fact. Little sprinkles of black stuff are settling all over my hands and arms when I hear a voice from somewhere outside of this machine that I now fear may become my second home, if I can't figure out how to get my hand out of the little back nook I have jammed it into.

"Don't you know what you're supposed to do when the copier breaks?" the voice says.

"What's that?" I ask, although I doubt he can hear me with my face literally inside the machine.

"Run away, run away," he says. "It's the only way to make it to the top. Otherwise, everyone will know you're the loser who fixes the copier and they'll call you in for backup every single time the fucking thing breaks. Before you know it, you're retiring as the copy guy."

I consider that this is actually very good advice, except for the fact that I don't know the loser who currently holds this position to get me out of my bind, or get my hand out of the copier for that matter. By some miracle (I may be using all of mine up this week), I give one hard tug, and my hand is free, saving me from a pretty humiliating explanation that I'm not sure I can even come up with at this point.

So, trying to regain my cool, I turn around to inquire, "So who's the loser that currently holds that position? I need backup."

He's cute—in a smuggish kind of way that I don't normally like. His tie is swung over his shoulder. You can't pull that off unless you're sure it won't hurt your cool factor. I normally never like guys that know they are good-looking because, well, they know they are good-looking. And, in my experience, this means they will never let you forget that, or the other fact surrounding good-looking men: that they know there're a million more where you came from—and if you don't like what you're getting, he can simply turn the corner and pick up the next girl in line.

But I'm a different person now, I remind myself. And that means I shouldn't judge people on first glance anymore. That's so PWW (Preworkingwoman), and as far as I'm concerned, she went out with that stack of press releases I tossed last night.

"For future reference, it's Donny Gold in accounting. But I think he's just in it for the chicks, so be warned. This time, since you're new, I'll help you out. But for the record, I never did this, and I have no idea how to use this thing. I'm Seth, by the way."

"Lane." I put my hand out, and I'm thinking how exciting this, my first possibly romantic encounter, could turn out to be, how absolutely perfect this could turn out, when he notices the particularly unromantic Band-Aid collection on my hand.

"Nice look," he says, flitting his gaze up to my face and back down to the accessories in question, as if he'd done this a million times and could turn just about anything into an opportunity to turn a girl on.

"Thanks. It's all the rage in Milan."

I watch as he bends over to check out the copier situation. And the view of his end doesn't elicit any complaints from my end. Looking directly at his ass like this, though, I can't help but hear Tiffany's comment in my head, "They're all assholes." With a butt that cute, surely a guy couldn't be all bad, right?

"So what department you in?" he asks.

"Mergers and Acquisitons," I say, finally getting the hang of the name after answering the phone that way no less than twenty times, considering the string of words together so many times they no longer held any meaning.

"Cool. I'm in accounting. Those are, like, two separate worlds around here—like the Jets and the Sharks. We're not really even supposed to be talking to each other." He put his finger over his mouth as a signal of secrecy.

"Really? Why's that?" I ask in a breathy voice, quickly getting swept away with the idea of intrigue and secret meetings à la James Bond—complete with slick form-fitting leather skirts and décolletage-revealing evening gowns.

"It was a joke, Lane."

"Oh. Yeah, that's right; only the investment and trading sides are protected by, um, smoke walls," I say, trying to impress him with my vast knowledge of the financial world. I tug the sides of my blazer to show I mean business.

"I think you mean firewalls," he says, turning around and smiling at me.

He pivots back to the copier, and within seconds, a crinkled, burnt paper emerges from deep inside. "I've found your culprit. Looks like it was stuck between your A and B slots, right by the corpus opperendi."

"How'd you know all that?" I am truly amazed.

"Again, it was a joke, Lane."

"Oh."

He snaps a succession of drawers and doors closed, slips his paper onto the glass and successfully makes a copy.

"You do impressive work," I comment.

He shows no hint of being flattered. Instead, stony, he issues a reminder. "Like I said, this never happened."

"And what happens if I do, say, accidentally, let it slip?" I venture to find out.

"Well, I guess you'll just have to take your chances." And with that he disappears out the door.

Again, I note, very cute butt. Very cute.

Asshole?

By the time 5:30 rolls around, I am done with mindless copying and taping and organizing, and my head is so fuzzy from focusing on the same thing for so long that there is no way I can attempt to actually figure out the conversions right now. Instead, it seems quite the natural time to write my daily journal entry.

This may be the first time in my life that I said I would do something every day and actually did it. Maybe this is only the second day, but I am still impressed with myself. I think, though, the dedication is partially due to the fact that the job, itself, despite what I said yesterday, *is* boring and virtually brainless, and so, I need to remind myself that I am actually a writer, with a real career, that actually means something to me, and that the pursuit of that career is why I am here in the first place.

I'm just opening to a clean page of *Diary of a Working Girl*, when a little envelope appears at the bottom of my screen. I have an e-mail! Tom has yet to e-mail me, and nobody else I know has this address, so I'm guessing it's probably some announcement about new coffee in the kitchen, or some warning about leaving dirty mugs in the sink, from someone who has an even less brain-taxing job than mine.

But, I couldn't be more wrong. It's from the copy guy, Seth.

Lane,
    I very much enjoyed being your knight in shining armor in the copy room earlier. I hope you are impressed with my technological genius. I was not very impressed with your technological abilities at all. But, lucky for you, I am willing to overlook that. I do hope, however, that you are genius in the area of sparkling dinner conversation, because I would like to see if you are free on Thursday.
—Seth

Seth,
    I am glad to hear you are willing to overlook my inefficiency in the area of copy machines. I am not making any promises in the

area of dinner conversation, but I will let you know that I am an
expert in the area of accepting free dinners (before you wonder
about the meaning of this for the next twenty-four hours, yes, I am
a gold digger and I expect you to pay for every cent of the meal
☺). I would be delighted. You pick the place. I'll meet you at the
scene of the copy disaster. Say six?
Best,
Lane

Now, before you think me the absolute smoothest woman in the
world, you must remember that A) I am a writer, and therefore,
more than able in the words department; B) I have a job to do here,
and therefore, must put any sort of neurosis or self-doubt that
might normally accompany male endeavors to the back burner;
and C) I am now part of this new, nonbeauty world, where my
confidence has skyrocketed overnight to a level that can even stand
up to the sort garnered from the best haircut, an outfit from Gucci,
or probably even plastic surgery.

Day Two and I already have a date. A date! That is, I have a date
with a very cute guy—and really, I guess he's not all that smug—
and it happened so quickly, and he has really nice lips. And I bet
he's a great kisser. Sometimes you can look at someone's lips like
that and just KNOW. And when that happens you just have to tell
someone. I need to tell someone. It is never any fun to have a date
without the opportunity to gloat about the date and dissect the
possibilities of the date from every angle with your friends. So I
sign on to my instant messenger to contact Chris.

Footnote: Exclamation points cannot under any circumstances
be omitted from electronic correspondence. They are the very cor-
nerstone of the entire communication framework, along with

funny faces and the need to act much bolder, funnier, and wiser than you actually are.

Lame2001: Hey baby!

Photoguyforguys: How is the working woman today?

Lame2001: Daahling, I couldn't be better.

Photoguyforguys: So are you gonna tell me why or am I going to have to guess ☹?

Lame2001: Well, it's a lot more fun if you'd just guess.

Photoguyforguys: For the love of God!

Lame2001: Patience is a virtue, dear...

Photoguyforguys: One I've never seen you exhibit...

Lame2001: What about that time I was on a waiting list for TWO WEEKS for that Laundry dress? Huh? And then I had to wait to get it hemmed after that!

Photoguyforguys: This is becoming tiresome. Would you just get on with it already?

Lame2001: I thought you'd never ask. Well, I have a date!

Photoguyforguys: (Warning: Cheesy saying ahead.) You go, girl! Who with?

Lame2001: He's in accounting. And he has a very nice butt! His name is Seth.

Photoguyforguys: Boring name AND boring job. How Lane, I mean, um, lame.

Lame2001: You're just jealous!

Photoguyforguys: You got me.

Lame2001: I knew it. You are sooooo transparent.

Photoguyforguys: And you're not, Miss Boy-Crazy Stacy!

Lame2001: You have a point. Still, am very proud of my rapid success.

Photoguyforguys: Well, you are very qualified for the position...

Lame2001: Let's hope so! Toodles! And, oh, photo 26—exact look-
    alike!

Photoguyforguys: 26! That one was mine! I won it fair and square!
    Let me at him.

Lame2001: No can do.

I am just closing out that instant message window, when another
one pops up from Tiffanybabeoliscious. This is so much fun! Now
I have coworkers, I have more than one IM pal. Joanne never uses
it—she thinks it is the downfall of society.

Tiffanybabeoliscious: I heard you've got a date with Seth!

Lame2001: That was very quick!

Tiffanybabeoliscious: Good news travels fast! Want the scoop?

Lame2001: Sure . . .

Tiffanybabeoliscious: Well, Seth used to date lots of the girls around
    here, until he started going out with Evelyn Grainger in accounts
    payable. But he dumped her bitchy ass last month. She's going to
    be sooooo jealous when she finds out!

Lame2001: Ooh!!!!!! Intrigue!

Tiffanybabeoliscious: Totally! Lucky girl! He's sooooooo cute!

Now, can things get any better than this? I am now like an office
celebrity. People will be whispering and looking at me. I am already the subject of gossip! This is so exciting. Evelyn Grainger—
watch out! There's a new girl in town! And that's me!

Initial excitement out of the way though, I attempt to calm
myself.

While I am trying out a new life and a new way of meeting
men, I will resist the urge to daydream about Seth every second

until Thursday. I will not write his name inside hearts on Post-it notes. I will not picture him naked. I will not squander away hours imagining how he kisses.

But don't I sort of have to? I mean this is no regular date. This is the first in what I hope will be a series of tests to determine whether Seth is my M&M. This is serious business. I have to throw myself into this head-on. Give it my all.

It's my job, after all.

Which is why I am keeping a diary to record these very things! Of course! As I said, it's my job.

Day Two: You know, it's funny, when every single man you encounter has to be thought of on such a serious level, there is a lot of pressure. Do I throw myself into thinking about him or don't I? Do I or don't I? Hmmmm... The best way to answer such a question would be to enlist the advice of a friend.

But my friends would not provide the answer I am looking for. Which is to definitely begin thinking about Seth, Seth, nothing but Seth from now until Thursday.

Without friends who can provide the proper answer, I will have to refer to my oldest friend in the world: my checklist book, to make sure I haven't missed any important points.

Checklist # 127 Seth
1. Reads NYTimes: ☐
Notes: Requires additional research
2. Has job that will allow for romantic trips to exotic locales; always insists we fly first class, feeding each other sorbet with a tiny silver spoon: ☐
Notes: Must ask Tiffany about this (but not too soon, as don't

want to appear after money, which is not important part of this
checklist item).

3. Puts passion above common sense/practicality: ☑

Notes: Did help with copier, even though obviously has fear of
retiring as "copy guy," also used phrase "knight in shining armor."
Didn't mind asking me out even with ex-girlfriend still on
premises (must add "possible conspiracy" as additional checklist
item).

4. Is British (depending on nature of remainder of checklist,
this can, on occasion, a be fulfilled with valid British
heritage documented on family tree, but British accent is
most desirable): ☐

Notes: Although does not exhibit verbal signs of United
Kingdom origin, did (as mentioned above) refer to "knights,"
which is surely a British sort of reference.

5. Makes me get That Feeling: ☑

Notes: Did enjoy rear view; if memory serves correct, also
experienced three heart jumps (1) when he did sexy eye-
flick thing; (2) when I received very direct e-mail regarding
date; (3) when I was trying not to write his name inside
hearts on Post-it notes or picture him naked.

6. Knows how to be direct, (Richard Gere, Pretty Woman):☑

Notes: See # 5.2 above.

7. Has roses waiting for me when I get home (even when I
am working at home, he always finds a way): ☑ Notes:
Really should wait on this item, since no chance for proof as
of yet (and is a two-part question, technically requiring me to
be done with this assignment and back home to prove), but
am getting extremely great feelings about this and have just
decided after reading article about it, never to ignore
woman's intuition.

8. I am unable to pass a Victoria's Secret without dashing inside to find some new lacy, sexy thing with all sorts of straps that go God-knows-where to surprise him with, and when I do, he never says something as ridiculous as, "You must get dressed now, we are meeting my parents in ten minutes": ☑
Notes: <u>See #7 above, re: woman's intuition.</u>

9. He is so beautiful, maybe not to everyone, but to me, that I wake up in the middle of the night and spend hours just staring at the angle of his jawline, the arch of his brow: ☐
Notes: <u>Although beautiful without a doubt, have learned that beauty can be fleeting and therefore will refrain from checking off until at least one month. Maybe one week. Definitely not until tomorrow night.</u>

10. If we ever do argue, it is always with bitter rage, arms flailing, and tears burning in front of a fountain in Central Park or by the tree in Rockefeller Center, or somewhere equally cinematic. But, then, without fail, we make amends—always meeting in the middle of the route between his home and mine (as we both have the urge for reconciliation at the same moment); and come together in the most passionate lovemaking both of us have ever experienced (once we've gotten inside, of course), and thank God that we have found each other. After, we spend the evening laughing uncontrollably at the littlest things, like the way he says parents with the same A sound as in apple and coming to unique realizations about things—like how amazing it is that people now only drink bottled water, when before they'd never thought twice about drinking from a tap: ☐
Notes: <u>Again, probably best to wait on this one until actual argument ensues; judging from past experiences, this means at least until second date.</u>

11. Witty statements are always on the tip of his tongue: ☑
Notes: <u>So far, so good. But with today's myriad sources for pickup artistry (e.g. Maxim, Stuff, Men's Health), men can fizzle out on the wit front after initial encounter: This item subject to change.</u>

12. He teaches me things I never even knew I had to learn: ☑
Notes: <u>Reference copier incident.</u>

Friends till the end, my checklist and I part ways, one of us slipped into my attaché case, the other back to my journal.

With all of that possibility, how could anything go wrong? But haven't things gone horrifyingly wrong before with equally promising checklists? Then the question of the hour (and I really haven't much longer to figure out the answer) is: How do you recognize your M&M?

The next couple of moments are occupied with a vacillation between doubts that any Prince Charmings actually exist, and doubts about my ability to recognize him should he actually surface. Each side of the equation has its horrors.

If there is no such thing as Prince Charming, then whom will I wind up with? A not-smart-enough, not-funny-enough, but sweet and thoughtful guy, who I'm not really in love with, but eventually stay with so long that there's no turning back? Or if I don't settle, will I become the proverbial bird-woman (I know it's really cats, but I much prefer birds), doomed to a long life of loneliness and excrement cleanup? And, on the other hand, if he does reveal himself to me, what if I am too stupid to recognize him? What if he's drunk and he says something inappropriate, like "Nice rack," and I turn my head and present him with the palm of my hand and, defeated, he rejoins his friends and never speaks to me again? What if this has already happened? This is a horrifying thought.

And the thing about horrifying thoughts—after you have just broken up with a perfectly decent man, who is smart, has a great job, supported your career, thought of sweet things to present you with on dates and holidays, and has told you on more than one occasion that he is never happier than when he is with you—is that they lead to more horrifying thoughts.

What exactly was wrong with James? All of my friends had nothing but rave reviews. They thought him witty, funny, a perfect match for me.

I think back and try to figure out where it went sour. I'd always fancied myself so fortunate when I'd see him with his family—they dote on him so! And when we were with his friends, I couldn't help thinking that since they were so wonderful, it could only support the fact that he, too, was wonderful. The few times we went for romantic dinners, I'd look around the room and feel lucky to be with him (former checklist item; now proven to be misleading). Or was it that I was lucky to be with someone?

I am about to hang up my pen when I have another insightful thought about the men of the Traveler's Building that does wonders to lift my spirits:

They are everywhere (eating, running, walking, typing, talking). I was right about that part at least. It is truly amazing. All you have to do is jam a paper in the copier, try balancing three coffees on a tray, drop a pen, and they come running. And as you know from my earlier rantings and ravings, this is not the norm for me. I am not normally the woman like in those Impulse commercials. There are no men I've ever met before who suddenly bring me flowers.

But now that the initial question has been answered, now that I've proven that placing yourself in a setting like this can increase the possibility of meeting men and scoring dates, does this mean out of the tons of men I see that there will be one who will be The One for me? I guess the next frightening question is: Does increasing the odds increase the likelihood that you will meet that one soul mate?

Six

Mr. Right Now

During a very inspired moment on Wednesday (mood buoyed by a trip to the downstairs shop, during which my telephone number was requested by three—yes, three—different men, one of whom carried my bag all the way to the entrance to my floor), after a long day of typing up memos, faxes, and letters, and shoving time in between to pitch an occasional story idea or two, answer an e-mail, check my voice mail at home, check out the men around me, I attack my *Diary of a Working Girl:*

> I think that every single girl should have the option to visit a financial institution at least once per week. I have taken this on as my anthem, replacing my old (pathetic, and so never before revealed) one: That every single girl should be able to have a camera tune into them on a Sunday when they are trying to

while away the day alone, so that it can be broadcast into homes around America and everyone can feel sorry for them, like in the movies.

Despite the fact that I might be falling in love with Seth, I am still able to rejoice in the attention of other men. I made a concerted effort, when allowing that other boy to carry my bag (containing exactly one small coffee), to stop comparing him to Seth (who I've already surmised has a more romantic way about him, a nicer butt, and a more confident demeanor).

When I was smiling like a schoolgirl today in the cafeteria with Tom, and he asked me what was so damn amusing, I resisted the urge to say I am in love. Instead, I said "Oh, I'm just thinking how happy I am here!"

And he said, "You really must have needed to get out of your apartment badly, Ab Fab."

Since love was in the air (in the air surrounding me, anyway) and I couldn't stop thinking about how great it would be when Seth and I are going out on double dates and business dinners with Tom and his girlfriend, I brought the subject of her up.

"If you don't mind me asking, how long have you been with your girlfriend?" I asked. I was already picturing the four of us watching a polo match, dressed in white.

"Well, as a matter of fact, I do mind you asking, but three years, if you must know," he said.

"So, how'd you meet?"

"I wasn't aware I was lunching with a representative from the Spanish Inquisition. But, if you must know, and I'm sure if you've asked, you must, I'll tell you. I get this strange feeling that if I don't, you'll just keep asking until I do. So here goes.

We were introduced by our parents, who'd met on vacation and apparently had nothing better to talk about than their unfortunately single children. My mother pushed and pushed until I said I'd go out with her—Whitney—and so, finally I did. That was three years ago. She's a real estate broker. She's from Westchester. And that's all you're getting. Happy?"

I thought it was rather strange, him being so snippy about her, and not once saying something like, "She has the most amazing sense of humor," or "You'd really like her." I always hoped that would be the sort of thing a guy would say about me when I wasn't around. But I chalked it up to the fact that some people just don't like to discuss their private lives and went back to imagining what mine would soon be like.

After work, when I'm taking a sip of a frosty Miller Light at the long oak bar at Due South, the pub across from the Traveler's Building, I begin talking about Seth, who I'm still set to go out with tomorrow. We are at this bar because Joanne is suddenly very interested in my male-rich environment and wanted to see what I've been gushing about for the past few days. According to Tiffany, some of the guys from work spill over here so I thought it would give Joanne a taste. But there really aren't that many people here at all. What could they possibly be doing? Working?

After I've told her about how great it will be when Seth and I start double-dating with other work couples she shoves a palm in my face.

"Oh no. You are not doing this again. Not when you've got so much riding on this assignment." She shakes her head, taking a sip of her cosmo and grabs for her box of Parliaments.

"I don't know what you're talking about. I'm not *doing* anything! I'm just preparing myself for my date. I'm working overtime, if you must know the truth—picking out my outfit, taking it to the dry cleaner, scheduling manicures and pedicures. It's a lot of work, Joanne." *I* don't even believe what I'm saying as it's coming out.

"Are you out of your mind? You know exactly what I'm talking about. You did the same thing with James, and you've done it with every other guy you've ever gone out with. You build it up so much in your mind that the only thing you can get after that is disappointment. Just take things as they come. Do you think Peter and I sit around staring into each other's eyes all night when I get home from work?"

I had pictured this very thing many late nights alone in my bed, but I'm guessing that would be the improper response by the way her face is turning green.

"No, Lane, we don't. I get home. He asks why I didn't feed the cat before I left. I ask him why his wet towel is still lying on the floor from yesterday and then we fight about what we're going to eat for dinner. And *we* love each other. That's life Lane. Not this fantasy world you're living in."

Why is it that any time you are getting the tiniest opportunity to be optimistic someone has to come in and ruin it with talk of this "real world" we're all supposed to be living in? When I'm miserable and I call Joanne up to cry, she unfailingly keeps putting the phone down to say things like, "I love you, too, honey," and "Oh, babe, can you rub my back for a minute?" But now I'm looking for her to support my positive outlook, she has to tear it to shreds and stamp all over it. I don't know what to say.

"Is everything okay with you guys?" I try, deciding I'd rather not get into an argument at this particular moment.

"Yeah, it's fine," she says and finishes the second half of her cosmo in one sip.

And I'm trying to support her and bring her spirits up by whooping at her fantastic victory over the potable when, out of the corner of my eye, I see one Mr. Tom Reiner. And next to him, wearing the scowl of the century, is the girl from the picture on his desk, Glamour Shot hairdo and all.

I turn in my seat to face the bar so he won't see how shocked I am at what this woman looks like in person.

I've got my hand over my face and Joanne asks, "What? What? You look like you've just watched a credit card company repossess your entire wardrobe."

It's too late. I can't hide. He's seen me. And the hostess is taking him to a table, which requires him to cross right by me. I'm hoping I can seem supportive and complimentary, but I've just never been good at hiding things.

"Ab Fab, fancy seeing you here," he says, looking more at my feet than my face. His *girlfriend* is looking at me from head to toe and back again in that horrible way that, that, well, *I* do when I'm sizing up the competition, which is ridiculous, since I am practically definitely maybe going to marry Seth.

"This is Whitney; Whitney, this is Ab, um, Lane, my assistant."

I put my hand out, and it takes her a second to take hold of it with her dragon-nailed hand. When she does, it's with a birdlike grip I can barely feel.

"Charmed," she says, clearly not meaning it. And then she turns to Tom and says, "I think we should go to the table now. If we're not going to a *real* restaurant, then the least we can do is eat at a table—rather than at the bar—like civilized people."

I look at my plate of boneless chicken wings here and should probably feel like a barbarian, but instead, I stab one with a fork and go, "Mmmmm," waving them off, with a closed-mouthed, mid-chew grin.

Tom looks as if he's going to flash that award-winning smile, but thinks better of it, waves and follows his Ivana Trump look-alike to a corner table.

"That's your boss?" Joanne asks, with disbelief.

"Yeah, why?"

"Well, he's so—young. And cute. How come you never mentioned him?"

I look at them; she appears to be fixing his hair, licking her finger and trying to smooth down a flyaway. I would have never guessed he'd be one for the mother type. I'm relieved I can't see his face.

If I could pick a woman for Tom, she'd be wonderful, stylish, smart, funny. I'm mentally cataloging my girlfriends to think of a single one, but I'm the only one who doesn't automatically receive the "And Guest" invitations these days.

"What's to mention? He's a sweet guy and all, but definitely not M&M material. Did you catch a load of that tie? And anyway, he has a girlfriend."

"Whatever," she says. "I've had enough of downtown. Wanna head back to the real world?"

"You know what you need?" Joanne perks up in the taxi, as if she's just found the cure for cancer. "You need to have some random hookup with a guy that you do not have to worry yourself sick about with stupid questions about him being your Kit Kat or whatever."

"M&M."

She doesn't skip a beat. "It's unnatural dealing with this twenty-four/seven. I think you're in danger of going mad and I don't mean that in a romantic HBO version of *Hamlet*'s Ophelia sort of way, so don't even go there. It's hard enough meeting anyone, wondering whether you should go on a second date, much less whether you can spend the rest of your life with them, before you've even had dessert. I really am afraid you may short-circuit. That's it. We're going uptown to a posh spot where none of these guys would ever go."

The jury is still out on whether or not I am going mad. It is possible, perhaps, that some might say I am a smidge too excited about my date with Seth. But as far as I'm concerned, I'm merely enjoying myself. Thoroughly. The pressure is there, but only a bit, since I'm still only in week one, and everything seems to be progressing swimmingly. Still, I'm never one to argue when it comes to meeting Mr. Right Now, who has many merits, which are thoroughly indisputable.

Mr. Right Now is Joanne's term. She's always telling me I should enjoy the single life because, once you are in a serious relationship, "You'll never be able to touch another man's ass."

I can't imagine being so unhappy with your own man's ass that you'd want another one, but I will never judge Joanne's relationship again. The one time we'd gotten down to talking about her sex life and she said they had sex on average once a week, I nearly fell off my seat laughing. What kind of relationship is that? Certainly not one I'd ever imagined. I'd thought it was a joke. Apparently it wasn't.

First she grew angry—eyes widening to perfect circles, brows raised so high they disappeared into her hairline—and glared at me like she was about to pounce. But after the scariest twenty seconds of my life, all she said was "Lane, you'll never change, will you?"

So now I just concentrate on my own love life. To each his own. And since I haven't technically seen Seth's ass yet, I'm free to do whatever I wish, with the bonus of my imminent date to keep me from feeling desperate should my mission fail. It's the best of both worlds really.

Twenty minutes and an eight-dollar cab ride later we are ordering another round of drinks at Cherry in the W Hotel. I have spent the last decade trying to meet men this way, and it has never proven successful before, but there's always that stubborn inkling of hope in the back of your mind that *this time* will be different.

"You're so lucky you're single," Joanne says, and I can't believe she's bringing this up again.

For someone who fancies herself knowledgeable in the ways of the world, she sure doesn't know the first thing about how unlucky the single life is. And I'm just about to start in about how before I met Seth the weekends stretched out ahead of me like torture tests—a series of never-ending hours to be occupied by various modes of distraction (mainly complaining about how there's nothing good to eat anymore; in desperation, eating something fattening; complaining about how I just ate something fattening; wondering what I'll eat next)—punctuated only by overindulgent sleeping jags, when I feel a tap at my shoulder, and hear the words, "Excuse me."

I jump, and in the process, land my pink drink right in the lap of the unfortunate speaker. The first thing I see is a wet lap. And then I notice that the wet is rather embarrassingly placed over the crotch of a rather exquisite pair of navy pants, which, looking up, I notice, is actually part of a rather exquisite suit, over a sleek button-down shirt, on a rather nice frame, and, finally, topped by one of the most beautiful faces I've ever seen on a man. Watery blue eyes, small, in that sort of squinty, sexy way, strong brows (I am an avid fan of the strong brow on men), a well-defined jawline, and almost non-existent lips. Most people like big, full lips, but I like tiny, skinny ones. There's no reason, really. I just do. Perhaps it's something to do with those Ken dolls I played with as a kid—they all had the tiniest lips. And I might add here that this guy knows exactly how to choose a tie. His is a beautiful, discreet, checked pattern with a hint of blue that perfectly compliments the shirt and the eyes and—whoa!

"Do you have the time?" he asks in an English accent (an English accent! I've spilled a drink on the most beautiful man ever to step foot in a W Hotel bar, who has, above all things coveted, an English accent!), as if nothing has happened.

I want to apologize, offer to lick it off if necessary, but, instead, look at my wrist, and say, "Six-thirty." Thank God I'd settled on that watch at Century 21. Apparently miracles never cease!

"Great. Then I've time for you to spill one more drink on me before my dinner meeting. What'll it be?"

I look over at Joanne, and in that no hands/words needed language that we communicate in, ask how to proceed here.

And in the no hands/words needed language, she lets it be known through a flick of a brow and the slightest turn of a cheek, that I should order another cosmopolitan, introduce myself, and attempt to refrain from regarding him as an obsessed 'N Sync fan would Joey Fatone.

Gosh she's helpful when she doesn't open her mouth.

"Are you sure I shouldn't buy *you* a drink?" I venture.

"Oh, not a chance. Then I'd owe *you* something, and I'm rather enjoying things in their current state. Now that you feel bad for making it look as if I've taken a pee in my suit, you've no choice but to sit here with me while I finish my drink. It's the only polite thing to do."

Polite? I would have stayed there with him until he begged me to leave, calling over bouncers to rip my arms and legs from him.

And then, with the most subtle gesture I have ever been witness to, he calls the waitress over, passes his credit card into her palm, and orders up one "mountain" of napkins, a cosmo for me, one for Joanne (even though she hasn't nearly finished hers yet) and a scotch for himself.

A scotch! (I am tipsy and highly attracted to this man, so using exclamation points to excess is now unavoidable.) I've never spoken with anyone who drank scotch. (!!!!)

"Do you ladies just pour drinks over innocent men for kicks, or is it a professional sort of thing?"

"I'm a, um, a writer," I say, catching myself from saying I am somebody's assistant. Or even worse, that I am undercover looking for the love of my life; I wonder exactly how many milliseconds it would take after saying something like that until he "forgot" his dinner meeting actually started five seconds ago.

"Well, why so glum about it, Hemmingway? Tough day on the keys?"

(!!!!) "I'm, uh, working through a really tough assignment right now," I say, thinking how simple it sounds in those terms—like when somebody advises you along the lines of, "You'll just have to move on."

"I'm Lane, by the way," I say, changing topics before my size XXL mouth gets me into trouble. "And this is Joanne," an elbow in my ribs prompts me to add. My gosh, this man is beautiful. He's beautiful in the sort of way that makes you very aware of the presence of estrogen in your body. (!!)

I experience a full-on flush of paranoia/neurosis/jealousy as Sexy British Man shakes Joanne's hand. I cast myself in the role of sixth-grade girl uncomfortable in her own skin, hating her best friend whom he might actually wind up liking better. And as I try to tell her without words, "This is my ass!" I semiconsciously shake my hair in what I hope is a sexy gesture. (!!!!)

"Joanne has a boyfriend," I say in knee-jerk fashion on behalf of said sixth-grade girl, before I realize what I've done. Idiot. My eyes widen when the knowledge that my pettiness has now escaped through osmosis from its hiding place in my head out into the world.

Sexy British Man smiles as if I've said the funniest thing in the world. This action further encourages the busy little she-hormones that have now infiltrated with their sexy gear (biological versions of flatirons, long-wearing mascara, and multicolor concealer) into every muscle, organ, and bone that make up Lane Silverman. The result is rapid rotation of hair twisting, décolletage caressing, and lip pouting that I can only hope looks as sexy as I feel (!!!!). When I nearly knock over cosmo number two, I am feeling less than confident that my hopes are being realized.

Before I can drag in the reigns on the tornado of activity that is currently my female sexual reproductive system, the sixth-grader once again takes over and I am overcome with how tall and skinny Joanne is. In yet another universal imbalance, my friend looks stunning, despite the fact she "doesn't understand" how anyone can bear to wear foundation, blush, or lipstick; "It's just so gross to put stuff on your face." The girl looks stunning, even with the Hello Kitty T-shirt and anti-fit paint-splattered jeans that must be twenty sizes too big for her.

I urge sixth-grader to retreat, but, still find myself moving closer to the bar, turning my head from Joanne, to block her from the conversation, anyway. I wave off responsibility in the face of biological instinct (the she-hormones have begun unpacking the heavy artillery: their anticellulite seaweed wraps, instalifting serums, collagen injections). I dismiss any further misgivings with the rationale that I've gotten a bit rusty at this sort of thing what with my own noncompetitive status at work these days.

"I'm Liam. I don't have a boyfriend." We find this amusing. We'd find anything he said amusing.

Liam, as it turns out, is here (I swear to God) trying to set up the U.S. edition of his magazine, *Beautiful*. He owns a publishing company. Well, his father owns it anyway (!!!!). *Beautiful* is a well-known magazine in the U.K. I've read it!

"Oh my gosh, the list is so long," I say, when he asks me which publications I contribute to. I feel a sharp pain in my calf and realize Joanne has just given me a swift kick. I hadn't realized she was so strong. I am suddenly reminded of a commercial from my youth, where dancers are dressed in black to look menacing, and they sing a song that goes, "You tell one lie, it leads to another, tell two lies, leads to another," and then I think of the saying "white lie" and consider that this one is more of a slight beigey lie that couldn't really hurt anyone, too much, anyway. All I want to do is meet a man that I don't have to feel any pressure about and here I am bringing work into the whole thing again.

"How long are you here for?" I ask, smoothing my hair back behind my ears.

"For one more month right now, while I find an office and work out all the legal details. And then I'll be back one month after that to get the project off of the ground."

"Are you staying in this hotel?"

"No, actually we have an apartment just down the road."

It's probably all marble and filled with artwork in heavy gilt frames. I bet there's a huge claw-foot tub, with a hands-free phone next to it, so he can work right around the clock—even while soaping himself up with the scents of L'Occitane (!!!!). I love a man who's devoted to his career.

"Where are you?" His voice lifts in the most adorable way at the "you," which could justifiably refer to my brain—which has momentarily vacated to a junior four apartment in the Louis the XV style—as well as my residence.

"I live in the Village, and Joanne's on the Lower East Side." I love saying I live in the Village—it sounds so bohemian and free-spirited.

"One of my favorite restaurants is in the Village. Have you ever been to Union Square Cafe? I guess that's really Union Square, but it's close enough."

Have I ever been to Union Square Cafe? I do get to go to a lot of fancy restaurants, for reviews and parties—another great job perk—but I hadn't yet been to that one. This didn't stop me from lying though, for absolutely no apparent reason.

"Of course. I think it's divine." I don't think I've ever used that word in my life. Somehow, through all of the hats I have been wearing lately, I have found myself in Zsa Zsa Gabor's.

"I go to business lunches there quite often. The service is outstanding, and the food is out of this world."

I'm shaking my head and moaning "mmm" like a complete moron. When I catch myself, I ask, "So are you having lots of meetings with writers and editors to pull your staff together?" feeling the confidence finally make that welcome transfer from my martini glass to my brain.

"Well, we haven't really nailed down the whole team yet. We do have a few people in mind, though." He lists a couple of really big names that just about everyone would know from their presence in the society pages, and so, I assume my personal inquiry should end here. It's not as if I can compete with those people.

"Have you got anyone in mind that you think would be good? What about yourself? Who did you say you write for again?"

(!!) M-m-m-eee? Who did I say I write for again? Oh yeah—nobody you ever heard of? I can't say that. I just can't. *Tell one lie . . .* "Well, I'm doing a lot of work with *Cosmopolitan* right now." It's true really—this assignment *is* a lot of work—and it is going on right now. And then I remember my most recent success. "And the *Post*."

"*Cosmo*, really? That's just the sort of background we're looking for. Why, I just mentioned that as a place to recruit from today. Would you be interested in coming to work for us?"

Now, hold on. He hasn't seen my writing or even heard of me before, but he wants me to come work for him? It sounds crazy. But, I guess, when you drop a name like *Cosmo*, it gets you in the door. That's why Lisa gets to write articles about the real-life stuff that happens to her, and I normally don't. With experience like that, what else do you need to know, really? I don't want to seem too eager, so I try to ask some more questions before I jump on his lap, screaming "Yes! Yes!" And the questions I pose about circulation, percentage of local content and design change are enough, I think, to make me sound like a true professional. So, I quickly seal the deal.

And then, before he dashes off for his meeting, we seal another, very sweet deal. "I hope you don't have any policies about dating people you work with, because I have to leave for my meeting now, but I have decided that I will not leave this spot until you agree to have dinner with me tomorrow," he says.

Me and policies about dating people I work with—I hold myself back from throwing myself on the floor in a fit of laughter, and from the hyperextended shape of Joanne's cheeks and its ripened hue, I figure she is doing the same.

No matter how great Seth already is in my mind, Liam is stunning and charming already—absolutely no imagination required on my part. And I mean, come on, he fills the British requirement (without stretching the category to breaking point with proof like talking about knights!) (!!!!!!!!!!!) As I feel my anticipation once again tighten around my lower abdomen, I think Joanne's advice was right on the mark this time around: Mr. Right Now, *indeed*.

Now, she rescues me again: "Didn't you say that event tomorrow night was cancelled, Lane?"

"Yes. Yes. The event. It is. It's cancelled. I love you—I mean— I'd love to."

Seth can wait. I've still basically got the whole two months left! He smiles and his eyes glimmer, even in the dim light. The effect is absolutely stunning. And when he takes my hand to kiss it—so slowly and softly—and then says, "Why don't we meet at Sushi Samba at eight o'clock?" I am not sure I have caught my breath enough to muster a response.

But, miracle above all, I manage to say, "That sounds great. I can't wait." Perfect. I'm a walking nursery rhyme. Hickory dickory dock, Lane please block your mouth up with a sock.

He kisses Joanne's hand, not as lingeringly as he did mine—believe me, I watch very carefully—says, "A pleasure," and turns to go. "Cheers."

And the back of this man is just as perfect as the front. There are shoulders so broad you could enjoy a leisurely picnic on them. And then there is, peeking slightly from the hem of his jacket, a beautiful, round ass. I am so hot I could easily be employed for egg frying. Seth, who?

"Holy shit," Joanne comments, I think, because she's caught the same rear view.

"Get your eyes off my man's butt," I say, snapping in that I-take-no-crap Z-formation. "Remember? When you have one man's butt, you can't have another."

"I'm just looking," she says, putting her hand up in defense and looking a bit forlorn.

"Is he not the hottest man in the entire universe?" I ask, not so much for approval as for a starting block to getting down to a conversation I am more than ready to start at this point. Now that there is really something to talk about there is no stopping me.

"Those eyes," she says with a far-off tone.

I finish the thought, "Those lips, that butt, that accent—"

"All right, all right, I get the picture," Joanne says. "But," she continues, and I don't like the sound of that *but* one bit, "You have really weaved quite a web for yourself here. You'd better hope you get that article finished, now that you've allowed him to think you're a regular contributor to *Cosmopolitan*."

Really, enough already with the reality checks. She's CNN—all bad news, all the time. "Like I'm not already worried to shreds about that. You don't need to make it worse."

Apologetically (shocker), she says, "Okay, okay, just don't get so head-over-heels for him right off the bat, alright? You don't know him at all yet."

"C'mon, I know that! He's just Mr. Right Now! You're the one who said I should have a fling with someone outside of the office in the first place. You know what the deal is. I'm not even thinking about him anymore."

Despite what I said to Joanne, during the taxi ride home, my head is spinning with Liam. I think about our date on the following evening (What am I going to wear? How will I lose twelve pounds by tomorrow night? Which magazine was that twenty-four-hour water diet article in?), and the fact that said British magazine mogul has offered me a position writing for his magazine in the U.S., on the sole principle that I write for one of the most successful magazines in the country, which I haven't exactly, er, written for yet.

Not that I am going to continue thinking about him, because, first of all, he doesn't even work in my company, and so he is off-limits as my M&M anyway, but, wouldn't it be just amazing if we wound up falling madly in love and then worked side-by-side at *Beautiful*? We'd go to press events and Patrick McMullen would snap our photo and the fashion magazine correspondents would ask who I was wearing, and they'd toss their heads back in laughter when we both replied, "Gucci." We'd topple Anna Wintour from her reign at the top, and when he went up at the Magazine Publisher's Association Awards to accept the title of Best Women's Magazine, he could say, "I couldn't have done it without the love of my life, my wonderful Lane." Now that is a life I could get used to! (!! !!!!!!!!!!!!!!!!)

Seven

One Enchanted Evening

So, it was with glee that I left work, headed out on a little-black-dress shopping expedition, went for my complimentary blow-dry with the hair guru of France, cashed in a favor for a free manicure (from a nearby spa I have written about before), and dolled myself up for my big date. I took Swen's advice and opted for the simple black dress—a strappy model that shows off my two always-skinny parts—my shoulders and back. I wasn't sure if the chocolate croc shoes quite went with it, but they were so elegant that when I put them on, and inspected myself at just the right angle, craning my neck back just so, I kind of, sort of, almost could fancy myself Audrey Hepburn in *Breakfast at Tiffany's* during that glamorous party scene, and so I made it work with a brown beaded necklace.

"Where *is* that Rusty Trawler?" I asked the mirror.

It would do.

Liam was early. Or maybe because I lost track of time peering into my vanity mirror pulling and piling my hair back to see whether a high chignon might suit me and dramatically reciting, "Fred, I'd marry you for your money anytime," I happened to be a bit late. This alone didn't actually take all *that much* time, but that got me questioning the croc shoes to such lengths I felt positive some battle-ready fashionista would point out my fashion faux pas and mortify me on my first date. I stood in the doorway positive the shoes were fine, and then that they were not fine, until the time I was already supposed to have been sitting across from Liam. And even though the walk would have taken ten minutes, I wound up wasting five bucks on a taxi, lugging along a larger purse that could accommodate safer black pumps in the case of crippling croc-shoe insecurity, and cursing the traffic on Park Avenue along the way.

He is sitting by the bar, drinking another scotch when I arrive.

"Stunning," he says. "Absolutely stunning." And then he leans in and gives me a kiss on the cheek, just close enough to my lips to make me want to turn my mouth to his and start making out with him right there at the bar. I wipe the *Ally McBeal* hallucination from my mind as he asks, "And how is the *auteur extraordinaire* today?"

"Perfectly wonderful, and you?" I reply, noticing my voice lift at the end as his does.

"Well, I conquered the world, saved the day, and managed to have some time at the gym, too. All in a day's work, you know."

"Of course," I say. I consider I had kind of done the same, as during the course of the day, I garnered three numbers in one trip to the cafeteria with Tiffany (if that's not conquering the world, what is?), saved the day with an expert excuse for Seth—sample sale at Girlshop.com—and although with all the primping, I hadn't made it to the gym, I might as well have because the heroine of my current read, *Jemima J.* had done enough exercising for the both of us in the chapters I'd read this morning. That had to count for something. I suck in my abs in case it doesn't.

The hostess arrives to take us to our table, and when we get there Liam scoots around to the seat I head for and pulls the chair out for me. I have never in my life had a man do this on my account. I didn't think people did anymore, citing women's lib as an excuse to forgo chivalry. I'm sure that's exactly what feminists are fighting for right now—first the right to vote, then a female president and, *finally*, one day we can all hope for an end to door opening and chair etiquette.

Still, I'm not that naive. Believe me, I know that just because a guy acts like he is in it for more than the sex, that doesn't necessarily mean he really is. But I choose not to focus on that possibility just yet. This is the first date, before any flaws are revealed, malevolent intentions discovered, or, on the other hand, (but not with a suave guy like Liam) that, nice as he may be, he is a crap kisser, and even worse in bed. And, aren't *I* in it just for the sex anyway?

In the bliss that is first-date discovery, I indulge myself in allowing his cologne to waft through my nasal passages and cause fluttering in my chest as he, very expertly, slides my chair in. It is enough to make a woman swoon—that is, if people actually did swoon, outside of period novels and miniseries.

"So, do you come here a lot?" I ask, rather impressed that he knows the restaurants on the Citysearch Best list when he doesn't even live here.

"Well, I know some of the people who run this spot. Business associates, you know."

The guys I normally go out with only know people that wait tables, not the ones who own them. This is quite a change. I can't help it, but I am suddenly picturing myself jet-setting to the coast—I don't know which one, just the one people mean when they say, "I'm off to the coast"—wearing black Jackie O sunglasses and a string of pearls about my neck.

And, he really does know everyone, from the waiters to the chef, who comes out in his puffy white hat to see how we are enjoying our sushi, and sends out some special dishes for us to sample.

I feel like a celebrity, or at least, what I imagine a celebrity would feel like. I was a bit worried about conversation topics, since we hail from such distinct walks of life, and even prepared a little list before I left the house (working out, restaurants, the overabundance of commercialism in the modern world), but such efforts turned out to be completely unnecessary. Liam is hysterical and a very smart conversationalist.

We both order up fruity cocktails, which are the house specialty here, and Liam raises his glass. "To the blue and pink contents of both of these glasses staying where they ought, rather than on my lap," he says, flashing that panty-tightening smile.

"Cheers to that," I say, trying to sound a little British and continuing to attempt a sexy look as I navigate the forest of fruits, straws, and kitschy stirrers sprouting from my glass. I notice that in superhuman fashion, Liam has smoothly removed his straw, dumped the fruit into the glass and gently placed the stirrer on the table. This starts me wondering what types of superhuman tricks he can perform with the jungle of straps, hooks, and lace that are my undergarments.

"Is there anything you don't like, Lane?" he asks, scanning the menu. "Because this food is designed for sharing."

"Er, no," I say, not wanting to sound unsophisticated in the world of sushi. It's like the world is divided into two sorts of people—those who eat the skin of eels and find the word "fatty" an attractive culinary adjective, and those who stick to cooked crab and avocado. I know the importance of choosing the right team here. So, I push my fear of slimy sea animals aside in hopes of having the perfect date.

When the waitress returns for our order, Liam ticks off roll after roll of things I can only imagine have spent way too much time on the bottom of the ocean, and I smile like he's ordering up ten pounds of caviar and warm blinis. I hear the word mozzarella in there somewhere and relish in the knowledge that at least that's one thing I can recognize.

"So, tell me more about who Lane Silverman is," he says, and I almost suffer a heart attack thinking we'll be talking business and I'll be lying up a hurricane the whole night, until he adds, "Aside from the award-winning journalist. This is, of course, a strictly business-free dinner."

Breath once again escapes my lips, proving I have survived and successfully evaded the storm's path. A business-free, *Cosmo*-free, M&M-free dinner—it's a nice thought, and now that I'm feeling comfortable with Liam, actually seems like an attainable possibility. And so, I try to find something intriguingly sexy to start off with.

A glance around the room for inspiration reveals lots of stylish women with perfectly straight hair and logo'd handbags fashioned in all sorts of fancy French bread shapes; men in crisp collared shirts and expertly weathered denim or freshly pressed slacks. This is not very conversation inspiring, until I notice a couple kissing at a corner table.

I reach for television dating show vernacular. "Let's see, I enjoy long walks on the beach, kissing in the moonlight, and water sports." Where *do* they come up with that stuff?

"Oh my God, I can't believe it! I knew we'd be a perfect match when I spotted you across the bar—or rather, when you spotted my pants under the bar. (Eyebrow raise.) Are you also fun-loving, a people person, and (deep breath here) a dog person?" He places his hand across his chest, mawkishly awaiting my answer.

I can't believe British cheesy dating show contestants are so similar to American ones. I thought they'd at least cite toast, afternoon tea, and something about the Royal Family. I guess it's true what they say, people are just people, no matter where you go. "Why yes! I do believe it must be fate. I also hate to play games, am a first-rate kisser, and a perfect 36-24-36, looking for someone who's ready to settle down and start a family." Suddenly, I panic that he might not get the joke and instead confuse me with some silly girl who wants nothing less than to tie a lasso around some guy and use him to play out her own personal fairy tale.

I am not that kind of girl. I know that men are living, breathing beings and not just some composite pasted together from male leads in movie posters ready to be plugged into your dream life at random. (Although, if you took a Brad Pitt, crossed him with a Ben Affleck, sprinkled a teensy bit of John Cusack—that would be one hell of a guy.) Anyway, I'm too young for kids.

"I hope you don't hate all types of games," he says lowering his lashes, and although I might normally relate this next action to a greasy pickup artist, when he winks at me, it is extremely sexy and on the mark.

And relaxing once again into our apparently kismet connection (just kidding), I realize this is the perfect opportunity to bring the conversation to the next level. I imagine a sexy guy like Liam is into sexy women. "Well, I only indulge in those involving feathers and hot chocolate sauce," I reply.

"I'll check if they have that on the menu for dessert," he says.

Inexplicably, I feel the need to keep recrossing my legs under the table.

Liam has served as such a great diversion from everything—

perhaps too great, I think, as a sinking feeling takes over my chest when the check comes and it becomes apparent we'll be parting ways soon. I know I shouldn't care so much. I barely even know him. And I obviously can't like him a lot because this is just supposed to be a little pre-getting-down-to-work-at-finding-my-M&M-to-start-on-the-path-to-award-winning-journalist fling. Still, I've never been very good at good-byes.

I don't know how those women play it cool and just go home after a perfect date without a second thought. I know that's exactly what you're supposed to do; say something like, "Well, it's been grand, but I have to wake up early tomorrow, so I'm off to bed." This sounds a lot easier than it really is. I am already imagining the way he would nibble on my ear, while firmly holding my hair back, by the time he's passing his credit card to the server (which he does without even allowing me to grab for my purse— a move he accomplishes by taking hold of my hand and shaking his head—tingly, warmly, coolly, wow!), because the conversation tickled around the topic of sex—in a fun, not raunchy, way for the larger portion of the evening. Random thought: What you are finding sexy and fun while you're doing it, would probably appear raunchy and cheap to an outsider, or more specifically, to a woman not on a date, who's jealous and constantly rolling her eyes at your conversation (not that I have ever been this woman before).

And after my pink, orange, and teal cocktails, I am feeling ready to rip his clothes off and ask for a chocolate doggy bag. Especially after he'd spoon-fed me a warm chocolate ganache, bite-by-bite, refusing to stop until I'd finished each and every drop. The entire time it was as if I was playing a role in a movie, and as soon as we paid the bill, someone would yell, "Cut!" and then this whole thing would come to an abrupt end. We'd get up, Liam would return to his real life persona—bumbling, awkward, hardly able to float above flirting level—and I'd revert to daydreams for fulfillment. Things like this just don't happen to me.

So, when we finally stand up and head for the door, I have no idea what is about to happen. Half of me hopes he asks to come up for the proverbial (wink, wink) cup of coffee and then it's random affair done, on to more pressing matters; but the other half of me doesn't want this to happen—hopes instead Liam will be a gentleman and rather than scoop up all of the spoils right now, will save that juicy stuff for another time—like someone does when they really like you and respect you, too.

"It's not like we've got all the time in the world, silly!" I say to myself in my head, or so I think.

"Time for what?" Or I've said it out loud and now sound like I'm auditioning for a Broadway rendition of *Sybil*.

"Er, oh, I was just looking at the time, sorry."

"Are you dashing off to meet some other bloke now, then?"

"Of course. He's picking me up in just a half hour at my place." (*Bloke*, adorable word—ahh, swoon.)

"Well, then, I'd better escort you home quickly," he says, "so I can send him on his way."

I know this is the most childish of games we play with ourselves, but the idea of a man being jealous of another fictional man who might be showering you with fictional attention is the most fabulous idea. And even though there will be no sending of anyone on anyone else's way, the idea that he even thinks to say this allows me to put myself under the sort of mental manipulation that I will dissect through telephone conversations for weeks to come, whereby this statement must obviously mean he wants to be exclusive with me. I'll have Joanne in a constant state of stage two non-listening in no time.

And as we start walking back to my apartment, I relax a bit, because I've just bought at least another twenty minutes of fantasy
time.

Well, I'm sure here you're wondering what happens next.

Will she be a diva and just go for it?

Is the combination of multicolored cocktail consumption and
the temptation of a breathtaking British man—who has basically
just had sex via chocolate with yours truly, understands bad dating
show jokes on the first try, *and* boasts the nearly nonexistent duo of
claw-foot tub ownership and Cocoa Pebbles addiction (aw!), and
apparently surgeon-worthy quickness of hand (as evidenced by
cocktail jungle manipulation)—going to send her straight on to
what the birds and bees have been whispering into her ear all evening, as was her Mr. Right Now mission anyway?

Or is this hopeless romantic, well, hopeless, and saving herself
for a possible future Liam encounter, despite the fact that she
knows someone like Liam will just further complicate her current
predicament?

As I lie here in bed, wearing nothing but the blankets around me,
all warm and tingly, smiling from ear to ear, I'll tell you what you're
dying to know.

The best thing about our walk is that we barely spoke at all. He
was holding my hand and lightly tracing his thumb back and forth
across the back of mine, and that very block that I'd walked along
a million times before seemed shiny and new and brilliant ("When
did they plant those baby trees?" and "Isn't that coffee shop with
the cane chairs just the *cutest*?") Every building was magnificent
and regal; every light took on a warm glow.

Cars must have passed, but I had no recognition of them at all.

Even as I recount now, I see empty, carless streets—a scene whose every yellow painted line, whose every awning, lamppost, and NO PARKING sign existed solely for our benefit. Normally, I'd find silence a bad thing and make a fool of myself, attempting to fill the void with useless chitchat surrounding meaningless topics. (Why don't they make crustless bread if that's the posh way to eat sandwiches? is one I keep for such occasions.)

But this was infinitely nicer. If a camera was following us, it would doubtless have stopped at our feet, which were perfectly in step, and then lingered up by our hands, which were so warm and probably emitting a halo of green light—a manifestation of feeling, and then zeroing in, finally, at the space between us, which was getting smaller and smaller as we continued south.

When our stride was interrupted at the northern corner of Union Square by a red streetlight, we slowly turned our heads toward each other. He looked at me, smiling without actually moving his mouth at all and then, as of their own accord, his lids slowly descended, snuggling his beautiful eyes beneath feathery skin and lashes. That rarely achieved, age-sixteen-potency wave of warmth and chill overtook me, starting at my chest and moving slowly down. And he moved his face close to mine. First, his lips hovered just millimeters away. I could feel them, soft curves and moist warmth, although he hadn't yet allowed them to actually touch my own. His breath was audible—such a strikingly personal sound—and I could feel my back, lungs already shaking in anticipation. Soft as a feather floating to the ground, finally we touched in an explosion of Magic Kingdom proportions. Neither moved for what couldn't possibly have been less than twenty-seven years.

When I was sure I would tumble down, right there at the corner, our lips parted and, ravenously, we searched inside each other's mouths, while his hands made their way at once around the back of my neck, on my cheek apples, at the lengths of my hair.

Although his collection of Park Avenue ladies probably hadn't prepared him for such forwardness, I just couldn't help myself from at least feeling, if only over the pants, that stellar ass I'd been doodling on all available paper scraps all day. ("What could you possibly need all of these for?" John asked when I'd inquired after an extra notepad for the third time.) Liam's butt was like one piece of Godiva chocolate daring me from a plate within arm's length for hours—I had to have it. I felt him smile mid-kiss in acknowledgment, so I gather it was just fine by him.

The light switched from green to red and back again ten, maybe twenty times.

WALK. DON'T WALK. WALK. DON'T WALK.

We didn't care.

A solitary honk.

Again, we didn't care.

When we parted and lips and tongues reluctantly returned to rightful owners, he lingered for a moment, his lids still low, as if his mind couldn't quite let go just then.

I was a *femme fatale dangereuse*. Ahhh. The power in my left pinky alone could transform a man into a pillar of salt. Now that was something.

And when finally, his sparkly blue eyes were revealed, he whispered, "Woah. You are amazing, Lane. I could stand here and do this forever. Breathtaking."

I really couldn't have imagined it better myself.

For once, I was glad my building had no doorman, because the things we managed to do standing upright in front of 555 West Thirteenth Street would surely have been grounds for eviction.

Who knows how long we would have been at it if Mrs. Kramer from the third floor hadn't returned from walking her Chihuahua and let out a big "Ahem!" to prompt us to move out of the way.

So . . . if I were a Girl Scout, and they had a patch for self-control, I would have used a big plastic safety needle to sew mine on proudly. Saying good-bye at my door after we'd gotten the pan all warmed up like that was one difficult feat, let me tell you. But, since I am not a Girl Scout, and I am not supposed to be liking Liam this much, and should not, by all rights, be smiling this much in my bed, fantasizing about the butt under the pants of a man who does not work at my company and is not allowed to be my M&M, I, for one brief second, taste regret. I should have just gone for it. Any girl in her right mind would have gotten it over with. Out of the way. Just cleared the path to achieve the real goals.

But then the dreamy effects of the cocktails. The wonderful movie of memories I get to play in my mind. Common sense is, once again, a quality lost on me.

Executive assistant-y duties are becoming second nature to me by the following week. I'm finding my way through the ins and outs. It turns out Seth is a wonder at converting currencies, and even though I have pushed our date off for next week, I somehow still manage to delegate this responsibility to him. In just one hour he brings the sheets back to me at our established meeting place— the copy room—and I couldn't be more thrilled. I'm so efficient! (.)

Tiffany and I have lunched more than once, and although we work not twenty feet from each other, we mainly communicate through instant messages, talking about this one and that one—I absolutely love office gossip! Who knew I'd been missing out on such a precious pastime for so long? And John, sweet as he is, is a bit of a gossipmonger himself. I'm not sure what his motivation is, but he's taken to e-mailing me all sorts of links of wild animals on the Internet and writing the words: "Tom's Boar," "Tom's Tarantula," "Tom's Barracuda" to identify a boar, a tarantula, even a barracuda who happens to remind him of our boss's girlfriend. I feel badly for Tom, since he's so nice and all, but I can't help thinking there must be some redeeming quality in her if he is in love with her. How important is a bad haircut, bad nails, bad attitude, and bad manners anyway?

Tom himself hadn't one bad thing about him, as far as I could see. When I get in each morning he's already on the phone with Europe, I imagine making deals or wheelin' and dealin' or something. But he acknowledges my arrival with a friendly wave all the same. My "To Do" pile is always in the same wire basket next to the entrance to my cubey. Each task is always clearly marked with instructions, which uniformly include the words "please" and "thank you." The work is easy and nobody's staring over my shoulder all day. I get the job done and so I'm left alone. If every boss was this logical the entire boss-joke genre would probably just fade away.

Sitting at my desk using my post-work free time to spell out L-I-A-M in writing utensils, I realize something amazing. There are no curved letters in his name! I am just realizing there are also no curved letters in my own name when it occurs to me that I probably shouldn't be going out with Seth at all. Time has speedily arrived at the day before my second date with Mr. Right Now, and my heart, and all of my filthy thoughts, for that matter (which I conjure up at variously inappropriate times of the day) now all belong to Liam. Liam. Wondrous, probable sex-god Liam. He is standing before me, naked, nibbling at different bits of me, while I am bringing coffee to Tom, taking telephone messages, filing papers. On other occasions, he is standing me up against a wall in some alleyway, ravaging me, *Nine and a Half Weeks*–style, ripping my skirt up out of the way.

I am having the best imaginary sex life. And it's so good, I don't even want to share it with my friends. I want to keep it all to myself. And I kind of have to, because the only people I could really share it with are irritatingly rational and have this awful habit of reprimanding me for doing the wrong thing.

When Joanne asks me how things are going, I say, "Oh, perfect."

"Excuse me, I must have the wrong number," she says, and proceeds to push in the buttons in a rather annoying fashion, "Hello? Hello? I'm looking for my friend Lane, the one who feels it necessary to announce to me every detail of her life, including when she's about to pee. Any idea where I might find her?"

And when I inform her I have absolutely no idea what she's talking about, she ignores my blatant lies as if I haven't even spoken.

"Oh, no. You've got it bad. The Mr. Right Now Backfire. I've seen this before. It is rare, but it happens."

I could all but see her shaking her head, rolling her eyes, burying her face in an open palm. And so, I do the best thing I can think of—pretend.

"Really, Joanne, what the hell are you talking about?" The Backfire. Damn. Please don't let it be the Backfire. Not happening to me. Not right now.

"Now, instead of spending your time fantasizing like a lunatic about someone at work before you get to know them—a path, which might, despite the ridiculous route, actually help your situation—you are spending your time fantasizing like a lunatic about someone who will not only *not* help you with your article, but will probably break your heart. He was supposed to be a Mr. Right Now! Lane, what have we learned in the past!" (I am not putting a question mark here because she is clearly not waiting for an answer.)

And so she goes on, "Did I not tell you just to sleep with him and get it over with! Then he could've just been an asshole and not called you the next day and you'd be on your way to finishing this article! Have I not taught you anything!" (Again statements posing as questions.)

The Backfire. The Backfire. I am a victim. My heart is racing with the severity of it. I swipe my desk surface clear of the writing utensil design of Mr. Right Now's name. As if that might help. As if that might somehow prove Joanne wrong.

You know what? I realize, as I'm reconstructing Liam's name with my writing utensils (I feel lonely without it), a horrible, awful, embarrassing fact: I don't even know his last name.

"I bet you don't even know his last name," she quips.

"Sure I do." It's Backfire.

"Well, what is it then? Backfire?"

"I'm not having this conversation," I say, growing annoyed and falling into a Liam panic mode, despite the fact I am surer than ever that after tomorrow I will obviously *never* have any interest in him other than a professional one.

I swallow a chuckle at the memory of Mrs. Kramer's "Ahem!" I'm totally getting used to the idea of saying good-bye to romantic Liam and hello to bossman Liam. I do wonder, though, how much room he's got under his desk? Strictly professional. Definitely. Maybe it's one of those desks that are really more like a table with lots of room for all sorts of "meetings" one may opt to hold there. . . .

"Well, I'll just say one thing, and then I won't bring it up again, ever."

Right. Because they'll be no need. Because I'm never going to think about him again, except as my boss, *Mr.* Backfire. Is there . . . ahem . . . anything I can do to, er, I mean, for you, Mr. Backfire? "Yes?" I ask, indignantly. If I could just, somehow, make this out to be all Joanne's fault, maybe I can go through with sabotaging my career by throwing this assignment in the toilet and sleeping with a future boss. Then I could just go ahead and look forward to many bawdy evenings with one Mr. Liam Backfire. Right?

"Don't forget what you have at stake here. You've got your whole career riding on this assignment and with your head in La-La-Liam-Land, you'll never do what you have to do."

I guess not.

Hmmph. Well, I'll show her, anyway! I'll have sex with Liam, and it will be great, and then I will just continue on as planned and that will show her.

Doesn't sound like such an awful plan, now does it?

When I go over this conversation in *Diary of a Working Girl*, I realize with even more severity just how right Joanne is.

I am making this assignment very difficult on myself. But what about my happiness? How many times do you get to meet Mr. Right?

Judging from the throngs of twenty- and thirty-something women heading out to bars on the weekends with blown-out hair, painstakingly applied makeup, and fuck-me eyes, I'm guessing not very often. What if Mr. Right is Liam? And, look, my first week is only half over and I've already got a date with Seth—I've put it off, but men love when women play hard to get, don't they? Isn't this what everyone is always telling me I do wrong? For someone who's never had a lot of prospects before, I think I'm on a pretty good track. And writing in this diary (that's you!) each day will make the process of actually writing the article simple enough. I think I've got a firm hold on the situation. So, it won't matter too much if I just stop writing about this project for a bit, and switch to oohing and aahing over Liam.

CENSORED!!!!!!

Eight

Serafina

Tonight Liam is taking me to Serafina. The only other time I've been to Serafina, a very rude man in dark sunglasses did not "Give a shit if you write about nightlife, even if it's for the fucking *New York Times.*" He handed my business card back to me like it was one of those donation sheets being peddled by a posing blind man in the street. And, therefore, like a man rejected in an offer of marriage, I hung my head low, and pushed my way out through the throngs of would-be entrants to leave the way I came. I hadn't really wanted to go that time anyway. It was a friend of mine who was dying to get inside and mix with the Hiltons and the Keisselstein-Cords.

I never understand the allure of places like this. Why set your sights on going somewhere that doesn't want you in the first place, and then insults you by charging sixteen dollars for a cosmo? If you did get inside, you'd spend the whole night worrying that your fake Gucci would be pointed to and sniggered at anyway.

I'd rather my local pub, where they're always glad to see me, and would never think of charging me more than five dollars for a drink of anything.

I've also been quoted on more than one occasion, commenting on the likes of men who frequent these establishments. "They are just wannabe scenesters and model-chasers. I can't even stand talking to them. It's always, 'And were you in the Hamptons last weekend? And have you been to the Mondrian in L.A.?' Screw that!" I told Chris one night, after a couple of hours at Lotus. I was only there because I had to review it. I couldn't care less about actually going.

"So why did you have your hair blown out and your makeup done? And why did I have to travel all over Soho with you to find a new black tank top, even though you already have twenty-five?"

"Because I'm here for work! I do have an image to uphold," I told him.

So, I have made it very clear that this is not my type of man, and that if one ever *did* ask me on a date, well, I'd rather eat my own hand than spend an evening with someone like that.

Now you're probably asking why, then, am I actually going on a date with a guy like that (not to mention daydreaming, night dreaming, coffee break–dreaming, subway ride–dreaming about going on a date with a guy like that)?

First of all, he wasn't wearing sunglasses when I met him, at night, in a bar. Second, he can't possibly be part of that ridiculous scene—he's British! And, third, I've already gone on a date with him to a thoroughly acceptable spot (Sushi Samba has already been around for at least a year, which means it's no longer the hottest, newest, rope-burn risk any longer) and had a fantastic time, and so I know firsthand he is not like those other guys, dropping their jaws at the sight of pin-straight blond hair and a size twenty-three waist, showing clear as day, between a half shirt and low-rider jeans.

Also, there is that butt. And those lips. And that tongue. And . . . *oy*!

The food at Serafina is good enough, and I note with some pleasure, that he knows the difference between Blue Point and Malpêque oysters and orders his filet mignon at the perfect medium rare. Tonight Liam is wearing a shirt so blue, his eyes are running the risk of blinding passersby with their brilliance. They might just be the eighth wonder of the world. We split the most wonderful bottle of some French Le Something 1994 Cabernet, and I am feeling, if possible, even more warm and fuzzy than when I first spotted him at the entrance to the restaurant, just one half-hour earlier.

The dinner goes by without a hitch. I can't talk about my job, for obvious reasons, and so, I steer the conversation to more relevant topics—mainly him, him, and him.

Thankfully, he doesn't mind talking about himself at all. Normally, I might find this annoying, but his life is so wonderfully fascinating, I find myself wanting to know the color shirt he wore when this happened, what sort of toothpaste he was using at that point, whether he preferred his potatoes mashed or scalloped.

In his first year of grammar school, Liam had a teacher by the name of Mrs. Smithy, who made up a song with everyone's name in it, followed by their hobby, so that the whole class could get to know each other. She'd asked every student to tell the class their favorite hobby on the very first day, so she could put the song together, and each child acquiesced with answers like "drawing," "painting," "swimming."

When she got to Liam, he hadn't hesitated for the slightest moment when belting out, "kissing girls." He had an older brother, and apparently, this was all he spoke about. Liam was a "sponge" back then (I note here that I love that word, and ask politely if he would mind if I use it in an article).

Obviously, the teacher asked him to select another, and to that request, he said, like a cautious attorney, "I'll have to get back to you."

To hear him tell it, Mrs. Smithy nearly had her eyes roll back in her head at that response and promptly called his mother up to school to discuss the situation.

After the meeting, Liam overheard his mother telling his father about what had happened. The father was laughing and joked, "Looks like we've got ourselves a little gigolo, there." Liam's mother was shaking her head trying not to laugh when she spotted Liam listening at the room's entrance. "I'm a gigolo! I'm a gigolo!" He skipped about chanting the mysterious word.

From that moment on, he had a new nickname. Gigolo's mother let the teacher know that he also enjoyed the hobby of piano playing, which he hadn't—yet. So, she signed him up for lessons, the fruits of which, to this day, remain the ability to play the lower key arrangement of "Chopsticks." Since I am well versed in the upper portion, we are now due for an ensemble the next time we are at his apartment, which is fitted with a piano—all of their family homes are now—just as a joke.

That is one very expensive joke, I comment, and he just waves it off, as if to say, "Money is nothing to me." And while this might normally be taken for a very showy display, I find it endearing and, well, sexy—although I can't say exactly why.

When the main course comes out, we are covering the ground of his fascinating high school years, during which he became the top rugby player, a sport, which, even after his very thorough explanation, involving a makeshift napkin chart—a real cloth napkin! (What a loon! He said he would pay for it, obviously)—I still have zero understanding of.

He once had his heart broken "right in two" by a woman five years his elder. She was a neighbor of his—twenty-five, when he was merely twenty. All the while they were having their "affair" (as he called it because it was the biggest secret Gigolo's ever had), neither of them told a soul; she would remark things like "You're too young for me," and "You know this can never last."

But he would toss those comments to the wind. She was just rationalizing to herself about being with a younger man. Obviously, she really loved him. He couldn't love this much alone. Besides, she'd told him she did. Sure it would be at the oddest times—after she'd had a particularly bad day, the sole purpose of a 3 A.M. telephone call—but she would let slip those three words, and after so much wanting, craving, when Liam would hear them, they were savored. But later, it would always be the same: He'd ask her about it; she'd deny ever saying it at all. It was very tragic. When I teared at the recounting of it, Liam collected the tears from the corner of my eye with one, soft, sensitive, romantic finger.

Even his finger has a deep soul, capable of rich emotions that most men can barely comprehend.

"You can; you can," I gently persuade after he admits he is unsure if he can go on with this story he has never shared before.

He makes an amazing recovery and bravely forges ahead with

the narrative. After she abruptly cut him out of her life, he insists he hasn't been able to truly bare his heart to another woman.

The poor thing, I find myself thinking. There is so much pain in the world. I resist the impulse to jump across the table and stroke his face. I declare my one mission in life: If it's the last thing I do, I will get Liam to bare his heart to me. After all, I am a different kind of woman. I am Ab Fab; I smile at the name's creator—the boss who belongs to that other world that is threatening my happiness and my sanity. It is striking, though, how sweet everyone is in that "sinister" place. Ab Fab. That really is funny. "Ab Fab, can you bring the faxes?" I get the urge to share it with Liam, but I don't want to interrupt the history he is now sharing with me about his childhood summers.

Liam has a family home in Provence, where, and I swear he says this, he "would love to take (me) in the summer, when the weather is so divine, it's like heaven on earth."

I am overcome with hatred for that stupid, awful woman who took his heart and couldn't even appreciate it. At the same time, I am consumed with the desire to show him with every inch of me, that I can love just as she can, only infinitely better. I bet they never even went to his home in Provence. Ha! Score one, Lane Silverman.

Obviously, though, I am not serious. Obviously I cannot fall in love with Mr. Right Now Backfire. Obviously, I cannot see his home in Provence. I don't even like the country (although you can wear all of those great Liberty print sundresses that never seem right in the city). I am not even close to falling in love with him.

This time, he does order one warm chocolate cake with crème fraîche to go, and asks, would I mind if we share it at my apartment?

His place is out of the question, as his father has surprised him with a visit and is staying there right now. "I suppose we could go, but then we'd have to share our pudding with him."

He is so witty and, oh my God, I can barely wait to see what the hell we are about to do with our dessert, but I am so ashamed of my tiny, dingy apartment that I almost abandon my mission. "Sure we can go to my place," somehow comes from my mouth anyway. I hear myself say it; I feel myself get into a taxi, and then with the distinct feeling that Omar Tuama, the taxi driver, is enjoying the view from his rearview mirror, I once again feel Liam's hot breath close to my face, and then his lips and then his tongue, and then, wow!

He doesn't seem to lift even an eyebrow at my rickety old lobby, with its lack of chair or couch or even table, my close-to-death elevator, or even my tiny apartment. Not that I would care if he did, this being our last time together and all. In fact, he comments that I have done "great things with the space." He adds "It's very charming."

I return the compliment: "You are very charming. And so I will get the spoons," I say, heading for the kitchen.

"There is no need for spoons," he says, pulling me back from the kitchen.

And while I may have thought myself well versed in the cannon of things one could do with a warm chocolate cake and crème fraîche, I must now admit I have barely scratched the surface in the past.

Despite what you may think, not a lick of it finds its way onto my sheets. Liam is very skilled in the chocolate and lovemaking department. And, this time, going to sleep, with nothing but my sheets around me, I don't have to think over the Liam I spent the evening with to keep myself warm. I now actually have the Liam I spent the evening with to keep me warm (although I swear this will definitely, positively be the last time).

And with an arm looped under my side, and another one stroking my middle, his mouth lingers for a while by my neck and ear. He says right into my skin, "You are such a breathtaking woman." And the breathtaking woman and the breathtaking man fall asleep.

And, not three hours later, when I wake, turn, and stare at this wonder in my bed, looking adorable and so human snuggled in my faux fur throw, and lean in and start kissing him, gently on the neck, and move to his cheek, and eventually, onto his mouth, he does not once protest and say, "I'm sleeping!" as other Mr.'s Not-the-One have in the past.

In fact nothing he says is really audible at all. It's more like this hungry, I-want-you language that only the both of us understand. I couldn't even explain it to you, because really, no two other people have ever experienced something like this. Truly. Too bad this will be the last time they do.

Nine

Plan B

All through the following week my assignment becomes more difficult to concentrate on. The millions of men around me have become faceless, barely noticeable. And that is probably because my plan to sleep and desist has gone awfully awry. I realize the full extent of this one night, when I once again am taking in the lovely length of Liam's bare limbs and tight buttocks. After a few too many glasses of wine and a whopping four hours doing the most enjoyable things, glancing at my sleeping wunderkind, I get a fabulous idea. I absolutely cannot believe it has taken so long to come up with this! It was staring me in the face (and plenty of other places I won't mention here . . .) the whole time! Lane Silverman is about to save the day—*and* her sanity.

Quietly, I tiptoe to my computer and pop an e-mail over to Karen, my editor at *Cosmo,* suggesting I switch the whole thing around, and say instead that meeting The One happens when and where you least expect it. In my excitement and urgency, I add some convincing arguments of both personal and professional natures that seem appropriate and poignant. Glancing back at Liam (who's just made the cutest little grunt) and reading it once again over a glass of wine, I am amazed that I was able to capture my feelings so perfectly in words, and so I click and send.

I am really thinking like an award-winning journalist now. What's the award journalists get? The Nobel prize? The Pulitzer? Whichever it is, I'm surely on my way. And so I find myself on the way back to my Mr. Right Now Backfire turned Mr. Right.

But when I am awoken at 7 A.M. by the jingle of a new e-mail, I delicately slip out from Liam's arm and over to the computer to learn that my editor doesn't quite see things in the same way. What is she doing up so early anyway? Sitting poised, ready to record the hour, minute, and second I screw up? She probably writes it in her day planner: 7:00—Monitor Lane Silverman's screw-up status.

Lane,

While I am so glad you find me the most thoughtful, wonderful, fantastic, open-minded editor you have ever worked with, I regret to inform that you will have to stick with the original plan. Yes, Liam does sound absolutely "dreamy" as you put it, and a "real" British accent does put him on a whole other level, but it looks like you'll have to table your bloke for some other time, sweetie. If it really is an "otherworldly" love, perhaps the two of you will be meant to be in your next life. I guess this is what they mean when they say, "Sacrifice for your art." I do hope that you don't think me a cold bitch for this, but if you really want to go for it with Liam, then I'll pay you a finder's fee for the story idea and pass it along to another writer. That's the best I can do. This is *Cosmo*, after all—not some supermarket tabloid—so consider your choice wisely. But from what you've told me of your electricity, cable, Saks Fifth Avenue, and Citibank Visa bills, I gather you'll want to stick with writing the story. It's your call, darling.

Best,

Karen

P.S.: If you decide to skip out on Liam, would you mind passing my number on to him? Thanks. You're a peach.

Surely I did not mention the tower of bills, ready to topple over on my desk to my editor at *Cosmo*. I would never do a thing like that. It's so unprofessional. So childish. So obviously NOT ME.

Let me just take a look. . . .

Crap. I. Am. A. Moron. I take a moment to collect my hopes from the basement, where they have now crashed down and look over at the two hundred pounds of fleeting happiness on my bed.

There is a reason people use the phrase "too good to be true." I am about to become well versed in it.

I'll have to continue as planned. There is, however, no way I am giving Liam's number to that girl. She's probably blond and five foot ten, dressed perfectly in a matching sweater set and trim leather pants. In your dreams, Karen.

So, I e-mail Karen back, letting her know that I will absolutely wash Liam out of my hair as of this moment and continue on as planned with the article. I do apologize, I add, but it seems I have misplaced his number, and therefore, will unfortunately be unable to pass hers on (noting, of course, if I should ever happen to run into him again, I will surely do my best to play the part of that chubbiest of cherubs—Cupid).

One month, one week, and one day left.

Time for a new plan.

Ten

Plan C

And with that, my one night of peace and normalcy and bliss since this whole thing began is over. Time to call in the troops for Plan C. I e-mail Seth first thing when I get to the office to see if he is up to going out this evening. I spend the better portion of the day silently reciting the mantra, "Seth is The One. Liam is not." I type it into a Word document over and over again under the thought process teachers enlist when they have children write over and over on the chalkboard, "I will not pull Sally's hair." The possibility of hiring a hypnotist to permanently implant this idea into my brain crosses my mind more than once. I will not think about Liam.

I will not think of his soft, squishy lips, the sweet smell of sweat on his body, or the way he was trying to tell a scary story that couldn't be completed because of the laughing spells that infectiously overtook the both of us.

Seth. Seth. Seth. *Seth's Good Points*, I name a new document, type the words at the top in bold, and begin a bulleted list:

- Excellent copier repair skills
- To date—not one instance of typing "their" where he meant "there," or vice versa
- Cute butt (not as cute as Liam's)
- Sweet
- Flirty
- Works at my company
- Is very good at converting currencies

I am just stapling this list as an addendum to Seth's official checklist when I realize: Currency—Liam seems to have a lot of that. Thus far, he isn't miserly with it, either. The first gift of a dozen white roses was absolutely gorgeous. The card read, simply, as if I'd written it myself, *!* The second was a tastefully naughty powdery pink teddy from La Petite Coquette. (I have been going there, promising myself to return tomorrow, and never having any intention of doing so ever since I was old enough to realize my tastes far exceeded my budget.) The card read, *Wear me.* I said, "You don't have to ask me twice." The third was another arrangement of twelve white roses, sent to my apartment with a card that read, *These are so beautiful. I can't help but think of you when I see them.*

Could you just die?

And you know what else? Liam makes me feel so sexy. He's always telling me that sex has never been so fulfilling before. So "innovative." I am sexy in sweatpants. I am sexy in an old T-shirt. Basically, I am just sexy. As a matter of fact, I am existing inside the warm confines of a sex cocoon, where even crossing the street serves as an aphrodisiac. Career, family, friends, all come in a definitive second to the main attraction of life—carnal knowledge.

Can you feel any closer to someone than when they are walking towards the spot where you are standing—arms grazing sides you have bit, licked, sucked; mouth opening to reveal the tiniest peek of a tongue that has been intimate with peaks and valleys of your body's topography that now feel illicitly exposed, though covered in clothing?

I am a beauty queen, a goddess. Why has no man made me feel this way before?

Checklist #128 Liam (Last Name TBD)

1. Reads NYTimes. ☑

Notes: No actual proof, but, media career basically demands this, so, definitely, yes.

2. Has job that will allow for romantic trips to exotic locales; always insists we fly first class, feeding each other sorbet with a tiny silver spoon: ☑

Notes: Lives in exotic locale! Works in exotic locale! Has family summer home in exotic locale! Duh!

3. Puts passion above common sense/practicality: ☑

Notes: Reference memory of warm chocolate cake (stain from which he still cannot remove from his shirt), also reference little powdery pink thing from La Petite Coquette which defies common sense with its very existence as a $380 non-supportive series of lace strands that serve no purpose other than to be anti-practical and pro-passion.

4. Is British (depending on nature of remainder of checklist, this can, on occasion be fulfilled with valid British heritage documented on family tree, but British accent is most desirable): ☑

Notes: No family tree necessary! Woo hoo!

5. Makes me get That Feeling: ☑
Notes: <u>Reference dates one to five, as well as the 23,400 or so minutes since I first saw him during which skirking responsibility, dropping things, and completely forgetting where I am going and why are commonalities.</u>

6. Knows how to be direct, e.g., Richard Gere, *Pretty Woman*: ☑
Notes: <u>See #3 above. (warm chocolate cake incident)</u>

7. Has roses waiting for me when I get home (even when I am working at home he always finds a way): ☑
Notes: <u>Twice! no women's intuition needed here!!!!!</u>

8. I am unable to pass a Victoria's Secret without dashing inside to find some new lacy, sexy thing with all sorts of straps that go God-knows-where to surprise him with, and when I do, he never says something as ridiculous as, "You must get dressed now, we are meeting my parents in ten minutes": ☑
Notes: <u>See newly acquired Victoria's Secret credit card bill.</u>

9. He is so beautiful, maybe not to everyone, but to me, that I wake up in the middle of the night and spend hours just staring at the angle of his jawline, the arch of his brow: ☑
Notes: <u>Although am aware that beauty can be fleeting,</u> HOLY SHIT !!! !!!!!!!!!!!!!!!!!!!!!!!!!!!!!!!!!!!!!

10. If we ever do argue, it is always with bitter rage, arms flailing, and tears burning in front of a fountain in Central Park or by the tree in Rockefeller Center, or somewhere equally cinematic. But, then, without fail, we make amends—always meeting in the middle of the route between his home and mine (as we both have the urge for reconciliation at the same moment), and come together in the most passionate lovemaking both of us have ever experienced (once we've gotten inside, of

course), and thank God that we have found each other. After, we spend the evening laughing uncontrollably at the littlest things, like the way he says, parents with the same A sound as in apple and coming to unique realizations about things—like how amazing it is that people now only drink bottled water, when before they'd never thought twice about drinking from a tap: ☑
Notes: Have actually shared this criterion with Liam, and he insisted we act out an argument right in front of Central Park fountain (Rockefeller Center tree obviously not up in springtime). He was fantastic actor, screaming, "How could you possibly have made love to that Frenchman when you knew it would tear my soul right from my body, leaving a gaping hole that will always bear your name!!!!!!" We then met at the top of Union Square, dramatically made amends, and went home to, well, you know. Giddy and sweaty, little to no effort was required to find folly in the fact that he wears tight red underwear! And doesn't plan on changing this habit anytime soon!!!!!!!!
11. Witty statements are always on the tip of his tongue: ☑
Notes: Best to date (via telephone): "Why am I not in your bed being naughty right now?"
12. He teaches me things I never even knew I had to learn: ☑
Notes: Slimy sushi—tolerance, chocolate cake versatility.

All of my friends could have moved to Costa Rica and I don't think I would have minded in the slightest. Of course, I'd act all teary-eyed when we exchanged good-byes and well-wishes, but all I'd really be thinking is, okay, hurry up and go already so I can get back to Liam! What's the holdup?

Liam would never waste time with pleasantries and formalities like that. He gets right to the point. He shows me he can't stand to have the distance of clothing between us—no matter how filmy and sheer the garments I've taken to wearing around him may be.

The second he arrives at my door, he says, "I haven't been able to think of anything but you all day."

He begins unbuttoning buttons, often tearing garments right off of my body (the expense is nothing in comparison to the intensity of the display). He'll barely even close the door before we are on the floor straddling each other in never-before-seen ways.

You might think this an odd way for a millionaire to conduct himself. And I would agree. He tosses aside all of the stereotypes of his class. He is much more like a leather biker jacket sort. He'll curse at any opportunity—just toss profanities around like adverbs, as in, "This steak is fucking fantastic."

I'd never known cursing to be so sexy. It adds such intensity to everything.

"You are so fucking hot," and "I want you so fucking badly."

And there are other things, too. He never wears underwear outside of the office.

"It's utterly excessive," he says.

He does have a point. Why take the trouble to put them on, wash them (they are the bulk of laundry loads anyway), when they'll only wind up on the floor for the better portion of the evening? He believes smoking is one of the most enjoyable pastimes.

"All of the greats die young," he says in the face of cancer and emphysema.

Seth, I'm sure, displays equally meritorious qualities.

My plan starts off smoothly enough and we meet at the copy room at 6 P.M. Seth is sarcastic and dry in the humor department, which I rather like. But when we get to the little bistro he's selected for dinner, I do compare it to the posh eateries I've dined in with Liam (now Bemelman's Bar and Butter and Industry Food have been added to the mix), and even though I don't normally like that type of suave guy, my entire opinion of this genre of men has now changed, and I realize that, prior to this Liam experience, I had built my opinion about an entire portion of the population around a stereotype and have now mended my ways.

And when we order salads for appetizers, I remember the decadent oysters that Liam and I have shared and can barely bring myself to move my fork to my mouth. When he orders his steak well done, I nearly hide under the table in embarrassment. When the dessert menus are handed to us, Seth says, "I couldn't eat another thing." Here I ache for a warm chocolate cake in my bed.

The conversation floats by somehow, but I can't remember anything that either of us has said, because only my body is here. My spirit is facedown on my coffee table, Liam on top, doing things I've only before seen on the Spice Channel. Therefore, it is probably no shock to you, that when the taxi pulls up to my apartment, and Seth goes to kiss me, I turn to offer my cheek, give a quick thank you, and scooch out of the cab without so much as glancing back in his direction.

I know I'll be sorry for taking this opportunity to forge ahead so lightly. I should feel worse right now. But right in the middle of my first real "love affair," the conflict, the forbidden nature, only fuels my fire for Liam. I'm throwing the world away for Liam. I love the sound of that. It is a novel in itself—a true love story, where, on the path to passion, a trail of devastation is left behind. It's us against the world. In the end, I'll be broke, jobless, without a chance of success. At my all-time low. Liam will save me.

He'll pooh-pooh such frivolities as a career and say, "All that matters is that you and I are together."

When I'm down, he'll pick me up, showing me that what we have is more important than any stupid article. We'll jet off to Provence and enjoy the simple things in life: the crisp taste of the first wine of the season, appreciating its "legs" and "tannins," swirling glasses and rolling our tongues like experts; a walk in the meadow; a car ride to the coast. The sweet smell of grass and fruit will waft in through our open windows at night, where we'll lie, naked and spent after a full day of making love.

It is quite obvious that the only reason my career was so important to me in the past is because without it, my life would have been empty. But now I see there is no article, no book deal that could make me feel the way I do now. The choice is that there is no choice to make. Everything's coming up Liam.

Eleven

Sexy Scents, Sangria, and Samantha Smells Something Rotten

During that weekend, my third as a nine-to-fiver, I don't fret over the fact that I am not seeing Liam at all, as I have so much magazine article writing to catch up on, especially after the way we squandered the entire last weekend on my bed, in my tub, on my couch, on the kitchen floor, and I know that he is very busy setting things up for *Beautiful*. The nobody's-ever-heard-of-them publications I still have regular assignments with have been leaving me messages about missed deadlines for the first time ever, and it has been hard for me to take these seriously, since they are part of a life I no longer lead.

My article in the *Post* came out yesterday and my mother has phoned each and every Long Island resident to make sure they know about it. And that felt really nice, since the pieces I write for magazines and papers she's not familiar with have all been "so cute for you, honey." A name like the *Post* is big my-daughter's-better-than-yours currency. But what felt even better was when I walked into my cubey, hung up my coat, and saw my article hung right there in a delicate white driftwood frame.

I called Tom directly.

"Did you do this?" I asked, looking over at him through the glass and pointing to the frame.

"I have no idea what you're talking about," he said matter-of-factly.

"Did you get my article framed?"

"Must have been one of those number crunchers with a crush on you," he said, trying to sound aloof. "I hear them talking about you all the time in the men's room. It is quite good, though. Congratulations. I'm impressed."

"Well, thank you," I said, so glad to have made a friend like Tom.

I am simultaneously filled with joy at the fact that I've had an article published in the *Post*, and angst-ridden at the fact that I cannot share this triumph with Liam, as he will doubtless wonder what I have been doing signing on with employment agencies.

I calm myself with the idea that I don't need to share details about other parts of my life with Liam, because the only part of my life that matters is the part I share with him. I never talk about my friends. He doesn't need to listen to details about conversations with my mother, the banalities of the day-to-day. Everything is trivial compared to our love.

Did I mention that this week he told me he loves me? We were walking by the West Side Promenade. The sun was setting. A street vendor walked by hawking roses.

"I'll take them all," he said.

That dreamy Liam hunkered me down with forty-five roses, counting each individual one as he pulled them from the white plastic tub and placed them into my hands. When the man walked away, and thorns were sticking me all over (a detail I would never ruin the mood with), he ran his hand through my hair, resting it finally on my neck, stared into my eyes for a good minute or two, and said, "I am falling in love with you, Lane. I never thought I could love again, but you've broken me down. You've taken me from the shell I've built up."

I wept. I did. It was a surprise. Not an expected, boring natural progression. No. It was a wonderful, spontaneous surprise.

With a finger, he secured one of my salty tears and brought it to his lips. After savoring part of me becoming part of him, he said the words I could swear I'd heard before in a dream: "You complete me."

It is truly amazing how Liam is *always* coming out with the exact words I'd wished a man would say to me. When he said that—so perfectly put—it was like a déjà vu.

Today, without Liam, I have to write a fragrance story. I actually enjoy smelling all of the different samples that have been mailed to me over the last week, imagining what Liam will say when I wear each one. He loves perfume.

"You smell like sex," he had once said to me when I was wearing Frederic Malle's Musc Ravageur. He's never afraid to be raw like that.

Since my mood is pure desire, I decide to name the piece, "The Ten Sexiest Scents" and come up with cute phrases like "Eau de Ecstasy" and "Liquid Lingerie."

It is amazing how simply enjoyable these tasks are when you can incorporate the emotions of love you are experiencing into them. Liam is my muse. I am an inspired *auteur*.

I also have put off writing the article about Lisa, and so going through all of those notes now, I piece together a witty narrative about her life as connected to the beautiful clothing, shoes, and accessories in her fabulous closet. This is not exactly what the assignment originally was, but with these small publications, you can really do whatever you want, as long as the final product is good. I wish I could say the same about the *Cosmo* piece, because I would now be done with it, and could go on to concentrate on enjoying bliss with Liam if that were the case. That would be one utterly sexy article, to say the least.

But when I think of my now cutely decorated cubey and Tom and John (who is blossoming nicely in actual communication, in addition to the virtual sort), I think I would miss the chance to be with them, even if it's only going to be for a short time more. It is strange how things turn out, isn't it? I decide to pop an e-mail over to Lisa to thank her and let her know how things are coming along with me.

Lisa,

I want to thank you again for the wonderful morning I spent in your home. It was a pleasure to go through your life in such a personal manner and to celebrate your sartorial history as well. I am very proud of the article I have written about you. I think you will be delighted. I also thought you would be happy to know that your advice was very helpful, and I have since gotten a fantastic assignment from *Cosmopolitan* for which I have combined my love of men and my love of talking about myself ☺. More to the point, I have been assigned to take a corporate position in the world of finance with the goal of meeting a man I will ultimately fall in love with. The only hitch is that I have two months to achieve this. Although the pressure is almost insurmountable, I am delighted at the challenge and really hope this will bring my career to a new level. I would love to catch up with you again once I am done with this piece and tell you all about my experiences. Your piece in *For Her* will be printed in the June issue.

    Thanks again for everything.

Best,

Lane

Putting it down in words like that, I realize two things. 1) I am lying through my teeth. I feel no pressure at all. I can barely bring myself to think about my assignment. Failure at achieving the goal at this point seems to be the only possibility, and I couldn't care less. I have something far more important—I have love. 2) Explaining my assignment to someone else, who I deem a worldly and respectable woman, I realize it is the most ridiculous thing I could have gotten myself into.

I am a complete maniac. What the hell was I thinking? Was I so far gone that I really took a want ad, a breakup and a pile of bills to be signs of my destiny?

I crash my head into my keyboard making all manner of jibberish appear on-screen when I remember the half-heart formation of paper clips, the horoscope, all of the "signs" I used to ruin my life.

This is it. This is what they mean by temporary insanity. Where, God, did you hide the rewind button?

I could pop an e-mail over to Karen right now and have the whole thing done with. I'll still get the finder's fee and maybe just keep my Smith Barney job until the *Beautiful* position starts. And now I know Liam so well, he would never dream of asking to see my clips, so it won't even matter whether I've actually written for *Cosmo* or not.

I go so far as to open a new e-mail and type in Karen's address— one very slow keystroke at a time—but at the ".com" something holds me back. My fingers freeze and, as of their own will, hit the backspace key until I'm staring into a blank field.

I'll do it tomorrow.

I suddenly need a cocktail. Getting Chris's answering machine annoys me to no end. What is the point of having friends when they are not there when you need them? I cannot try his cell because he is strictly anti-cell and refuses to even allow me to keep mine on when I am with him, much less purchase one of his own. I have a momentary lack of all common sense and decide to call my mother.

When we are through, I need something more along the lines of ten cocktails.

"I told you this would happen!" My mother says when I reveal I am not going to be able to complete the assignment. She really thinks the sole reason you give birth to children is so that you can always have someone you can say I told you so to. I know this because she actually informed me of that very thing once. She was trying to be cute when she said it, smiling and playfully hitting my arm, because we were having one of those days of acting like schoolgirls—shopping and eating chocolate and drinking wine.

But I knew she wasn't kidding.

She only said she was kidding after my face turned sour and I began reciting a list of times that could actually prove this was my sole purpose in her life. "You said 'I told you so' when I broke up with Andy, Evan, Patrick, John, Rick, Timothy, Raoul, Jasons One through Three—"

"I never even *knew* there was a third Jason!"

Rather than return her joking smile, I continued, "When I fell off my bicycle; when I wanted to be Wonder Woman and jumped off the roof and twisted my ankle; when I wanted to be Mary Lou Retton and I cut all of my hair off and cried."

This time, I am in no mood for reminiscing. Besides, I can only blame myself for calling her. I already know she wants me to chuck this whole "article thingy" because she is a strong proponent of Liam. Her voice takes on a distinctive shrill every time his name comes up, and I can virtually see her Cheshire cat grin through the receiver.

This is not because my mother has done something so logical as to meet Liam and discern that he is a good person with high morals, who treats me kindly. And it is also not because she possesses psychic qualities that enable her to see that Liam does in fact have the best intentions and will one day ask for my hand in marriage.

I wish I could say it was that deep, or even respectable, for that matter. But it's not.

The reason my mother has founded the Liam fan club is that she has concluded, solely through my descriptions of what he looks like and sounds like (the G-rated version, of course), that he is not familiar with off-brand groceries. Which is to say, that he is rich. And to her, this is as glaringly obvious a sign of the perfect man as a slot machine ringing and buzzing with coins dropping down all over the place is a hint that you've won the jackpot. If she were to design a slot machine, rather than fruits or palm trees, she'd probably use little depictions of men driving Mercedes, men steering yachts, men holding out Amex Black Cards, and men escorting women into Tiffany's.

If a guy I am dating happens to, say, live in my building (which is a "sad place for a man to live, okay for *you* of course"), have a roommate, or work for a not-for-profit agency, in any of the arts, or do anything with his hands, and it doesn't work out, she'll say, "I knew it wasn't meant to be. He just wasn't right for you." Just like that—whether he had been given a commendation by the mayor for running into a burning building to save small children in a fire or invented a cure for cancer or spent his spare time teaching Braille to the blind.

Don't get the wrong idea about my mother. She is not walking around posh hotels with a metal detector, stopping at the bejeweled man fetching the loudest beep. She herself is no Joan Collins, riding around in limousines all day, fully coiffed and sipping sherry with one pinky out. In fact, quite the opposite; this is a woman who demands ice cubes for her glass of "mer-lotttt."

But the way she explains it is that being as I "will never make any *real* money of my own with my little writing thingies," she is constantly worrying about my welfare—picturing me in tattered rags, begging for change for subway fare.

"It makes me sick darling, just sick as a dog."

Apparently, this sort of worry is not so all-consuming that it gets in the way of her daily trips to the diner or her weekly hair appointments, or her monthlong vacations to the Caribbean—during which her deep concern doesn't require anything as excessive as a telephone call. But it does make for a comforting welcome home.

"Oh, honey, let me see how skinny you've gotten from making no money and driving your mother into an early grave with worry, just so you can keep up with your writing thingies."

"Just forget about this silly little assignment and make a go of it with Liam," she is saying into the phone. "Billy, come down and get your dinner! Your father is going deaf, I swear. And did I tell you about the party your Aunt Anne is having next week for cousin Kelly's college graduation? She's making some crazy crunchy granola kind of food. I told her to just order from Cluck Cluck Chicken. You know how they have those great mashed potatoes and the cucumber salad? And the barbecue sauce is divine. And I offered to make my pasta salad. You know the one with the Italian dressing and the broccoli that I made for your birthday last year? Did I ever give you that recipe before? You just have to get that multicolored, twisty pasta—I think it's spinach and carrot or something like that; otherwise they just dye it to have the different colors, but either way—and then you boil it up, al dente, and then you drain it, defrost the broccoli, and just toss it all together with the whole bottle of dressing; you should use the Wishbone, it's really tangy. And that's it. So, do you think you can bring Liam to the party, then? Everyone's dying to meet him."

Liam to the party. Liam to the party? Perhaps if I want him to go running and screaming all the way back to London by foot, I would ask him to go to the party. (I table this for a backup plan should I decide I really need to rid myself of him for this assignment.) My family, thinking he is royalty, and doubtless asking all sorts of questions about Prince William and parties at Buckingham Palace—too embarrassing to even think about.

Liam is not the sort of guy that you imagine playing with your dog. He's the sort of man you imagine doing it doggie-style with. And the latter is more the man for me anyway. I never once added a checklist box that reads, "Compliments my mother on her twisty pasta salad." That is too commonplace to even consider. We don't even walk on earth, much less on the streets of Long Island.

And besides, I remember Liam saying, "Family parties are not my thing. Why people feel the need to waste a perfectly good Sunday acting like they're interested in hearing who's got high blood pressure, who's headed for a divorce, and who's filing for bankruptcy because they blew too much on trying to outdo their suburban neighbors on the twisty shrubbery competition is beyond me."

I'd had the family-pleasing boyfriend before; I'm falling asleep just thinking about it.

Still, I can't help allowing my mind to explore how wonderful it would be to go home for once without anyone inquiring why it is that I am still single and whether I would like to meet their coworker's son Jason. And if so, would I let a little thing like ulcerated adult acne get in the way of my feelings for a very nice person?

But that would be nothing compared with the fact that Sunday evenings have now transformed from the loneliest time in the world to a cuddle and giggle fest of movie rentals and microwave popcorn, during which, if my phone rings, I can take the role of oblivious coupled friend to my single girlfriends calling to chat because they can't bear the loneliness of a Sunday evening—rather than me being the one who is nasty to my coupled friend when she tells me, through a mouth full of microwave popcorn, that she can't talk because she is in the middle of cuddling and giggling and watching a rented movie.

Come to think of it though, *tomorrow* is Sunday. And I still have not heard from Liam since our last night together. Surely he can't be so busy that he cannot spend one moment with me the entire weekend.

When I hang up with my mother the walls of my apartment seem like the most depressing apartment walls that have ever been. Just moments earlier, they were blossoming with memories of Liam, lovely Liam. Now, they are just reminders of his absence.

That is ridiculous.

I am not the sort of insecure girl who panics at a few days of silence from a gorgeous, successful British man, just because he could have any girl in the world he wants.

Still, I do feel deserted.

I can honestly feel a cactus growing right inside my chest. It is prickly and painful and it is the most horrible sensation I have ever known.

Disturbingly, though, there is something rather sensationally *dra-*

matic about the pain and the insecurity and the blankness of my walls. This sort of pain is anything but ordinary. It is epic.

Isn't this the way I'd always wanted to feel? So in love that it hurts? So tormented by emotion that I would dash my life to shreds?

I am so lucky! All those years of Joanne telling me I had no idea what love was all about—I held strong, and I have finally been rewarded.

I could just sit here all night and stare at the blankness that is my painful separation from Liam. And so I stare. And I stare.

Hours go by.

I check the time. When it says three and three-quarter minutes have passed, I check another clock. And one more.

Well, time is nothing in the face of true love. And so, if I've spent minutes that feel like hours staring at the blankness that is my painful separation from Liam, that's plenty dramatic. Right? Right. Besides, I'm getting to that state when you've stared too hard and no matter where you look, there are little dots of color where there shouldn't be. Like in the middle of my literally blank desk wall (which is blank because it is waiting to be hung with magazine articles from *Vogue* and *Elle*, penned by *moi*, but which now I'm thinking would look so much better with a picture of Liam and I), and right in the middle of my otherwise blank computer screen. Which just goes to show why I definitely need to go out right now.

So I strain my memory to think of someone to go out with (who is not a guy I should be dating but I'm not interested in, or a guy who I am in love with even though I shouldn't be and who isn't around anyway), and I remember that wonderful girl from the temp agency with the great shoes—Samantha.

It turns out Samantha is actually in public relations (hence the

nice shoes), and left her job at one of those humongous firms because she "felt the company was just taking money from clients for
absolutely no reason whatsoever, and that every single project I
worked on was pointless and of really no benefit to said clients at
all." And to make matters worse, she was placed on horrible accounts like medications for venereal diseases and panty liners for
thong underwear and so she had lots of difficulties feeling important in the world in general and most distinctly, when it came to
talking about her job to anyone at all.

When she reveals this information to me, we both suddenly realize that we had once spoken about two years ago, when she was
calling around to see if writers were doing any pieces on either
venereal diseases or panty liners that you can wear with thongs, as
she was assigned to organize a very unnecessary trip to the venereal
disease medication plant and the panty liner factory all at once,
since, as luck would have it, they were both located in Iowa.

I distinctly remember a girl calling me about this and breaking
down in tears, and when I gingerly bring this memory up, she re-
calls the conversation, too, and we both can't believe that she stuck
it out for so long afterwards.

So now she has decided to do something more important with
her life and felt that advertising might be a step in the right direction. Ms. Banker had pointed her to a boutique advertising agency,
but when she went on the interview, she discovered the agency
handles panty liners and so she just ran out of the office right at
that moment without explaining a thing to anyone.

"I described my whole situation in detail to Ms. Banker, and so
I couldn't believe she sent me to that agency knowing full well
which accounts they handle!" she says over our second glass of
sangria.

"I believe it," I say, with the sort of camaraderie you can only have when you share negative feelings about the same person. And then I go on to divulge my theory about how Ms. Banker likes to break people down before building them up again.

"Oh my God. You are so right!" she says, waving her head back and forth, as if I've just figured out the murderer in a whodunit.

I am a genius—when it comes to solving other people's problems, that is. "And therefore, what you have to do is go back to her now, and she will surely do the right thing for you, because that is the way she plays the game," I inform her, in my most I-am-a-clairvoyant-wonder-of-the-world voice.

"That makes total, fucked-up, no-sense sense. That is *exactly* what I'll do."

"Cheers to that," I raise my glass to a girl who can curse freely with someone she has just met.

After a third glass of sangria, I get that wonderful warm feeling that comes when you make a friend that you have a hunch you will wind up loving forever and will get to be bridesmaids for when each gets married. We have already covered jobs; apartments (she has two roommates—one cute British guy and one annoyingly tall and thin British girlfriend of his); places of birth—she is from California (although doesn't have that stupid happy-all-the-time L.A. attitude that New Yorkers normally associate with people from that region); and now we are at the all-crucial-but-you-never-want-to-bring-it-up-when-you're-dating-someone-as-to-risk-seeming-like-a-show-off-topic—men.

She brings it up, for our fifth cheers of the night, the one that marks our entrance into word-slurring and dangerous clumsiness: "To hoefully, one day fining a man worth a hill of beas in this city full of scenesters and cute but nah sessy men."

I really couldn't have said it better myself. Except, of course, now I have Liam, who is neither, and is absolutely perfect, despite the fact that I haven't seen him since Tuesday and still don't know his last name and must break up with him immediately.

"Hey, I have a crazy idea," I offer.

"Wha's that?" she asks, wiping a dribble of sangria from her chin with her palm. We've had too much to drink and probably couldn't even speak clearly enough to order another drink, but of course won't realize this until tomorrow, when we start questioning how bad of an impression we've made and send cute e-mails to cover up the embarrassment of anything we may have done.

"I met this guy at my offsse who's asssolutely gorgeous, knows a thing or two abou copy machines, and's a nice ass. I mean a grade-A, genui nice ass."

"So whasss wrong with 'im?" she wants to know, rightfully so.

What is wrong with Seth? The only thing I can think of is that he's not Liam.

"Obviously, something is wrong with him if you don wanhim."

"Well." And I stop myself, because I really don't want to tell her that I'm seeing someone, as I feel we've been bonding so much that I can't really build this huge wall between us right now—you know, then I will be a "them" and she, an "us." But I can't very well say I've already been there and tossed him, so I have to fess up.

"I'm kind of dating someone," I reveal delicately.

She says the magic words, "Do tell," with a smile, rather than a jealous or angry look, and so I get to spill the whole romantic saga of my current predicament and take the floor for pretty much the remainder of the evening, a state, despite my attempts at changing and bettering (since I feel like an attention-starved, self-centered bitch when I do this), is still pretty much my very favorite thing to do.

When I'm through, she surprises me with a whopper of a comment and I wonder if she is Joanne's long-lost twin.

"He sounds like a fuckinnasshole to me."

I am shocked. Had I not just told her about the roses and the "I am falling in love with you" thing? Had I not told about the skipping of the underwear and the beautiful restaurants and the broken heart and the chocolate cake?

"And 'you complete me' is a line from *Jerry Maguire*!"

Is it?

Holy shit, it is!

But so what?

Don't I myself blur the lines between my own fantasy life and movies all the time? I explain this just means we are kindred souls.

"Don't you think it jussa li'l bit odd tha you ha'nt seen his aparmen? Tha you don know his lass name?"

What is it with everyone? "He's got company righ now ann is my faul tha' I dunno hissname. I never assed."

Samantha's got her head resting on her crossed arms now, and she's shaking it back and forth. She lifts herself for a second to say, "You juss better be careful. He sounnns way too cool for school."

When her head bangs back down on the bar she murmers into the wood, "I think I better go ta bed."

Twelve

Practicality and the Pickle

I spend the better portion of Sunday morning putting cold compresses on my head and downing water. I am glad to feel sick as hell because at least it serves as a distraction to those awful doubts Samantha tried to plant in my head. She doesn't even know Liam! Though I can't blame her for thinking those things because he does *sound* too good to be true. But, lucky me, he is really that good. Samantha is obviously one of those women who walk around with a negative attitude about men, thinking Mr. Right doesn't exist. I can relate to that because it wasn't too long ago that I spent an entire day cursing fairy tales, counting couples, and entertaining the very same thoughts.

But, oh, how love can change you! If I'd upheld that negative, defeatist attitude and thrown my hopes into the trash can for a boring safe guy, look what I would have missed out on. I am so lucky to have been able to bring myself out of the dumps right in the nick of time. I just picked myself up, got myself a new life, and look how everything turned out. I couldn't be happier.

I guess I'd be a *bit* happier if Liam worked at Smith Barney and therefore my article would have been a success. But I'll be done with all of that soon enough, when I back out and then—bam! Perfect life, here I come. I'll pop that e-mail over soon enough.

"You complete me!" It's actually funny how similar we are. I'm *glad* he said that. It just goes to show that we share more interests than I'd even thought before. I can picture the both of us, just watching love stories all day long, lying naked, taking breaks to make love to each other, ordering in chocolate cakes. . . .

Two gallons of Poland Springs later, a bit of regional-calling coddling from my grandmother ("poor baby!"), and I am a new woman. Joanne and I are going to the café down the block to have some coffee (and chocolate for me).

She'd called me a little while ago and said she needed my advice about something. Joanne never takes anyone's opinions seriously, so I am very interested in seeing what this is all about.

Maybe she's thinking of becoming a writer and she wants me to advise her on how to get started! That would be so great. We could find some really cheap office space somewhere and get cute, but cheap, Knoll knockoff furniture from Ikea, or maybe we could get an article placed about our office and Knoll would design it for free!

And then we could work with our desks facing each other and share the burden of pitching, and when editors are nasty, we will be there for each other so it won't seem all that bad.

I wear my most intelligent, sensitive-looking outfit so that I will look the part of trustworthy friend and literary mentor. This is a lightweight powder blue cashmere T-shirt (soft and warm), a sweater tied about my neck (this is the editorial equivalent of a doctor's stethoscope) and vintage denim (they say I'm still down-to-earth), but with no holes or anything, so they come across as chic and not just old and ratty. And even though we are just going down the street, I wear black heels, to show Joanne that you really need to dress more adult in this industry.

Now that I am not monopolizing our conversation with complaints about my love life (or lack thereof), I am free to be a better friend. I am happy to have the opportunity to help her out. I probably have been pretty bad over the past . . . eight years, or so.

This can be a whole new start for us. Joanne will look up to me and ask things like, "What's a dangling participle?" and I could say . . . well, maybe she could ask something a little easier.

It's a little bit overcast today, and so I don't really need the sunglasses, but I feel like they are so elegant, and really pull the whole outfit together, so I keep them on.

"Joanne!" I exclaim when I spot her walking my way. I'm really so excited about the whole prospect of our partnership that I can barely wait for her to come out with it. I do the double air-kisses to get her into the swing of things.

But she says, "What the hell are you doing?"

These things take time.

It isn't two seconds after she's sat down when Joanne starts crying. Maybe I shouldn't have worn the heels or done the double air-kisses—maybe it's too much to handle all at once. I hadn't known she had the ability to do something as sensitive as cry. She's normally either bitter or happy—sadness she finds a wasted emotion.

"What's wrong?" I venture, afraid the world may be coming to an end, and well, sort of disappointed in realizing this is probably not a career call after all.

"It's Peter. We're—we're breaking up."

Peter and Joanne splitting? "But you're an institution!" I say.

"I know, I know."

"But I've looked to your relationship as a standard for greatness forever! What could have possibly happened?"

"Lane, I've been trying to tell you for a while now. We have not been getting along at all. It's just arguing about the loud music, the friends that are always following us wherever we go, like we're fucking Puff Daddy and Jennifer Lopez. And look what happened to them."

"But you're so in love! I see the way you look at each other."

"Love isn't everything, Lane."

"Don't be ridiculous! Of course it is!"

"Sometimes you have to be practical. Peter doesn't have a job. He's thirty years old. And he refuses to go the nine-to-five route. And while I understand having dreams, I cannot live with his would-be Moby derangements anymore. We have no money. We never get to go on vacations. We never get to eat out or do anything. I want things. I want a family. You know?"

"Money isn't everything. I mean it's nice to be able to go to Bergdorf right when the seasons change and buy whatever you want before it sells out, rather than pine over things and by the time you've saved up enough to buy it it's gone already. But money isn't everything! The idea of struggling together—making your own entertainment like in *Breakfast at Tiffany's* in that scene with the masks—that is so lovely!"

"Lane! Stop it! This is not a movie! This is real life! And I can't afford to pay all the bills by myself! And neither of us has a rich patron to foot the bill."

She does have a point. Wouldn't that be so nice though? A patron. I'd never considered that option before. It would take a lot of pressure off scrapping this article if I didn't need the money.

"So how does Peter feel about it?" Peter—a second father, really.

"He said he's never giving up on his dream. He thinks I'm too hard on him and said I should know he's nothing without music and he can't be with someone who can't see that. He's sick of the fighting, too. He said he'll never be as practical as I am. We both agreed it's the best thing."

Love being thrown out the window for practicality's sake? Is this really happening? Love conquers all. Doesn't it? For someone who's been in a relationship for five years, with someone she truly loves, to pick up and leave is just crazy, right?

"Are you sure you shouldn't just give him another chance?"

"I've given him a million chances," she says, taking a slurp of her black coffee like it may save her life.

"Well, I'm sure you guys were just caught up in the moment, saying things you both didn't mean. Why don't you stay with me tonight and cool down. I'm sure it will be better in the morning."

"Thanks, Lane. I'd actually love it if I could stay with you tonight. But I'm sure nothing will be different in the morning. Thank God I've got my career and such a great friend. Otherwise I'd really be left with nothing now. I can't imagine what it's like to break up with someone and realize you've thrown away your whole career and lost touch with your friends. That's why I'm always so proud of you, Lane. No matter how lonely you've been, no matter who you've gone out with—as crazy as you've gotten with some of them—you've never lost sight of your career goals. I know I don't say it a lot, but I am very proud of you, Lane."

You know—she's right. I've complained my fair share. Sure I have. And I've procrastinated *a bit* in the past. But in the end, I always pick myself up and keep pitching and giving my all to those boring, meaningless articles that I have been assigned. People are always complimenting me on how I push myself, and I never really pay attention. But it's true. How many people can just make themselves wake up in the morning and work—oftentimes with no assignments and no hope of assignments? I really have put a lot of effort into my career. And it has always been so important to me.

Is it possible I'm taking too big of a risk with Liam? I'd always thought that Joanne and Peter were the perfect couple. They were always embarrassing me at restaurants, smooching and whispering. They spent every night together. This all seems so strange. What if Liam and I don't work out? What if I wake up one day, having thrown my whole assignment, and with it my career, out the window, and Liam and I break up?

It cannot happen. It simply cannot happen.

I'm suddenly glad I haven't sent that e-mail to Karen. I will make this article work. I will find a way. I am a resourceful woman. I can definitely find a way. But first things first—Joanne.

We spend the rest of the day doing the things you do when one girlfriend is mourning a breakup (unless of course, that girlfriend is me and you're sitting on your couch crying your way through *Cinderella*). We drink lots of wine. We make fun of the bad things about Peter—he wore bikini underwear; he drooled on his pillow; he couldn't go to sleep without calling his mommy to say good night.

When this method of entertainment wears thin, we go for pedicures and gossip about the celebrities in the magazines. I suggest a wickedly caloric meal, but Joanne doesn't believe in such things (her parents were hippies and raised her on organic sprouts and couscous). So we settle for take-out from the Chinese restaurant and watch stupid high school movies—*Bring It On, 10 Things I Hate About You, She's All That*, while the leave-in conditioner works its magic under our shower caps.

"We should do this more often," I mutter as Joanne is smoothing a green mask around my face.

"You know what would be really fun?" Joanne asks.

"What's that?" I inquire, tasting, by accident, a bit of green mask.

"If we went outside like this, went into the deli, and just acted totally normal—as if we didn't have green crud all over our faces."

I'm so glad Joanne is taking this so well that I'd probably go outside naked if it would keep her smiling.

"Sure! Why not?" I say, tossing caution to the wind and spinning my key ring around my finger as if I'm cool as a cucumber walking outside my apartment looking like a cucumber.

In the childish spirit we're in, we opt for the stairs and race down. Joanne wins (only because I let her, of course—you know— to raise her spirits) and I'm pretty breathless by the time we reach the front door of the lobby. People walk by. Oh, I hadn't thought of them, only the guys in the deli, who already know my style from my multiple pajama expeditions. A couple is walking hand in hand, staring at me and Joanne like we've left our minds somewhere in the paint jar and when they reach us, Joanne turns to me.

"Do I have anything on my face?" she asks in coquette-l'il-ole-me mode. I totally lose it and by the time we get to the deli there are skin-colored streaks of laughter-induced tears running through my otherwise green face.

The idea is to keep a straight face and not act like we're doing anything out of the norm, but every time one of us tries to open our mouths, we just start cracking up.

The guy behind the counter tries to be funny. "My, you guys are looking kind of green."

This isn't very original. Regardless, we fall crouching to our knees, holding our stomachs, unable to catch our breath from laughing too hard. Forgetting I have green on my face, I rest my temple against the side of the white counter, and when I remove it there's a green print.

"Oops," I say, looking at the splodge and Joanne's trying to say something, pointing at the mark, but it's as if she's given up language all together, so she just lets out a laugh instead.

"You spit on me!" I exclaim, and here we are literally lying on the floor in hysterics.

"Testing out the new color for fall, Ab Fab?"

Did somebody say Ab Fab? Because there's only one person who calls me that and there's no way he's just seen me lying on the floor in my pajamas looking like a pickle in a shower cap.

Joanne looks first, and with the boldness that comes after you've just changed your entire life with one decision, stands up, reaches her hand out, and says, "Great to see you again!"

"The pleasure's all mine," he assures her, looking down at me as he says it.

"Hi, Tom. What *are* you doing here?" I ask, and rise, smoothing my top down, as it's the only thing I can think to do to improve my appearance.

"Well, I just went to see a movie at that theater down the street and I remembered you raving about the bagels here. So I came to check it out. You know me and the carbs."

I hadn't even remembered telling him about my deli. I guess I'm like EF Hutton—when I talk, people listen.

He's wearing nice Gap-type jeans, in a distressed finish. Jeans are really idiot-proof. All men shop at the Gap; you have like, five kinds to choose from and you can't go wrong. And without a heinous tie, jacket, and collared shirt he's actually rather striking in a crisp white T-shirt.

"So did you go to the movie with Whitney?" I ask, not seeing anyone in the shop who looked like a possible candidate for Tom's companion. Unless you count the guy with the three shopping carts sitting at a corner table very loudly gargling Vanilla Coke. I can just hear Whitney's voice as she enters a place like this: "Daahling, you really should hire a new assistant. Anyone who'd frequent a drab place like this isn't really the type of person you want to be associated with."

"Whit—oh, no. I, um, went with a friend but he had to go meet someone right after the movie. Left before the credits even began." Tom scans the room as if his "friend" might magically pop up, lets out a deep breath, and looks back at me.

"I see," I reply, wondering why he is being so utterly odd, I mean, aside from the obvious reason of attempting to uphold a conversation with a girl in pajamas with her hair in a shower cap and green goo on her face, a girl who just happens to be your assistant, and now, possibly, insane.

Joanne had picked two Heinekens from the fridge, which the cashier had obligingly uncapped, and handed me one now in a brown paper bag.

"If I haven't told you already, Ab Fab, this is a fantastic look for you. Fabulous."

"*Vogue*'s calling it Military-Schlump-Shower-Cap-Chic!" I exclaim as I wave good-bye and push through the door.

"Too bad *Tom* isn't single," Joanne states as we turn the corner.

"What?" I ask, blinking my eyes in the most forceful way I can muster. I know he looked sort of nice in his casual attire, and he'd obviously just had a fresh haircut. And his cologne did smell sort of like a fresh spring day. . . . But still—this is Tom we're talking about! Mr. Nice Guy. Mr. Boss Man. Not Mr. Hottie Man.

"I just think he's cute is all. And obviously he has no problems holding down a job. What did you say he is? A vice president?"

"A managing director actually. But never mind! He's totally not your type. And anyway, he *does* have a girlfriend. You met her, remember?" I'm not sure why I am screaming now, since Joanne is right next to me.

"All right, all right. It was just a thought. But you know, if I didn't know better, I'd say you like him—ooh!" she says, and pinches my butt.

"Yeah, I love him. We're gonna get married and live happily ever after. You happy now?" I mock like I'm making out with my paper-bagged beer "Ooh, Tom. Oh, don't touch me there. Tom Baby, is that a cucumber in your pocket or are you just happy to see me?"

I'm still mid-smooch, soaking my paper bag with saliva when I hear, "Bye, ladies. Have a nice night."

Tom. Great.

"He definitely didn't hear," Joanne assures me.

"There's no way he could have, right?" I ask, wiping away the possibility with my hand.

"No. I could barely hear you with your tongue all up in that paper bag."

She's right. There's no way. Sheesh. I'm such a worrywart sometimes! So what if my boss thinks I'm kissing a paper bag that I'm pretending is, him? (Right?)

We get back upstairs and I'm peeing with the door open while Joanne is finishing her beer and I'm pretty sure I hear a sob.

"Are you crying, honey?" I ask. It was bound to happen some-time. You can't very well break up with the person you thought you'd spend your whole life with and not shed a few buckets of tears. Even if you happen to be stoic, logical Joanne. In fact, each and every one of the day's distractions was an intricate part of a strategic plan to get Joanne to clear her mind from being so strong and wear her down to get it out. You've got to get things out. It's the only step to really getting down to how you feel. Otherwise you'll live in a constant state of denial.

When I come out she's shaking and there're no tears coming out, but they are definitely on their way if the lakes forming at the corners of her eyes mean anything. Her mouth is so contorted she can't control the drool beginning to make its way down to her knee.

"Oh, poor baby," I say, rubbing her hair.

"It's just, I wish he would just be more practical for once."

There's that word again! I don't want to argue with her at this point, but I think I really need to advise her on this one.

"Joanne, you know, with some people, love isn't about practical-ity. It's about romance and sweetness. And that's how Peter sees it."

She lifts her head up, tears now welling up, and places a firm palm in my face. "Lane, do not start with this shit now."

I remove her hand from my face and start rubbing it, softly, and say, "Just hear me out here for a second."

And I don't know where I get this insight from, but it really sounds quite professional. I explain to her that maybe that very im-practicality is what she loves about Peter. And yes, it can be annoy-ing when he's not getting much work, and having no money obviously sucks. Especially with the warm weather coming in and all of those adorable peasant blouses to choose from this season, and the beaded sandals and the dangling earrings. But that he loves his music, and that his passion for that is what made her fall in love with him in the first place. I go on to remind her that *she* is the practical, rational one in their relationship, and that is what makes them so perfect together. They complement each other. He allows her to enjoy the fly-by-the-seat-of-your-pants-ness that she never allows herself. And he gets brought down to earth when he needs to by her strength and logic.

"He's probably at home right now thinking about how much he wants you back," I finish with authority, and cross my arms, pleased with myself. "The phone's over there." I point to my desk.

"Lane Silverman," she says my name as if shocked this sort of speak is actually coming from me, "that just may be the most logical thing you have ever said on the topic of love. Maybe you've learned something in spite of yourself. Now, if only you'd throw out your damn checklists and follow your own advice, maybe you'd be okay."

But Liam and I are different. We don't need to concern ourselves with such trivialities. Our love makes everything work perfectly. Even the fact that we are not together right now. It's not sorrow, it is sweet sorrow—because even our separation is part of our love. We are Bonnie and Clyde. We would never discuss dishes. We'd toss them all and get a whole new set if they were ever an issue. When you're both equally romantic souls, the whole equation is entirely different.

My doorbell rings while Joanne is mid-conversation with Peter.

"No, I'm sorry. No, you shouldn't be sorry. It's my fault. No, it is. Yes. I love you, yes, yes. No, no. Yes." It pulls me from the thought I'm silently mulling over: that other people's love when not serving to make you depressed on account of no love of your own to speak of, is normally just plain boring, but that this time I am glowing with my favorite people reuniting. I figure it must be Chris, since he is my only building friend, and visitors have to buzz to be let in. And so, I decide to get one last kick out of the now very dry and tight mask (which is probably peeling my skin off right now).

I open the door and scream, "Raaahh!"

And I am jumping up and down like a wild animal when I see it is not Chris.

It is Liam.

Surely this is not happening. I mean I have worn mud masks in front of old boyfriends. But Liam and I don't exactly have the mud-mask sort of relationship. Lane! Stop being so silly! Of course he won't mind. It's just once! Everyone has beauty rituals to maintain!

"Have you seen Lane?" he asks.

"Liam!" I say in a sweet, high-pitched voice as if I don't look anything less than sexy. I go to kiss him, but he pulls away.

"Maybe I should come back when you are back to normal," he says, and I'm pretty sure he is not kidding.

"Don't be silly! Joanne is just leaving," I say and pull him into the apartment and run into the bathroom to wash the mask off.

"How are you, Liam?" she asks as she hangs up the phone.

"I'm okay. I hadn't realized I was walking into a sorority house, but I'm okay."

Joanne is all giddy and I can't see what she's doing, but I hear Liam scream, "Gross! Stop!" And when I walk out of the bathroom, rubbing a towel around my face, I see her squishing him in a huge hug, nestling her green face on his blue polo shirt.

"It's the sorority ritual," she says. "All the guys who enter have to go through it."

I know this act. Joanne is testing Liam, and with that tone she's taken on, I can tell I'll be getting an earful tomorrow. God help the man who doesn't pass Joanne's test. Or rather, God help me if that man happens to be dating me.

I never thought they'd like each other too much. They are very different people. I, myself, am a totally different person with each of them. Joanne and I talk about, well, everything—stomach problems, work problems, how big Mariah Carey's ass has gotten, how annoying my mother is. But with Liam there is no need to be negative or share things that are so commonplace. When we are together we normally talk about—our love, or we spend hours going through the different homes he owns around the world, and what it will be like when we go to each. It's much better that way. Why do I need to bring up such trivialities with Liam when I've got Joanne to share them with?

Two hours later, Liam *Kampo* (last name mystery solved) and I are once again in my bed doing wonderfully devilish things that are far more interesting than discussing Mariah Carey's tush. I am so lucky! And to make things even better, Samantha calls me, feeling chatty, because it's Sunday and you know how that goes, and I get to say that I can't speak because I am busy giggling and cuddling—and I swear—I am crunching microwave popcorn as I say this into the phone.

See Miss Smarty-Pants Samantha—he is here and we're having a wonderful time together! I'm sure she'll apologize for what she said the night before, but instead she screams, "Forget about Liam!" and hangs up the phone. I remember what it's like to be the lonely one on a Sunday, and so I don't get angry at her hostility. It's actually quite romantic, Liam and I beating the odds together, surprising all the naysayers.

Thirteen

Playing Dress-Up

I am wearing my Liam confidence on my face as I enter the office on Monday, which serves as a fantastic enhancement to my black dress and faux pearls. I am literally glowing as I hang my overcoat up on the doorway to my cubey.

"How was your weekend?" Tom's voice asks from my telephone. It has become a habit for him to call me, rather than walk five steps out of his office into my cubey.

I think he prefers this habit because it is easier to be a different person when you are on the telephone than it is face-to-face, and he sometimes likes to act like he is a powerful boss man, rather than the sweet down-to-earth man that he actually is. (Or maybe he is madly in love with me and can't bear to see me, knowing in his heart that I must—being so radiant these days—owe my heart to another? Hah!)

Being the master of human nature that I am (this is one of the blessings of a writer, along with poverty and carpal tunnel syndrome), I sarcastically take on the role of unimportant underling during these conversations, saying, too sweetly, things like, "And shall I bring you a cup of coffee, and purchase a *cadeau* for your *petite amie?*"

He smiles through the phone, I imagine, but tries to retain an air of professionalism and says, "No, that is fine, just what we spoke about, please," referring to whatever small task he has asked me to perform.

But today I just say, "Absolutely perfect," and start going off about the articles I've written (as I do still need to remind him that I am an intellectual literary sort outside of being his assistant, even if I am maintaining the role of unimportant underling while on the telephone).

"I'd love to see some of your stuff," he says, and I remember who the articles are for and decide to change the topic. I've talked myself up so much already, I might be a bit embarrassed and deflate his image of me. I'm quite sure he wouldn't see a woman's closet in the same way I would.

"So, what can I do for you?" I ask.

"Meeting in my office in five. Grab John, too. And one more thing—I'm glad you opted against Military-Shlump-Shower-Cap-Chic today."

I'd almost forgotten.

"John!" I scream over the maroon cubey wall.

"Yes, dear," he moans like a beleaguered husband, and I think in wonder, how he has really warmed up to me.

"Tom wants us to meet in five minutes in his office."

"Cool. I'll swing by and pick you up and we can catch a ride over together."

I love office humor. It's a whole other sort of humor that you just don't get when you're sitting by yourself at a computer all day. At home, I used to laugh really loudly and then comment about whatever it was that was funny, in hopes that one of my neighbors might think I lead an interesting life and ring my bell to start up a conversation. Not surprisingly, this never worked.

"So, looks like there has been a lot of movement in the telecommunications sector as of late, what with the merging of companies that have Internet telephone capabilities and those that have vast numbers of traditional telephone customers already. I have in mind a couple of companies that I think would hugely benefit in the long run by pairing their assets and I'm going to need to get together a massive proposal by the end of the month."

John and I are shaking our heads mechanically in our meeting, as one feels they ought to when someone is delivering a long-winded speech, wondering where to rest our gazes, fidgeting with invisible strands of hair, lint, etc. John is eating a doughnut at the same time and I am in wonderment of how I don't even want a doughnut because I am now so focused on being slim in order to feel my most sexy when having sex with Liam. Sex really does wonders for diets. I should write an article about this. (I would just like to point out that I am still listening while all of this is going through my head, because listening, thinking something else, and taking notes at the same time are skills I have mastered as an interviewer/writer.)

And Tom goes on: "John. I need you to run the numbers on these two companies." He hands him a computer printout. "Really look at it from every angle. I need numbers of clients who use the telephone for business, for business and personal, for personal only. I need average usage per month. I need peak hours. I need customer interest surveys on new service areas. I need concerns over these new service areas, frequently asked questions, et cetera. And of course, I'll get the other guys to do the merger projections."

"No problem," says John, who I'm sure is happy to get this project, because when he is not running numbers and doing research, he is really doing nothing at all. I suggested the option of writing a novel in his spare time, but he put the kibosh on that notion, saying he would rather research things on the Internet. Different strokes . . .

"And Lane. I have a bunch of letters on Dictaphone for you to draft here. But as soon as all the data starts rolling in, I would like you to take a more active role in this project. I know you're good at creative presentation, and I thought about what you said about the job advertisement, and I'd like to see how you would organize and design a piece like this."

I am loved and appreciated and actually sense my brain getting larger inside my head. I know I can do this, because I have written many press releases and marketing materials in the past (maybe not many, but the ones I have done were fantastic), and feeling very qualified and professional, I venture, "Will I be getting a raise for a change in job duties?"

First Tom looks at me as one would a woman barking at an empty subway seat, and then that one-sided smile pops up, and he says, "Smith Barney does not give raises after the first three weeks of employment, Lane."

I had to try. "No problem," I say with visions of Prada heels being snatched from my hands.

"But I will, however, take you both to dinner at a fabulous

restaurant of your choosing when we are all through. And make it a nice, expensive one. It's on the company."

This is a very wonderful prospect and I am still feeling all fuzzy from being appreciated and sort of promoted, and so the world is right once again. "Great. I know this really great new restaurant that serves ten types of caviar and makes these fantastic flavored blinis, and I have the perfect outfit to wear that I just picked up at . . ."

"Lane, why don't we just get started on the project first? Okay?"

I make an aye-aye, sir salute with my hand (all of a sudden worrying that I've perhaps done the SS salute by mistake).

"Just remember, Ab Fab, this is not a proposal for a hair salon or a clothing boutique, so try to stay away from flower images and any shade of fuchsia, lavender, or teal, okay?"

And you might think that sounds condescending, but it's not, as Tom knows I am smart (he has just told me this) and he is just teasing, as he likes the opportunity to call me Ab Fab and use it in context. I enjoy being thought of as the fashionable, young member of the department anyway, and so smile and ask, "What about baby pink? It's all the rage for lips right now and since the piece is all about communications, it might come together nicely."

He just shakes his head and turns (I see the half-smile before his back is to me though) and says, "Alright kids, that's all for now."

Over the next couple of weeks, the project is shaping up nicely, and I get to schedule meetings with the design and reprographics departments to choose paper and graphics and fonts. I am an integral spoke on the wheel of a very important American institution. And this project is sort of what I imagine being an editor is like. Often, when I finally see my published articles, I am disappointed by the design chosen and imagine what I would have done if I'd been given the choice. I always thought I would be really good at that. And bringing the fruits of my labor to Tom at the Friday afternoon meeting during my second week on the project, I can see he is truly impressed.

"You really have a flair for the creative, Ab Fab."

When he says this, I want to say something that might be helpful about his tie collection, but stop myself.

Only it comes out anyway. "You know, I can really work wonders on men's wardrobes, too." My eyes widen with the knowledge of what I've just let slip and my mouth takes on the shape I imagine it would if I'd swallowed a bug.

"All right. Let's have it," he says, head shaking. "What's wrong with my wardrobe, Ab Fab?"

I begin to explain that it is really the fault of the girlfriend when a man is dressed poorly, a point that is half joking and half serious, as everyone knows this is true, and most men can't dress for crap—except for Liam, of course, who wears those beautiful blue shirts that bring out his eyes, and . . . and really that's mainly all he wears.

Odd, actually. I picture a closet like Lisa's filled only with blue shirts. Press a button and a cool breeze of blue shirts goes whizzing by. Only, I rather hope a tour of his closet would be more like, "And this is the shirt Lane tore off me in the movies, and this one is the one that lay on her floor for a week while we had a nonstop sex-a-thon."

Anyway, I already know Tom is not the sort of guy who reads GQ for the fashion and couldn't care less about looking anything besides professional and clean-cut, which is merely a job requirement. He did look so nice when I'd run into him on the weekend though in his simple, risk-free jeans and T-shirt. A makeover would be so much fun!

I decide to start small, although I can't help but wonder why his

girlfriend, if she is as awful and controlling as John says, lets him walk
out of the house in those ties. Although, judging from her Glamour
Shot and dragon nails, I guess it's entirely possible she's actually
picked them out. Had them monogrammed on the reverse side.

"It's really just the ties," I say, as gently as one can say such a
thing.

Tom is amused, rather than hurt, but mocks like I've just stabbed
him in the heart anyway. "Well, what do you propose I need to
change about my ties?" he inquires, staring down at the one he is
wearing today, which is some sort of homage to modern art—
Mirot, I think.

It looks strikingly similar to a shower curtain I had from IKEA,
in my college dorm room.

"It's the kitsch factor, really," I say. "A tie is supposed to subtly
enhance your suit, not the other way around." I cock my head
here, to appear sweet, and not like an evil enforcer of the laws of
fashion.

"Well, then how about you take me shopping for some new ties
after work one day next week? I'll have to look presentable when
the big meeting comes around."

This is a fantastically fun proposal, and I think, a really cute article idea for a men's magazine. Perhaps *Men's Health* or something
like that. "Mr. Corporate Ups His Stock With a Makeover." I really like that one. I mention it and say that if we get the article
placed, he could probably get all of the ties for free.

"What's wrong with my stock?"

"Oh, I just . . ." I'm fumbling for an answer that doesn't sound
mean, because really, what *is* so bad about his stock?

He saves me. "It was a rhetorical question, Ab Fab. Just let me
know."

Tom doesn't really seem like a person dying for his fifteen minutes of fame, so I skip the part about how they'll probably want to do a photo shoot if the article is a go.

I can't help but ask this though: "Won't your girlfriend mind another woman picking out your ties? That is a very territorial sort of thing, speaking as a woman." If Liam's assistant had him gallivanting around town, peeking in his dressing room, and straightening his trousers, I'd probably turn to stone and crumble into a sandy heap formerly known as Lane Silverman.

He glances at the Glamour Shot of Whitney—with her hazy soap opera eyes and feather boa—and his look turns cold.

"It's fine," he says and turns away. "All right. Back to work."

She really must be awful.

I type up a quick pitch to *Men's Health*, and e-mail it over, since they already have me on file from the tons of past rejections. I feel hopeful, because things have been going well in the breakthrough department since the *Cosmo* thing (which I'm going to start figuring out how to tackle straightaway), and so I mention that assignment and the one for the *Post*, to bolster my reputation.

Perhaps now I really can just get any assignment I want. Imagine the possibilities. The blank wall in my apartment will soon be covered over with framed copies of my *Vogue* column, next to snapshots of Liam and I—surely there's room for both—and I am considering a rich mahogany for the frames when an e-mail signal appears at the bottom of my screen.

Lane,

   Thank you for your article inquiry, and although it is a good idea, we really only work with VERY seasoned writers, and I am afraid

you just don't have enough experience under your belt right now.
It does sound like you are doing lots of things at present, so I am
sure in a couple of years, we will be able to work together. I am
sorry to be so frank, but today my inbox has been flooded with
pitches, and I must tell the rules to all, so I can free myself from
having to answer all of these inquiries and concentrate on things
that NEED to be done.
Best,
Jim

It has been a little while since I have gotten such a rejection.
And the memory of the regularity of these things, when I was
stuck in the pitch-reject loop all day, every day, brings back that
cold, empty feeling that makes me want to lie on my couch eating
anything and everything with a fat content over fifteen grams.

But then I think of Tom and John and what has just happened
in that meeting, and the really important assignment I have been
trusted with here (surely worth millions of dollars to the company)
and it doesn't actually seem all that bad. It is not the first time since
I began working here that I am happy to have some positives balancing out the negatives.

I recover almost immediately. Which allows my mind to begin
thinking clearly again, and consider other publications that might
want my piece. The *Post*! I already have a contact there, and they
did say I should continue to contribute ideas. Now I'm thinking.
So I pop off an e-mail to my editor over there. With renewed hope
I continue working on the big phone proposal.

My editor over at the paper answers almost immediately with an
enthusiastic thumbs up, and while Tom acts like it's just another
item on his To-Do list, he is, I think, a bit excited about the venture.

The following Friday, Tom and I are scheduled for a grand tour of the best men's clothing shops in Manhattan in search of not only ties, but also new suits, button-down shirts, shoes, and everything. I have called ahead and spoken with the publicists to okay the photographer, and, of course, for some of the promised freebies—which I don't think Tom is quite as enthusiastic about as I am. I guess after spending years with no money in your pockets, you have a very esteemed view of freebies, but if you have money in your pockets, they just occupy more space in your closet. Nope. I can't imagine it.

He does his best to seem excited though, ("Bring on the freebies!" he teases) and if I'm not mistaken, Tom quickly assumes the role of pseudo-celebrity-for-a-day, acting embarrassed and humbled when passersby begin gawking (which they always do with a photographer around), but secretly enjoying the whispers and hubbub ("I saw him in a movie once; isn't that the guy from that Ford commercial?"). This is surprising. Tom doesn't seem the look-at-me type. But that's just the thing that makes it, well, endearing. Like I've just got a peak of something.

I imagine Liam, on the other hand, would be used to this sort of thing, being at the almost-head of a huge media giant. He would enjoy the whole thing outright—signing autographs, ready with quotable remarks. But Tom is no Liam.

I thought a lot about this comparison when I went to preview the stock at the shops over the weekend—to pull things for Tom. I couldn't help it, because selecting the clothing for him, and thinking about things like his waist size and inseam is very personal and causes you to think about someone without any clothes on. Also, I was overcome with that wonderful feeling you get when shopping for a boyfriend. You know, when you get to say things like, "Oh, he has *very* long legs," or "He wouldn't dare wear anything with a logo" to the salesperson, who is fancying a fantastically handsome man and enviously inspecting you.

Only, of course, Tom is not my boyfriend. He's just my boss. A very sweet boss, whose inner thigh I happened to have measured, but a boss all the same. And he has a girlfriend. And, obviously, there's Liam—who spends more time in my own bed these days than his own, making the most of his time before leaving for London in just two day's time. This will probably kill me, but I can't think about it. The break will be good for me. Or at least for my career, as I've only two weeks left on this assignment and just one bad date ending in a snubbed kiss to show for it.

At Calvin Klein, Tom emerges from the dressing room, and I nearly keel over.

"Oh. My. God," I can't help but say, whistling like a horny construction worker. He is stunning. The pale green shirt, the tie in a subtly darker shade of green, a deep charcoal suit, which is draping and hugging in all the right places over his surprisingly athletic build. When he does the little spin (with his arms out and his eyes wide in expectation of my reaction), I notice—and I know you've caught wind of this observation pattern by now—a fantastic butt.

Simply extraordinary.

Of course I can't see the entire butt. But there is just enough peaking out below the jacket that I can surely get a taste of what the whole thing looks like. And it is extraordinary. I know I have said this already, but wow!

"So, what do you think?" he asks, looking just the perfect mix of unsure and sort-of, kind-of confident.

There is a certain joy in teaching when two people come from different backgrounds, isn't there? I mean, you know, with friends, which, at this point, I guess we are. Not every boss has your article framed for you, right? I guess I hadn't really thought too much of it, since I haven't had too many bosses to compare Tom with. But that really was very nice. My own mother hadn't even thought of that. And the way he just had it hanging there for me when I arrived the next morning. That was very sweet.

"You look breathtaking," I say, shaking my head to emphasize the point and trying to keep my eyes on his face, rather than grazing up and down his body, which again, I might add is really something else. Lucky boa-wearing bitchy girlfriend.

Not that I care. Liam is already Rico Suave—no education necessary. But there isn't all that much fun in that, is there? There would be no makeovers in Liam Land, as Liam is perfect right off the rack. But we have all sorts of fun doing other things, different things.

"Really?" he says, raising his eyebrows here in an adorably unsure way.

"I'm sure your girlfriend will just melt when she sees you like this."

Here, he does what he always does whenever she comes up. Clams up. Turns around to go back into the dressing room. I should probably stop bringing her up if it gets him so upset, but then, what is he doing with her if she is so bad? He doesn't seem like the sort of person who'd stay in it just for his parent's sake.

I wonder if maybe one of them is dying and this was their last wish. I could see if that is the case.

"Wait a minute, we've got to take the photo," says Bill, our baseball cap–wearing, gum-chewing photographer.

Here's where I switch into creative mode, suggesting we go by the sleek leather chair and pillar and have Tom sit right down, with his back bent a bit and his legs open, in a really casual sort of way. If there's one thing I know, it's what positions a man looks best in. Bill agrees with this (surprising, since photographers usually have their own vision of what they want to shoot, and just politely nod and smile at suggestions from people who think they know what's best). Of course, he has Tom do all sorts of other poses—some standing (during which Tom seems to be getting a bit red in the face) and one where he is checking his watch, which looks quite professional.

And right after he puts down his hand after this shot, he looks right at me and smiles and then unsmiles and does something very un-Tom. Something, I'm imagining his evil girlfriend and evil girlfriend-loving sick parent would hate.

He says, "I saw you checking out my butt."

And although those words alone—from Tom—would have been enough, it's the way he holds my glance that gets me rouged.

Before I have a chance to really consider that my boss has just accused me (if rightfully) of looking at his ass, and that he seems to have enjoyed this, his unsmile returns to smile position and I am free to rationalize that I have imagined the whole thing.

Taking full advantage of such freedom, I smile back. Ahh, denial.

"Thanks for this. It's surprisingly enjoyable," he's saying, un-fazed with the photog snipping some unposed shots.

"You're welcome."

Tom nods, smiling and turns back to the dressing room.

For the second time today I am extremely happy to be friends with Tom. I've never had a male friend like him before. It's different. Rather nice.

Since everything fits so well, Tom decides to take the whole lot, and the publicist has arranged to give him a forty percent discount. It's really a great deal. The day goes on. Pink, Brooks Brothers, Burberry, Bergdorf Goodman, Emporio Armani. He's mastered subtle tweeds, light checks, pinstripes.

At the end, Tom insists on taking me for dinner, but I explain that I have "a prior engagement," which is to say, one of two last romp sessions with Liam before he goes home.

I settle for a quick glass of wine at The Peninsula's pricey Pen-Top bar, which, I add, after choosing it, will cost as much as an entire meal anyway. He can expense it, so it doesn't matter that I've made a decadent choice to top off what has felt like a thoroughly decadent day.

Now, if I can just zoom out for a moment, I would like to pat myself on the back for never having told Tom or anyone else at the office about Liam, as it has been hard to keep the secret, since everyone knows that offices and gossip go hand in hand (especially offices inhabited by the likes of John and Tiffany). And let's face it, when you're happy, you want to let the whole world know. Don't think I haven't missed the wonderful jolt that goes along with coming in, after a fabulous evening, and gloating about it.

Joanne made me promise to keep the Liam thing quiet. "Just in case it doesn't work out and you do meet someone at work."

I couldn't see any chance of that, but I just didn't feel like mingling my two worlds anyhow. Like stripes and polka dots, they didn't seem to go together.

But what happens when you start socializing with people from work outside of work is that you inevitably start talking about personal things that you shouldn't. Tom is back in his own suit now, which although not nearly as sexy as the new digs, does suit his personality, in a way. To me, he feels like the old Tom again. And I think, he probably feels the same way, as he is back to being sarcastic and wry.

"I'm just like Julia Roberts in *Pretty Woman*," he says, "but, of course, without the red hair, knockout legs, and, well, obviously the sex with Richard Gere."

I am so glad that Tom and I are buddies. This sort of friendship will surely last even after I have finished at Smith Barney. Surely.

"And without being a hooker—or is there something I don't know?" I say, suggesting he may have a second job.

"I'm not the one with the *secret appointment* . . ."

"It's not a secret," I say.

"So, what type of appointment have you got? Another fabulous writing assignment? Making over men all around town so you can get them to look just the way you like them? You're staging a coup, aren't you? Little by little, one by one, you will get everyone with a Y chromosome to dress just as you want. . . ." He's waving his fingers here, like I'm doing something *Twilight Zone* worthy.

"No, I'm just meeting Li—" and I stop midsentence while knowing full well that Tom is a smart man, and no matter what I say here, he will now know that I am seeing someone who is probably a *someone*. Shit. I am getting panicky. My palms are clammy. I am not sure why, because it is pretty clear at this point that I am not going to meet someone who is *someone* at Smith Barney, and so I shouldn't really care. But I do.

Word will get out, and everyone will know I am involved—by the time it churns through the rumor mill (I hear those HR people are the worst) I'll be listed as married with children. But the wine is going to my head a bit, and this is actually a good thing, because I relax and realize that Tom is not a gossipmonger.

I can't picture him standing by the watercooler talking to anyone about anything, much less any*one*. It's fine. So why do I still feel irked?

"I didn't know you were seeing anyone, Lane," he says, and I note that this is the first time he's used my real name in quite some time. And I'm not sure if it's because I value Tom's opinion and I would like to see what he thinks of Liam, since everyone else I know seems to have a negative view, or if I just want to bring our friendship to a closer level, but I decide to spill the beans.

And so I go on. And on. And before I know it, I'm telling him how wonderfully suave Liam is, and how he knows all the right places to take me and all the right things to say. And I don't think this is really why I like Liam so much, but I can't talk about all of the intimate things—the under and over the covers things. He asks all of the questions that someone really interested in what you're talking about would—where'd you meet? How long have you been together? Is he nice to you? Is he very proud of your career? But he never once offers an opinion. Only listens to the answers and shakes his head every now and then.

This method proves very powerful in allowing me to continue gabbing away, and I tell him about how I'd dreamed of meeting someone like Liam my entire life, and how I was so afraid I'd never meet The One before, and about all the nights I'd spent alone in the years previous.

"I can't believe someone like you would ever be alone," he says, which I think is very sweet.

In the taxi ride back home, I am a bit nervous that I've come off as a very shallow girl, one really worthy of the nickname Ab Fab. All I've spoken about is expensive dinners and nice clothing and how successful and good-looking Liam is. While I was talking, I didn't mean it to come out this way. I'd only thought I was explaining why I love him so much. But it's very difficult to explain something so mysterious and all-powerful, and so I'm sure Tom understands that. But why do I keep worrying that he thinks I'm awful?

Fourteen

A "Splendid" Good-Bye

"I'm really going to miss your ass, I mean, um, you," Liam is saying, as he runs his fingers through my hair. We are on my couch, the scene of what will most likely be our last encounter (we are both exhausted now) for a month. I love the way his fingers feel on me. I love the way he looks in a reclining position. It has been a whole month and I am still feeling the tingles from every touch, rather than being bored or disgusted by his presence. In all honesty, this is the first time since high school that my interest has been so strong in just one person. And Liam is smart and funny and successful. I really think this could be it for me.

Lying here with him right now, the thought that I'll have to concentrate on the article after he leaves flits in and out of my mind. I'm wishing we could just lie here forever. Although, holding in my stomach in this sitting-up position could become a bit painful. It occurs to me again that I would give up this article for him, if that's what it would take to do this every day of my life.

I'll bet the job at *Beautiful* will start as soon as he comes back. So I ask him about this.

"I don't want to talk business now, Lane. Let's just enjoy each other," he says soothingly.

And I guess he's right. I am kind of ruining the mood.

He continues, "When I'm sleeping all alone in my lonely bed in London, I'll be thinking of you. I'll have only your love to keep me warm."

It's not really that cold now, since it's spring and all, but it is a wonderful thought. And he probably has central air-conditioning, which can get extremely chilly.

Thinking over the last month, I sigh at the dreamy haze over the whole thing. The memories weave together in the most beautiful patina of images. We fit together perfectly. The candlelit dinners, the exquisite lovemaking, the randy late-night telephone calls from his office, imploring he come over immediately. And then there was that hint about going to Provence (which was never brought up again, but still, the summer is very far off), and other future-oriented allusions, like restaurants we must try and movies we must see. Then there are the gifts and the compliments: "You are so beautiful," "My god I love the way you kiss!" and most of all, the feeling—there is no way in the world I can feel this much without him feeling the same way. It's just not possible.

Before he leaves, he takes a full hour to gush over how much he will miss me. He takes another half hour to kiss me good-bye, and before he finally leaves the door, he grabs both sides of my neck, looks me in the face, and says, "Splendid."

Fifteen

The True Meaning of Splendid

Is there nothing more moving than the feeling of woe resulting from two lovers who cannot be together? I take to wearing black, like a Sicilian widow and speaking in low, hushed tones.

Tonight, after I inform Samantha, "And the last word he said was, 'Splendid,'" I sigh and look to the ceiling, as if heaven is up there in the air ventilation duct.

"What's splendid?" Samantha is saying. She takes a sip of wine, leans her elbow on the bar, rests her chin on it, and with a deep breath, continues, "The fact that he is separated from his *loooooooovvvvvvve*? That he is woebegone and devastated? How *will* you be able to live without each other for a whole month? Oh the horror! The horror!" She throws the back of her hand to her forehead here, all Scarlet O'Hara–like.

I am really getting sick of all the negativity surrounding me these days. I note that when Liam returns, I'll have to set up a meeting between the two of them so that she can see how great he is once and for all. I bring the conversation round to a topic I'm more comfortable with. "So where is Mr. Seth taking you tonight?"

This is their third date. I am so thrilled for her. I mean, Seth is a good, down-to-earth kind of guy. He's not my type at all, but everyone's got their own checklist.

"He did the sweetest thing the other day!" she says, smacking my arm—rather roughly.

"What's that?" I ask, wondering whether there's another side to Seth that I may have missed.

"Well, I told him that I had to start reading the *Wall Street Journal* every day now that I'm working for that financial advertising agency, and so, he ordered me a subscription. He instructed them to put a little card with the first delivery, and it said, "To the financial wizard-to-be!""

I can't help it, my eyebrows raise and the corners of my mouth descend into a frown.

"What?" she asks. "Isn't that sweet?"

"Sure!" I say, trying to act like I've never heard anything more romantic. It is *thoughtful*. But really. A newspaper? And a *financial* newspaper at that? Even the way he phrased it. Surely something passionate could never be paired with the word 'wizard'? What could be more *un*romantic?

"Lane? Are you in there? Don't you understand that the most romantic thing someone can do is to think of something unique that would be important to only you? Flowers take no effort, honey."

Right, and that's why florists can't even order enough flowers on Valentine's Day and Mother's Day, right? I'm starting to wonder if Samantha and I are really meant to be friends at all. She's just so—weird. I mean Joanne is obsessed with the whole practicality thing, but at least she's good for a romantic Pete story every once and again.

"Name one thing that Liam has done for you that showed he really knew *you*. Not that he knew women, but that he knew Lane—what makes her tick. Did you ever mention something and then he remembered it and commemorated it with a unique token?"

Well, Liam and I don't really talk about me all that much. We don't really talk that much at all. But that's because we don't *need* words. We speak the language of love. And that involves fingers and toes and stomachs and thighs. . . .

But, you know, I do know quite a lot about him. I know about his family, his business, his multiple global dwellings, his money, his favorite restaurants, and that he is allergic to broccoli. I guess it would be accurate to say that he doesn't know much about me.

But that is so easy to fix!

I'll just bring up the subject of me and I'm sure he'll be delighted to spend an entire evening poring over my photo albums—the mall hair from high school, the snaps of me crawling out of my diapers. It will be a hoot!

Here we both look around at the crowd, because it's getting a bit tense between us. Samantha is very hostile. I spot a man who I'm sure is British across the bar. He's got that tallish air and a great, pointy nose. But it turns out that the distinguishing factors of British men are not very distinguishing, as he turns out to be from Staten Island, and uses the phrase "fouggetaboudit." I guess sometimes things aren't what they appear to be.

Samantha is actually meeting Seth here in a few minutes anyway, and while you'd think that could be awkward, it really turns out to be just fine. It's funny, though. Seeing them together really is quite romantic. They do seem to fit nicely. And if I didn't know any better, I'd think that that odd tugging in my heart when he whispered a little joke in her ear and she laughed was . . . jealousy. Me and Liam have lots of secrets. Lots. Or we *will have* when he comes back anyway.

B_y the time Wednesday rolls around, and I haven't heard from Liam yet, I am so impatient, I can't help but take out the scrap of paper he wrote his phone number on and stare at it. I know I said that I would wait for him to call—since this is the way things are supposed to go, but, really, the pressure is too much to bear. And I really want to get started telling him something about me. I've rehearsed a whole narrative of the time I was in the play of *The Wizard of Oz* in the fifth grade and I came in with all of these rewrites of the script, whereby Dorothy and the scarecrow fall in love and get to live in Oz.

I stare and stare and stare until the numbers form one blurry mass.

I shouldn't be worried. He's just very busy. He only has one more month to tie up all of the loose ends before he moves to New York for good and then we can be together forever and we'll have plenty of time to learn more things about each other.

But all of the negative vibes coming from my so-called friends have started to get the best of me. I mean, I've managed to keep myself busy at work most of the time, what with the big meeting coming up soon, but every time I write something in the *Diary of a Working Girl*—it's just doubtful, stupid stuff. My mind is getting me into an hysterical, paranoid state. I keep hearing that phrase in my head, "Too good to be true." I can allay my fears for a few minutes at a time by replaying some of our wonderful moments in my head. I can still feel him—heavy and lovely—and I remember that smell, and I know this has always been my dream. And I have it right now at this very moment. And so I try to remind myself to enjoy it. But in the end this hollow feeling creeps in. It's just love, I'm sure. Of course, I am not yet familiar with all of its symptoms. But just to feel better, I'd love to just speak with him—even if it's only for a second.

And then I'm sure that he will be the wonderful, sweet, romantic Liam that I know and everything will be perfect. I'm sure. I probably shouldn't even call. He's probably going to call me any minute. He probably just doesn't want to bother me at work, and by the time it's five here, he's so tired he just falls asleep by the phone waiting to call me.

So I'll just work and not think about it at all.

This works for about ten seconds until all of the words I am proofing on my page say, "Liam."

Without any effort on my part, my hand picks up the telephone, dials the number and I sit, waiting, shaking. And finally, after nothing—no ringing, busy signal or anything else, a recording picks up and says, "The number you have dialed is incorrect, please hang up and dial again." All the ones and zeros you have to dial on international calls are so confusing that I have no idea where I've gone wrong. Or how to fix it.

I try again, altering the configuration a bit—the zero first, the two ones second. I'm in tears at this point. It's horrible. Something as simple as a phone call seems to be the sole thing keeping me from him. After each failed attempt, I am slamming the phone down on the receiver now.

"You okay, Lane?" John asks over the wall. He can stand up and look right over, since he's so tall, and he does this now. It's too late to say yes, because he sees me crying and shaking.

"What's wrong?" he asks, coming around to my cubey and, after hesitating for a couple of seconds, puts his hand on my back.

"Nothing, nothing." I stare through the line of buttons on his shirt. And without shifting my gaze, I do my best to undesperately explain my desperate needs. "It's just, do you know how to make an international call? I thought I did, but I can't seem to make this number go through."

John takes a look at me; I feel him take my energy in with the sort of expression that shows someone knows there's something more going on here than an incorrectly dialed phone number. But being the shy type, John would never come out to suggest something as bold as that.

"Sure. Let's see," he says, holding the paper close to his face.

And like an angel from heaven, he dials the number for me, puts the receiver to my face, and I wait intently, so happy to hear the double-ring sound. But when a woman's cockney voice answers, "Tate's carpet cleaning services," I am completely thrown off course and not sure what to say.

Of course! This is just one of his family's other businesses. He hasn't mentioned it before, but maybe he just doesn't like to talk about it. After all, carpet cleaning isn't very glamorous. Although, I'm not sure how carpet cleaning fits under the media umbrella. But don't smart investors dabble in *all* sectors of the marketplace, just to balance things out? I've definitely read that before. Yes, a "balanced portfolio" is what it's called. It's all making sense now. Doesn't Phillip Morris own Kraft? There's no obvious relation there. See, silly! You're just getting crazy now. I instruct myself to take a deep breath. And then I take a deep breath before venturing, "Is Liam Kampo in?"

"Liam? You mean Liam O'Neill?"

Is it possible he uses another last name at this company? Why would he do that? Maybe they keep the carpet cleaning all hush-hush because again, it is so unchic, and so he uses his mother's maiden name for this end of the business. I am so desperate I will tell myself anything in order for this to be true, for this to be the right number.

"Yes. Can I speak with him?"

"Hold please," says the woman on the other end. The seconds I am waiting feel like hours, days even, and the Muzak version of "Oops! I Did It Again," is not doing anything to soothe my mind, or my stomach, which is doing this crazy flip-flop thing because I feel as if the fate of my entire existence depends on whether or not Liam picks up the line. An innocent Post-it note is suffering a slow death as I tear it apart piece by piece.

"Hello, Liam here," says a voice.

But it is not the voice I know. Not the voice that said, "Splendid," to me on that last evening. This is a distinctly Irish voice.

"Hello? Anyone there?" the voice asks, but I can't bring myself to speak. I just sit with the receiver to my face, thinking that maybe, if I just stay on the line and don't hang up, then there is still a chance. I feel like a prank caller, breathing heavily into the receiver, until . . . finally, he hangs up. *"Wanker."*

And the busy signal comes, and there are no tears in my eyes. There is no expression on my face. I fear I will have to get this telephone surgically removed, because I cannot command my hand to hang it up. Questions are running through my mind. Why would he give me the wrong number? Why hasn't he called me? And although I play with the possibility that perhaps he just wrote it incorrectly, I'm not buying into this theory. I feel deceived.

I try to ground myself with the memory of his hand tracing

around my eye. For one second I can close my eyes and know the feeling.

But, embarrassingly enough, it is only a matter of seconds until I start down a road of self-doubt that can only lead to bad things. My stomach feels unusually large. I am chiding myself for my fast-food binges, the gym sessions I never got to. I am suddenly an over-anxious, calling too much, fucking too poorly, badly dressed, conversationally challenged moron, with a big nose and a horrible personality. I feel as if I've eaten bad fish—sick to my stomach, and suddenly I could fall asleep right in my chair, sitting up straight, with the phone to my ear. The pile of papers in my inbox seems impossible to look at, much less sort, type, fax, format. I have to go home. I can't be here now. It's the only thing to do.

I can't bring myself to face Tom right now, as I know I will start crying the second I try to speak. So I dial his extension instead.

"What is it, Ab Fab?" he asks. "Got a new project you'd like to make me a guinea pig for? Going to give me a new hairdo? A mullet? Mohawk? Pluck my eyebrows maybe?"

And he's being funny, and part of me would love to laugh with him right now, but I have that distinct feeling in my chest that I am not part of the rest of the population right now. I'm someone who can't laugh with the crowd at present, like when you've just had your wisdom teeth out and your friend calls to tell you she's going out to your favorite bar.

"Um, I'm not feeling very well. Is it okay if I take the afternoon off?" The last word barely comes out as my voice trails off.

"Everything okay? Can I help you at all?"

He's concerned and that feels nice, but really, I just want to be alone.

"That's okay, thanks."

"Well, call a car then, I don't want you standing outside trying to get a taxi forever. No, never mind, I'll do it for you. I'll call you as soon as it's here."

I don't want to wait here, but I don't know what else to do. I'm actually glad that Tom made a decision for me, because I doubt whether I would have been able to do something as simple as raise my hand to hail a cab.

When I hang up with Tom, I am just sitting, staring at my computer screen. I can't even shut the thing down. I can't put my coat on. All I can think is how stupid I have been to once again put all of my eggs in one basket. Every time it doesn't work with some guy, you promise yourself that the next time, you won't let yourself get swept away, you'll keep your sense of self and just hope for the best without letting it get the best of you—but that never works when you're in the middle of something.

My feet are somewhere below, but I can't feel them at all. If I could, I would try to kick myself in the ass. I am so stupid. But I guess I don't have to kick myself in the ass. Life has already done this to me, as if to say, "Wake Up! This is not reality!" I am again thinking of myself as the old woman with the birds, perhaps canaries. They seem nice. Yellow.

"Hey, Lane, don't let him get you down," John is whispering, and bending down next to me. It doesn't occur to me that I've never mentioned anything about Liam to John, and that he must have a very sensitive side to see what's going on here.

I just say, "I know, I know," and start shaking my head from side to side.

I'm so pitiful, but I don't even care.

It's a miracle that I make it down into the car service, and this is in no small part thanks to Tom, who pulls one arm after the other through my coat sleeves as one would with an infant, shuts my computer down, leads the way to the twenty-sixth floor and into the elevators, past the turnstiles and the guards, through the courtyard, and to the car.

Of course, it's pouring rain and I don't have an umbrella. In a masochistic way, I am glad for this. It's the perfect scene for a perfectly horrid turn of events. Tom is holding his suit jacket up over my head.

When he helps me into the car he looks at me, as if he'd like to say something, opens his mouth, and says, "I—" but then stops and closes his eyes. When he reopens them he whispers, "I'm here if you need me," and passes me a slip of paper.

I take it, without looking. I am numb and say thank you but I'm not sure if it was actually out loud. After a second, he puts the blazer around my shoulders, gently closes me inside, and the car drives off.

The driver tries to make small talk with some comment about cats and dogs, which I guess is referring to the rain, but rather than egg him on, I act like I haven't heard. Every store we pass seems to be there just to remind me of Liam. A pet store—Liam has a dog. A shop called Good—I remember him using that word. A coffee shop—he likes his black. The driver misses my block and I find my voice somehow, to tell him this. And even though I would normally be incensed by something like this, I behave very unNew Yorkeresque and barely even notice. Instead, I watch the raindrops hit the window and eventually slip down until they are gone. Like my relationship with Liam. Like the idea that I'd met my M&M. M&M, M&M, M&M . . . I say it over and over until it is just "mmmmmmmmmmmmmmmm." It, too, is nothing now, a meaningless nothing. Like my article and my career, which I'd foolishly tossed away for a fantasy.

When I get to my apartment, which is dark in the way only

rainy days can make a space, I don't even bother undressing. I just throw myself onto my bed, next to an open window, which affords the raindrops the chance to hit me every now and then, and fall into a deep sleep. In my dreams, Liam is sitting with a beautiful girl, tall with long black hair to her waist, and they are looking at me in my bed and laughing hysterically and he keeps saying, "Splendid, absolutely splendid."

By the time I wake, it's 11 P.M. My breath tastes stale; my bags are strewn on the floor. I'm wearing my coat and I'm soaked through with sweat. I'm so thirsty, but I don't want to stand up.

The phone rings.

On the desperate hope that it might be him, I throw the blankets from my body and run for it.

"Hello?" I ask, breathless.

"Hey, what's up?" It's Joanne.

"You'll never believe this," I say, and tell her the whole story. All I want to do is run through the episode from beginning to end, feeling the faster I get it out, the faster it will all be over.

But now that she's just worked everything out with Peter, she feels like a relationship guru, and so she keeps interrupting with irritating detail-oriented questions like, "So what time exactly did he leave your apartment on that last night?" and "Did he write the number quickly?"

Each time she stops me it's physically painful.

When, finally, I'm done, she sums it all up. "What an ass. Well, at least you know now, before it's too late."

And I'm listening, and thinking that it is already too late, and wondering why people always say this, when obviously, you are already hurt. Then the oddest thing happens. My mind turns to a picture of Tom, not in one of his beautiful new suits, but in that funny globe tie, making that half-smile, amused by something I'd just said without meaning it to be amusing.

And that made me think of before I'd met Liam—when I walked into that office with hope and confidence and felt like the whole world was mine for the taking. If I could have just gone with my head instead of my heart, just this one time, maybe everything would have been okay.

Still, I think, If I get anything out of this experience, I've made a fantastic friend. Tom had been so kind to me earlier—it turned out in the end to be a good thing I'd told him about Liam. I feel the need to call him. Thank him. I fumble for the paper he'd given me in the car, wondering if it was his number, but I can't find it anywhere. I give up the search when I realize that I couldn't deal with that world right now, the one where I was failing to do what I set out to, and finally, I'd have to face the reality of it all.

"Yeah, before it's too late," I say.

"There must be someone at work you've spotted," she says, looking towards the future, which is very easy to do when it's not you who's right in the middle of a major crisis.

And then I hear a beep, signaling another call. Again, my heart jumps and I squeeze my palm into a fist, thinking just maybe, just maybe.

"Hello?" I say, clicking over. It's a friend from college I haven't spoken to in quite some time. And of all things, she wants to know if I feel like meeting up for a drink. And at any other time, I'd doubtless have all of the catty resignations about this—her calling out of the blue when obviously I am the last one in her telephone book, the fact that there'd been some boyfriend whose presence in her life marked the end of my presence in her life. But at the current moment, she fills the exact qualifications I am looking for in a companion: She is not male, and she doesn't know anything about my current state of distress, something now that I'd gotten it out, I don't feel the need to think about anymore.

"Sure," I say, "How about The Reservoir?" suggesting a little neighborhood spot.

I don't change. I don't apply deodorant (despite the unattractive aroma emanating from just about every inch of me). This is a pity expedition (embarrassing, but much more mature that I actually recognize it).

By the time tomorrow rolls around, I'll need a new plan, and most importantly, a new attitude. But for now, the only thing I want to think about is getting drunk. One thing at a time. I figure this first goal is something I can at least succeed at. And if I've learned anything in the past month, it's that successes help—no matter how small.

The Reservoir is pretty packed. And mainly this appears to be due to the fact that it's the middle of the workweek—everyone's in after-work garb, and although I might look to be in the same boat, I can't feel the rift between them and me could be any wider.

Whenever you've had a breakdown and cease to worry about the little things that consume your thoughts every other day of your life—hygiene, projects at work, eating—there comes along with it, the freedom from responsibility that I imagine lunatics enjoy. And with that sort of no-worries attitude, I am actually good company to Jenn: not calling her on anything she says, like Pearl Jam is a better band than Nirvana (a topic I would normally argue to the death); acquiescing to her every desire—"Let's sit near those cute guys," and "Why don't we play pool?"—not commenting on the extra weight she's put on or the "Rachel" 'do she's wearing nearly a decade after its popularity has waned; or asking why she hasn't called until tonight.

Fidgeting in her barstool, her face takes on that look you get when you've caught the eye of someone from the opposite sex. Ah! I remember how this used to be such an enjoyable pastime for me! Before my hopes and dreams had been dashed about.

All of a sudden she is more animated than she has been all night. She shakes her overly feathered and voluminous, dark hair back. Are all women this transparent? I wonder. If so, then maybe it's our fault that men get the best of us. We never play our cards close to the vest like they do. If you give everything over to someone, obviously, they won't want it. Everyone knows that. So why have I done this very thing? This, I am right at this moment quite positive, is the reason Liam does not want me anymore. I've been accused of it before. But games have just never been my style.

"There are so many guys here!" says Jenn.

"Ya think? I hadn't noticed," I say, and honestly I haven't. I feel like everyone is faceless, a bunch of Mr. Potato Heads sans eyes, ears, noses, and mouths. And then (as she readjusts herself once more, pulling her shirt down over her skirt) whomever she'd been making eyes at pushes his way through the crowd to her.

"How you ladies doin' tonight?" asks her stranger, never even looking at me as he speaks. He pulls the rim of his Yankees cap up and down again. He's sort of cute in a boyish way.

"Good," Jenn says, dragging the word out and nodding her head up and down.

"I'm Liam," he says.

Oh, no, he didn't.

"Excuse me, did you say Liam?" I ask his back, which is still towards me.

"Um, yeah, is that okay?" he asks to Jenn's face, raising his eyebrows to her, as if to say, "Your friend is insane."

He doesn't think I can see him, but I catch the whole thing in the mirror behind the bar. I don't really feel the need to excuse myself to this person, who is too stupid to realize there is a giant mirror in front of him, but still, I say, "I just wasn't sure I heard you right," half attempting to swallow my words.

Jenn begins to ignite the memories I have of her by being totally disloyal and sending me down the river by shrugging her own shoulders in agreement. "Yeah, she's bonkers, she said half-kidding."

I have to agree. I am bonkers. I am totally and utterly nuts. I have lost all semblance of reality. But surely it has to mean something that this person's name is Liam when here I am right in the middle of a crisis over my Liam. Since this Liam is obviously a jerk, it must not be a good sign.

Liam and Jenn are exchanging pleasantries and I'm doing what The Other Girl always does—smoking, taking extra interest in every inhale and exhale, peeling the edges of a coaster, and checking myself out in the mirror, while taking long, slow sips at my straw. Every so often I look at my drink as if it is the most interesting thing I have ever seen. (Who does this fool? Ooh, ice! Bubbles!) After a few moments, I take to looking around at people, you know, moving my head from one side of the room to the other, in a half attempt to act like I'm looking for someone (and not drinking alone at a bar) and partly just to keep myself entertained.

I can't help but notice that everyone seems to be talking to someone of the opposite sex. I imagine that they are all in love, planning trips to the Caribbean, and ready to head home to have amazing sex. I notice a couple at a corner table. She's pretty in an unassuming way, and he is dressed down in a sweater and jeans, definitely the intelligent and funny type that doesn't have a big ego. They are speaking in the most hushed tones and their heads are so close their foreheads are touching.

I gather, in a very scientific way, that only a girl lapping around in a pool of self-pity can, that this guy would be perfect for me, and therefore continue to do what any lonely girl would do: Mentally I tear his companion to shreds. Her boring J. Crew look—she must be frigid; her plain-Jane hair—probably doesn't own a shred of lingerie; her driving moccasins—surely a rich girl who just doesn't know what life is all about. She probably doesn't even work at all, just has Daddy pay the mortgage. I am shaking my head in disgust at what men see in women, and why they don't see it in me when suddenly, there is a shot of 151 in front of my face.

"Bottoms up!" screams Jenn's new beau.

The one other time I'd ever had this shot, I was playing hostess at a New Year's Eve party. It was during the first of my relationships with a Not-Funny-Enough, Not-Smart-Enough, but sweet and in love with me guy. One thing I knew I was handing out pigs in a blanket, the next thing I knew it was noon the following day. Therefore, I'm sure you can see why the shot seems like a good idea to me at the moment. I clink cheers with the two idiots I am making company with and let the exceedingly hot liquid make its way down my throat. A bit dribbles down my chin and I go to wipe it, but a pile of napkins is thrust in my direction before I actually make contact.

"Can I get that for you?" asks a redheaded guy.

Can someone really ask that in an attempt at a pickup line? Surely this could be awarded some type of cheesiness citation. But I am feeling the effects of the alcohol already (this is strong stuff) and, well, I'm actually delighted at the attention.

"Sure."

The couple in the corner is now kissing, it feels, just to show me how happy they are. Redheaded Guy wipes my chin, taking his time, and probably less interested in the possibility that some alcohol has made its way to other regions, and more interested in the possibility of exploring those other regions, he expertly trails the heap of napkins along my cheek and down my jawline towards my neck.

I am disgusting and cheap for allowing this, but I don't care. Mid-wipe, my cell phone rings. Whatever I may have said about getting past everything and tomorrow being the start of a brand-new me, well, I forget all about that, and consider the possibility that this may be Liam. Without thinking, I grab my purse, take a look at Jenn, who is already lip-locked (even in this hurried state, I am in-tune enough to guess from her behavior that she's probably here for reasons similar to my own), and run out the door to answer the call in quiet.

I'm sure it's Liam.

It is.

"Hello?" I say, trying to keep the world straight by leaning against a wall, as it is currently spinning uncontrollably.

"How's it going, sweetheart?" he asks. And now that it's really him, I'm not sure what to say. But the way he said sweetheart is sending all sorts of pins and needles into my stomach and I remember this feeling and it is fantastic. Does this mean it was just a case of mistakenly writing the wrong number? Or is he calling to seal the deal now that he's given me ample time to call and find out the truth?

Instinctively (or rather, because I'm drunk off my ass), I swim past the pins and needles and find my bitchy woman-scorned tone.

"Liam, I want you to tell me right now what the hell is going on here?"

I am not sure how he will react to this because I have never used any tone other than the adorable sex-kitten variety on him before. But whatever effect the bitchy woman-scorned voice may have had is somewhat diminished by the long pause that follows. Rather than concentrating on keeping up this tone, I am deciding whether this is a guilt-driven or shock-driven pause.

And then the silence is broken when he starts to laugh. First it's a small, light hiccup of a laugh, and then it's a full-blown, all-out yuck-fest, with intermittent sighs to catch his breath.

Laughing? Wait. This is a good sign.

No, a great sign.

He has no idea why I would be angry. He thinks I am putting him on. Yes! This is perfect. Obviously, you cannot feign this type of laughter—never, and now it is so clear. I was being paranoid. A lunatic. Perhaps I should be admitted to an asylum.

I get that wave of relief that comes over you after you wake up from a nightmare and discover that whatever horror you'd gone through was not real. Of course! It was just that he'd mistakenly written the wrong number. Hadn't that been exactly what Joanne was trying to get at when she asked how quickly he'd written the number? And I'd just ignored the question. Joanne, she's so smart! (I now choose to ignore her final summation of the situation, which involved the word "asshole" on the grounds that I was telling the story only from my point of view, which you know is only one side of the truth.)

"You're bloody hysterical, Lane. You know that? I wish I could give you a big hug right now."

"I wish you could, too," I say, trying to sound cute.

"Are you waking up for work now?" I ask, imagining it must be like five in the morning there, and his hair is probably so adorably pushed up on one side.

"What? Now?" he asks, and I am suddenly confused and paranoid, thinking I've caught him in a lie and he's not in London at all. His voice is rather clear for just having woken up.

But then he calms my fears again. "No, yeah, well, I set my

alarm to make sure I'd catch you when you'd probably be coming home. I just wanted to tell you that I'm thinking about you. And chocolate cake. And your bed. And your floor. And . . ."

That last *and* can only mean one thing, and that is exactly what I've been dying to hear. I really couldn't have fantasized about this telephone call any better than it really is going, except that I probably would have added, "I love you, Lane," somewhere in there.

But, still, this is perfectly fine. I am worlds ahead of where I had been just seconds earlier. I am feeling normal again (albeit having trouble standing up straight), and so I leave all of the negativity (and my off-again friend Jenn) behind and walk home talking with Liam on the cell, discussing all of the things we wish we could do to each other. And I start to tell him the story about *The Wizard of Oz*, and he's listening, he really is, but he has to cut me off in the middle to get ready for work. Which is totally understandable. At least I got a bit out. I'm sure I'll get a chance to finish up the bits about the wedding scene and the Tiffany diamond he offers to Dorothy the next time we speak. And when finally, I am in my bed once again, sure we are absolutely perfect—Liam and I—where hours earlier I lay in the lowest of spirits, I feel that once again, all is as it should be.

I get to work the following morning by the grace of God. I am so hungover I can barely see, and even though there is no sun in the sky, I am wearing the darkest sunglasses I own (okay, the only sunglasses I own, but you get the point). And now that everything is back to normal on the Liam front, I really have to get serious about the project we are working on, as tomorrow afternoon is our meeting with the telecom companies. I have to make all of the final decisions, and proof all of the copy, and make sure that the order is perfect before it goes off to the printer. It's a long day, and it's not really until noon that my brain is at a fully functioning level. John is very sweet to me, and gathering that I have drunk my sorrows away a bit, he keeps bringing cups of water by my cubey.

Tom doesn't really seem to be himself today. The only conversation we'd had was in the morning, when I'd returned his jacket and let him know that everything was just fine with Liam. And if I'm not mistaken, he was a bit short with me then—avoiding my face when I spoke to him, and since then, his door, which is normally open to us at all times, is firmly closed. Perhaps he's angry that I took off early yesterday, in the middle of such a big project over something that was obviously blown out of proportion, and so I make sure to work very hard today to show him that I am still dedicated. I'm sure if the meeting goes well, this will all blow over.

It's after midnight by the time I have the proofs one hundred percent ready. I have never been pegged as the detail-oriented type, but I have taken extra-special care on this project with every single dot of ink that will wind up on the page. With a project like this, there is so much riding on the deal—employee bonuses, jobs even—that you can't help but feel a strong sense of responsibility, above and beyond the sort that comes with naming the wrong hue of lipstick that Sarah Jessica Parker wore to the Oscars.

But all of that extra time making sure that each statement follows the *Strunk and White* guidelines, that each date is formatted in the exact same manner, and that every single page looks absolutely perfect, our print department will now have to work overnight to get the piece done. I use my womanly charms to ease the situation, arriving with a big smile and sodas for all, and keep the guys company for the first couple of hours—handing out cookies and candy from the vending machine. And while I'm sitting on a high stool, watching the guys work, I wonder if perhaps I'm not dragging this day out because when I no longer have this project to use as an excuse for procrastination, I will be back to panic mode as I will only have one week left before my article is due.

Before I know it, it's 2 P.M. the next afternoon, and I'm in the conference room, removing the cellophane from the sandwiches and salads I've ordered for the meeting. At each place, I gently lay down a copy of our proposal, which really is stunning and very convincing. The solid metal cover—in the shape of an old-fashioned telephone, bound with an actual, real telephone cord, looks just stunning.

An hour later, we are beginning and there are over fifteen people gathered to listen to what Tom has to say. He looks very professional in one of the suits we'd bought at Thomas Pink, and when one of the women from AT&T compliments him on his tie, he looks over at me and winks. I feel a wave of something unfamiliar during the second she takes to smooth her finger over the tie—something like pride, but with a tinge of something else that causes me to watch the whole scenario and follow her freakishly long fingers until they are firmly curled around her coffee mug at the other end of the table. I mean, he has a girlfriend *and*, I can't help but think, this is a *business meeting*; she could be a bit more professional.

He takes full control of the meeting. We'd gone over his spiel the day before, John and I acting the part of the potential clients, unable to help ourselves asking stupid questions like, "That's all well and good, but what type of dressing is on this salad?"

As I said, he wasn't in the greatest mood, and so, didn't even crack that half-smile once. But, today, he couldn't be more smiley or gracious.

In fact, when he gets right down to business, I am really blown away. I have never seen him do his thing before, and it is impressive. He is charismatic; he knows what all of the charts mean; he has the answers to every question: "The largest portions of users . . ." "In American and international studies conducted via . . ."

With each point he makes, you can see the faces at the table take on a look of surprise and interest, as if they've just heard something that they wouldn't have expected to. And although I am there really just acting like an important part of the team, to make our department seem much larger and stronger than it actually is, he never once treats me with anything less than the highest respect.

The meeting is long—literally six hours—and by the time we've wrapped it all up and called cars for all of the attendees, it's ten o'clock. I figure that Tom will be wiped out, but just the opposite; he is electric with energy from our apparent success. I am awestruck by how dedicated he is to his job. It's like, well, like me. I know that feeling of getting what you want because you worked hard for it. You can see that he was made for this position. He shines under the pressure; thrives on the challenge. Tom Reiner, managing director extraordinaire.

When we are all back by our desks and packing up, he walks over to the cubes and says, "We really all must celebrate. C'mon, we don't have any work tomorrow anyway. We deserve it. You guys have done a fabulous job, and Mr. Tamaka has already called me from his cell phone, hinting that this is pretty much a done deal. I couldn't have done it without the two of you. I promised you a fabulous dinner, and that's what you're going to get."

"I would love to," John says. "But my girlfriend and I are celebrating our anniversary tonight."

John has a girlfriend. Of course John has a girlfriend. He is sensitive and intuitive and sweet. I, on the other hand, am a shallow jerk, suspecting that he is bad with the ladies. God, can I be shallow. I look at him now, smiling, as he really is such a sweetheart, and surely, a fantastic boyfriend. I remember the other day, when I was so upset by Liam, John was so sensitive to my feelings. He knew exactly what to say, and what not to say. A girl would be lucky to have someone so intuitive and caring to go home to. I look at him now and notice the slight lines around his eyes and his mouth—smile lines. John is a good guy—not the kind you come across every day. I guess if you let them, people can amaze you every day.

I'm more than willing to make this night last, as now that the project is done and it's back to the reason I'm actually here, I couldn't be more delighted for an excuse to drag the night out a bit longer.

"Well, it's just you and me, Ab Fab," says Tom, now, apparently over whatever I'd done to upset him the other day, looking at me with that half-grin I've grown to love once again.

"Sounds good to me. Where are we off to?"

"This is a celebration, so how about my favorite spot—Union Square Cafe? My cousin is the owner, so we won't have any problems getting a table. I hope you won't mind dining among the swanky," he raises his eyebrows here to indicate that he thinks I'm a posh girl at heart.

"Not at all." It will be nice to be at a spot that Liam loves, like he's there with me in spirit.

Sixteen

The End of an Era

In the car ride over, Tom is sitting way over on the other side of the cool, leather seat. He's so far away that I need a megaphone just to speak to him. This is quite different from the last time we'd gone out together at the Pen-Top. I consider that a girlfriend like his must have a guy on a pretty tight leash to keep him that glued to the opposite window, and I wonder if she's questioned him about the new suits and gotten angry when he said I'd picked them out.

But at the restaurant, the table is so small that it is just the opposite setup—we are so close that reaching for a slice of bread or the butter cup means that our hands touch more than once. The first couple of times it barely fazes me at all, but after the third time, I notice that I allow my hand to linger just a bit—without even thinking about it. When I look up at Tom, I am almost embarrassed at what I've just done. Maybe it's the fact that I haven't seen

Liam in over a week now, or just the thrill of the success we're sharing. I can't read his expression at all. It is, I guess, what people mean when they say "blank."

But during the elation that follows a period of stress, a strong sense of camaraderie is not a rarity, and so after a momentary lapse of he's-going-to-think-I-like-him neuroses, during which I rationalize that it was absolutely nothing at all, I manage to forget about it.

"I'm sure you've got something fabulous in mind for an appetizer, so what will it be?"

I'm eying the oysters, but fear that Tom is a meat and potatoes sort (he is) and that this will make him feel rather how I did during my sushi date with Liam. So I suggest the most normal-sounding thing on the menu—macaroni and cheese.

"My gosh, I take you to a beautiful restaurant and you order macaroni and cheese? You must be very easy to please. My kind of gal."

When he says this, I remember the first time he called me a gal and think, now, that when he says it, it doesn't sound lame at all— just cute, actually.

"What about *your* gal?" I mimic the word. "Is she easy to please?"

And he buries his head in the menu here, avoiding the question for a minute. When he lowers it, he's taken on that blank expression again, looks me right in the eye and says, "Well, I've got something to tell you, Ab Fab."

I brace myself for something awful, monumental, something.

"I would absolutely love the macaroni and cheese."

It takes me a second to realize it's a joke, but then his mouth turns up at the corners, and so does mine.

He says, "I was worried you'd want to order something like oysters, which for the life of me, I cannot stomach."

"They are so good, though!" I say.

"I know in your fab world it's all about the hottest, hippest slimy cuisine, but I'll let you in on a little secret, Lane." He leans in here and lowers his voice to a whisper. "Stick with me, kid—you may not be able to tell from just looking at me, but I am actually so ahead of the trend that to the common eye it actually looks like I am behind the trend. Think about it."

Is this a jab? Mark of Tom being supremely above frivolous trends? Hysterical joke? I am trying to figure this out when my train of thought is interrupted.

"Your waiter, Terry, has just ended his shift. I'm Liam. I'll be taking over for him. Are you ready to order?"

Now, I haven't looked up yet. As a matter of fact I'm looking right at Tom. And our waiter, whose British accent I heard from behind my head, has not yet seen my face. But, I swear to God, that is MY LIAM'S voice. I know it can't be. He's in London! He's not a . . . a . . . waiter! I just spoke with him two nights ago, from his "flat." He wished he could be in New York—and that's because he's not in New York—he's in London—missing me, and wanting to do things with me and chocolate and he couldn't do any of those things because he is not in New York, he's in London. He's the owner of a publishing company, and we are going to make *Beautiful* the most successful American women's magazine. And this is his favorite restaurant!

Yet, I can't bring myself to look up and prove that my paranoia has finally gotten the best of me.

"Lane?" Tom asks. "Are you ready to order?"

He's said my name. If this is my Liam, he will probably be curious at the mention of my name and walk around to look at me. Since I can't bear to move, to enable this slight, ridiculously impossible possibility to become anything more than just that, I wait for this to happen.

But I can smell his cologne wafting before I even see his face. It is, make no mistake about it, Liam's cologne. But lots of people, I'm sure, wear that cologne. And many of them, I'm sure, can have the same name. And in one fluid movement, I get a surge of confidence, turn my head, see him, throw my hands over my face, and drop my head to the table.

"Lane? Lane? Are you alright?" Tom is asking, so sweet, but, strangely, not so surprised.

"Lane, I can explain," I hear Liam saying from somewhere next to me. I can't find words. I don't even know what the words would be. Nothing makes sense. All the insecurities I was suffering—thinking myself crazy—when, really, I was right on the mark. So stupid! The signs were all there. He is a fake, a liar, and I fell for it all. Because I wanted someone perfect—good-looking, successful, smart, funny. I really asked for it. I'd said it a million times: He was too good to be true.

"I just wanted to impress you," he's saying.

And finally, I turn to look him in the face, and he looks so stupid—that jawline, that hair—they'd both evoked so much pleasure when I'd let my eyes rest on them in the mornings in my bed, but now they just seem phony and disgusting. I can't bring myself to find words. I look to Tom and he is trying his best to find his plate interesting. And Liam goes on to reveal my stupidity, my naiveté to my boss, to the entire restaurant.

"We're good together, you and me—we both just want the fairy tale. You know, the Sundays reading the *Times*, the brunches. It doesn't matter that I'm not exactly what you thought. It's the fantasy you're after. Wasn't it great? The best time of your life? Those are your words! Lane, you know it's true. It is. What's real anyway?"

And as if things weren't bad enough in their current state, a new element is added. A waitress wearing the same uniform as Liam—a white top and black pants, bow tie and all—appears at our table, looking less than happy.

"Liam, do you want to tell me what's going on here?" she says.

I'm imagining if this will be his boss, and he will now be fired for creating such a debacle, so I am dumbfounded at what comes out of her mouth.

"Liam? Who is this woman? Tell me!" Liam looks from me to her and back again. And rather than look her in the face and answer her, he waits for another second, probably too scared to speak, until she can't wait any longer, and figures it out for herself.

"You *have* been cheating on me! Haven't you? Haven't you? I cannot believe that you would do this again! What did you tell her this time? That you're the heir to the throne? Or a member of the House of Commons?" And then she looks at me and shakes her head, "You poor, stupid girl," she hisses, and storms off.

The words are so vindictive, and shouldn't really hurt, considering the source, but they feel so accurate—and I feel the water leaking from my eyes onto my hand, which is holding so firmly on to the stem of my now shaking wineglass, that I am afraid I might crack it in half.

Poor Tom—scenes are not his thing—is really doing his best to maintain his dignity right now, with the whole restaurant staring at us. And I know I need to wrap this up, get out of this place, and never turn back.

And finally, the words come to me. "You know what, Liam? That's disgusting. You're disgusting. And I've never read a fairy tale that ends with the guy turning out to be a complete phony. You don't have any idea what I want. You have no idea what life or love, for that matter, is about, and I guess, neither do I. But that doesn't change the fact that you are a pathetic fucking loser, and I never want to see you again in my entire lifetime. Never. The only thing I regret is that I now have to be ashamed of myself for being such an idiot, for believing in something that was so horribly unreal. Have a nice life. Tom, can we go now?"

Tom throws some twenties onto the table for our wine and, placing his arm around my shoulder, leads me outside. Once we are in the cool air, I can finally breathe, but unfortunately, with the breath comes more tears. Lots of them. And it's that sort of wailing that you normally reserve for times when you are alone, watching *Steel Magnolias*, nursing a lethal case of PMS. And I'm crying for Liam, but also for everything that I had ever dreamed that Mr. Right would be. If anything ever proved to me that my perceptions were totally off the mark, it is this. I have been foolish. Stupid, even. And I'm saying all of this out loud, although it's not exactly audible, what with the wailing and the sniffling and my inability to control my tongue properly. Tom is perfect. He's just rubbing my back and wiping the tears off of my face and not saying a word.

This goes on for about ten minutes, and then I take a deep breath and look at him for the first time, really, since we've been standing outside. And the way he's looking at me, it seems like it's his heart that's been broken rather than mine—that's how sympathetic he looks. And when I see him break into a gentle smile, I do, too. And then, like so often in the aftermath of hysterics, I start to laugh. And then he starts to laugh. It all seems so ludicrous.

"Did you see his face?" I ask.

"You could have caught flies in his mouth, he was so shocked," Tom says.

"Yeah, and I can't even imagine what's going on in there right now."

"Probably crying like a baby," Tom says. "Lane, I just want you to know, it's really his loss. It really is. You are a fabulous, wonderful woman, and anyone who tries to manipulate the things that make you so wonderful is just the lowest sort of person in the world."

That just may be the nicest thing anyone has ever said to me. So I sort of want to hear it one more time. I mean, I'll be swimming in doubt for probably the next year of my life, so it will be nice if at least this stands out in my memory.

So I ask, "Really?"

He takes my hand and says, "Please don't ever forget that." And then he asks, "Do you want me to take you home, Lane?"

And I look at him, and he's so sweet and gentle and patient. It's as if he knows me, not on the physical level that Liam did, but in that way of the couple at the supermarket—the way in which you know exactly what someone needs. And in the past, I might have taken this to mean something more than friendship, but I am done with presuming such frivolities, like imagining Tom would leave his girlfriend and declare his love for me and that he would be The One and then we'd all live happily ever after, the end. Things just don't work out that way in real life. If there's one thing I've learned through this whole disaster, it's that.

Love, if it even exists, just doesn't happen to girls like me, who've built their entire hopes for the future on an intricate web of mystical daydreams. It happens to those who have a realistic approach and understand that the funny-enough, smart-enough, but not stereotypical heroes are sweet and gentle and able to open their hearts and minds to you. It happens to those who understand the firewall between real life and fiction-based expectations—the line that should never be crossed. And those like me, who keep holding on to the fantasy, will live a life of loss and disappointment.

I nod my head to indicate that I would like to go home. The walk is short, less than a couple of blocks and the cool breeze is even more sobering. I feel empty, like everything I've ever known is gone. Tom will go home to his girlfriend, who, to me may seem like the worst match for him in the world, but who is a real, veritable human being and not some lame fictional character from a book. He is practical and smart, and I am not. And that is why I am alone, going home to shelves and shelves of books harboring would-be M&Ms, who exist only in the minds of those like me, who have nothing else to keep them company at night—not because no wonderful men exist, but because nobody could ever measure up to that perfect image you have created, no matter how many men you surround yourself with every day.

My phone rings and rings the weekend through, but I can't bring myself to answer it. Whether it is Liam or Tom or Joanne or Samantha or even worse, my mother, I can't bring myself to face anyone. I'm in no mood for I-told-you-so's or even for things-will-be-brighter-tomorrow cheers. For the first time in my life, I know that the only place I can find the answer is inside myself. Unfortunately, myself does not come with any sort of road map.

Seventeen

The Exorcism

On Sunday, though, I wake up with a renewed sense of hope. The ideas I'd been mulling over for the past twenty-four hours have formed some sense in my head. Of course, in the aftermath of what has been the hugest realization I have ever experienced, I am still just trying to get my mind around everything I have learned. I spent the better portion of yesterday in mourning. I've mentally waved good-bye to everything I'd thought life was about since I was a little girl. And although shame has played a key part in recalling my actions and emotions of the past, there is a process that accompanies letting go.

No matter how unhealthy and ridiculous my M&M ideals may have been, they were so much a part of me that I am not sure who I can be now. Even when I was at my lowest points, gluing glitter to "Anti-fairy-tale-ism" posters, I knew who I was; I knew the ins and outs of my life, my value system. There wasn't the faltering, the wavering that accompanies the unknown. I always knew what I would have one day, what I wanted. I had a plan, and even if my fantasies were detrimental, they kept me company. They dictated what I would do, how I would act, how I would feel.

There was no question, no way for me to take an alternate course. I didn't have to think, I just had to hope and dream and wait for the day it would all come to fruition. After all of this time, my friendships were dictated by my role—the lonely one, the one who called to complain about a dateless Saturday night. The question in my mind reminds me of when I left my college dorm for the last time to start my adult life: Who will I be now? The unknown can be a scary thing.

But after spending yesterday concentrating on the difficulty of the loss, today I wake seeing a lightness that hasn't occurred to me before. The pressure that I felt to find that one perfect person— that culmination of every daydream, every journal entry, a bit of Hugh Grant, a slice of Tom Cruise, a lover like Richard Gere—has completely disappeared. My entire life, I've walked around with that weight, that ghost of the M&M haunting me.

He hovered in the corner of my bedroom, clucking his tongue at every boyfriend who wasn't a fabulous kisser, at every lover who couldn't go all night long. He sat at the empty seat in restaurants when my companion didn't hold my hand or stare deeply into my eyes at the moment I deemed appropriate.

He laughed on my couch when I opened the door to reveal a boyfriend who hadn't bought flowers for a special date that I'd built up in my mind. He was always ready with an "I told you so" when a wonderful man presented me with a thoughtful present— a new cordless phone with a very professional headset, "Because a talented writer should look the part," rather than the perfect pair of earrings or sexy lingerie.

He'd frown menacingly at the one who, instead of ripping my clothes off while I cooked what I'd envisioned to be the most romantic meal for two, spent the time downloading MP3s from the Internet to create a song list that he hoped would commemorate our perfect evening forever.

Now that I see him for what he is—someone who controlled my thoughts and my life for that matter, I want to make sure that he is gone from my other haunts, the spots I'd visited in the past that served as clear indications that I was a have-not, as compared to all the haves that surrounded me.

My first stop: Central Park. As much as I'd always loved this urban oasis, the trees, the reservoir, the funky dancing Rollerbladers, the playful dogs, the majestic cityscape, I feel I'd never really gone through a day there without focusing on how alone I'd felt. I need to clear my head of these hindrances, and start anew, and with the glorious spring weather in full swing, I can't think of a better spot.

I am not looking for diversions today. I pack no book; I bring no Walkman to listen to love songs and separate myself from the real world. I want to become part of the present and live for today—the real day, rather than the ideal far-off one.

When I enter the park at Sixtieth Street I notice Rollerbladers, bikers, runners in brightly hued clothing, and of course lots wearing the urban uniform—black. I see a hot dog vendor selling his treats. I decide to indulge in one, rather than worry that I'll have to maintain the perfect body for the perfect man. The smell is fabulous, salty and strong. I notice the spiciness of the mustard, the sweetness of the ketchup. It is the absolute best lunch I have ever had.

I walk past a bench where a couple is sharing a hushed conversation, their eyes oblivious to passersby. And, here, I smile. Rather than taking the role of the have-not, I am a have, and what I have is so precious and has taken so long to figure out that I once again recall that last day of college. But this time I remember the other set of feelings—the splendor of victory, the freedom, the feeling that you can have whatever you want in this world.

Normally, I find the rolling hills and the wide-open space of Sheep's Meadow a lonely place in the face of the couples sharing wine and cheese from a picnic basket, tossing around a Frisbee. My eyes always skip over the single people enjoying the sun's rays or indulging in some magazine reading, never seeing the smile on their faces, the serenity of their experiences. Instead I have always focused with tunnel vision on the pairs, never considering the possibility that a solo venture could be anything but lonely.

But I am not that girl anymore. When I do spot couples, I am delighted in the knowledge that I have learned the secret they share. And as I see them, I begin to grasp more and more what this is all about. There is no such thing as perfection. And while they may seem as happy as newlyweds right now, and probably genuinely are, they have faced lost jobs, weathered arguments, worked to make their sex lives fulfilling. Perhaps one has thought about cheating, maybe one already has. One has probably gained weight, lost hair, suffered through illness, questioned their happiness, felt bored. At one point, they had to tuck their fantasy person deep into a drawer and throw away the key to accept what a real relationship is. They had to make sacrifices and concessions for things. They had to accept reality.

Love is not the perfect dinner conversation or an all-out boink-fest. It is not someone ordering the chicest appetizer or saying the perfect thing when you open the door. In short, it is none of the surface things you pick up from leading men who know how to keep the heroine dying for more. Love only happens when you are willing to forgo all of those stereotypes of perfection and exchange them for an appreciation and love of the unique things that *your* someone does, to the best of their abilities, to make you happy. And while I know it is fruitless to revisit the many relationships I have destroyed in ignorance of this understanding, many of the scenes play in my mind anyway, and I can only hope that in future scenarios, I will recognize the everyday wonders that fall outside the stereotypical mold.

With the death of the M&M, the power of happiness lies in my hands alone. And I have to wonder: Will I be capable of discerning not only the good bits, but which concessions are the right ones to make? How much is too much to give up?

Although I am glad to have rid myself of my M&M ghost, I have become so comfortable with him that the idea of leaving him behind for good seems daunting. I will have to start life anew. It feels like mourning. My black ensemble seems pointedly appropriate. I have carried and nurtured this dream and had it keep me company on many a lonely night, and now I have to let it go. I get the sense that I should be tossing something into the river to start fresh, like when I was little and we celebrated the Jewish New Year by scattering bits of bread into the water. But what would it be? Liam springs to mind as an appropriate choice.

But really, I shouldn't be angry with him. I now see that I should be thankful that he allowed me to see the world for what it really is. Despite the lies, he was just as sad and foolish as I was. It is not so difficult to see how he got to that point—that very far-gone and ridiculous point. Was he really so much more far-gone than I? Was I not creating my own reality, just as he was? Perhaps I'd wished him into existence. If I hadn't been so open to the whole scenario, it wouldn't have worked.

The lovemaking we had shared was very much like a movie—two characters playing the roles they had spent a lifetime creating. Had I not already created my own Liam the very first time we'd met? Had I not weaved together the pieces of his life as I wanted to see them? I'd pictured his bathtub, his family, his home in Provence. I'd fancied that I could unbreak his allegedly broken heart. I'd loved the drama. I'd pictured us making love before we'd even kissed. I'd outlined the way he would tug my hair, the way his kisses would start out slowly and build up to deep, hungry cries of passion. And the prophecy fulfilled itself.

It wasn't real. I could see it so clearly now—the chocolate cake, the ravaging kisses. This was less of an exchange between two people and more of an act—what we both thought the script of love should read like. And when I thought back to the compliments, the moans, each time my name was repeated after the words, "Oh my God," they are now empty, not for me, not inspired by me. And that is what was missing from the puzzle: The fact that I could have been interchanged with virtually any lovesick girl. Lane Silverman was never there.

When I get home, I decide to create my own rebirth ritual. Rather than sit on my couch and go through tape upon tape of movies that have helped fuel my ridiculous existence, I decide to do a little housecleaning. Since I am going to start a new life, I need to rid myself of the artifices I've employed in the past to propagate my deceitful life.

I start with my bookcase. After two hours, I have lots of shelf space available and four boxes of love stories. I am not going to throw them away. These books are not bad, after all. It is I who did not know how to put them in their proper place. Now I know that I can only blame myself. What I am going to do is put them in the storage area in the basement until I am ready to revisit them.

Next up is my collection of films. Looking at each one, I see hours and hours of time wasted, weekends, days I could have spent working, living. I can't blame fate for the days I spent feeling jealous, watching and crying and considering myself unlucky. And with each tape I remove, I laugh. This whole time I've been tricking myself, hiding them in drawers like an alcoholic locking a liquor cabinet, rather than admitting there is a problem.

"I'm Lane and I'm a love-a-holic."

When I take the books and files to the basement, I feel quite sure that I will have no need to look at them again. And once the super locks them inside the storage room, I feel light as a feather. I am taking a step I should have taken long ago. I know that in the future I will be able to revisit my cherished books and movies, but not for fulfillment; it will be for entertainment only. But before that time comes, I have a lot of living to do.

When I return to my apartment again, I don't get that lonely feeling I normally do on a weekend without plans. I am not saddened by the single place settings of bowls, glasses, plates that are stacked in my cabinet. My single-servings of chicken cutlets and hamburgers tucked away inside Ziploc bags in the freezer do not serve as reason to shed tears, to despise couples walking hand in hand down the street. I feel no need to sit at my window, counting those whose fortunes outweigh my own. And please don't misunderstand. I have not resigned myself to the fact that I will never love. I have just realized that I hold the key to love—that I've held it all along.

Eighteen

A Painstakingly Researched Article

When Monday rears its head, and I am at home, having taken the day off to begin my article, I feel the pressure of this assignment in such a tangible way that I can barely bring myself to sit down at my computer. This whole experiment has blown up in my face. I have learned something, but not achieved my goal. The pressure of finding my M&M, of having to truly think about what it takes to be with someone forever caused me to realize that I was not equipped with the realistic notions required. If I had taken a step back and seen what was really going on—seen that the perfectly good men I was tuning out because they did not send tingles up my spine at first sight were probably worth a thousand Liam's—perhaps I *could* have done what I set out to do.

And despite what I had originally thought, it's not the geographical environment that you are in that makes it possible to meet The One. It is the environment within—your heart, your mind, your willingness to take someone for good and bad, your willingness to forgo fantasy for reality. If you can do that, then you can find happiness in love. If you can't, then you will always find some sort of excuse as to why not—geography being only one of them.

But the fact remains that I have an article to write. I feel like a fraud, having posed as a real, dedicated writer, when, if you really think about it, I have behaved like a stupid little girl. Now I have to act like an adult. And the only thing an adult in this situation could do is to take her experiences and write the best article she can think to write and convince her editor that this is, in fact, the better story.

Only I'd tried to change the assignment before, and it hadn't gone so well. After all, magazine editors are not in the business of helping Lane Silverman to find out the truth about love. They are in the business of getting the story—no matter what the price.

I try some meditation to clear my mind, only I don't really know how to meditate, so I just sit in what I hope is the lotus position, with my fingers on my knees and my eyes closed. Far from being relaxed, all I can think about is the fact that I am about to toss aside the biggest career opportunity of my life. After five minutes of this, I get up and decide to just jump in. If I write the best story ever, if I convey the magnitude of what I have learned and experienced, then perhaps everything will turn out okay in the end. This will have to work. It is the only way.

And I haven't even finished typing in the name of the file in the "save" window when a tiny envelope appears at the corner of the screen. I am sure it can only be some kind of bad news, probably an alert from the *New York Times* online that there are now ten women to every man in Manhattan—signaling that now that I've come to my senses it is actually too late to do anything about it. But it's from Lisa, successful Lisa who probably never had to dash her hopes and dreams to bits just for an article assignment.

Lane,

I am just getting back from a week at the Cape, and I'm glad to hear that the article you've written about me is to your liking. If I think I know you at all, I'm sure it is fantastic. Congratulations on the *Cosmo* gig, but darling, from what you've written, I feel I need to give you the sort of advice that only experience can provide. Never, never put such unnatural stakes on something as organic and wonderful as love. I know it does seem impossible to find it sometimes, but believe me, honey, once you have opened your mind to delight in each smell, taste, and sensation of that heavenly emotion, you will see that it is not something you can just will into being.

It takes time to appreciate the subtleties that make someone the love of your life. Even those who feel they are victors in the game of love at first sight, when ticking off the reasons they love someone, will never mention a beautiful face or a great pickup line. Love is in the subtleties—and two months' time will never reveal that sort of thing.

Your predicament is probably confusing and worrying but listen to your heart. And no matter what sort of lessons you have learned, please don't ever forget that mysterious power known as fate. Love, although possibly not the ideal you'd thought upon setting out on this venture, does, above all else, have a mystical element, and happens when you least expect it. You can quote me on that.

Please give a ring if you need anything.

XOXO,

Lisa

It is no wonder that Lisa has done so well for herself. She is one very smart woman. Without even telling her how the whole scenario worked out, she knew what would happen. But she did bring

up one thing I'd tossed away with the rest of my romantic notions—fate. Am I still willing to believe in this? Is Fate Avenue a
dangerous one to turn down? It does take some of the power from
your hands and at present that is a scary notion.

I type the word atop the blank document on my screen in capi-
tal letters.

FATE

I bold it.

FATE

I look it up in the dictionary.

fate (fat) *n.*: The supposed force, principle, or power that pre-
determines events.

It is too large an idea to think about at the current time.

I erase the bolded, capitalized letters and table them for the future. For now, I need to know that my future is in my hands. I need
to write an article saying so, for all the world to read.

The only thing I can bring myself to chalk up to a higher power
at this point is the fact that Lisa has offered her services just when
I've made up my mind to change the direction of the article. I
know that I had asked for a similar change when (wince) Liam was
once lying in my bed, to receive a very definite answer of no. But
if Lisa believes I can do such a thing, than I am sure that she can
help me to make Karen see it through her eyes. I pop her a quick
e-mail asking for her opinion and advice and it turns out that
Karen is actually a good friend of hers. She is sure we can work this
out. She tells me to pour my soul out into this article, finish it up,
and then we will present it to Karen together.

With this huge weight off my shoulders, and the opportunity to
publish the article and keep my career moving in the right direction,

I should be happy. And although I have decided that my recent experiences have changed my life for the better, the fact remains that this is not the happy ending I had hoped for. Couldn't I have learned the lesson *and* found someone anyway? It definitely would have made for a much better story, and, let's face it, a much happier me.

Fate. The word comes to me again. I try to resign myself to fitting this idea into my understanding of love. But I can't quite comprehend where it might go. I'm holding a single piece of a very large puzzle and no matter which angle I look at it from, which side of the table I try to work it into, it doesn't seem to fit. If love is about finding the ability to love someone for who they are, doesn't that mean it really is all up to you? Haven't I tried to twist—in reality—the hand of fate with very dire consequences?

Perhaps fate is angry with me. Is it possible this is the reason I haven't met anyone, because I have played with fate, attempted to control it? If fate can bring two people together, then fate can also decide that you will never find true love, no matter how much you open your mind and alter your expectations. This idea brings me back to the point where I start worrying about the future, perhaps not in the same way as before, but worrying all the same. Maybe Lisa, as smart as she is about most things, is possibly wrong here. For now, I'll have to make myself believe this and carry on as planned.

DIARY OF A WORKING GIRL

Once upon a time, I was a little girl with long pigtails and lots of plaid, pleated skirts. Like most girls my age, I amassed and coveted a large collection of Barbie and Ken dolls. But probably a bit unlike most girls my age, I spent hours pairing the couples. Now I know what you're thinking. They all look exactly alike! And you are one hundred percent correct in that assertion.

But, early on, somebody very wise taught me that it wasn't what was on the outside that mattered, but what was on the inside. So, after I'd spent long hours working out the life stories of each Barbie and Ken, I decided which male candidate was perfect with each female candidate. I named each one. Sally, a lover of the outdoors, animals, and any type of adventure sport, had dreamed about finding a man who knew how to make life exciting every second of every day. He would always have a fantastic excursion planned for the two of them. After a hard day of white-water rafting or climbing Mount Everest, though, he would never be too tired to think of a wonderfully romantic way to express his love for her. Rather the opposite, all the while they were rowing or grabbing hold of rocks, he would compose rhymed couplets of love poems in his head, and when they lay in the sun, sipping mint-infused iced tea and staring into each other's eyes, he would recite his words of love to her. Sally, therefore, was paired with Marco, who, graced with strong limbs and nerves of steel, was an aesthete adventurer, and because he was raised by a widowed mother who'd spent her days spinning tales of her wonderful late husband and speaking of how true love never dies, even after your lover has left this world, was a romantic soul like no other.

Each identical blond doll had her own story, and her own unique love match. The Barbies, though, were just the beginning of my affair with love. The next several years marked my fascination with cinema. It was the era of *Grease* and

Xanadu. While my friends loved the films for thier campy music, leg warmers, hot pants, and synchronized dance routines, I held them close to my heart for a very distinct reason. I'd watch them over and over again to learn exactly what the sort of man you can fall in love with would be like. From Danny Zuko, I learned to covet danger, good looks, dark hair, and leather jackets. I also took note of the fact that a great guy is one who's not so easy to attain. It would be difficult to make it work with The One—but the work was worth it in the end if you'd get to fall in love on a carnival ride and have the whole school sing about it.

From *Xanadu,* I'd garnered that you'd need to be an inspiration to the one who really loved you. They couldn't imagine life without you and they wouldn't have any trouble at all conveying that to you. He would have to be creative and talented, sensitive and open to change.

Books only increased my research cannon. The leading man was now the captain of the football team. He'd ask you to the prom even if his friends disagreed. He'd defy his parents to steal a moment with you and his kiss would send actual electricity coursing through your veins. He would cherish every inch of your body, and literally shake when the opportunity to touch it presented itself. If he'd lost you somehow, he'd devote years to the challenge of getting you back, or die trying. He'd grow up to become a successful, wealthy world traveler, and he'd sit patiently while you shopped, got your hair colored. He'd eagerly participate in frivolous escapades, have a Cracker Jack ring engraved at Tiffany's. He'd gladly leave his bride at the altar for you, and given the choice, would throw his career into the trash just to have one minute with you.

Fast-forward to my mid-twenties. By then, Ken dolls and movies had been joined by yet another litmus test—the real test—actual men. And none of those men ever broke my heart. I never gave them the chance. No matter how sweet the sentimental deed (an e-mail with the words "I'm thinking of you:" an all-nighter dedicated to helping me edit an article) he couldn't stand up to the checklist of characteristics I'd compiled through my research. *But he's not the best kisser. But he didn't ever whisk me away to the Caribbean. But why didn't he want to have sex every single night? But how could he not make lewd suggestions at a restaurant?* And after it became clear that he would never allow me to check off those boxes, I would have to put the kibosh on the relationship. I had to find The One. And apparently, he was not it.

Often, after the fact, I'd pass a coffee shop where we had laughed on a Sunday, seen a movie we had both hated and made fun of for days, or come across someone who had a Yankees cap as ripped and torn and aged as his was and I'd feel a loss. And sometimes, in my mind, I'd miss him so much that I would build up our relationship in my mind. Only now I'd fill in the checklist boxes by imagining what a rekindling would be like—in my script, he would do all of those things this time. And when we would reunite, and he failed, once again, to meet my expectations, I'd be devastated all over.

So, there I was, just two months ago, with a string of failed relationships under my belt and a freelance writing career that didn't offer much in the way of male contact, when I woke one day with what I fancied to be a marvelous idea. What if I increased the chances of meeting Mr. Right by taking a position in a male-dominated industry? Increasing the odds absolutely must increase the likelihood that I'll bump into him, right? (Well, we'll get to that later.)

But just changing geography would have been too easy. I had to complicate matters by bringing my career into the picture. I pitched the idea to this very magazine. We all chat about how difficult it is to meet men in the magazine business, don't we? Don't others always advise us to "get out more?" Isn't work always cited as a top place to meet Mr. Right? Well, this magazine seemed to think so. And so, under an agreement to meet Mr. Right in two months and describe him in three thousand words, I swapped my writer's notebook and my late mornings in pajamas at my home office for an attaché case, an adorable camel-colored overcoat, and one very official-looking name badge, with the sole purpose of finding The One. This might sound extreme, but you know that saying about desperate times calling for desperate measures. Well, at least I thought I knew what that saying was about.

After seeing *Pretty Woman, Cinderella, Romeo and Juliet,* and reading *Bridget Jones's Diary* and *Confessions of a Shopaholic,* it seemed the ridiculous was actually a crucial part of finding The One—a precursor even. How could I fail? And walking through the doors of my new office on that first day, it didn't seem there was a chance of anything but success. An explanation of the scores and scores of men (tall, short, bespectacled, with long hair, with short hair) seemed to require an exorbitant amount of expletives just to convey to my friends. Out of the thousands that walked past me, rode in the elevator with me, ate lunch across from me, one of them had to be The One.

During my first few days, I made diligent notes about the

men I came into contact with—noting which I thought might fit my profile. I did my part. I looked cute, dressed in my best shoes, had my hair done, came up with witty comments, even read the financial pages (and that was some feat, let me tell you). One day, I met a nice enough guy who rode into the copy room like a knight in shining armor to save me from the big bad Cannon color machine. Everything seemed to be coming together perfectly. Like a movie. Like a book.

And then, like any good story, the conflict entered my life. Let's call the conflict Liam. The conflict had strikingly good looks, a winning smile, and above all else, a way with the ladies. And to make the whole scenario even more complicated and star-crossed (oh, the romance of it all), the conflict did not work at my office. I would not, could not be with him!

Oh, but I would and I could and I did. And all the while I was entranced by my forbidden, romantic (and not too bad in the bedroom) conflict, I was ticking off the little boxes on my list of qualifications for The One—at this point, my life's work. Great in bed—check; aggressive—check; smart—check; sparkling conversationalist—check; master of anticipation—check. The only problem was, the conflict, despite all of his seeming perfection—his hysterical personality; his insatiable desire to perform all manner of wicked deeds with me, on me, above me, below me—turned out, in the end, to be a fraud.

And the fraud, when brought to light, blamed me.

He—the liar, the cheater, the creator of a false identity—blamed me.

The audacity.

The sheer ridiculousness.

The truth.

It was true. I'd been caught in a web of my own weaving. Before we'd kissed, before we'd even had our first date, I'd dreamed him into my own reality. I'd consulted the checklist! I knew what I wanted, and I knew he was it. Only he wasn't it. But that's because nobody in the entire world *could* be it. It only exists in my Barbie doll case, tucked in my mother's attic; it exists in my boxes and boxes of movies and books; It exists in those days and days in Central Park when I'd muse about what each coupled man was to each coupled woman. The only place it doesn't exist is in reality.

And this was a place, through my own romantic and ignorant imaginings, that I'd managed to put off a visit to thus far. And the landing was a bumpy one. But it had to happen sooner or later. And the only thing my speed dating experiment had done was to purchase me an express ticket there.

But once you've mourned the passing of The One, whom you've created and kept as a companion since the days when tricycles were your main mode of transportation, through the dateless wedding receptions, beside you on an otherwise lonely Saturday night, you come to realize that his death is really the best thing that could have happened. His death gives you the opportunity to live, to see each man you encounter for his own unique wonders, which needn't fit into a confining mold. And while I may not have found The One at Mankind, Inc., I have found something far more important. I have found the ability to love. So now, with all those hopeless romantics out there, I remove my mourning veil and look forward to a love far better than any on the silver screen—a love that's real.

I'm happy with the piece, but I can't help but wonder what is missing. That awful word keeps coming back to mind—fate. Perhaps if, after I'd learned the error of my ways, I still managed to meet someone wonderful, who I could fall in love with, I could see that fate plays a role. But as far as I can see at the current time, fate is a whole separate idea, filled with words I used to melt at the sound of, like "predestined" and "meant to be." And as much as I would like to believe that I could return to that type of sensibility and indulge my yen for such frivolities, I now see the danger involved with that line of thinking. I'm not going back there for anything.

So, I e-mail the story over to Joanne to see what she thinks, and I attach a file I'd typed up of *Diary of a Working Girl*. I wanted her to see where I'm coming from, the daily ins and outs of my debacle with love, even though I imagine it's too long for her to actually read.

I ask in big bold letters: ***Do you believe in fate?***

If anyone is rational it's Joanne. She might as well have invented the word. I am quite sure she'll keep me free and clear of all sorts of ridiculous thoughts.

I am impatient for her reply. At the ten-minute mark, I resist the urge to ring her. At fifteen minutes, I dial, shaking. I feel as if my entire existence is dependent upon whether or not Joanne agrees with my point of view, and more importantly, whether she believes in fate.

"I am not finished yet. Chill out. I'll call you back. Breathe."

And with that she hangs up. It's harsh, but I realize, necessary.

I attempt to while away the time by checking my horoscope online.

With Venus in your house, love is on the way. Don't forget to look where you least expect it. But remember, looking alone won't bring your special someone to you. You have to trust in that wonder of all wonders—fate.

"Ha!" I say out loud to no one in particular.

I glance at the stuffed bear on my bed.

"Do you believe that crap?" I ask Teddy. I look at his torn ear, into his ready-to-fall-off eye.

"Do you?"

He's not saying a word. I throw him on my bed, shaking him like someone who's fainted to get his attention.

I repeat the question, "Do you?"

Defeated, I throw myself onto the bed next to him.

"Oh, Teddy," I say, "is there such a thing as fate? Can I allow myself a touch of the mystical if I am ever to hope to steer clear of my old, silly ways?"

I am staring at the ceiling, looking for the answers, and seeing only a bunch of hairline cracks in the plaster when my eyelids begin to droop. An exaggerated yawn leaves my mouth, and I decide it's time for a nap. It's been a long time since I have napped. Two months, roughly—the time when I'd started working at Smith Barney. (I once measured my overhead storage bin to see if I could fit inside, but alas I was too large.) I always had mixed feelings about them before. On the one hand, you feel guilty for sleeping when you should be working. But on the other hand, when you wake, refreshed, sometimes the answer to your quandary is right there.

I began this ritual in college when I'd spend hours and hours downing Diet Coke in front of my computer and taking breaks only to scream at the musical theater majors to stop singing those damn operas in the damn hallway while I was trying to write a damn paper. And then I'd just take a nap (the opera singing was actually quite nice as a lullaby) and bam! the answer to why a certain poet chose to use the word *twilight* would be right there. If I'd ever been in need of a miracle like that, I was in need of one right now.

So with that four-letter word, *FATE*, lying heavy on my mind, I bury myself in the mountain of pillows around me, turn down the blankets, and curl into the fetal position. As my breathing starts to slow, I take comfort in the fact that I am falling blissfully into slumber.

Nineteen

One Fateful Day

Although it is only five o'clock when I lie down in my bed, I sleep the whole night through. When I wake, holding Teddy in a head-lock, looking out the window to my right, I see it is so early that the sun is barely even lighting the sky. It looks like "naps" are not really something I'm capable of handling anymore. This was more of a vacation, only without actually going anywhere, no tan to speak of, and a wicked case of jet lag.

At the mirror, I let out the sort of yawn that only single women can partake in—a screaming one, where you open your mouth so wide you can see every filling. It's not the feminine covered-mouth sort you attempt in front of a man. And as I'm staring at my mouth in amazement—how many fillings do I have anyway?—I begin recalling my dreams.

In one rapid, nonlogical sequence, I was Sleeping Beauty, my hair not a mass of human hair, made up of separate strands, but instead a lump of one-dimensional orange colored in with a marker and contained by a heavy black line drawn around. I'm lying in a bed, locked up in that infamous dark tower, holding an arrangement of flowers—a few white lilies—when the plump, jocular fairy god-mother of Cinderella fame taps me on the shoulder, briefly inter-rupting my sleeping spell.

I turn to look at her and ask, "Are you Fate?"

She looks at me and smiles, waving a glowing Fourth of July sparkler in the air, tracing loops and spirals with each movement, completely ignoring me, even when I throw the flowers onto the stone floor and begin stomping on them.

Until she finally says, "Aren't those sparklers so much fun? Here, try one out."

She hands one to me and I look at it, thinking how fitting it is that when I finally do get a fairy godmother she turns out to be a wacko. She's trying to write something in the air with her sparklers, but the blaze fades away before I can make the letters out.

Finally, I rip them from her hands and say, "Listen, I haven't got all the time in the world here. Would you mind answering my question already? Geez."

The fairy godmother looks like she's about to sock me one, which isn't very fair considering it's my dream, and I don't think my subconscious is filled with heavyweight aspirations. She com-poses herself, lights another sparkler, this time holding it still, and takes on a whole new demeanor.

"I am, indeed, Fate, my dearie. And I am here to tell you that you have really been pissing me off. I mean, I have been with you dur-ing your entire lifetime, and now you just up and desert me because of one stupid British guy! Whatever happened to devotion? Do you remember that rainy day on your family trip to Massachusetts, sum-mer 1980, under the palace you'd constructed from sheets and two wing chairs? And don't forget your first kiss with Christopher Tamin; if I hadn't brought you tumbling off of your bike and onto his driveway, would you have that memory now? It is true that sometimes you do go off the deep end. Believe me, we fairy godmothers have had many a laugh over you, but that doesn't mean you should shut me out for good. Stay true to yourself, okay? Oh, and here's another sparkler for the road. Aren't they just a hoot?"

And she disappears.

"But—"

I need to ask what she means, to find out when I will be ready. But she is gone. And this stupid sparkler is really hot. Great. Thanks for the help. If that's my fate, I'm left thinking; then I may be in some serious trouble. You may not take much stock in dreams, but I do. I dreamed I would be a writer all the time when I was a little girl, and here I am. I even dreamed which college I would attend, and that's where I wound up. Dreams for me are very, very important— just as important as my horoscope. Or maybe more. No less. Okay, equal then. Just put it this way, they're important. So it would have been nice if the one that contained the answer to my question seemed a little bit, what's the word? Sane.

Is it me, or do you have to figure out every single thing in your life by yourself? What do you have to do to get a little help once in a while? Change your career? Throw yourself into new situations? Put your life on display for the entire world? Wait. I've done all that already and apparently I still don't know which end is up.

Just as I'm considering pitching a column where I get to complain all the time (now, I'd never run out of material for that one), I remember another dream scene. Those little mice and birds from *Cinderella* are scurrying about a human form—pinning a shoulder here, an inseam there. This form is not me. It is male. It is Tom. He is wearing that Calvin Klein suit and flashing the half-smile.

When the tiny tailors are through with their alterations, he is giving a tour of his office building to them. Nobody bats an eye at a gaggle of animated characters walking the halls of the Traveler's Building.

At the elevator, he is pointing to the red and white buttons and saying, "Yes, red is up."

In the cafeteria, he is scooping up vegetables from silver bins and explaining, "This is the lettuce and this is the carrot, and here are the tomatoes."

The mice and birds are elbowing each other and belly-laughing. One little bluebird is attempting to flirt by singing a sweet song and nestling into Tom's neck. Next Tom is holding a copy of the telephone presentation in one hand and hammering a hook into my wall, where my *Vogue* column would one day be. When he's fixed the silver piece onto the wall he stands back and says, "Well done, Ab Fab, well done."

When that flirty bird flies into my window and goes to sing in his ear again I shoo her away thinking that blue is *so* last millennium.

And as quickly as he'd appeared, he is gone.

I look at the wall now, awake, thinking how stupid I have been all of these years to keep pursuing these dreams of being a writer, of meeting my M&M. Is it really worth it if every little success is so hard to come by? The article, I think, is good, but at what price? And why the hell did I decide to throw both of those challenges into the same boat? If I hadn't, perhaps I'd still be in possession of one triumph.

But why in my dream was Tom hanging something up in my spot of honor? Is it possible that Tom may have found his way into my heart? Is it possible that he is (dare I use this word) my M&M?

From habit, I consult the old checklist. I know, I know. I'm like a heroin addict—just one more time, I swear!

I just spent an entire weekend growing up and realizing I am totally irrational and that love is nothing like I thought it was and now I am right back where I started. But old habits are hard to break, and *come on*, you know how melodramatic I am. I was overreacting. I was upset. Hurt. Angry. But that was with Liam. Surely Tom is nothing like Liam.

This is totally new territory here. So, of course, this is a totally different scenario. Of course I need the list. Where else can I turn? I need guidance, and I just told you about my fairy godmother, so obviously I'm not getting any help there.

And so I scan the list. As I open to a clean checklist I get a flush of warmth, like coming home. Why did I ever think I needed to grow up? Obviously I do know about love—look I'm getting $7,500 just to write about it! They wouldn't pay that to just anybody.

"Ha!" I laugh out loud as I begin reading over the boxes at speed-reader pace to find one—just one (!)—that Tom might, possibly, at a certain angle, fall under. I feel one would do. Yes, one would definitely do. Only I do not have to speed-read. I know every single item by heart. And in seconds flat I know there are none to be checked off. None. Tom is none of those things I wrote.

Checklist #129 Tom Reiner
1. Reads NYTimes: ☐
Notes: Wall Street Journal devotee.
2. Has job that will allow for romantic trips to exotic locales; always insists we fly first class, feeding each other sorbet with a tiny silver spoon: ☐
Notes: Has recently been changed to the MD in charge of New York—based negotiations only, so this is out of the question

(but wonderful for assistants who will no longer have to convert currencies).

3. Puts passion above common sense/practicality: ☐
Notes: <u>Dressing-less salad?</u>

4. Is British (depending on nature of remainder of checklist, this can, on occasion be fulfilled with valid British heritage documented on family tree, but British accent is most desirable): ☐
Notes: <u>This item is, from this moment on, officially struck from the checklist!!!!!!!!!!!!!</u>

5. Makes me get That Feeling: ☐
Notes: <u>Shopping, dining, post-meeting, did experience momentary twinges of strangeness in his presence. But cannot one hundred percent testify to the particularities... Well, err... definitely premature.</u>

6. Knows how to be direct, e.g. Richard Gere, *Pretty Woman*: ☐
Notes: <u>Actually, have no idea how he feels about me. Shit! Wouldn't be pulling strands from my scalp in frustration if I did. Ouch!</u>

7. Has roses waiting for me when I get home (even when I am working at home he always finds a way): ☐
Notes: <u>Gave me flowers on first day. Also, there was the framing of the article and the dinner we were supposed to have, but which was ruined for obvious reasons (See checklist #128!!!!!!!!!!!). Still, none were technically delivered to my residence.</u>

8. I am unable to pass a Victoria's Secret without dashing inside to find some new lacy, sexy thing with all sorts of straps that go God-knows-where to surprise him with, and when I

do, he never says something as ridiculous as, "You must get dressed now, we are meeting my parents in ten minutes": ☐
Notes: <u>I could definitely see myself showing up at his office to test this item. On his part, this is barely applicable, although he did compliment the color of my underwear on my first day.</u>
9. He is so beautiful, maybe not to everyone, but to me, that I wake up in the middle of the night and spend hours just staring at the angle of his jawline, the arch of his brow. ☐
Notes: <u>Haven't yet, but have also been obsessed with #128.</u>
10. If we ever do argue, it is always with bitter rage, arms flailing, and tears burning in front of a fountain in Central Park or by the tree in Rockefeller Center, or somewhere equally cinematic. But, then, without fail, we make amends—always meeting in the middle of the route between his home and mine (as we both have the urge for reconciliation at the same moment); and come together in the most passionate lovemaking both of us have ever experienced (once we've gotten inside, of course); and thank God that we have found each other. After, we spend the evening laughing uncontrollably at the littlest things, like the way he says, parents with the same A sound as in apple and coming to unique realizations about things—like how amazing it is that people now only drink bottled water, when before they'd never thought twice about drinking from a tap: ☐
Notes: <u>When Liam did this it was so much fun. I remember this ancient, shrunken woman wearing the largest red glasses I have ever seen stopped right in front of us at the fountain and so he screamed, "I would have died for you Lane Silverman! How could you have made love to my best friend while I was in a coma in a hospital bed in Paris?" Oy. Have no comment yet for Tom. Perhaps could count pretzel argument?</u>

11. Witty statements are always on tip of his tongue. ☑
Notes: <u>Now this is definitely true.</u>
12. He teaches me things I never even knew I had to learn: ☐
Notes: <u>Firewalls? Did not really have to learn, though. I mean,</u>
<u>when will this ever be of use to me?</u>
13. I love the way he looks in his gray boxer briefs: ☐
Notes: <u>Although am now kicking myself for not having done so,</u>
<u>could have snuck a peak at Calvin Klein, as flimsy dressing</u>
<u>room curtain was not exactly the height of security.</u>
<u>Unfortunately, missed the opportunity, and therefore unsure if</u>
<u>he even wears boxer briefs(?) Hopefully, does not wear those</u>
<u>ugly red bikinis with mesh...On brighter side, he has a much</u>
<u>talked about nice butt.</u>

So he is actually the one item I hadn't memorized—witty. But, now that I think of it, one out of thirteen is not a fantastic score. It wouldn't get you a passing grade in algebra, it wouldn't get you a driver's license, a thumbs-up on a psychological exam, or a discharge from a hospital bed.

I scan through the older checklists. You know what? Every guy I've ever dated, liked, pined over, appeared to be all of those things I held so important.

There might, possibly, be some flaw in my logic. I briefly thank God that I have already written my article and that it is not a video docudrama I am creating here, in which people would be able to see that I am at this moment violating every single thing I "learned."

I scan my apartment for cameras and lower the shades just in case—you never know.

You know what though? After the initial disappointment of realizing that Tom fits into only one single category, (but if you think about it, actually tons of penciled in ones—"excellent diet;" "nice boss;" "provides wonderful nickname;" "is great candidate for a makeover story," and dialing my grandmother to discuss this (she is the only one up at this hour and tends to agree with everything I say); I realize something awful.

Tom has a girlfriend. A girlfriend who takes Glamour Shots. A girlfriend who doesn't like to eat in pubs. A girlfriend who has nails the length of the Nile River. Still, a girlfriend all the same.

I'm tearing through my closet for my most woe-is-me attire, something befitting an unrequited lover (purple, maybe?) when it hits me. She's the sort of girlfriend who takes Glamour Shots. A girlfriend who doesn't like to eat in pubs. What I'm saying is, I am *so* much better suited to Tom than she is! Anyone can see that.

I'll win him over. And that will fulfill a whole new check box— that will make him "a challenge!" I can do it. I am now scanning my closet for challenge-ready garments (red, definitely) with which to begin my venture. And just when I get to a skirt that I never even knew I owned that is really sort of ugly, but the only red item I can find, it dawns on me—I don't have any idea if Tom likes *me*.

How will I get to the bottom of this? I'm now tossing the skirt onto the floor over the purple dress, ready to search for something in the Sherlock Holmes range (a wool blazer—it is spring, but you know what they say about fashion and function) when my eye catches the printout of *Diary of a Working Girl* on my floor.

And, I realize with a jolt of excitement that I have recorded every single thing that Tom has ever said or done for me ever since day one at Smith Barney in *Diary of a Working Girl*! Genius! Now I've got the outfit—a wool blazer and matching pants, a great tweed hat with front and back bills and a string that ties on top (don't ask me why I own this), and even this pipe I'd gotten at a Dunhill event (it's so great when I find a use for these random freebies)—*and* all of my clues ready. I'll just have to read between the lines a bit, which is just my specialty, something I have been doing my entire lifetime. Maybe after this, I will be so good at spotting clues I can start to write mystery novels in the manner of Nancy Drew. I used to love those when I was younger.

So I get dressed, grab the printout, three colored highlighters (you have to color code for organization), and a portable Post-it flag pop-up gadget, and I go where any girl would go when she needs a trusted friend to take her through a challenging journey— to the café, for one very large latte and one warm, always loyal friend, a chocolate croissant.

As I take a seat outside the café on my block, I am delighted at the sensation of home, of belonging, that I feel in my tiny corner of the universe. This is, indeed, another thing I had taken for granted during all of those years working at home. I mean, where else in the world could I sit in the glaring sunlight on a very warm May morning in head-to-toe wool without anyone batting an eye? (It's actually getting a little toasty under all this wool but it really looks great.)

Across the street a group of people are walking, loaded up with shopping bags, and I remember how much I loved the lunch hours I would take right here, playing Guess What They Bought. I see the young and would-be fit drinking their fat-free morning coffees in their designer workout gear and running sneakers (toting the spinning and après-workout sneakers in logo'd gym bags) on the way to overpriced gyms chosen because the owner is known for helping models drop ten pounds before catwalk jaunts.

And here I recall all of the days I promised myself I would run upstairs to go to the gym, but just ordered another cafe mocha instead, rationalizing that I can't very well go to the gym when I am smack in the middle of a writing streak. You just don't have the benefit of those sorts of excuses when you are doing the nine-to-five thing. I am thinking how peaceful this whole scene is when a deliveryman from my corner deli passes by.

"Where have you been, *chica*? We've missed you!" he says.

"Oh, you know, I'm *sooo* busy these days," I say affecting fabulousness.

"The big writer girl! We miss our celebrity. You haven't gotten so big that you've forgotten about us, have you?"

In my little world, I am a big fish. I am "the writer." I'm the one who runs into the deli to share my newest article about how to lose five pounds in five days with the sandwich makers, who are truly excited to see my name in print, and never once say they've never seen that magazine before. If I take a seat at a table at my deli, with a draft printout and a red pen, they will lower the music so I can concentrate. But in the big world, I am a little fish—I am the one who writes for, "who is that again, Laney-pooh?" And you know, there's definitely something to be said for the former.

"Of course I could never forget you. I've been gone for a while, but, you know what? I'm back now. I am back," I say, to myself, rather than to him, partly because I am so happy to be done with the article (providing Joanne doesn't say it absolutely sucks) and partly because I am so caught up in my Sherlock Holmes persona that I feel pregnant with purpose and renewed energy.

He winks and waves me off, and I watch as his familiar figure—white shirt and pants, blue apron strings tied about his neck and back—gets smaller and smaller. And with that comforting image fading in the distance, I get to reading. I am prepared for this venture. My highlighter awaits, uncapped and ready to pop out the clues.

I am so enraptured by my reading (Did I mention how good this is? Too bad they hadn't asked for a novel rather than just an article) that when my cell phone rings, I jump roughly 10,625 feet in the air, and when I have returned to earth, I am amazed I have not bumped my head on a stray bird or a small helicopter. It's Joanne. Strangely, I feel confident about her answers. And then I lose the confidence. And then I tell myself to get some confidence. And then I regain some once again.

"What's up?" I ask when I can't take the back-and-forth game my mind is playing anymore. "Well, I've read your piece and the *Diary of a Working Girl* and I have some feedback for you."

"O-kay," I drag this out, wondering why she is acting so un-Joanne and not coming right out with it. In a panic, I begin to consider that maybe it is the worst collection of words ever to hit a page and that Joanne is holding back because she is afraid she will burst out laughing if she speaks too quickly. Perhaps my elation caused me to see everything through rose-colored glasses (I hate this saying, because I actually have rose-colored glasses and just because the color is different, I still get the same reaction from things, but it seems to fit here) and the piece was actually crap. I mean, after all, hadn't I just shoved all of my teachings aside the very morning after I'd written them? I am a sham. I am a fake. I have let my people down. I didn't even have them yet and already I let them down. People like me should never have their own people. It should be right on your driver's license: "Under no circumstances should this human being ever acquire any *people.*"

I should rip up my article and throw in the towel and maybe get a job at the deli. I could still be creative with sandwich making. Look at those beauties Martha Stewart concocts. I can sculpt delicate cucumber flowers by dragging a fork along the sides, maybe throw in some unusual veggies, like radishes. Perhaps I can carve sandwiches into the shapes of hearts and stars. People can start writing articles about *me*. "Lane Silverman—Queen of Bread," or "You Won't Believe What's Between Her Bread," or something like that, anyway. (I'll leave it to someone else this time.)

"Where are you?" she asks.

"I'm at the café down on University Place. Why? Do you want to join me?" I would love the chance to talk face-to-face, to get a reaction about this whole Sherlock Holmes look, because, really, I think I may be onto a new fad. And if it's bad news she's going to give me, then at least I won't be crying into my cell phone sitting here all by myself. If you're going to be melancholy, it's much better to have someone there to sympathize with you and maybe she'll even want to go into the sandwich business with me.

"Er, yeah, I'll be there. Wait for me."

She doesn't say good-bye, just hangs up, and I take comfort in this one traditional Joanne-type action. It can't be all that bad—whatever it is. I go back to my reading. I'm going so fast, because it really is an interesting story, and before I know it, I'm coming to the day of the shopping expedition—Tom and mine. I remember that day now. His discreet appreciation of the attention, the adorable way he'd slipped into the limelight, so innocent and child-like. Aha! A clue. Hadn't he done that whole speaking without words thing? Hadn't he—errr—noticed me looking at his ass and . . . liked it? Hadn't he offered to take me out to dinner? It had been so easy to speak with him over cocktails, effortless even. Didn't he look defeated when I'd spoken about Liam? Like I'd crushed the very life from him by confessing my love of another? Like he was ready to declare he'd never love anyone ever again if he couldn't have me? Hmmm. I'll tag that bit with a yellow Post-it flag (this one signifies *maybe*) and come back to it later.

But as I read over the encounter at the Pen-Top I begin to feel ashamed—it looks as if I talked about myself the entire time. It looks as if I was a completely selfish cow whom he could never like. Oh, no! I really am like those Ab Fab women. Maybe the name wasn't as nice-sounding as I'd first thought. He hadn't told me anything about himself that night.

But maybe this is a good sign? Maybe he was just so completely engrossed in me that he wanted to know every single detail about my life. Compare that with conversations I'd had with Liam the Fraud. He had never once allowed me to talk about myself. And while at the time I'd been enthralled, wanting to know each and every detail about the life of Liam—now that I think back, I can see that is just awful—he hadn't been interested in *me* at all. I'm torn between tagging this a good sign (red) or a bad sign (green) and, once again, decide on a yellow, when I realize that I am out of yellows. I look at the pages I've already gone through. On the side of each and every page there are yellow flags. I am getting nowhere. I think of that song, "it was all yellow." That really is a sad song. Frustrated, I dramatically bury my head in my hands.

"Tom, I wish you could just tell me what you think!" I say out loud to my yellow-trimmed papers.

"About what?" a voice asks.

Great, now I've gone mad. I am imagining that my paper is answering questions.

"Well, can you answer this?" I ask it, "How does Tom feel? Huh?"

I let out a sigh, pick up my highlighter again, and shake the fleeting thought that perhaps this stack of papers is a real-life fairy godmother.

"About what?" the voice says just as I'm putting highlighter to paper at the part where Tom is asking me to take part in the merger project.

This is getting rather frightening. But at least if I do go crazy, I can go out like Ophelia, and maybe wear one of those white gowns and crown myself with wildflowers. And then I have a thought and try out my hypothesis by asking, "T-Tom?"

"Yesssss?" I hear the voice again.

And this time, I look up. I look to my right. To my left. I hear a light-hearted chuckle, this time coming distinctly from behind me.

I turn, and my eyes are drawn to the most elegant sight. A single chocolate crocodile stiletto shining in the sunlight atop a table, a true thing of beauty.

I'd know that shoe anywhere. God knows I struggled enough in maintaining ownership of the thing. It is my shoe. But what is it doing at a neighboring café table? As perfectly majestic as it looks there, it does seem odd, sort of like, well, a talking stack of paper, I guess. As much as it is inspiring article ideas: "The Shoe as Art," "One Woman's Shoe, Another Woman's Masterpiece," it does seem strange.

I hear the voice again. "Do you recognize that shoe?"

Again the voice is behind me, even though I am facing the other direction now. And when I turn, I see a single bright-yellow sun-flower. And when I look up, the sunflower holder is none other than the man I am currently investigating under a blinding um-brella of yellow—Tom. I am happy to see that there is no flirty bluebird on his shoulder. I have enough of a challenge on my hands right now.

"What? What are you—"

"I'm here on official business," he says.

"I'm sorry, I, um, I meant to call in sick again," I scramble for an excuse, realizing that Tom is still my boss, although he *could* be my love interest. And without the *Beautiful* job, and unsure about the future of my article, he could potentially be my boss for some time. In the midst of my investigation I'd forgotten to call in. God! Another selfish act on my part. He'll probably be glad if I give up my job.

I cup my hand over my mouth, ready to produce an Oscar-worthy sick-person cough when he scoops my hand away from my mouth and into his dry, rough palm.

"That's okay. I can see you are *severely* under the weather. I wouldn't *dream* of having you chained to a computer all day getting my whole team sick with spring-fever-itis. I hear it can be quite devastating."

Wait. That's a joke, right? (Did I not check off checklist #11 regarding witty statements.) He's playing around with me. So maybe he's not angry. And come to think of it, I don't think it's standard procedure to make a personal appearance to reprimand a no-show employee. And he *is* holding my hand, and it's definitely not in an attempt to check my pulse—that is, unless there is a new method of pulse-checking that involves rubbing the underside of one's palm in a slow, methodical, extremely pleasant manner.

I'm searching, trying to place that look in his eye. It is absolutely not anger. But it is not lust, either. And it is not the standard-issue look that Hugh Grant gave to Julia Roberts in *Notting Hill*, that seemed to say "I am a devastated human being without you." Yet, it is equally, no, *far* more wonderful. It is a look that only someone who appreciates the Tao of Tom would understand. It is a look just for, well, me—and it is (clue!) the same look he gave me at Calvin Klein. I am reaching for a red Post-it flag when he rises from the seat he'd just taken, drops my hand, and, I think, may be leaving. I want to scream "No!"

But it turns out I don't have to scream at all. He just fondles the bow atop my hat and says, "Another new look from *Vogue*, Sherlock?"

And before I have a chance to answer, he walks to the table where my slender, sexy shoe is scintillating in the early morning glow.

He scoops it up, muttering, "How the hell do you walk in these?"

And I smile, because I actually love the fact that Tom does not appreciate the beauty of a good heel. I'd just noted that a minute ago when I read over a time I'd tripped leaving his office and he'd said the very same thing. It just wouldn't befit a man who prefers a sunflower to a rose to understand the dictums of fashion. And I'm so clearly enamored of the beauty of a sunflower-type now (I'll have to add this to the checklist), and I am sure that were he to have gone with the status quo on even something as trivial as flower selection now, that he would not be the man for me (which I am very much hoping that he is, given the fact that he has just presented me with a flower and held my hand in a non-pulse-checking manner). Anyway, didn't I read somewhere that roses are out? Maybe we'll start a whole new botanical trend!

And then, (thank you, fairy godmother/fate/wacko from my dream!) he does the most adorable thing. He takes the shoe, kneels down before me, and reaches under the hem of my pants to slide my shoe off. Only, when he sees what I am wearing over my feet he stops and looks up at me with his eyebrows all bunched up, shaking his head.

"Can I ask why on earth you are wearing slippers?"

"Well, I didn't have any brown leather shoes other than the ones you just brought here, and so I thought these brown leather slippers would do just fine. Don't you think they look cute, though?"

"Ab Fab, I can't believe I'm saying this, but I almost understand your logic there. And yes, they look absolutely adorable."

And as he slips the right one off, he takes my foot in his hand (free pedicure; thank God) and kisses it! His lips are so tickly on the side of my instep that my leg jerks uncontrollably and I kick him in the face.

"Okay, so I'd better remember you have ticklish feet," he says, rubbing at his jawline, "and one hell of a swift kick."

Maybe that wasn't a "traditionally" romantic moment, but in a weird way it was much better than anything normal. And when he regains his composure, he places the shoe on my foot, looks up at me, and says, "Ahh, the perfect fit."

That look once again says something to me—it says that it isn't the shoe he is talking about—it's me! Case solved! Look at that, the clues came to me! I am the best detective in the entire world!

Our first kiss, which one would imagine to be a strikingly passionate, beautiful display, ending with the other café patrons rising for a standing ovation, whistling and clapping their hands together, wiping tears from their eyes, turns out to be absolutely nothing like that at all.

First of all, we both close our eyes before our faces are close enough, so we wind up doing one of those awful teeth-banging things, at which point Tom winces and says, "You know, Ab Fab, for a romantic, you are a seriously crap kisser."

I smile here and say, "Well, you're a pretty crap kisser yourself."

At that point, he says, "Well, maybe just for this first time we should keep our eyes open, as a safety precaution."

And you know, keeping your eyes open is actually a wonderful way to kiss. As we move closer and look at each other, our lips taking each other's in, I can see the extraordinary way his eyes dance, turning up a bit at the corners, tiny lines forming. I can see his eyes so clearly that I notice they are actually made up of millions of tiny specks of green and brown and even gray that together make up the most spectacular hue. It is breathtaking.

And his lips! They are so soft and plump—the opposite of what I usually like, but such a wonderful change! I'll have to add this to the checklist! I mean, now I actually *have* my M&M, I don't really need the list, but old habits die hard.

With no teeth-banging this time, it is just moment upon moment

of soft touching, deep kissing, a bit of lip-tugging—overall a perfect mixture of movements. I could write an article on it: "The
Perfect Kiss," "A Kissing Equation" (not that I'm thinking about
articles smack in the middle of the quintessential romantic moment of my life).

Just before we part, someone screams from across the street, "Get
a room!" At that Tom pulls away, not saying "to hell with PDA-
naysayers! This is my Lane and I want all the world to see how
much I love her!"

Instead he remarks, "See that? I am with you for nearly a minute
and I'm already causing scenes. The Ab Fab lifestyle—I wonder if I
can take it."

But already I know he could take it, wants to take it.

And so he goes on, "There's just one thing I have to clear up.
You really think I have a great ass?"

And right here, I venture something I know is very un-
Tomlike—I grab for it.

"Not bad," I tease.

"I'm glad you approve, because I know what a high priority
your checklist gives to looking good in boxer briefs," he says.

And I'm just about to correct that it's gray boxer briefs, when I
think, WHAT? How the hell does he know about the checklist,
and for that matter, what the hell did I write for him on this item?

And then it hits me. Being that I had just read the very passage
that praises his ass myself, I knew he'd seen it all.

"So you know?" I venture.

"Oh, I know."

"Whoops," I say.

"Whoops is right. Looks like I'll have to find a new assistant
now. One who isn't in it to score with her boss."

"So you don't have any problems with all of this?" I ask, know-

ing the whole thing probably appears a *bit* complicated to an outside party.

"I do have one problem, Ab Fab. If you're going to continue to
stand here with your hand on my ass, it's only proper that I be allowed to do the same."

And so we walk, hands on asses to grab a taxi to the Traveler's
Building. In a dreamed-up version, Tom would probably forsake
his responsibilities to be with me for the day. But in the real world,
whose merits I am becoming increasingly keen to (I only whined
for about ten minutes in the taxi), today is the day that Tom seals
the deal on the telecommunications merger. And as I'm the only
assistant he has at the moment, he needs my help.

Now, I know what you're thinking. You're crouched on your
couch or at a table in a deli eating an overpriced custom-built
salad, or attempting to pick up sushi with chopsticks and hold a
book and read it at the same time, without dripping soy sauce God
knows where, and you're thinking—I knew it! Tom actually does
say the perfect things and do the perfect things. Lane gets to go
back to her old ways and they live happily ever after.

But most of all, you're thinking, don't I get to see them together
doing all of that wonderful romantic stuff? Don't I get to see how
Lane's romantic sensibilities play into the picture? Does she ever
stay down on planet Earth? Or is she unable to separate herself
from her fanciful ways? And does she get to see that ass without the
confines of clothing? How the hell did Tom find out about her
feelings on said ass anyway? And what about that article?

Well, sister, put down those chopsticks and turn the page. After
we've come so far, you don't think I'd leave you hanging like that, do
you? Especially when you know how I am about happy endings. . . .

Twenty

Happily Ever After

Well, I do wind up with one standard-issue fairy tale-ism in the end. We do live extremely happily ever after. But I'll tell you, Tom is Tom and there's no leading man quite like him. I've thought and thought, and I can't find one male character to compare him to. But that's actually the best part of all. I could have never dreamed him up, and those little quirks are precisely the things I love about him more and more every day. My checklist is now officially four pages and growing.

For instance, I'd always thought a couple should sleep in each other's arms all night long, my leg slung about his thigh, his arm resting under my neck and the other about my back. And, yes, we'll start off like that most nights. But right before I fall asleep, when he thinks I already have, he'll do this thing where he'll whisper my name to check I'm in dreamland.

"Lane? Lane?" he'll venture.

And when I don't answer he'll slide his hand out from behind my neck, peel my leg off of him and spend about five minutes shaking his arm out, whispering, "I have no feeling in my arm."

It is with all of my might I pretend to not hear any of this and maintain a straight face. When he has finally got feeling back in his arm, he'll turn over the other way and go to sleep with his butt directly in my face. It's a very cute butt, as I've said before, so I really don't mind.

He knows I like to fall asleep cuddling, so he does his best to maintain this little convention for me. I don't have the heart to tell him I know the truth. And you know what? It doesn't matter at all to me, really. In fact, I prefer it, because he makes up for it in the early mornings, when I catch him turning back over, sneaking his arm back under my neck, dragging my leg back around him and kissing me on the cheek, or stroking my hair. It really is adorable.

And while Tom so clearly has the most sentimental and admirable intentions at heart with every gesture, every word, they don't always turn out perfectly. There was the time when he was planning a vacation for us. For weeks, I asked and asked about what he referred to as "the big surprise." All he said was that I should have my passport ready and to pack lots of skimpy swimsuits, especially the one with "all of those stringy things." Of course, I had to pack a lot more than just skimpy swimsuits.

When you have no idea where you may be off to, and your mind is taking you to all of the majestic destinations you may be dashing towards, it is very difficult to know what you should pack. So, basically, I packed everything for a Caribbean fantasy vacation. I had years of *InStyle* magazine celebrity vacations to fuel the fire.

The full-length evening gown would be for our black-tie eight-course dinner, where we would dance like Fred Astaire and Ginger Rogers (although neither of us knows how to do any of those ballroom dances) on a dance floor that juts out over the Caribbean sea, lit with elegant torches and twinkling white lights, the sounds of birds chirping and the air redolent of bougainvillea.

And then there are the practical items—the sneakers for exploring deserted islands that the concierge would arrange for us to be dropped off at, the proper woven hat for a lazy day of fishing, a driving outfit with gloves and Tod's moccasins (so what if I've never driven before?). I needed a sunset-watching velour Juicy zip-up hoodie for the crisp night breezes, which I would pull up around me and Tom would say, "Come here, let me keep you warm, my darling."

There's the pareo I would need to wrap about my waist when we emerge from our private infinity pool to sip champagne and strawberries on our terrace. I couldn't forget the array of white garments to accent the rich teakwood and bamboo furnishings with white upholstery, lush greenery, and Italian tile floors when we come inside, after a midnight stroll on the shore to create the perfect seduction scene before we step into our open-roofed bathtub, glancing up at the twinkling stars while I scrub his back with a loofah, drinking white wine and munching on caviar.

From the number of imaginings I'd indulged in before I even finished packing my suitcases, vanity cases, and suitor, you might be throwing around the idea that I have fully reverted to my fantastical ways. And in many respects, you would be correct. As it turns out, some of us are just woven from an imaginative cloth. And when we attempt to bury that part of ourselves, we are really burying the part of ourselves that makes us who we are.

That's what Joanne tells me, anyway. And with that outlook I get to stay the way I am, so it works out rather nicely.

The trick is, for us Over-the-Rainbow sorts, to remember that the fantasies are wonderful in and of themselves. They weave together this whole other world where all sorts of fantastical things happen all the time. There, frogs turn into princes, sunny days never run out, and whims are always satiated exactly as you would have them be. And this world is one that I am not willing to let go of—ever.

It was only a matter of days until I dragged those boxes back out of my basement, tore off all of the tape I thought would hinder me from unearthing the paraphernalia inside and, once again, reunited myself with my beloved books and movies. Now I have my own love, I don't get sad at the endings. But after we watched *Pretty Woman* and I got all quiet at the end, Tom said, "Ab Fab, don't tell me you want me to charter a private plane just to go to the opera, which I'm sure you've never attended before in your life."

Boy, what kind of a spoiled girl does he think I am?

"It doesn't have to be a *private* plane," I said.

He smiled curiously and then just held me in his arms, whispering in my ear, "Don't ever change, Lane. Please don't ever change."

I hope he doesn't think I've forgotten about the opera.

So you might think that when we got to the "big surprise" and found ourselves right smack in the middle of a Caribbean hurricane, which did not enable us to enjoy outdoor dinner/dancing escapades, driving trips, or open-roofed bathtub evenings, that I would have been devastated, having built it up so much in my mind.

But, my darlings, that couldn't be farther from the truth. The reality of our trip, as awful as my hair looked (I spent many unfruitful hours looking for a converter for my flatiron), as wet as our clothing remained (I spent many hours attempting to dry them out with a hair dryer), was a wonder in itself.

We spent the whole time in the room, which I guess we could have done anywhere in the world, even at home. But Tom was so sweet, making up all sorts of games and declaring holidays like "Crazy Saturday" where we had margarita-drinking contests and wore snorkeling apparatuses in the bathtub (Tom had to coax me into that one—I tell you, those goggles are pretty unflattering), and he even brought some sand, as wet as it was, and a couple of lounge chairs into our room to create our own little beach. It's amazing how much fun you can have when you live life as it comes.

The pretrip fantasies, though, did not go to waste. After Tom had read my *Diary of a Working Girl*, he took the liberty of calling a publisher friend to take a look at it. It turns out that while I have had a world of trouble in the past coming up with ideas for articles, I have no trouble at all coming up with ideas for novels without even trying. (Did I not say this before?)

Diary of a Working Girl is due out in a few months time and I have a three-book contract to keep the romantic books coming. So now, every single wonderful scenario I play out as I do such simple things as pack a filmy pink dress has a very definite, very fulfilling use. I instructed Tom that he would have to do some romantic research himself, as it helps when you have a strong leading man to draw from. But after he came to bed in a Fabio wig with a shaved chest, I could see he wasn't taking his research very seriously. Although I have to admit that the shaved chest was actually rather nice.

And I guess, if you fill your time with enough fantasies, one of them is bound to be true once in a while. Remember Swen? The voice mail guy I'd kept on hand for a fantasy whenever the need for one arose? Well, soon after all of the amazing things began to happen to me, I once again reached his number in error.

"I couldn't be happier for you, my little sugar plum. I insist you come up to my brownstone for a splendidly decadent meal, caviar, oysters, and all. Bring your dashing Tom, too."

Dashing—only Swen could use that word and get away with it.

When Swen's butler, Harris, brought us into the sitting room to meet Monsieur Swen, he was (I swear this is true!) in a smoking jacket, running his fingers through his shoulder-length blond hair, sitting by a crackling fire.

After the kisses and the "Oh my God!" exclamations of our premier meeting were through, he said (and I quote), "You'll have to excuse my appearance, I've just come in from a rather long day on the slopes."

Can you believe it? Tom still can't get over that one.

"I knew you were a witch, Ab Fab," he said.

But despite the fact that this one musing did in fact turn out to be true, the important thing to remember, should you read any of my books in the future (remember that is Silverman, S-I-L-V-E-R-M-A-N) is that the stories I conjure up are just fantasies—they have a place in your mind and in your heart. Of course, I would never fully be able to follow that line of thinking myself, but since you are my people, I feel a certain duty to say that, even if you choose not to listen.

And while some of you might prefer the magical stuff of fluffy, frilly love, others, apparently, like the tough stuff—the stuff where people struggle and endure pain. And under that category would fall *Cosmopolitan*. When Lisa called Karen and began to plead my case to renegotiate my article assignment, Karen almost fell off of her seat laughing.

She literally said to Lisa, "Hold on, I have to unbutton the top button of my Paul & Joe pants. I'm laughing so hard I'm about to burst."

Lisa, even sweeter than I'd first thought, was more than ready to defend me to the death, since she assumed Karen was laughing about the fact that she knew I couldn't finish the article after all.

But when she finally caught her breath she said, "Lisa, how many years have you known me? I am one of the toughest editors in the business. Now do you really think that I didn't *know* this assignment would cause Lane to have a meltdown and reconsider her notions of how to find love? That setup she came up with was the most ridiculous thing I've ever heard in my life! Two months to find The One! God, I've been trying to do that for thirty-five years!"

"So you wanted her to have a breakdown just so that she could write the article about what she learned?"

"Of course! I could tell from those articles she sent me—you know the ones from the magazines nobody's ever heard of—she was great, but a little green on instinct," Karen exclaimed.

"But what about when she asked to switch the topic and you denied her? And what about asking for Liam's number? That was pretty low, even for you."

"That was all part of the game, darling. I couldn't let her give up that early, she would have never gotten a story out of giving up so quickly. And as for Liam, that was pretty funny, huh? We hung that e-mail up by the watercooler. It's a classic!"

"Well, I'll tell you this, you did get yourself one damn good article, but Lane wins in the end, since after she finished her article denouncing every single thing she'd ever held to be true, she found the most fantastic man ever."

Lisa says Karen got silent here and after a moment, she said, in a tone pregnant with thought, "Tell her to e-mail me the manuscript right away. I've got an idea."

Obviously, I was completely overcome with rage when Lisa recounted this exchange to me.

All of that time! All of that stress! Unbelievable! It's no wonder I could never get anywhere with those editors before—they are totally insane, not to mention mean. What if I really had gone nuts and spent the rest of my life in a drug-induced haze. Would she want me to write the article about *that*? Once again, I had to wonder why I want to continue doing this for a living. There has to be a better way. Once again, the sandwich idea popped into my mind—innocent, meditative cucumber flowers. . . .

But you know what? When Karen called me, after she'd read the piece (and absolutely "adored" it, by the way), she had the audacity to ask me to thank her! Thank her for nearly sending me to the loony bin!

"Oh come on! Look what you've learned. Look at the great piece you've given me. You should be very proud, Lane."

"Hmmph," was all I said, and believe me, I never thought I'd speak to a *Cosmo* editor like that.

"All right, you're mad. But I have a proposal. Since I've heard that you did wind up meeting someone after you finished this piece, I would like you to do a follow-up—you know, give the ladies out there a little hope that after all the rough stuff, there comes all the great stuff."

Now that definitely sounded like something that was totally up my alley, but I was mad, okay?

"I'm not sure I want to work with you again," I said, not sure where I'd suddenly acquired this enormous set of balls.

"All right," she dragged that out, like I was bargaining with her. "Fine. If it's four dollars a word you want, then that's what we'll give you."

I was silent. I couldn't believe she had the audacity to think that my feelings were nothing but a bargaining chip to me. Surely my dignity cannot be bought for four dollars a word!

"Okay, four-fifty, but that's my final offer."

Well, what's dignity, really? How could you refuse an offer like that? My feelings are all fine now anyway. And, of course, I owe it to my people. They need me. They are my people. (And you know how I feel about my people.) And it gets better than that. They liked the story about my wonderful Tom so much that they want me to continue writing about our trials, tribulations, romance, and growth for every issue! After all of that time reading about other people's romances, not only do I get to have my own, I get to let other people enjoy it! What could be better?

Tom was hesitant at first, since he's so private and all, and there were to be photos of us with each column. But when I insisted he wear the globe tie and finally showed him the first story about us, he was touched.

He said, "How could I deny you the pleasure of telling the world how wonderful I am? I won't take no for an answer, Ab Fab."

Could you just die? He is so sweet. And you know, I think he's getting a bit too into this whole celebrity thing. He's begun checking Page Six every day to see if there's any news about us, although he says it's just to "learn more about the world of Ab Fab." But it's so adorable I don't have the heart to tell him I've caught on.

I'd insisted that Chris shoot our photos for the column, since he's the only one who consistently takes great pictures of me. When we arrived at Chris's apartment to shoot our pictures for that first issue, he was staring intently at a Polaroid, smiling. So I walked over to see who it was.

"Number twenty-six?" I asked.

"Oh Lane, number twenty-six is right."

"Did you finally meet him?" I asked.

"Meet him? Oh, I did a lot more than meet him."

"So was he everything we'd hoped? Witty, funny, intelligent?"

"Oh, no, he's absolutely none of those things at all. In fact, he's completely thick."

"So then why are you so happy?" I asked, extremely confused by this.

"Because now I can stop this ridiculous fascination with him and get on with my life."

Surely this couldn't be. I mean, we'd always joked around about how amazing these guys probably are (any seriousness was entirely on my part), but there's no way he really entertained the idea that he would one day fall in love with the guy from the Polaroid that he'd never spoken a word to other than photographer lingo like, "Good. That's good. Now to the left. Now stick your butt out. Spread your legs a little wider."

Well, I guess that could be construed as something pretty intimate, but you know what I mean. Chris—levelheaded, always together, Chris—was just as much of a dreamer as I was! Who knew?

"Your article really helped me get through the whole thing. I knew you had it in you."

Now that you know how our future turns out, there's the little unresolved matter of the mushy stuff you are definitely due to enjoy, being that you stayed by me through all of the crazy times. Before Tom took on the role of Prince Charming and showed up with one very stylish pump, he had a little nudge from a real-life fairy godmother, who for once skipped the lofty, empty statements and got straight to the point. Let's call her Joanne. For all the times my faithful friend implored me to remove my head from the clouds, when she read my article and my question about fate, along with the entire two hundred and fifty pages of *Diary of a Working Girl*, she took matters into her own hands.

She, the forward-thinking, rational woman that she is, realized I had, in fact, learned a very important lesson about what meeting my M&M is really all about. But she also knew that I had a history of taking things a *bit* too far. Pairing my now sullen outlook with the hints that had revealed themselves to me in my diary, she came to the same conclusion that I did—that Tom and I were a perfect match. Only, she came there much quicker than myself.

Waking the next morning before seven (I really should have realized how uncharacteristic this was for her at the time), she took the liberty of leaving a message for one Mr. Tom Reiner that she had a very important package for him. And while I was preparing for my investigation, she delivered the package herself and sat and waited while he read every word, clucking his tongue and muttering things like, "My tie was not *that* bad! I've had it since the first day I worked here. It's a monumental tie, really it is," when he got to a portion that riled him up.

She also said he blushed quite frequently.

And when she asked, "What? What part are you up to?" he just acted like he couldn't hear her. Tom, as we know, is quite a shy guy when it comes to people knowing his feelings, so you'll imagine my surprise when Joanne shared the next bit with me.

When he was through, my insightful pal asked outright: "You broke it off with your girlfriend way back before Lane ever even started probing you about her, didn't you?"

Before he answered, she whipped out her own copy and backed up her argument with legalese like, "If you'll refer to page twenty-two, section three which reads, 'I asked Tom how a girlfriend could ever allow her man to walk around in a tie like that and he just turned away and said "It's fine,"' It is a very clear indication to me that a private man like you was just unable to share such a personal matter as a breakup with someone whom he had very strong feelings for because he was afraid of the possibility of rejection. Am I correct in this assertion, Mr. Reiner?"

Joanne has honed these contract negotiation skills over many years of arguing that, no, her production company was not going to pay for a doggie au pair to stay on set at a photo shoot to keep a model's purse-accessory pooch company.

"But I gave her a note that told her how I felt on the day that she left here in a state over Liam—page two hundred—and she never said anything to me about it!"

Joanne just said, "Tom, if I know Lane, and I think I do, she would have told me all about that note, had she seen it. Was she not flustered? Is it not possible that she lost it?"

Joanne tells me he took on a face like he was figuring out a quadratic equation and then said, "But what type of a girl takes a job just to find someone who fulfills the requirements of the man she has been dreaming about since pigtail-days?"

But even before Joanne could go on with the three-pronged defense plan she had prepared, citing cinematic obsessions, weaknesses for all things whimsical, and even (this is so sweet) how lovable and human this all makes me—after all it is why she is my best friend—he answered for himself.

"The kind of girl that has used her magical powers to cast a home-brewed, black-magic love-spell on me. I'm even talking like her now, with run-on sentences and audibly hyphenated words. I'm using exclamation points!"

She says his voice lifted here and he began laughing uncontrollably.

When he'd gotten up from falling on the floor in hysterics and let out a big, long sigh, he said, "If she wants a fairy tale, then by God, she's going to get one! Now where are those ridiculously pointy shoes she hobbles around in and hides in her overhead cabinet in case she feels the need to change in the middle of the day?"

Joanne says he was a man possessed at this point, trying to decide between the croc and the caramel-colored Jimmy Choos I'd splurged on at a sample sale. He held them both up and proclaimed, "For the life of me, I will never be the kind of man to understand the unique merits of one pair of shoes as compared to another!"

But just as Joanne was about to offer up the suggestion of the croc, he recalled reading that passage in my diary and suggested that would be the perfect choice.

Joanne smiled triumphantly.

Now maybe needing your friend to approach your would-be love interest to show him the light is not the quintessential picture of romance to a love story–phile, and I'll admit this bothered me a bit for a moment or two (three, tops) but that's not the point, now is it?

The point is that it is *my* romance. And it is a *real* romance— fabulous in its reality due to all of the pieces of me, fitting with all of the pieces of him. Different pieces with bits sticking out here and there, some in the right places, some in the wrong places—but bits that each of us has a place to contain within us. And, well, it does make for a good story, which everyone is always saying is a necessity for a lasting love. So that actually makes it better than a traditional romance.

That's what Tom said when I suggested we do a retake and maybe stage the whole thing in a more *Hope Floats*–type of way— maybe he could take a picture of himself and I could learn how to develop pictures and then I'd come across one of him before a pickup truck holding a bunch of flowers and then I could run out and hug him and he could toss me into the truck and we could ride off into the sunset.

He's right—who *am* I kidding? I would never want to learn how to develop photos, with all those icky chemicals and stuff.

You already know the next part—the shoe, the flower, me as Cinderella (which is, by the way, another dream come true), the kiss, the hands on asses.

There was a lot of work to do on my last day at Smith Barney. When finally, the papers for the merger were signed and everything I'd ever fax, file, or e-mail for the Mergers and Acquisitions Department of Smith Barney was faxed, filed, or e-mailed, I began packing all of the personal belongings I'd accumulated in the last two months. I took down the tiny card Tom had given me that first day with the flowers, I untacked the job-well-done posters he'd fashioned on expense day.

John stood up, looking over the cubey wall.

"You two were so obvious," he said. "I think that blind guy in the cafeteria knew before either of you did. Sheesh, some people are so slow."

John, master number-cruncher, discreet perfect-boyfriend, clairvoyant.

"Well, I'm glad we served as a great source of entertainment for you."

"You know? I hate to admit it, but I'm really going to miss you. But it's just as well, because I couldn't very well e-mail images of animals that remind me of you to *you*."

"Ab Fab, can I see you in my office?" Tom asked into the telephone.

I leaned back in the chair to glimpse him glimpsing me.

"And don't even think about touching my ass. This is a place of business after all."

"I would never do a thing like that," I replied, hand over heart, eyelashes fluttering at him through the glass, loving this office-romance thing so much that I really hated to think this was my last day.

"So, what can I do for you?" I asked as I plopped down into the seat opposite his desk, wearing the croc heels, which I had changed into when I'd arrived.

"Well," he began, trying to look very serious and failing, like a *Saturday Night Live* skit where the actors can't keep a straight face. "You really did a great job on the design for that presentation. And apparently it worked."

"I'm sure you had *something* to do with the success of the meeting," I insisted.

"No really, it was all you—that woman from AT&T called and said, 'You know, I was on the fence, but that beautiful design brought me to my decision.'"

I rolled my eyes to emphasize that I was not buying this brand of logic.

"Whatever you want to believe, but either way, I would like to outsource all of our proposal designs to you. We pay a lot for that sort of thing and I know you really enjoyed it."

"You're not just doing this because I'm your girlfriend?" I asked, and as soon as I did, I realized the mistake I'd made.

What the heck was I thinking calling myself his girlfriend right away like that? I find myself once again scanning for spy cameras to foil my rep as a relationship guru.

"No, actually, it's despite the fact that you're my girlfriend."

See, that's why they pay me the big bucks!

Adorable man, really.

Did I mention he was wearing that awful tie that day? The one with the golf clubs? And did I mention the fact that he went back to wearing awful ties and the same old suits he had before?

As long as I'm mentioning it, I might as well tell you that I wouldn't have it any other way. I want Tom to be Tom. *Sometimes*, when we're going somewhere really special, and I go out and buy him a new shirt or pants he might claim otherwise, but on the whole, really that's the truth. I'm even starting to believe there might be something to his "ahead of the trend" theory. I actually read in *GQ* recently that kitschy ties are making a comeback!

Tiffany and I shrieked in instant message mode after I spent hours typing in what had happened, while she sat quietly (this means no typing), a few yards away in her cubicle. (We have just gotten so used to communicating this way, and I'll miss her, so I figured this would be an apropos good-bye.)

Tiffanybabeoliscious: Get out! ☺

Lame2001: Isn't it amazing?!?$#%**

Tiffanybabeoliscious: Which part? 🌐

Lame2001: Me and Tom, of course!

Tiffanybabeoliscious: I couldn't think of a better match. But you have some seriously jealous women on your hands now!

Lame2001: Do you think?

Tiffanybabeoliscious: Oh baby, I know! Do you think yours is the only instant message window I have open right now? Why do you think I didn't type a word all through your story? I was sending instant messages to just about everyone on our floor! 🌐

Lame2001: You really are the queen of gossip. 😛

Tiffanybabeoliscious: But you wouldn't have it any other way. 🌐

Lame2001: That's right sister! So you better keep feeding me the gossip when I'm outta here.

Tiffanybabeoliscious: It is my duty and I take it seriously. And as long as you've spilled all of your gossip to me, and you promise to keep a secret, I've got something for you....

Lame2001: What? What?!!

Tiffanybabeoliscious: I've got a special someone right here, too.... 🌐

Lame2001: Who? You're absolutely killing me here.

Tiffanybabeoliscious: You really haven't guessed?

Lame2001: Oh my god! Out with it already!! 🌐

Tiffanybabeoliscious: Deep breath ... John.

Lame2001: John across the cubey wall?

Tiffanybabeoliscious: Who do you think forwarded him all of those images of Tom's ex-girlfriend? ☺

Lame2001: No way!

Tiffanybabeoliscious: And by the way ... there is no 'spaghetti incident.' John made that up so you'd start wondering about Tom, because he thought you two would be great together. 😃

You know, it's not really that crazy. I could definitely see how they would compliment each other. After all, opposites attract, and if you let them, people will shock and delight you every day, and in my case, even if you think you've already got them pegged. And believe me, when I finally got John to admit to his "secret" relationship by justifying that the only one in the office that you have to worry about when it comes to gossip is his girlfriend, and he agreed to have dinner with Tom and I (definitely spaghetti), it is easy to see that those two are just perfect together.

When I left at the end of that day, I had to sign a whole pile of contracts about confidentiality. At the bottom of the pile, which was about twenty pages thick, I came across a pink sheet. I began reading the same jargon that the others started out with.

"I, Lane Silverman, ex-employee of Smith Barney, promise to maintain under the strictest confidentiality, blah blah blah," when I came to the part about what it was that I was agreeing to.

"I will devote this entire weekend to getting to know Tom the Boyfriend and will not once return to my apartment during the entire period spanning from Friday, May 29th to Sunday, June 1st."

I brought the pile of papers into his office and said, "I've just one problem with this last document."

He took a deep breath, folded his hands, prayer-style on his desk, and said, "Yes?"

"Well, I need to go home and get some clothes first."

"I regret to inform you that you'll do no such thing," he said, very matter-of-factly. "There is no need for clothes where we are going."

Friday night went, to quote someone I once knew, "splendidly." And for that matter, Saturday and Sunday, too—all of which were spent in Tom's apartment—which does not have one inch of marble or a claw-foot bathtub. It does have lots of ugly black leather couches and Barcaloungers and sports paraphernalia, though. This suits him perfectly, and after a little while, I'm sure we can work on it. If I subtly introduce a vase here, an Oriental rug there, he'll barely even notice.

True to his claim, there was no clothing necessary. And he is, without the need of suave rehearsed lines, a fantastic lover, who doesn't concentrate on creative positions and *Nine and a Half Weeks*–type scenes, but instead on smiling, and genuinely enjoying every second, without the need to say so with meaningless, faceless words.

And after, he strokes his hands on my little pooch of a belly and says, "Now *this* is adorable," and kisses it, and squeezes me so tightly I can barely breathe. This method of passing time in a bedroom is equally, if not far superiorly, effective (and if I happen to throw in an "Oh, Tom" here and there, well, I can't help myself). Only, it is not really a method. It is a natural, wonderful thing that comes from a place that Liam does not have within his otherwise flawless body—a heart.

And there were other wonderful moments aside from those on the bed—eating Chinese take-out wrapped in sheets at Tom's dining room table, fighting over the one fortune cookie, which I won (through a tricky maneuver involving pulling said sheet off of one very private area) and read aloud, which to our dismay, offered no deep insight into our future: "If no one hears the tree fall in the woods, has it really fallen?"

But it offered plenty of opportunities for jokes.

"If nobody sees Ab Fab's breasts under her sheet, are they really there?"

And, of course, that just lead to a thorough investigation to find out. (As it turns out they were.)

"If Tom wears his globe-covered tie with nothing else, is it still ugly?" I try my hand.

"Lane, that's really not the same kind of question. I see you're trying to be funny, but, c'mon—you can do better than that. But, hey, if you really want to see me in my tie, with absolutely nothing else on, I'm not going to argue. . . ."

The very last point I need to cover is one that is very important to me. And that is the little question of fate. And I got my answer one day while Tom and I were whiling away the day in Central Park, envisioning all of the most recent fights that the various couples spread out on blankets had gotten into.

He'd floored me with his imaginative description of a scuffle between a thirty-something couple. One very tall woman and one extremely vertically challenged man presumably came dangerously close to divorcing when she'd offered to let him sit on her lap in a movie theatre so he could see over a hatted individual sitting in front of him. And when Tom turned his attention from the couple, he settled the matter for me once and for all.

He said, "Ab Fab, it was nothing less than fate that brought you to apply for a job at my company that you were totally unqualified for in hopes of meeting a bite-sized chocolate candy, or whatever the heck you call it, to write an article about the most ridiculous thing I've ever heard of. I can't think of a way the gods could have given me a better gift."

And that's when he said for the first time, "I love you. Please don't ever change."

It wasn't poetry. It wasn't the way I envisioned it (and believe me, I've dedicated many a day to envisioning it). But it was true. And therefore, it was, rather than a dream come true, a truth that became a dream—one that I replay again and again.